The
Island House

The
Island House

A NOVEL

POSIE GRAEME-EVANS

ATRIA PAPERBACK

New York   London   Toronto   Sydney   New Delhi

ATRIA PAPERBACK

A Division of Simon & Schuster, Inc.
1230 Avenue of the Americas
New York, NY 10020

First Atria Paperback edition June 2012

ATRIA PAPERBACK and colophon are trademarks of Simon & Schuster, Inc.

For information about special discounts for bulk purchases,
please contact Simon & Schuster Special Sales at 1-866-506-1949
or business@simonandschuster.com.

The Simon & Schuster Speakers Bureau can bring authors to your live event.
For more information or to book an event contact the Simon & Schuster Speakers Bureau at 1-866-248-3049 or visit our website at www.simonspeakers.com.

Manufactured in the United States of America

10   9   8   7   6   5   4   3   2

Library of Congress Cataloging-in-Publication Data

Graeme-Evans, Posie.
   The island house : a novel / by Posie Graeme-Evans. —1st Atria paperback ed.
      p.   cm.
   1. Archaeology—Scotland—Fiction.   2. Life change events—Fiction.
3. Vikings—Scotland—Fiction.   I. Title.
   PR9619.4.G73I84   2012
   823'.92—dc23   2012010046

ISBN 978-0-7432-9443-0
ISBN 978-1-4516-7202-2 (ebook)

For Julian Blaxland
son of my heart
with all my love
(And because I thought you might like
the Vikings)

THE BONES of the brothers lay in the dark. Dust thick as cloth covered them, for the air was ancient and dead.

It had been a different world then, in the days of the Wanderer. A time when people turned from the old Gods, and slaughter stalked those of the newer ways. Gods are never replaced without blood.

The younger had died for love, seeking justice. The older was cut down as he'd expected to be, surrounded by his fighters. They were both betrayed.

But when they were buried, the bodies had been honored. Placed beneath a scarlet pall, weapons lay close to their hands—an ax for one and in the other's hand a sword.

All the grave goods were precious, the best that could be provided. The spoils of other places, other raids, there were cloak clasps of bronze inlaid with garnets and a collar of worked gold that would have glimmered, if there had been light. There was a knife, too, with a bone haft. Carved in the shape of an otter, this was a work of rare skill. The animal seemed almost alive, a sinuous fit for the palm of a dead man.

Sheep meat and a goat had been given for the journey, and there were apples in a silver dish beside their feet. Just before the tomb was sealed, the bodies were scattered with meadow flowers, and their murderers killed all the monks. It was a generous gesture. The dead must have attendants in the next life and, too, sacrifice paid the blood debt of betrayal. Murder, unappeased, makes the dead malevolent.

CHAPTER 1

S HE FIRST saw her house from the sea.

It lay on the cliff above the sheltered cove, long and gray with a roof that was darker than the granite walls. Close by was the crumbling stump of another, much greater building. Above both was the bulk of a hill, a sentinel.

Freya Dane stood up in the open dinghy. She clutched the gunwale as they rounded the headland. There was the crescent of the landing beach beneath the cliff, and she could see the path to the house. The place matched the pictures. She had arrived.

What had she done?

The dinghy plunged over a wave crest, and Freya sat down with a bump. She'd wanted this, wanted to come here, but the cliff had not seemed so high in the pictures. Now she was close to its walls, and that dark bulk was intimidating.

Freya glanced at the things she'd brought from Sydney: her laptop, a backpack, and a larger bag for clothes. Before the crossing, she'd bought basic groceries in Portsolly, the fishing village on the other side of the strait. They were there, too, in a box. With wet-weather gear, she had all that was needed for a quick trip. Why was she feeling such anticipation? She should be *angry*. She'd made this journey *because* of him, not *for* him. And there was plenty of room for anger because of what he'd done—not just to her either.

Was it only the day before she'd been in Sydney? Freya saw herself, like a clip from a film. One last, brave wave to her mother at the air gate—anxiety unacknowledged on both sides—then the turning, the walking away. The last scene from *Casablanca*.

She half-laughed. Ah yes, they were all stoic, the Dane women—Elizabeth had trained her well. *Stick the chin out, get on with it.* So she had.

But she hated flying, that was the thing. When the plane took off, *any* plane she was on, Freya expected to die. One day, she knew, the joint confidence of all her fellow passengers would falter; and when that innocent, blind belief—the certainty that hundreds and hundreds and *hundreds* of tons of metal could (a) get off the ground and (b) stay up in the air—ruptured, it would all be over. They would drop from the sky like a brick, screaming.

But not this time. *This* time work got Freya through that endless night and the day that followed as the jumbo tracked on, indefatigable, over Australia and India, Afghanistan, the Gulf States and, as dawn broke, Europe.

After all, why terrify yourself picturing how far it was to the ground when you had only to open your laptop to allow another, equally powerful—though less terminal—anxiety to distract you?

"An Assessment of Regional Influences on the Iconography of the Early Medieval Church in the Romance Kingdoms." It certainly looked like a doctoral thesis on the screen—all those pages and words and footnotes—but, sadly, trying to write her way to the end was just as difficult at thirty-five thousand feet as it had been at her desk on the ground in Sydney.

The usual terror; deadline or not, Freya just could not crack the topic—and she'd chosen it. Her fault.

A wave slapped the bow of the dinghy, and Freya ducked. Too late.

"All right?" The man in the stern shouted over the engine; he seemed genuinely concerned.

She raised a hand. "I'm fine."

At least the air was cool on the strait between Findnar and the mainland. Freya hated heat—odd for an Australian—but Scotland made it easier to forget the steaming weight of Bangkok's air on that first night of travel. But then there'd been sullen London and the hell of Luton on a lead gray summer's day. Plane delays and zoned-out people in queues were Freya's own personal vision of Hell, and that final flight north had nearly done her head in. So little room, her knees pressed against the seat in front, *and* she'd been wedged between two braying idiots in business suits. Both of them pale, one half-drunk with a long, odd face, the other rowdy and sweaty.

An overactive imagination; it had always been her curse. Add jet lag, and Long Face turned into a donkey while Pungent One barked like a dog as the pair talked across her. Brits. They could all patronize for Home & Empire when they heard an Australian accent.

But she'd arrived at the coast in the far northeast of Scotland in the long summer twilight at last.

And, as promised by Mr. W. Shakespeare, there was the silver sea. It really was silver. She saw that as the cab from the airport dropped her beside the shops in Portsolly and drove away.

Sharp air—real air, after more than a day of canned reek—had rinsed Freya's mind as she walked down the twisting main street toward the harbor and that glimmering water. She was looking for a pub—always the best place to ask for directions.

Portsolly only had one pub, the Angry Nun. A small building of gray stone with leaded windows and a painted sign that moved back and forth in the gentle breeze off the sea, Freya liked what she saw, and her mood had lifted. She'd pushed the door open as the barman looked up from polishing glasses. Other faces turned to stare as she entered, and though Freya never had trouble asking for help, the observant silence made her self-conscious. The barman seemed amused as she leaned in close over the varnished counter. "Excuse me, but would you know someone who could take me across to Findnar tonight?"

The man had raised his brows. "Tonight?" He'd looked around the bar. "Walter, can you help the lady?"

The *r* had been softly rolled and the *a* more of an *o*. Beguiling.

Freya smiled as she remembered. Spoken language this far north was sweet and dark in the mouth.

One of the barstools swiveled as its occupant inspected her. Somewhere north of fifty, he had white wrinkles in the brown skin around his eyes. A good face, but he frowned.

Because she was anxious, Freya had jumped in. "I'm happy to pay, of course. Twelve pounds?" *Ten too little, fifteen too much.*

He'd stared at her with no expression Freya could read. Then, as she'd been about to up the offer—though she didn't want to— he'd said, "Best we go now. Wind's on its way. Put your money away."

He was wearing the boots of a fisherman, Freya had seen that when he stood, and storm gear had been hooked over the back of the stool.

Perhaps it was kindness from a stranger that had made her jumpy. "But it's a calm evening, surely? Just a soft breeze."

Walter Boyne had laughed. "Perhaps."

In the end, she'd hitched up her pack and followed him, and so, here they were.

The boat pitched in a dip between waves, and Freya resisted staring at the man in the stern. Why had he been so nice? She thought about that as the sky darkened above her head. At last, the long twilight was fading, and in Portsolly, across the water, first lights blinked on.

This place was nothing like her home, nothing like Sydney— even the sea smelled different—yet the day was dying into glory, and the green of Findnar's sheltering headland was luminous in the last light. Above, seabirds were settling in their rookery. Unfamiliar, harsh calls, a bedlam of honks and squawks, not like the evening music of wagtails and magpies.

And suddenly Freya was washed, swamped, by the thought of all she'd left behind on this fool's errand. All the safe rituals, the habits of her life. Work on the PhD she thought she'd never finish, meeting her friends for coffee or breakfast, Sundays with Elizabeth, even waitressing to pay the rent. Known things. Known people. And now there was anxiety and fear. And yearning. They'd come back, that unholy trinity, her companions from childhood; by getting on that plane in Sydney, she'd called them up again.

The dinghy grounded on the cove in a rattle of shingle. An urgent sea, shouldering behind, pushed the boat higher as Walter Boyne cut the outboard. The engine snarled and died, the sound rushed away by the surging water. Without comment, he clambered over the side to tie the dinghy to a jetty stump.

Freya called out, "Mr. Boyne, will my bag be safe on the beach? Above the tide line, I mean." It was good she sounded calm. She'd take the laptop and the backpack, the groceries, too, up to the house, but the bag of clothes was heavy.

The man was a pace or two away, a rope in one nicked and battered fist. He shook his head. "Mr. Boyne's my father. I'm Walter. Best we take your things to the house tonight. Big tide with a hunter's moon. Wait here, lass."

Freya's lips quirked. *Lass.* Were you still a lass at twenty-six? Perhaps he was being polite, yet there was a lilt to the way Walter said the word, and she liked the music of his accent, his courteously formal way.

Freya swung her legs over the side of the boat. She swallowed the urge to call out to that retreating back because she didn't want to be alone on the beach. *Don't be ridiculous. You chose to come, Freya Dane.* That voice in her head annoyed her. Often.

But what would have happened all those weeks ago in Sydney if she'd said to the solicitor, calling all the way from Scotland, *I don't want the place. Please arrange for the island to be sold.*

That had been her mother's advice, of course. She was a practical and dignified woman, Elizabeth Dane, but both qualities ran to sand with the first of the lawyer's letters. Corrosive regret, long strapped down beneath the armor of defensive resignation, had found a voice after Freya opened that envelope. "Why would you go to Scotland just because he's asked you to?"

But if she'd agreed with her mother, Freya would have smothered that faint, unacknowledged hope. The hope she was trying, now, not to recognize.

Coming to this place, to Findnar, might help her understand why her father had walked out of their lives all those years ago.

Freya knew Michael Dane was dead. She had seen that jagged little fact in the black type and careful lawyers' phrases. A sparse note that her father had drowned. She'd been surprised how much the news upset her—and, more strangely, her mother. They'd not talked about him for years because, stonewalled, Freya had stopped asking questions.

So there was no point, now, planning *the conversation*. No point scripting, in forensic detail, what Freya would say to her father, or what he would say to her, when they finally met again. The apologies (from him), the scorn (from her). Her fury, his penitence. Answers. *Reasons.*

Michael Dane did not exist. He was dead. They would never speak. The end.

Freya glanced up at the low gray building, now just an outline against the florid sky. His house.

So, Dad, I'm here. You whistled finally. And I came. Abrupt tears filmed her sight. Freya shook her head; *too late for that, far too late.*

The face of Fuil Bay changed, the surface chopped by a rising wind. Fuil. The word meant "blood"—Walter Boyne had told her that, shouting against the engine and the sea as they tore over the water toward . . . what? This moment she'd never expected.

Skirling air caught the girl where she stood on the beach, lifting her soft, shining hair, streaming it away behind her head. Freya shivered and chafed her arms. So, this was summer in Scotland.

A white blur swooped close. Panicked, she ducked from the yellow eyes, the slashing beak. *An owl?* Freya straightened and her heart lifted as she watched the bird ascend the face of the cliff.

Owls are good luck. Cheered, Freya began to ferry her things from the boat. All would be well. She could do this. The owl told her so.

Silently, behind her, a bright, small sphere rose in the eastern sky. Lassoed by Earth's gravity, the erratic orbit of the comet had circled back to the north after more than twelve hundred years.

The people had called it the Wanderer then, and the brighter it became, the more they feared its power. Wandering stars were omens of evil times.

But as owl-light died, Freya Dane turned her back to the stars. She did not see the Wanderer as it climbed the sky.

CHAPTER 2

I'LL TELL our mother it's your fault—you took too long making the sacrifice. We can't stay here." The whisper was fierce, but Signy knew what was going on—her older sister was trying to pull rank.

She made an effort to be reasonable—she was always the reasonable one. "Father asked me to, Laenna, you heard him. How was I to know they'd be tilling instead of singing?" Signy nodded toward the stone hut the newcomers used so often. They'd arrived on the island when Signy was still a baby, but every day since, the strangers crammed inside and sang at least seven times from well before dawn to deep in the night. Even the girls' father could not explain why.

But Laenna was jealous. She was older than Signy. Why hadn't she been asked to perform the sacrifice to the Sun? "If we'd got here earlier, we could have made the sacrifice to Cruach, taken the eggs, and gone."

Signy spoke over her sister. "But it's safe here, Laenna—they can't see us. If we wait, they'll finish what they're doing and go off and sing again. Then we can—"

"Oh yes, and what about the tide?" Laenna glared at her sister. "We'll miss it, and then we won't get back before Cruach leaves the world. The Wanderer will find us here, and that's worse. You know it is."

Laenna was impetuous, Signy was not. "If we run, they'll see us; there's hardly any cover. Besides, their God is powerful, and He'll help them catch us. We shouldn't take the risk."

"Oh, what would you know? You're just a baby. We've got Gods, too, lots more than them."

"Yes, but—"

"No! I am not going home until we've got the eggs. That'll show these idiots. They can't stop us taking what's always been ours. Come *on*." Said with the unshakable authority of fourteen summers to eleven, Laenna wasn't whispering anymore.

Signy desperately shook her head. They'd be heard!

"Don't you shoosh me, Signy." But Laenna lowered her voice. "You have to do what I say—Mother said. And we have to stick together."

"Hah!" Signy rolled over on her back. She would not look at Laenna; she was too angry.

"I'm not lying. Father said it too; it's dangerous if we split up."

Signy smothered a sigh. That was true at least; it *was* dangerous on the island now, and that was not fair. The newcomers seemed to think they owned Findnar, but that was not right. The clan memory keeper said the interlopers had arrived from the South just as summer began the year after she was born. They came in three boats—big, well-made craft with plank sides and woolen sails. They even brought livestock, cattle and pigs and sheep. The men and women dressed all alike in black and spoke a language—gabble, more like—that no one could understand then and still did not. But there were no children with that first group, and none had been born on Findnar since, which Signy and the memory keeper both thought was strange. Then, before the end of that first summer, the newcomers had begun to build with the stone of the island. A hall—square, not round—then the singing hut, and barns, too, in which they slept—men in one, women in the other.

They'd been friendly at first, but then as their second year on the island began, something changed. The people of the clan found they were no longer welcome when they landed their coracles in the cove. Even Signy and Laenna's own family, traditional custodians for generations beyond counting of the holy places—the ring stones and the great tomb of the ancestors—were made to feel like strangers.

The contest between the clan and the newcomers deepened year by year, and as Signy grew in understanding, she became fearful. She was not alone. All the clan women were frightened of what their men might do if provoked too far. No one had died yet, but that day might not be far off. Things were tense.

"Come on, Signy, please."

Laenna was wheedling, but her younger sister was sick of being bossed around *and* being responsible. She folded her arms. "It won't work."

"Sulk if you like. I'm not waiting." And Laenna was off at a crouching run through the seeding grasses; Signy had no choice, she had to follow. But she was right—as usual—for, as the girls sprinted along the cliff toward the gannet rookery, one of the new men saw them. He bellowed something loud and harsh, and two others dropped their hoes and began to run after the sisters. They hauled up their tunics, white legs flashing, screaming as they came.

Signy gasped. "Told you!"

"Idiot!"

The sisters, being young and thin and with a good start, actually made it to the marshy ground ahead of their pursuers, and they plunged in among man-high rushes; the ooze around the roots was cold and sloppy as duck shit. Just a bit farther, a bit farther, and they could hear the rookery now. All those eggs and chicks just waiting, if they could only—

"Ha!" Unfriendly hands dragged at Signy's hair, Laenna's hair. One of the strangers, bigger and faster than the others, had cut around the back of the meadow, and a mighty effort had got him to the marsh just as the girls peered out.

"Deo gratias!" Thanks to his God was premature, for Laenna

bit the man's wrist. Cursing, he punched her and Laenna fell to the grass. Like a dog will shake a rat to kill it, the man shook Signy's sister. "Little filth! Slut! Thief!"

A boy arrived. He was not much older than Laenna, and the man shoved Signy at him. "Take her. This one's mine." He grabbed Laenna's hair with his good hand. She was crying and choking as blood splashed from her nose, but he yanked down spitefully. "We know how to deal with heathen thieves." Laenna howled as she stumbled after him, trying to match his long stride, trying to pull his hands away.

The boy attempted the same trick. "Come on, you."

Signy was already standing, and she was not much shorter. She hit his hand away. When he grabbed, she growled, lifting her lips from her teeth.

The boy backed off. He picked up a rock. "I'll use this and I won't be given penance. Your heathen soul will rush to Hell." His voice was a squeak.

Signy didn't understand, but she grabbed her own rock and hurled it, hard. It took him on the side of the head. The boy collapsed to his knees, yelping.

"Hah!" Signy ran, faster than a hare raised from corn. No time for gannets now; this was all about her fool sister—they had to get back to the cove.

The world was a blur as she closed the gap. Her sister was wailing, begging for pity. *As if he understands,* thought Signy, *ignorant beast!*

At three paces, she launched herself. She took the man's knees from behind, and he fell hard, the breath knocked from his chest as he hit the earth.

"Come *on!*" Laenna hauled Signy up. Fear lent the sisters rabbit speed. They ran, lungs burning, until the shouting died behind them and, somehow, they'd found the cliff path.

Laenna panted out a promise. "My amber beads, Cruach, if

you get us safe home. I swear it, into the fire they will go." The necklace was precious—a gift for her first moontide—but she didn't care now.

It was hard to run on the narrow path, but they hurled around the first steep curve, past the lone young rowan, then the next bend, and soon they would be—

Laenna stopped as if hit. Signy collided with her sister's back. Her foot slipped from the path—she was falling!

Laenna yanked her back. Signy yelled, "What did you do that for?" And then she saw why.

Dragon ships were moored in the bay, and men, too many men, dressed in skins and homespun with swords and shields, were jumping into the sea.

Laenna said, softly, "Raiders. Nid told me. They've been seen up the coast. I thought he was trying to scare me." Under the blood and the mud, her face was white.

There was nowhere else to go. Signy grabbed her sister's hand. "Come *on*!"

They turned and ran back the way they'd come, too terrified to scream; breath and energy were needed for survival. At their backs a thudding crash began. The raiders had seen the girls and that noise, sword hilt against shield boss, frightened the sisters more than facing the newcomers. *That* noise meant death; now, not later.

The children hit the top of the cliff. They screamed as they ran toward the Abbey, past Laenna's captor, only now getting to his feet.

"They're here, they're coming. Run!"

If the man did not understand, he heard the bellow of approaching death. And then he was sprinting after the girls, he was past them, yelling . . .

"Brothers, Brothers, ring the bell. The bell! Raiders!"

That was the first night of the Wanderer in this world.

CHAPTER 3

N O POWER? What do you mean, no power?"

Walter was moving Freya's things from the dinghy to the handcart he'd brought down from the house. "Never had the electricity on Findnar so far as I know. But there's a gas ring in the house for cooking and a VHF radio for weather reports and contacting the RNLI. Runs on batteries."

Freya had just been tired before; now she was exasperated. "Why doesn't the house have power—and what's the RNLI?" She knew she looked ridiculous, hugging the laptop like a baby.

Walter hauled the clothes bag into the cart. "RNLI is the Royal National Lifeboat Institution, search and rescue for mariners. Like to ride?" He extended his hand.

Irrationally, Freya was angry. "I'll walk," she snapped. She heard herself. Surly. She stretched her face to a smile. "I've been sitting in a tin can for a day and a half. Walking's good." Walter had been a stranger only an hour ago and he didn't need to be this kind.

The fisherman said nothing, but he grinned as he bent to check the load. This one would walk up the track on her own two feet even if they bled. He picked up the cart handles and stepped forward. Two months, he thought, as he led Freya up the cliff path, three months maximum, and this girl would be gone. Autumn and the great gales would do it; that, and the truth of living on Findnar alone.

After a minute he looked back. "It's not so bad when you're used to it." He smiled encouragingly. Freya nodded; the gradient of the track was making it hard to speak. Walter slowed his pace without being obvious. "I've a cousin in Sydney; beautiful place I hear. Never been there, though, the bottom of the world."

"It's a nice city. Friendly." Freya tried not to pant.

"You'll miss it then?" The cart's wheels turned, white spokes catching some flicker of last light.

"I'm not sure, not yet anyway." *Liar.* Freya stopped and wiped her face as she stared across the strait toward Portsolly. She didn't like to be alone. At home there was always something to do, someone to see, gossip, work; but now it would be just her and this sky, this island. Could she do it—learn to just *be* in this place while she waited? For what?

A breeze nudged Freya. The man, ahead, was disappearing into the dark. She hurried after him.

Fumbling with keys, trying first one and then another, Freya said, "I hate to think of you getting caught on the open water, Walter; the wind's up. I can manage now, really."

She saw the glimmer of his teeth. "Well now, I'm thinking there's just a few little things I should—"

"Got you!" A key turned. Freya pushed the plank door wide and, stooping beneath a lintel designed for shorter people, entered Michael's house for the first time. And nearly killed herself.

Five steps led down to the kitchen; hurrying, Freya stumbled on a dip and pitched forward. Walter snatched the girl's backpack straps and swallowed a grin as she scrambled a foothold. "Perhaps it will be best if I show you how to light this house?"

Ruffled, heart thumping, Freya stood to one side, and Walter descended into the void beneath her feet. After a moment, ruddy light bloomed as he lit the wick of a lamp. With a shade of oxblood glass, it looked like a runaway from the set of a period drama, and behind him on the table stood its cousin—blue milk glass on a base of tarnished copper.

Walter waved matches. "Paraffin, these lamps. Just keep the chimneys clean, trim the wick each time, and make sure the fuel's topped up; you'll have no trouble once you've used them once or twice."

Freya nodded, bemused. These were actual functioning objects, not ornaments, and from the same era, there was a kitchen range. That ancient black bulk against the wall was intimidating—some kind of secular relic, like the lamps. She gestured. "What about the stove?"

"This?" Walter patted the monster fondly. "You don't have to cook on it—the gas ring's over there." He pointed. "But you'll find the old girl does well with a belly full of peat on a cold day—she's got a wet back."

"A wet what?"

Walter laughed. "Pipes, Freya Dane, around behind. Water's from a tank on the hill—gravity-fed." He waved toward a deep porcelain sink. There was a steel hand pump beside it. "Pump the pipes full and the water heats up when the stove's working—that's for your bath."

He set the lamp down on the kitchen table and lit the other. "Let me know how you get on next time you're over in Portsolly. Ask at the Nun. Anyone will say where to find me."

"I'll do that, but would you mind if I took your number?" Freya was unsure why that suddenly came out of her mouth, but she patted pockets, found a pen, and held it up. She said, encouragingly, "You could scribble it here if you like?" Was he reluctant? She offered a cereal packet from the box of groceries with what she hoped was a winning grin.

Walter took the pen, and Freya watched him write the numerals, chatting brightly. "And thanks again for bringing me over here. I really appreciate it." She went to get her wallet.

He waved a genial hand. "Whisht, none of that." Closing the back door gently, he was gone.

Whisht? What did that mean?

A quick knock, and Walter eased the door open again. "I forgot to say there's a cruiser in the cove. That's how you get to Port." He tipped an imaginary hat.

"Thanks." But Freya called out to the door as it closed. "Thanks for that . . ." Her tone faded as she stared around the empty kitchen. Michael Dane's kitchen.

She set the lamp with the red shade on the windowsill over the sink. The warm light was comforting, and as her eyes adjusted, she began to absorb her surroundings.

The kitchen was a useful size—not cramped but not so large it couldn't be heated quickly. The floor was flagged with pieces of natural slate; that would be cold in winter, but cheerful kelims broke up the expanse. *Winter won't bother me. I won't be here.*

Freya ran her hand over the scrubbed top of the kitchen table. It was massive, so large it must have been built within the room. Generations of islanders had sat at this table before her, before her father.

"Hello, Dad." Freya spoke without thinking. Eerie. She shook herself.

"I'm going to explore, that's what I'll do." There was no one in this house to challenge her. Walter had put the groceries on the table. "After dinner." Soup and bread, that would be easiest.

But as Freya began to remove the bags, the tins, the bottles one by one, she saw something she'd not noticed before.

Beside the cardboard box was a folder and a string-trussed package. "For my daughter, Freya Dane" was scrawled on the front of both.

Freya picked the folder up. His fingers had formed these words, shaped the letters. He'd thought of her, at least for that moment.

The edge of a chair seat caught behind her knees. A nudge to sit. Was this his chair? A Windsor carver, curved in the splats with a gentle hollow in the seat; the wood was mellow as honey.

Freya didn't want to put the folder down. It might disappear as he had. She watched herself place it on the table as carefully as an offering. From somewhere outside her head, she saw that she was shaking.

Eight remembers a lot. Four does too. Even at four she'd sensed her parents' unhappiness, and sometimes, after she'd been put to her bed, after the last story had been finished and she was on the edge of sleep, she'd heard them in the rooms downstairs.

Her mother, mostly. Shouting sometimes.

Michael did not shout, he spoke more softly.

Her mother would cry some nights. Then a door would slam— the downstairs bedroom, that's where Elizabeth went when she did not sleep in the big room upstairs. The room Freya thought of as her father's.

Those were the nights she did not go to sleep. She'd wait for him to walk up the stairs, wait for the door to the bedroom to open, wait longer for the light under the door to go out. Then she'd run from her own warm bed and burrow in behind his back. He never said much, just "Go to sleep. You'll see, it will be better in the morning."

But it wasn't. They'd pretend, of course, for her.

It was then that dread had become her companion, because Freya knew, she *knew,* that one day she'd come home from school and he'd be gone. And that is what happened.

Freya squeezed her eyes shut. *Why?*

From misplaced loyalty perhaps—but loyalty to what, to whom? Elizabeth would not tell her. Not when she was a child and not when she was an adult. Even now it was never possible to talk about the meaning of that absence in their lives, but there was anger. A rich vein of it beneath the surface of the skin, hers and Elizabeth's, too, with confusion at its core.

And now there was this. A manila folder. A package.

"For my daughter, Freya Dane."

She thought he'd forgotten. But why contact her now, and in

this way? Perhaps the folder would tell her that Michael had married again, that there were other children out there—half brothers and half sisters.

Freya got up with such force the chair squawked. "I'm hungry." The weakness was low blood sugar, bound to be. "And I'm not going to do this now."

She would make him wait as *he* had made her wait, all those years ago.

But at least, then, she'd had hope that one day the door would open and there he would be again—that he would ask her to forgive him.

She'd never worked out if she would or not. Tears or icy rejection? It depended on her mood.

Fingers stiff as twigs, Freya lit the gas ring as wind began to hunt the eaves of the house. The flame, when she struck it, was bright. A star in that dark room.

CHAPTER 4

RATHER THAN run for the doubtful safety of the Abbey, Signy and Laenna had scampered back to the rushes. Burrowing, they'd clawed their way to the roots, curling together in the mud like cats in a basket. And there they'd lain as the sack of the Abbey began, too frightened to move.

The invaders had begun with the chanting shed, but now all the buildings were burning, the sky was burning, as Findnar's newcomers were herded toward death and worse. Perhaps the raiders were demons, evil beings conjured from flame, creatures who feasted on blood.

The howls were the worst. Even at this distance, the sisters could hear men screaming. Who could tell if it was the newcomers as they died or the raiders about the slaughter?

They heard women's voices too. Higher-pitched, sobbing, screaming out one word, over and over. Mary.

It was owl-light now, that dangerous time half light, half dark, when things change their shape. The screams stopped, and there was a lower confusion of sounds. Smoke was thicker than mist. Soon there was only the crack of burning timber and the occasional shout as an invader found something or someone missed in the first chaos. Meat was cooking; the raiders must have killed the animals as well.

"Stay here." Laenna was pushing the reeds aside, wriggling away.

"No! Please, Laenna. Don't go!"

"I have to see what's happened. If they've gone, we can go home. Be quiet and lie still. I'll come back for you."

Signy tried to stop her sister, but Laenna pushed her down. She was gone before Signy could sit up.

The child closed her eyes and shivered. She should pray for help, but who would hear her? Her own Gods were at home in their parents' house, and Cruach had left the world for today. She could not call on the new God of this island either, the one the strangers worshipped—she did not know His name, and He would not know her. Anyway, He wouldn't help, why would He, when He'd just allowed his own followers to be murdered? Had He punished them for taking Findnar from her people?

Signy shivered. Her father always said Gods were dangerous if you crossed them. He was a shaman and knew such things. Maybe she should pray to Tarannis in the sky. He wasn't one of their usual Gods, but she knew he looked down on everyone; he was the fire God, too, and the God of thunder. The fires lit by the raiders had roared like a storm at their height and, even if the ring stones weren't his home, Tarannis might approve of the sacrifice she'd made, since Cruach, who lived there, was his brother. Yes, when this was over she would hurry to the stones to thank them both for the hiding place—it might be fetid, but the rushes were thick and had hidden them well.

Them. Where was Laenna?

Flat on her belly, Signy moved like a worm, knees and elbows propelling her through the ooze. Beneath the rot there was a hint of apples and mushrooms; if the marsh ever dried, this would be good soil. The strangers had come here for the same reasons her people always had; Findnar was a summerland of plenty.

Smoke hung, curtain high, above the smudge of Signy's face as she peered out. There was clear air close to the ground, but three handspans higher and the world was blanket-cloaked, smoke hiding the stars.

That, above all else, broke Signy's courage. If she could not see the sky, Tarannis would not see her. She would never get home, never; neither of them would. Tears fell, clean lines on her dirty face.

An owl came out of the smoke, pale as ash. It landed close, so close Signy could touch its feathers. It turned to look at her, gold eyes unblinking. A sign!

She whispered, "In the name of Tarannis, show me how to leave this place."

Soft as it had come, the owl left, swallowed by the dusk and the smoke. The child screamed out, "No! Don't go!"

A man's hand descended from the smoke-blanket. He caught Signy by the throat, and she was jerked into the air, flailing and coughing. Desperation turned fingers to talons. Signy slashed at the man's face, and she was lucky—long nails found flesh and gouged.

Blood filled the man's eyes. Bellowing, he nearly dropped her.

She wriggled and howled. A lucky kick did the rest as one of Signy's hard little feet found her attacker's balls. He staggered, yelping.

That was enough. Signy fled, fast as a hind, swallowed by smoke as the owl had been.

Breathless, choking, she thought she was running toward the cliff path, but she stumbled and fell. She'd tumbled over something. A body, facedown in the grass. A sudden gust of wind tore the smoke.

Signy stuffed her hand in her mouth.

Oblivious to danger, oblivious to pursuit, she knelt. The back of the skull was a bloody mess, broken like an egg. Without words, without tears, she laid her face against the unmoving back, the dirty homespun cloth. Laenna. This was all that was left of her sister.

The smoke thinned, and through it she saw the man. He was blundering toward her, an ax in his hand—a red ax.

When Signy fled this time, it was purely from instinct, no

thought in her mind but running and breathing. She ran from the light of the fires, ran and ran, and when she cried, the tears dried in the heat of that night—the heat of destruction.

Down the cliff path, down to the beach, down to the sea. It was nearly dark, but no moon had yet risen to expose her. This was all she could do, and perhaps, in the end, Tarannis was merciful, for the ships hauled up on the beach were unguarded—there'd been no need to leave sentries.

So the child hurried alone, in the shadow of the cliff, to the place they'd left their coracle at dawn, outside the sea cave.

She found their small craft smashed.

Like a wounded animal, Signy crept deep into the back of the cave, and from the pain that clenched her body she thought she might die, but in the end she only sobbed until she slept.

She did not see the comet as it rose against the clearing stars. She was too deep in the dark.

The long-necked ships would leave soon. They were being readied to push out from the beach on the swollen, full-moon tide.

The raid had been successful, and the vessels were laden with trade goods because the invaders had kept nearly all the younger nuns alive, though some of the older monks, those who'd tried to fight, had been killed. A loss, of course, but the remaining boys— those without beards—would be valuable; they'd likely be gelded before the autumn markets and sold on as merchants' clerks. And a large enameled cross had been looted from the chapel, along with a good, uncracked bell of bronze. Since there was always a short-age of bronze on the market, this alone would fetch a price that would put the raid into profit.

Reimer, the captain of the raiding band, was impatient at the slow start to the day. He was beginning to pace. A bad sign.

His men had eaten and drunk well after the raid—too well. After their days at sea, they'd gorged themselves on the fat sheep of Findnar's meadows. Mutton, though not as good for fighting men as beef, was relished after fish for so many days, and they'd also found jars of mead in an earth cellar under one of the barns.

"Men of God they call themselves—idiots and drunkards, that's what *I* think them. Our Gods crushed theirs last night. No contest. Eh? Eh, Thorkeld?"

Thorkeld nodded, keeping his eye on the work going forward. He was happy to agree with his volatile war leader, since doing so saved trouble and time. No contest. The lieutenant yawned, scratching his belly. A big man who had survived late into his third decade, Thorkeld was unexcitable. He commanded *Wave Piercer,* the second largest ship in the fleet of twelve, and he'd worked hard last night but, after so many similar raids this season, he was, unusually, feeling the effects. His ax arm, for instance. He'd jarred it torching the chapel; plus the smoke, noise, and ale headache from the aftermath was more annoying than usual. The Abbey folk had not offered significant resistance, however, except for one or two hotheads, who were easily dealt with. On balance, irritations aside, a good result. Today though, when he was both queasy and tired, Thorkeld had no relish for the long, cold voyage to come.

Perhaps he was finally too old for this life. He didn't enjoy it as much as he once had; maybe it was time to leave it to younger men and retire to his farm, paid for from twenty years of raiding, and breed sons. He'd earned that.

"I'll kill you!"

Reimer and Thorkeld turned to look at a fight at the water's edge. A wheat-haired youth in his late teens was choking another member of the war band. They were fighting over a coffer from the Abbey. Its lid was up, and vestments, one or two of silk, were spilling into the water.

"They'll ruin those if they keep this up." Reimer hated waste.

Thorkeld nodded and started off to pull the men apart. Reimer called him back. "No. It might help Grimor. He's been black since last night."

Grimor, the blond, was winning—his opponent was on his knees in the surf, blood from a split nose and a broken eye socket washing away in the sea. At last the defeated youth staggered to his feet, hands held high and empty; he waded out of the surf followed by Grimor's jeers and the laughter of his comrades on the beach.

Reimer grunted, transferred his attention back to the loading. "No word of the boy?"

Thorkeld shook his head. "No. Just classic inexperience—the kid was full of himself after the river village, and he thought this one was easy."

Reimer agreed. "A waste." His band had sacked a settlement at the mouth of a small river some days sailing from Findnar before they burned this monastery. The river people had been a tougher contest since they'd been armed and had more trained fighters among them, but Grimor's younger brother, Magni, had done well in what had been his first real raid.

Thorkeld continued. "I looked for his body this morning, so did Grimor. Nothing. Magni's dead, burned I'd say. He showed promise, though, and courage—that's something Grimor can take comfort from."

The war leader sighed. "You're right, you're always right, Thorkeld. But we can't let one boy's death hold us up." He was distracted watching the last women being stowed onboard. Reimer didn't want them damaged. Two of the three were handsome enough to fetch good prices at the markets, and the third was a real beauty, even with all her hair hacked off. "Would you look at what the Christians did to her? The hair!"

Thorkeld took his leader's elbow in the ribs in good part as they watched one of the men pull the girl to her feet—she began to scream, of course; they were all good screamers. But he agreed, the monks and nuns truly were fools. Why would you knowingly damage the looks of a girl like that? It would take at least a year for the hair to grow to anything like an acceptable length, and someone would have to invest the money to feed her while she was held back from sale.

Reimer sucked his teeth reflectively and watched the pretty novice struggle as she was carried to *Fenrir,* his own ship. The craft was the largest in the fleet, big enough to take thirty rowers on each side. The girl was gagged now and her hands securely bound, but even though she was filthy with smoke and scared out of her wits, her face was a pleasure to look at. And her body was at that early stage of ripening that Reimer, personally, found very attractive; the young ones were so much easier to deal with. In fact, as he watched, he made up his mind. He'd keep this one. It was a while since he'd allowed himself anything pleasurable from a raid, and he deserved something for his efforts, long overdue tribute, in fact.

His senior wife would not be pleased, but she'd come around; he'd just have to make sure she didn't harry the girl to a miserable death. But, in the end, what did it really matter—what was one concubine more or less?

"Careful! Look at that, Thorkeld. What is that great oaf *doing*!" The girl had wriggled so much the man who had her over his shoulder lost his footing, and he and his burden both fell into the surf. Having her hands tied, she hadn't surfaced. "Pull her up, you fool! Go on!" The girl was hauled, choking, out of the water.

Thorkeld was bored. He'd seen it too many times; this island had given all it had for the moment, and he was as impatient as his master to weigh anchor. "I'm sure she'll settle now, Lord."

At the last minute, Reimer had decided that the three best women should be placed on his own vessel, and Thorkeld agreed with the decision. There was no point putting valuable merchandise on any of the other ships, since, having been used by the crew, they'd be in a shocking state by the time they arrived at winter quarters.

Reimer nodded absently as he watched the crying girl pushed

over the side into his ship. As Thorkeld had said, all the fight in her was gone. "Good. Let's be away."

After the raiders left, when the tide had lowered once and come in again, Signy left the cave.

She was hungry and thirsty and numb with grief, but the sea had washed away the marks where the hulls had rested. The raiders were truly gone.

Now she must bury her sister.

CHAPTER 5

THIS HOUSE had a name, and Freya remembered it from the solicitor's letter. Compline House, Findnar Island, near Portsolly, KA33, Scotland—a mouthful with a twist that seemed uniquely charming when first read.

Compline. She'd looked it up. In monastic tradition, the last prayers before bed were called by this name—prayers of protection against the evils of the night.

Freya raised the lamp higher. She was reflected in one window of the largest room, at the very front of the house. In daylight there would be a view of all the western sky and the strait between the island and the mainland. The letter had told her he'd died out there. That night, in the water, there'd been no protection for Michael Dane; no search and rescue had come for him.

Lost at sea; the words had never resonated before now.

Abruptly, Freya turned away from the glass. Holding the lamp higher, she saw faint marks on the board ceiling above her head. This must have been two rooms once, and there would have been a corridor where she'd entered from the kitchen; someone had taken the walls out to open up this graceful space.

The place was sparsely furnished, yet each item spoke of a clear aesthetic. The chair of stainless steel and leather, a small deep couch and matching armchair, a glass table loaded with books and magazines—even the old station clock over the fireplace had been chosen for its design and style, not just price.

So, he'd had taste, her father. Unaccountably that made Freya angry—he'd not been around to show her how much he loved beauty.

She walked to the desk placed beneath one of the windows and ran her hand over the timber. Oak, planed and then meticulously sanded.

"Did you make this, Dad?"

From long ago, she remembered his hand holding a chisel as the other tapped on the end with a wooden mallet. He'd made her a bed once, and carved a bas-relief of her six-year-old profile on the headboard.

She banished that image. *Concentrate.*

Her father's desk was still covered with working papers, and there was a stack of books on the floor beside the chair just as if he had, at that moment, got up and gone to the kitchen to make a cup of tea. And there was a VHF radio. Small and bright yellow, it was the size of a TV remote. Freya thumbed the On button; the screen stayed blank. Her father had died six months ago. Of course the batteries were flat.

Ruby light displayed a bloom of dust on the sprawled possessions, the pot full of pens and pencils, the stapler. There was even dust on the paperweight—a snow dome of the Sydney Opera House, the sort of thing you'd give a child as a joke present.

Could she see him shaking it, or was that just imagination? *No snow in Sydney, Little Fee, except in here.* That was what he'd called her, Little Fee. Was that her laughter she heard, a happy kid? Freya stared at the paperweight, reached out, almost touched it . . .

No. She turned away from the black glass, away from the image of her face, one side in shadow, one side bright. Was it a trick of that strange mirror—to see her face so haunted and so strange? And younger, the face of the lonely child she'd once been.

"This is *rubbish.*" It was bracing to shout; the noise filled Freya with energy.

"What rubbish." She said it softly the second time. Freya wandered around the austere and beautiful room, trying to take it all in, trying to smell out the truth of Michael's presence.

What remained here? What was really left? His books—he'd collected them and no doubt knew the contents of each one. Floor to ceiling, the width of the entire front wall of the house was lined with his library, and there were even shelves below, between, and above each of the windows. "Lotta trips up that path, Dad. That must have kept you fit."

Freya slid a volume out from among its companions—there was almost no dust. These books had been frequently used.

Holding up the lamp, she saw a number handwritten on each spine in white correcting fluid; so, Michael still had his own system, and, if she looked, she knew she'd find his card file—there'd be no computer database for Michael Dane. "Writing time is thinking time, Little Fee." He'd always been a Luddite.

Freya nodded. *I know, Dad. I agree.* She, too, liked to write things first in longhand—an anachronism, but his anachronism. Some things remained to her, of him. And as a child she'd loved his cards, each one an elegant statement of his love for what he did.

Archaeology, of course. That thing, worse than another woman, the obsession that had taken him away; it must have been that. Family and archaeology—why had they been so incompatible, and why had she followed Michael into that same realm of the dead past?

Freya snorted. She knew why; any bloody amateur psychologist could tell her why. She wanted to prove herself to him, wanted to be better than he was.

Too late.

Freya shook her head, angry, not sad. *Can't please you now that you're dead, can I?* She ran a finger across the book spines as she walked the length of the room. Gradually, as she knew she would, she was absorbed by the names, the bindings, the range of topics . . .

She stopped. Of course! This library would be the most tremendous resource for *her* work. Freya laughed at the irony.

No power = no laptop = no surfing the Net, but with all that was on these shelves, she'd not even miss the Web for research—her father's books would get her to the end of her unloved doctorate. Michael's deep knowledge of his chosen subject, the archaeology of the so-called Dark Ages, the early medieval to be exact, and the resources in this room would provide all she needed and more.

Perhaps she *was* meant to come to this place after all. Perhaps, in the end, there were no accidents.

Freya Dane sat down at her father's kitchen table, the lamps placed on either side of the folder. She pulled it toward her. In that quiet room, the cardboard made a hushing sound as it slid across the plank top.

She opened the flap. It had an internal pocket, and in that was a solicitor's card. She scanned the plain black type—it announced that Hindhawk, Piddington, and Associates, Solicitors and Advocates, could be found at Kings Quay Chambers, 18 Balloch Court, Ardleith, KA33, Scotland. *Scotland* was embossed—a definite statement. Freya's lips quirked. Scots independence rose up from that small cardboard rectangle—no *United Kingdom* for these gentlemen at law, apparently.

She put the card aside. Inside the folder there was a mass of anonymous white pages, covered in her father's writing. And then she took in the meaning and feeling behind the first words of his letter before they blurred.

December 31
Close to Midnight

My darling Freya,

Perhaps it is the last night of the old year that has made
me write to you or perhaps because whisky, drunk alone,
brings feeling close to the surface.

Truth is always complex, but tonight I have, it seems, the courage to say what must be said between us. And also to try to record what has happened on this island, to set down the facts as simply as I can, because it is your right to know.

For if you are reading what I've written here instead of talking to me over a companionable dram at last, that will be because I've left instructions with my solicitors in Ardleith.

By now you'll know that Findnar belongs to you, with this house and all its contents. And this document will be placed where, hopefully, you will find it if and when you decide to come here. I hope you do. If I close my eyes, I can see you sitting here, at my kitchen table. That provides a little comfort.

Perhaps you do not believe that I am sad, desolate rather, that we have never met as adults? Believe me, I am. I have planned, so often, what we might say to each other, but each conversation in my head begins and ends with this. I want you to know that I have never, ever stopped loving you.

Freya blinked. There was a pain at the base of her throat, and it was hard to breathe. The words swam, and it was some minutes before she went on reading.

It's such a very long time ago that your mother and I parted. I don't know how much you actually understood, then, of the causes of the end of our marriage. I've often asked myself that question. Would it have been better if you hadn't known the ins and outs, or worse?

No answer to that question. I shall not write of such sadness now because I want to tell you about the life I've

lived here, and I want to explain an instinct I have long
cherished: that you, and only you, are the right person to
own Findnar after me. I'll try to explain when I have told
you a little more.

Of course, it will be your decision—and right—to
keep this place or to sell it as you please. All I ask is
that you read what I've set down here and suspend
judgment, if you can. This is the most difficult letter
I have ever written, but I am telling you the truth, so
far as I understand it.

I also want to describe something very odd—a puzzle,
if you like, or a mystery, the greatest of my working life.
I've not been able to properly decode the evidence either,
though I have found so many hints, gone down so many
false trails trying to do just that. Perhaps you will succeed
where I have failed. I hope that you do.

I know that you're close to the end of your doctorate.
By the way, I'm proud indeed that you have chosen to
become an archaeologist. For this conundrum, however,
you will need all the skills you have learned at university
and something more, something I believe you have in
your bones—instinct. I saw it in you as a child.

Do you remember that summer dig in Norway when
you were seven? Freya, you were a real member of our
team, not just a passenger, or the boss's daughter.

Did she remember? Freya swallowed. Of course she remembered. Sleeping in a tent with just her dad, dirty and hot in the
long, bright days, so happy grubbing in the dirt as they excavated
the streets of the trading port from a thousand years ago. And the
pride when, all by herself, she had found the enameled brooch and
brought it out of the ground, intact. *He* had been proud of her, too,
and there was a photograph of them both grinning—white teeth in
dirty faces—as she held up the treasure she'd found.

Nineteen years ago. Time was supposed to heal, to seal over loss. Freya cleared her throat noisily. *Did you expect this to be easy for either of us, Dad?*

Freya, this island gives up its secrets reluctantly. Some, from the recent past—the last six hundred years or so—I have uncovered, but some, one in particular, are much more ancient and intractable. And elusive; I did not know that, of course, when I came here. Perhaps you've wondered about Findnar—and why I bought the island.

Freya pushed back against his chair. "So, tell me, Dad." When he left Elizabeth, Michael had done two decent things. He'd signed over the Sydney house to his wife, and he'd never shirked his obligation of maintenance payments for Freya as she grew up. Her mother had told her that—grudgingly—after the letter arrived from Scotland.

To say Freya had been angry she hadn't been told didn't touch the sides, and the flare-up between the pair went nuclear. It still hurt not to have known that he'd cared about her, even to that extent, for all those years. Searing questions had been asked and avoided. *Why did he leave you, why?*

He was searching. We weren't enough for him.

For what? Jesus Christ, what was he searching for? There has to be more. You're lying to me; you have in the past, you're doing it now.

Freya blinked. She was sorry for some of the things she'd said to Elizabeth, and they'd made up after a day or so because fights were rare between them, but her curiosity *had* kicked in—and Michael was right. She wanted to know how he'd been able to buy Findnar, since Elizabeth implied her ex-husband was, so far as she knew, broke after giving her the house.

I resigned from the university too—did you know that? That place was part of the problem between your mother and me. I was never ambitious and Elizabeth was—for me, that is. I've always liked to dig more than to teach, and they knew that. I was passed over for tenure too many times, and I was never going to be dean, of course. Politics. Not my strong suit. So I ran away from Sydney, worked in the gulf, on the rigs. Entry-level jobs at first, roughneck and roustabout. I was leading a drilling crew inside two years, and I rediscovered my physical self. How to just be and not overthink everything—that saved me.

"Overthink everything." The pages trembled. "There's a gene for that?" Freya shook her head.

It was hard work, twelve, fourteen hours a day and dangerous, but very well paid. And I saved my dollars because with free food and accommodation I had nothing to spend them on (we were paid in US currency, tax-free, when the dollar was worth something in the world). I heard about Findnar from a Scot—we shared accommodation on the platform—a forced sale, he said. And the gulf was starting to heat up politically at that time so . . . I decided it was time to go. I flew to Edinburgh and choppered into Aberdeen, hired a car and drove to Portsolly. End of story. There was something about this place, and I didn't care about the remoteness, that suited me. Findnar was so cheap, though, of course, it's a while ago now, and though Compline had been uninhabited for years—another winter and the roof would have gone—I knew I'd have the time (fourteen days on, twenty-one days off) to restore the house. It turned out that the bank was desperate to unload the place for almost any price to set against the debts of the owners on the mainland,

and I had enough put by for a deposit. That got me a
mortgage, and I decided to work out of Aberdeen on the
North Sea rigs. Wilder, much, much colder, but it was
closer to home. And that's what Findnar has become. My
home. And slowly, Compline came good—as you'll see if
you look around. A lot of work, a lot of trips up and down
that path, but satisfying to see the house come back
to life.

And archaeology found me again because I was able
to pursue work on my own terms here.

I hope you like living and working here too, Freya.
If you decide to stay.

The soft light played with his words. "Sorry, Dad, not convinced I'm an archaeologist. There. Said it." Freya chaffed her
arms. Perhaps his voice in her head was amused as she read on.

Whatever you decide, my finds of these last years
are all cataloged. There are site plans, drawings, and
photographs, and I've stored the physical objects in the
undercroft—others will call it a cellar, but I know you
will understand what it is.

This house proper may be only a few hundred years
old but in the lower layer it's much more ancient, though
linked in style to the Abbey; that's what people have
always called the ruins beside Compline, by the way,
and "people" are right.

However, going further, it is my belief that parts
of Compline House are very much older than even
the monastic era. I feel they predate the turn of the
millennium before last, and it is this aspect of Compline's
past for which I have pursued dating evidence; it's
become a quest—the center of my being. And it feels
right, somehow, what I am doing here.

There are riddles in this place that I have never solved. But you? Well, you are different, you always have been. The head from me. The heart, the imagination from your mother. And that is why I feel compelled to tell you something I do not think I can share with any other person.

I have always thought of myself as a rational being, Freya, a person who deals with facts—so far as any archaeologist can. But there are other dimensions to this puzzle than concrete, datable evidence of the past. I am not able, any longer, to accept the deductions of my training, or my senses, alone.

Now, I look at what I have just written, and I see you shaking your head, yet it is very hard to find words to describe what I have experienced so recently on Findnar.

Lately, what I can only describe as visions have begun to disturb my sleep. These are not dreams, by the way—dreams have no structure—but what I see, what I increasingly hear, does. It is as if I am being given a new chapter of a story to absorb each night. The setting is always Findnar, and there is only a small cast of people, but the time is not our era.

Thraaaaaamp! Something hit the back door. Freya jumped, heart jolting. She rose from the chair. Another thump. Harder. This one rattled the handle.

"Hello?" She heard herself. *Hello—how dumb is that?*

Freya turned the key quickly and pulled the door open; wild air rushed past and riffled the papers off the table—absorbed in Michael's letter, she had not heard the storm rise outside, and lumps of peat had been flung out of an upended basket by the force of the gale; they'd hit the kitchen door.

It was hard to shut the night outside, but Freya forced the door to close. She picked up the scattered sheets of paper and did not sit down to the letter again until she'd drunk a hot, sweet cup of tea and lost the shakes.

> Recently, just before Christmas, there was a week of fine weather and I decided to finish some work I had started. In the autumn just gone, I sank some trenches in the circle of standing stones—seeking dating evidence of construction.
> To that point, the trial digs yielded little, but when I reopened a trench near the center of the circle, more digging yielded a number of remarkable artifacts. They were hidden—I'm convinced of that, by the way—but by whom it is impossible to say. Certainly pre the first millennium and utterly unique. I believe a crucifix I found there is the key to the visions—everything I have experienced began after I gave it away. You will find full descriptions of that piece and of each of the other objects in my notes. And please, Freya, look with particular care at the contents of the small lead box. Can you read Latin by the way?

Lead box? Crucifix? Freya frowned; archaeologists do not give away unique finds. Had her father been drunk by the time he'd written this stream of consciousness?

> Now, you may say that a lifelong interest in the past and constant study is generating all that I am experiencing—or that I am drunk.

Freya sat straighter in the chair and faintly smiled.

> At the beginning, I would have said you were right (in reference to the former, not the latter). Now, I am not convinced, and to engage with, to really examine, the

meaning of recent events, the objects I have found must be properly placed in their contexts—validated, if you like.

If you are reading this letter, I will not have achieved my goal. And if that is so, this is where I must ask you to help me, though I have no right.

It would be a miracle, I know, if you were able to find written records for the people whose names I shall give you, for I have not been able to. However, I feel certain there will be something. Even a crumb of information, no matter how small, will be important.

And you must search for the grave and the tomb. I am convinced they

The writing ceased.

"Tomb?" Freya turned the page over, held up the folder, and shook it. Nothing, except for a small, yellowing newspaper clipping, which fluttered down, mothlike, to the tabletop.

It was from the Ardleith *Herald,* and it was dated January 1. The column was brief, under an arresting headline: HEROIC RESCUE FAILS.

In simple language the article recorded the death by drowning in the early hours of the morning of January 1 of Michael Dane, PhD '52, born Sydney, Australia, but longtime resident and owner of the island of Findnar.

Dr. Dane, formerly an archaeologist, had died trying to assist a fishing vessel named *The Holy Isle* and its crew of two: Walter Boyne, fifty-seven, and his son, Daniel Boyne, thirty-one, fishermen, both of Portsolly.

The details blurred as Freya absorbed the facts. Walter Boyne had been there when it happened.

And he'd said nothing to her.

CHAPTER 6

SIGNY WAS starving. She stumbled as she walked the line where hard sand met shingle in the cove. She had to go back to the Abbey, to the killing ground; she must find Laenna's body and bury it. After that, she would look for food; there would be gannets' eggs, if nothing else. Then she would go home. She would find a way.

The last, steep turn in the cliff track nearly defeated the child. Just a few more steps, only a few, two more, one . . .

Signy collapsed on the grass as the sky whirled above her and settled to a high, blue bowl.

It was a warm day, quiet except for birdsong and the distant mutter and slump of the sea—perfect. But there was smoke in the air, an acrid tang.

Signy stared at the sun. "Help me, Cruach. Please." She knelt in the grass, holding up her hands to the white disk above her head. "Make my sister be alive. Make this all a dream."

A breeze lifted hair from her eyes, gentle as a mother's hand. "Ma, oh, Ma. How can I tell you?" Signy thought there were no more tears, but they came from somewhere as delayed shock punched her down and she saw, once more, her sister's crushed head.

"Poor little thing. Hush now, you're not alone. Hush . . ."

Signy froze. Perhaps the hand on her shoulder was kind, but like an animal she curled in on herself.

Let the blow be fast. I won't feel it if it's fast.

"I can help you." A woman's voice.

Signy opened her eyes. Only a little.

Soft, crumpled skin was framed in white linen; or it had been white once, but now the cloth was filthy. Robes of black wool hid the dirt better.

The smiling woman held out her hands. "There, see? I am a friend."

Instinct beat fear. Signy wrapped herself around the stranger instantly, twig arms stronger than any vine.

"What's that?"

A man spoke.

Signy buried her head in the woman's belly, quivering.

"Hush, Brother. She's just a child, badly frightened."

The man muttered, "Aren't we all?" He cleared his throat. "One of ours, Sister? I do not recognize her."

"No, Brother Cuillin. I do not know where she is from."

What were they saying? It was the same gabble all the newcomers spoke; Signy dared to open her eyes. The man was staring at her—his eyes were bleak. He was about the same age as the woman.

"A heathen child. Local. Has to be unless she came with the raiders. No good to us either way."

Why was his voice so harsh? The man seemed angry. Signy buried her head again, shaking—it was hard not to cry.

The nun, Sister Gunnhilde, put a finger to her lips. "Hush, Brother, you've scared her. At least she's alive."

Cuillin sighed. He was too tired to be offended. To help Gunnhilde, he bent to lift Signy, but the girl screamed when he touched her.

Gunnhilde put her arms around the child. "I'll do it, Brother. There, girl, no one will hurt you." She pulled Signy onto her hip and walked beside the monk toward the ruins of the Abbey.

Signy hid her head in Gunnhilde's neck. She did not want to see what the world looked like, not yet.

The adults murmured together as they walked. "How many of the community are left, Brother?"

The monk shook his head. Like Gunnhilde, his eyes were red from smoke and grief. "No more than a handful. Besides me, two brothers from the Scriptorium, Anselm and Simon, and only one of the novices; he hid in the combe."

Gunnhilde nodded. The combe was a small wooded valley beneath the Pagan stone circle, a sensible place to hide. "I saw Brother Vidor from the kitchen earlier, and one of my novices managed to run away also."

Cuillin caught Gunnhilde's glance over the child's head. "Praise be, Sister, for this at least." They'd both seen what happened to most of the Abbey's novice nuns.

Signy felt something wet drop on the back of her neck. Tears. She clung on more tightly.

They were close to the Abbey when Gunnhilde stopped. Slowly she absorbed the extent of the blasphemy and the horror. She crossed herself, as did Cuillin. "The end of the world. You were right, Brother—you told us the traveling star was a warning."

Cuillin's anguish was very great. "Why would God punish His servants in this way, Sister?"

Gunnhilde hitched Signy higher on her hip. She was exhausted, but there was far, far too much to do to acknowledge weakness. "Perhaps, in His mercy, God will tell us. Then we can make reparation for our sins." The nun walked toward the ruined buildings carrying the child as if she'd been a mother all her life.

Brother Cuillin caught up. "I forgot to say, there's another one. A heathen boy—he came with the raiders, I think. He looks like them, rather than her." He eyed the filthy child dispassionately. Black hair, black eyes, brown skin. The boy was blond, a superior type compared to the tiny native people. "I think he is dying, however. Perhaps we should put him out of his pain; it might be a kindness."

Gunnhilde stopped. She faced Cuillin, eyes snapping. "If God has given us these children, it is for a purpose, Brother. They will be treated as Christ. It is our privilege to receive them and to bring them to Him." She clutched Signy tightly and cradled the child's head to her chest, muttering, "The idea. The very idea!"

Signy did not know or care what the adults were fighting about; all she knew was that the old lady would protect her. That was enough.

It was many days before Gunnhilde was sure the boy would live.

He'd been caught in the Abbey as it burned. One of the roof beams had fallen, breaking both his legs, and he'd been trapped beneath it. Someone must have seen what happened, for the burning timber had been pulled away and the boy dragged outside. Dumped behind a pile of rubble, he'd lain unconscious for all that night and the day afterward until found by Cuillin. By that time, shock from burns and blood loss was compounded by infection.

Now the boy was lying on a heap of straw under the one piece of roof still left on the nuns' dormitory. Flushed and moaning, barely conscious, his eyes glittered beneath bruised lids. Signy, edging closer, recoiled from the stench of his wounds and the sight of his damaged face. Nausea made her forget hunger.

"You must help me, girl. We have little time if he is to be saved."

With sign language, Gunnhilde showed the Pagan girl how to drip water into the boy's mouth from an unbroken beaker. Then she hurried away to find medicinal plants in what was left of the Infirmarian's garden. First she must make poultices for his burns and then consider what to do about his other injuries.

Clutching the beaker, Signy sat back. She tried not to look at the boy, since flies covered his face in a black, heaving mass. When he attempted to move his head, they rose in a fizzing swarm and then settled back. In weakness and pain, the boy called out, *"Grimor!"* as slow tears bled from closed eyes.

Signy dropped her head to her knees, dizzy and weak. *I will not vomit!*

"*Grimor. Grimor!*" The boy was increasingly agitated.

Signy leaned forward. Perhaps he was calling to his Gods. She tried to coax the boy to drink, and he did not have the strength to push her hand away. His eyes opened wide and blank, and the two children stared at each other until his gaze clouded. He muttered something and sighed.

"Water." Signy knew he could not understand, but he frowned as if he had. He did not want her help. Did she care? If he really was a raider, he deserved to die in as much agony as Laenna had; she should be glad that he suffered, but that was hard.

This stranger was just one more poor, broken creature and, when he died, as seemed likely, he would pass into the dark alone, far from his family. Without the comfort of his Gods, or someone to perform the rites of passage, where would his spirit go? Unappeased, perhaps he would haunt them. That thought, if nothing else, made Signy sidle closer, and she tried to drop water into the boy's mouth. She was frightened of malevolent spirits.

"That is good. Very good."

The old woman had returned. She smiled approvingly as she pounded leaves and roots together on a flat rock with a hand-size stone.

Signy smelled wild garlic, and she saw plantain roots plus another plant with large, hairy leaves.

The old woman beckoned; she handed Signy a small pot. "Here, just a little at a time when I say." Gunnhilde mimed dripping the contents onto the mess of crushed plants.

Wary, Signy sniffed the liquid; she smelled honey. Her eyes brightened.

Gunnhilde knew the girl would not understand, but the sound of a human voice among such devastation was comforting. "Yes. It's nice, mead: just a little splash." She mimed the action, and Signy copied her. "That's right, good." The nun talked as she worked; at least the child seemed bright enough to grasp simple instructions. "Fermented honey—that's the smell; honey is a powerful healer, especially with comfrey and garlic." But Gunnhilde cast a worried glance at the boy.

This first poultice was for the outside wounds—the damage to the child's face and the burns on his body. For the deep wounds, and to control fever, she must brew simples of shepherd's purse and the bark and leaves of willow. But that would have to wait; the boy's broken legs must be set very soon, or it would be too late.

"Here, Sister, as you asked. And the rope as well."

Signy scuttled away. The man had appeared again.

Cuillin produced four broad stakes. Signy did not know, but the monk had split them laboriously from straight timber—the remains of a precious half-burned roof beam.

The man dropped a hank of flax rope beside Gunnhilde. He had not changed his opinion; it upset him to see the boy in such agony. "He's a lost cause, Sister. Smothering would be a kindness." Cuillin swallowed. *Help me, Lord, if it is your will.* "Even if he lives, the boy will be crippled and scarred."

Gunnhilde did not acknowledge the kindness of the monk's pragmatism. "God will guide my hand when I set the bones in his legs. I have all that is needed."

"But these are weeds, Sister. Weeds for broken bones and burns?"

The poultice was finally ready, and Gunnhilde knelt beside the boy's head. "These are not weeds, Brother Cuillin, they are weapons in God's armory." The nun waved her hands, and constellations of insects rose in a single mass. She slathered green slime over the wounded face and chest, though the boy writhed under her hands. "There, child, do not fight me. This will cool your face, I promise you."

Cuillin sighed raggedly. "I must help the others. Where is the girl?" Seeing Signy, he beckoned. "You. Here." His tone was impatient.

Signy backed away. She remembered the other man by the rushes, the one who had broken Laenna's nose; the newcomers were always ready with a hard hand.

"Make her come, Sister. You won't hold the boy alone."

Signy watched them. The woman was stubborn, and from his expression, Signy understood the man did not agree with her treatment. But she stared him down, and eventually, defeated, the man left, shaking his head.

Signy crept over to sit beside the boy. She fluttered her hands to drive the insects from his face.

Gunnhilde smiled at the little girl. She was sad that Cuillin had not seen what she saw now—a sign that the Lord's Grace was working even through these Pagan hands. She patted the child's shoulder approvingly.

Cautiously, Signy smiled. The woman did not want the stranger to die, and neither, now, did she. He was only a boy, and the good side of his face reminded her of Nid, her oldest brother, though the ruin of the other side was grotesque—fire had stripped skin and fat from the muscle beneath and left the twisted features of a demon.

Signy shivered. This might so easily have been her, or any of them on Findnar.

"Come, child, it is time." Gunnhilde spoke confidently, as if the girl understood each word. "His legs." She clamped her lips into a colorless line; this would be agony for the boy. She pulled back the covering of old sheepskins.

Signy came closer and looked where the woman was pointing. Gunnhilde mimed gently placing a wooden stake on each side of the boy's broken lower legs, and then wrapping the rope around to keep them in place. But each leg was swollen to twice its usual size, and the entire bottom half of his body was purple-black—shocking when joined to a chalk white torso. Abruptly the world reeled around Signy's head.

"Do not faint—he needs you." Gunnhilde spoke sharply. She, too, was sweating, and vomit clogged her throat, but there was work to be done. "Hold his hands. Like this. Yes, above his head. Tight. Do not let go."

Signy nodded; she understood. She lifted the boy's arms up and back, gripping his hands with her own. If he'd been stronger, he'd have fought her, but nothing was working in his mind and body, and all he could do was groan.

"I'll straighten the bones while you hold him. One leg at a time. Now!"

You can hear broken bone moving within its covering of flesh; you can hear the scraping click when two ends meet again.

The boy's hands convulsed in Signy's, frantic to be free, but she fought him, tried to hold his twisting upper body straight. They'd both heard pigs in autumn as they were killed; the boy made a sound like that as he tried to flail away from the agony. It was an assault inside Signy's head, but she swallowed the red mist of transferred pain—and then he fainted. That was good.

"This, first." Gunnhilde smeared more handfuls of plant slime on the broken, swollen shin. "And now this." Long strips of clean linen were wound around and around from knee to ankle.

Signy stared. Where had the old woman found the cloth?

Tears dripped on the nun's busy fingers; these had been spare shifts for the novices in her care. "Now the wood, then the ropes. They will hold everything."

Signy turned her head away. With eyes closed, she could concentrate as minute after minute, strong and still, she held the boy because his pain was so much greater than her own.

"Good." Gunnhilde looked up briefly. The girl was ash-pale, but white knuckles showed she had a grip like death.

And then it was done.

The old nun sat back on her heels and wiped green hands on the skirts of her habit. She was trembling. She gestured to Signy. "Let him go. You did well." She found a smile.

Signy relaxed her grip. Carefully she placed the boy's hands beside his torso again. He did not move. Was he dead? She looked at Gunnhilde fearfully, patting his chest.

But the boy sobbed a breath, muttering.

"He's still alive, praise be." Gunnhilde picked up the sack she'd used to gather herbs. "No more plantain, though, and only a little shepherd's purse." She sighed with utter weariness. "Tomorrow. I'll look for more tomorrow."

Plantain. Shepherd's purse. Signy saw an association between these words and the things they named as Gunnhilde drew out the last leaves in the sack. The nun had picked the current stock at dawn, when the dew was still on them; moon-infused water added greatly to the potency of the plants—everyone knew that.

Both were familiar to Signy, though her clan called them different names. She would find more, for the boy must have fresh green slime on his face and his legs. She surprised herself in a prayer. *Let him live, Cruach. Help him . . .*

CHAPTER 7

THERE WERE only a couple of places on Findnar where Freya's mobile phone actually worked. Inside the house the signal was uncertain—the bars coming and going depending on which way she faced—however, the top of the hill behind the house seemed okay.

It was piercingly cold standing on that smooth, green dome and shouting toward Australia. Sydney winter clothes were no help on this sharp morning of a northern summer.

"Hello, Mum. Sorry you're not home. I've arrived, got here last night. Long trip but no dramas."

Freya closed her eyes with the rush of images. It was true, the dramas had come later. "The place is amazing, like nothing I've seen. The house is really interesting too; nice."

Nice. That was an inadequate word for something so stamped with her father's presence. "And there are ruins—church buildings of some kind, I think. There's even a ring of stones." Freya was staring toward the east, toward the circle of tall gray stones surrounded by a wider ring of mostly broken monoliths. "Imagine that. My very own standing stones, so lots of things to explore. And the view is . . . It really is spectacular."

Freya looked down on Compline, roosting like a gray bird on the top of the cliff. Beneath, the strait between the island and mainland to the west was covered in a carpet of solid white. "There's fog on the water at the moment. It's very pretty—just like lamb's fleece—though I think it'll burn off a bit later, once the sun's properly up . . ." Maybe. If anything, the mist was getting thicker as she watched.

Why was it so hard to tell the truth, say what she really intended instead of well-meaning platitudes?

"Look, I should just let you know a couple of things. There's no power at the house because Dad never sorted that out. I guess there were fewer options, technology-wise, when he came here or he liked it that way. I have paraffin lamps, though—very pretty, colored glass and all that. Anyway, the problem is, I can't charge my phone on the island, so that means I can't call very often, but we can text back and forth and I'll pick up messages a couple of times a day. I'll reply as soon as I can, promise."

Freya glanced down at the battery strength bars on her phone. "This place is full of Dad's things, though. That's a bit weird." Her mother would be curious about Michael's house, though she'd pretend otherwise.

"I'll go over to Portsolly a bit later—Dad had a boat, and it's the nearest village on the mainland—so I'll try calling again from there when I've sorted myself out some. Still not sure what I'll do with this place, though. I might just stay for the summer and work on my thesis. It'll be a good place to work—no distractions; then I'll see if someone wants to buy Findnar. There must be someone out there who'd like an island paradise, even if it's not the Bahamas— all the tranquillity and serenity you just don't get in Mosman. Better go. Love you."

Freya cut the call. Glib. Elizabeth would know there was a subtext. And Freya hadn't mentioned the letter; maybe the isolation was good in more ways than one right now . . .

She looked down over Findnar. The island was shaped roughly like a teardrop with a dent on one side—that was the landing beach. As far as she could tell, the rest of the coast was cliffs, sheer cliffs and even more, bigger sheer cliffs. Wind nudged at her jacket, and she looked at the phone in her hand. There was another difficult call she had to make—but it was necessary.

She'd put the number into her phone, so after thumbing the keypad she pondered her new domain as the phone connected. And rang. And kept on ringing. "Please be there . . ." Six rings, seven, eight, nine, *but who was counting?*

"Workshop." Abrupt. Male. But not the person she wanted. "Workshop, hello?" The man's voice had an edge, the first time Freya had heard broad Scots sound anything but cozy.

"Oh, yes, hello, this is Freya Dane. I'm wondering if Mr. Walter Boyne is there please?" Silence for a moment.

"Hello?" She could hear the anxiety in her voice. She sounded neurotic.

"He's not in. Try later."

"Could I leave a message?" She wasn't quick enough. Freya looked at the phone in her hand. He'd hung up. She was annoyed now. Her friends in Sydney described a certain duck-and-cover look when Freya was pissed off. She wasn't laughing.

Freya hit Recents. This time the phone was answered a little faster.

"Workshop." Terse, definitely.

Keep it light, Freya. This is not your country.

"Hello there, Freya Dane again. I'm wondering if I can just—"

"I've said he's not here." The man sounded hostile.

Great. Just great. Freya locked her jaw; he'd hear her teeth grinding if she wasn't careful.

"Oh, please, I'm really, really sorry to bother you, but Mr. Boyne asked me to let him know when I'll next be in Portsolly. Turns out I'm coming over today from Findnar—you know, the island? I'd love to buy him a coffee if he's got a minute. And he told me there's a boat over here, but I don't know where it's moored." That was true—she'd not noticed any other vessel anchored in the cove last night.

The stress was genuine suddenly; this was a child's voice, squeaky and close to tears.

Workshop Man said nothing.

"Hello? Are you there?" Freya hated this. Her voice was *shaking*.

"Yes. I'm here. Go down the path, Freya Dane. There's a sea cave at the far end of the cove. Look there." The phone clicked, and the dial tone kicked in.

Freya felt like screaming, so she did. "Charming. *Just. Bloody.* CHARMING!"

A cloud of gannets wheeled up from the cliff protesting loudly— a mist of honking black and white. Freya felt absurdly guilty; perhaps there'd be chicks in the nests still—how irresponsible was she? "Sorry! Going now." A stage whisper.

For a moment, she paused. The fog was rising fast from the strait. Soon Compline would be shrouded in white; she'd better get going or she might get lost. *Lost? Findnar's not big enough. I might fall over the cliff edge, though.* Freya pulled her jacket tight; her wet-weather gear was all very well, but she wasn't wearing thermals. Maybe in Portsolly she could buy a hat of the keep-your-head-and-ears-warm variety—and gloves? Might be a good idea if she really was going to stay, even for a while.

Pushing her phone into a back pocket, Freya made careful progress down the track toward the house. The rain last night had left the mud slick as ice, but she could just see a line of smoke rising from the kitchen chimney; that was a pleasing sight, the first successful thing she'd done on Findnar—lighting that ancient stove.

Mist and smoke, quite similar in their way.

Freya sniffed and wiped her nose, dreaming of warmth. Maybe the water would be hot enough for a shower now, or a bath. Come to think of it, had there actually *been* a showerhead in the bathroom?

She zipped her jacket and pulled up the hood, half-contemplating the ruined walls of the Abbey near the house. Fog was starting to obscure the meadow, but from this height she could see the space the structures had once occupied. Ridges ran away beneath the grass, and mounds of rubbled masonry showed the buildings had once been extensive—surprisingly large for such a remote place.

Freya trudged on, sneezing. A louder sneeze; she stopped and wiped her nose. Below, in the mist, something moved.

Freya squinted. What was that? The air had thickened considerably.

Walter? Had he come back to find out if she was okay? She picked up her pace as the track flattened out, hurrying toward the blur of half-broken walls. Whatever she'd seen, it had been about midway between . . .

Close to the ruins, Freya paused. This was the place, wasn't it?

She turned in a circle. "Walter, hello?" There was no answering voice, but mist muffles sound. "Of course it does."

Why was it comforting to hear her own voice? *Because no one's here. That's why.* She'd been mistaken. A trick of the shifting light.

Feeling better after a bath—no shower, she must have been hallucinating—and breakfast (proper, sticky brown-sugar porridge from stored oats in the small pantry), Freya sat down at her father's desk. It felt like the right thing to do.

The small package lay in front of her. It looked like a present; did she still like surprises? Freya touched it with a finger. There was something hard beneath the wrapping. Metal? She picked it up—oddly heavy, for such a small thing—and shook it gently. It was solid; nothing shifted.

Freya put the package down and stared around the room. It seemed different, the mist beyond the windows adding white diffusion to the morning light. An elegant room, yes, but . . . sparse. Spartan, almost.

The couch, for instance, was a modest two-seater upholstered in charcoal gray wool (how did he get *that* up the track?), and there was only a single armchair beside it. With clean lines, it was a shade between gray and black, and this chair at the desk was its cousin—brushed steel and leather webbing.

A large rug—a tribal Afghan in reds and blues—covering most of the board floor was the one concession to color. And books, books, more books . . .

Frighteningly tidy, Michael Dane. Self-sufficient, orderly—that's what this room said.

Just like me. In Sydney, her mates had laughed at Freya. They'd called her She Who Puts Things Away, and it was true. She liked order; it was the only way when you couldn't afford anything but a studio flat.

That had got in the way sometimes.

No, truth to tell, it had got in the way a lot, especially with boyfriends. She did not easily share her meager space or enjoy having her things moved around. But no man likes being tidied away either; tidied out of her life, more like—more than one had told her that. But if there was fleeting regret, there was also rueful acceptance. She liked her own company and always had, liked a sanctum that was just hers.

You are my daughter, deny the genes if you can.

Freya jumped. It was a shock to hear his voice, as clear as if Michael had leaned down and spoken in her ear. She shook her head impatiently.

Sleep had pretty much abandoned her last night. The wind had been a presence, as well as the sea storming into the cove below as the gale rose—that, and her busy brain, which just would not lie down. She'd jerked awake before dawn, her body clock saying it was time for lunch. Of course she'd made herself wait before she ate breakfast to speed up the process of acclimatizing.

No wonder she was seeing things. And hearing them too.

Get on with it. Elizabeth.

Really, what with him *and* her mother in her head, Freya thought she might just go mad. All this isolation. She smiled. One day soon they'd find her raving, ranging over the hills, dancing naked among the standing stones.

Freya laughed. But there it was, still, the little parcel. She was reluctant to open it, for a reason she didn't want to analyze.

Sitting back in his chair, her feet up on his desk, Freya Dane saw what her father must have seen, working here.

On the far side of the double-glazed window, she could just make out the rough turf rolling away to the lip of the cliff. No one would call such an expanse lawn, but it was certainly green and, at this time of the year, growing well. If she stayed, she'd have to mow it—or get a sheep. A flock of sheep? There was a lot of grass on the island—shame to waste it.

It was an engaging image, sheep in an open boat traveling to Findnar. If the fog ever broke up, she'd go down to the cove hoping the unfriendly workshop man had given her good advice. Then *she'd* be the one on the water, but going the other way, toward Portsolly, toward the little town with its own guardian cliff hanging above in the sky, like a granite curtain. Meanwhile . . .

It was like diving off a high board, that moment. Her father wanted her to have this, and after reading his strange letter, she knew there had to be a reason.

Freya slipped on a pair of white cotton gloves. They were too big but lay ready on the desk, along with a selection of sable brushes and various dental probes and scrapers—the things her father would have used when coaxing dirt or calcification from the surface of something delicate.

Shredded, the wrapping revealed a lidded box not much bigger than one of her palms. It was made of lead.

She turned the artifact over carefully. Engraved on one corner was an equal-armed cross within a circle, and the lid was secured to the body of the box with a hinge that ran the length of one edge, held in place by a delicate bronze pin. It was a beautiful, simple object, but it was hard to open—the lid was dented, as if it had been dropped. It took Freya some moments of patient work, but inside was a snap-lock plastic bag, and inside that, interleaved with finest-quality tissue—and a small sachet of moisture-absorbing crystals—were a number of pages covered with tiny, dense black-letter writing.

Freya sighed. "Latin." She was properly annoyed with herself now—this was the language of so many primary sources. She'd taken two semesters at college but switched to medieval English, because Latin grammar and the declensions of all those verbs were too much of a slog. Now, rightly, she felt like a slacker.

"All right, Dad. Where are the card files?"

Freya pushed Michael's chair back and stretched. Lined up on the desk was a small battalion of her father's card-file boxes—she'd found them stacked and neatly labeled in a cupboard beside the fireplace. Now, after reading her way through years of his work on the island, Freya's head was stuffed with so many unanswered questions she needed a larger skull.

It was clear from the dates on the cards and the amount of activity recorded that Michael Dane only gradually recognized Findnar as a mostly undocumented archaeological site of great importance.

In his first year, each of the cards contained just a few dates with one or two brief descriptions: records of site observations, for instance, or where the walls of vanished buildings might have run as part of a survey of the remaining aboveground structures.

Then from around spring of the second year, Michael had begun to dig consistently. He'd started with the ruins Freya had seen from the top of the hill. Systematically sinking test trenches, he'd uncovered steps, drains, even the foundations of a cloister next to the remains of a church—a structure he thought was older than many on Findnar. Finally, he believed he'd defined the extent of the ecclesiastical buildings, and from that point, records of other finds increased.

By the end of the last year of his life, each card case was

crammed with documentation of Pagan artifacts, Christian objects, and also the burials he'd found. Quite a lot of burials, though these were mostly Christian, judging from their alignment and lack of grave goods.

But it seemed to Freya that Michael had become obsessed and possibly secretive about his work on Findnar, for she could find no mention of articles he'd written, or collaboration with other archaeologists.

She stared sightlessly at yet another site drawing of a find: the remains of a sword excavated in the area of the cloister.

She sat up. A sword—in an abbey? "So, where's the undercroft, Dad?"

In the kitchen, Freya stared at the staircase that led to the bedrooms. It climbed diagonally across the wall that divided the back half of the house from the front—the part that wasn't occupied by the dresser with its plates and cups and bowls.

And then she saw there was a door beneath the stairs, wide and not very high. A storage cupboard? She pulled back the simple bolt. The door opened on oiled hinges—it wasn't a cupboard, but it was dark in there. Freya hesitated after lighting one of the paraffin lamps but then ducked through.

Light picked out the edges of a steel staircase leading into the void below. The treads were fixed to the wall with massive bolts, and irregularities in the stone glittered like powdered glass as, step by step, she descended. Ahead, there were four small windows, through which daylight struggled. Freya had not noticed them on the outside of the building.

But something else was down there, something big. As she stood on the stone floor of what was, undeniably, an undercroft—a crypt such as a monastery might have—awe feathered her spine.

The granite obelisk was much taller than she was, and it was considerably weathered, but she was startled by the symbols carved on its surface. Touching the incised markings gently, Freya traced the lines. There were twining serpents and double circles with dots in the middle like the pupils of eyes, and something that looked like a hand mirror used by high-status women; she recognized that from finds she'd seen as a child. Memory nudged. The Picts. These were *Pictish* symbols.

She walked around the other side, and here there were Nordic runes. If they were Elder or Younger Futhark, Freya did not know, but one thing was clear: the obelisk had been reused, very deliberately, in antiquity, by two separate peoples.

She held the lamp higher and turned a complete circle. The placement of the stone was strange: it was planted in the floor near the bottom of the stairs like a tree that had somehow lost its forest, but the groined and vaulted ceiling placed this space somewhere between the twelfth and fourteenth centuries CE, as did the slender, twisted pillars that supported the roof and marched away into darkness.

As Freya's light traveled over the landscape of this new subterranean world, it did not touch the ends or edges of the space—so this was a very large area, possibly even more extensive than the footprint of Compline House.

And then she saw the storage Compactus. She couldn't imagine the difficulty her father must have had and all the time and labor it would have meant, but somehow he'd brought these steel cupboards down here and assembled them, piece by piece, panel by panel onto their tracks. Perhaps he'd had help—maybe Walter had lent a hand? The Compactus certainly answered one of the questions that had nagged Freya; here was storage space for his finds, and lots of it.

Was it locked? Freya pulled on the handle at the end of one row of cupboards—there were five—and the first rolled smoothly away from its neighbor. The shelves were organized and orderly, but they were packed, crammed with containers. Anonymous cardboard boxes with lids but all labeled, all cross-referenceable with Michael's records upstairs.

Freya scanned the numbers on the shelves and selected a box. In a nest of cotton wool was a gold torque, something a king might have worn much more than a thousand years ago. Michael's notes had said he'd found it when cutting peat for the fire—one of the random discoveries he'd made in what had once been a marsh.

She opened another and saw arm rings, also gold; these had been lying close to the torque in the bog. "You said they were here, Dad, and I didn't believe you." Only two boxes out of . . . who knew how many others.

Freya replaced the second lid very carefully. Findnar was a treasure-house—a really, really serious trove of precious objects.

She pushed the last cupboard back, and as she turned, her light slid over a surface that seemed to writhe—dark figures squirmed, all popping eyes and teeth like knives.

But it was only a carving, just a piece of blackened wood. Propped up against the wall beyond the windows, this panel was several meters long but narrow at one end and with a long, curved edge. It had been deep in shadow before, but now, etched in high relief, Freya saw the savage little figures were linked together in patterns; whorls formed by arms and legs, swords and axes spun out into ever greater circles of repeating motifs. There were animals too, many-legged horses and snarling hounds.

Freya put the lamp on the floor. She knocked with one careful knuckle on the surface of the wood. This was very old, Viking age at least, and museum quality, as were all the finds she'd seen.

She closed her eyes. Her head was tight and aching—as if there wasn't enough skin to properly stretch over her skull. Time to ask a few questions of the living.

CHAPTER 8

L ATE IN the morning a fresh wind pushed the fog away. Hauling on the backpack and zipping her wet-weather jacket tight to her throat, Freya closed Compline's back door. She resisted the urge to lock it.

The little cart was waiting in the shed, and Freya picked up the handles. It was heavier than it looked and would be cumbersome on the cliff path, but if she bought provisions in Portsolly, it would beat carrying them home. *Home.* Hmmm, bit premature that.

Head down against the wind, Freya walked the narrow trail to the cove. Natural buttresses forced the path to curve along its length, and she tried to avoid looking down at the rocks below. When she reached the beach, she put the cart down and flexed her shoulders, scanning the headland at the other end of the cove. The granite was black against the white sky, and it was hard to pick out detail except where light caught on the knobs and spines of rock, but there it was. A void, at sea level—a different shade of dark beneath a natural arch of stone.

Workshop Man was rude, but he was right. This had to be the sea cave.

Heartened, Freya trudged along the hard sand above the tide line. It was tough pushing the cart, so she tried pulling it. After a time her arms quivered with the effort, but she slogged on virtuously—this was better exercise than in any gym, and it was free. Of course, the real price would be paid when she tried to get out of bed tomorrow.

Closer to the headland, Freya began to appreciate how useful this sheltered beach must have been to the islanders. Sand and shingle sloped gently into the water, and landing boats must have seemed easy on Findnar compared to the rest of this difficult coast. And, too, the headland blocked the worst of the weather from the strait. The air was gentle in the cove, and warmer, a contrast to the cold buffeting she'd had on the cliff path.

Nearly there, now, nearly . . .

She could see the opening was many times her height though narrow, and a tongue of shingle licked out of its shadows.

But there was one further trial; swollen by water cascading from a rent in the cliff face, a stream guarded the entrance to the cave. The rain last night had turned the trickle to a minor torrent, and it would be hard going indeed to pull the cart to the other side.

Freya made a mental note. Enough with the wooden wheels— she had to get something with a tread for this cart and gum boots too for her; no, make that waders.

Panting, wet beyond the knees, Freya finally shoved the cart inside the cave. And there it was—a small cruiser, nothing elaborate but solid and well used. Amidships, there was a proper cabin for protection against the weather, and the seats inside were comfortably padded, including a high chair for the driver, plus there was a substantial panel-mounted VHF radio. Below there was space enough to sleep a couple of people on narrow benches; a tiny, simple kitchen; and tucked away under the nose, a microscopic toilet. Michael must have made the trip to Portsolly and back many, many times and in all weathers. Maybe, thought Freya, he liked exploring the coast as well. Comfortable and dry, that'd be his style.

A natural stone quay began where the shingle ran out, and Michael's craft was moored to a steel ring hammered into the rock. At high tide, as now, a wide channel in the floor of the cave floated the boat so that it faced an opening on the sea side of the cliff. At low tide, the craft would be beached high and protected as the sea retreated. A convenient and logical place for the only means of transport on and off the island—secret, too, sort of. If you needed it to be.

The wharf rock must have been used by islanders for a very long time, for there were steps chipped into the stone, and Freya noted, with approval, that a drum of fuel was placed well away from the water. It had a hand pump in the bunghole, and beside it was a new-looking jerrican. She picked it up. It was heavy, full of fuel—excellent backup. There was also a tin trunk and inside that were coils of rope, a rugged flashlight with spare batteries, plus a first aid kit. All good stuff, all well maintained and carefully stowed.

Freya had spent time in boats when she was a kid, and Michael had always insisted on safety checks and well-ordered equipment. It seemed nothing had changed. Some things never did.

As her eyes adjusted to the space, Freya saw the ceiling sloped down as the cave burrowed back into the cliff, its end lost in the dark. *Dark*—Findnar's specialty. She thumbed the flashlight anyway, but the battery was dead. Putting a fresh one in, she let the beam show her what was there.

Light played over an odd feature. High up at the back of the cave was a stone ledge; quite wide, it would be a good place to store stuff out of the sea's reach. Serviceable, definitely serviceable, and a good place to hide too. Freya restowed the flashlight. Somewhere to hide—was that a good thing?

Outside the cave, the sea had muddled to a low chop as Freya jumped down into the cruiser. She was pleased with herself; she'd judged the tip and sway of the boat well, and exploring the cabin, she found a safety vest stowed in a locker between the bunks. Time and salt had faded the sleeveless garment from violent orange to pink. It was larger than she needed, a man's vest. Freya hesitated but then, impatient with herself, tied it on. Michael had taught her to respect the ocean, for he, and she, knew what it could do. In the end, for him, respect and knowledge had not been enough.

Don't think about that now.

The wind off the strait pushed the sea higher, and the little cruiser swung on its rope when the surge rushed into the cave. It took Freya many attempts and much swearing to get the inboard engine to fire; like the flashlight, it had been a long time unused, and there was almost no juice in the starter. But as the motor rattled and coughed at last, reluctantly snarling into life, Freya nudged the boat out of the cave with a sense of achievement. Instinctively she picked the best moment to crest the incoming swell, and that pleased her too; things learned in childhood, practiced enough, stayed for life.

Once past Findnar's sheltering headland, Freya felt the force of the sea against the small hull as the restless swell turned muscular on the open water. It took strength and concentration to hold the cruiser's nose toward Portsolly when the sea wanted to go elsewhere, yet it was glorious to taste salt on the wind again, and there was nothing in this small bout of weather the cruiser couldn't handle. Michael had chosen his craft with care, Freya could feel that—he must have understood the strait so well, and yet it had taken his life.

Something nudged her. Something half-remembered—lines from a poem at school.

> *The sea does not care.*
> *It has no mercy*
> *And no memory,*
> *For what it has done.*

It took less than half an hour to cross between the island and the mainland, and as Freya entered Portsolly's breakwater, she throttled the motor to slow, taking time to putter toward the quay.

This was such a pretty place. White-walled cottages, some painted pastel pink or yellow, and working buildings of sober gray granite were backed and sheltered by sheer cliffs. There was a sense that the people of the town had come to terms with their changeable neighbor the sea long ago; they had anchored their houses to the shore like whelks or oysters—unwilling or unable to leave a place of such wild beauty.

Freya cut the engine and allowed the boat to drift toward the quay, making ready to fend the cruiser off. Could she ever fit in here—really learn to call Findnar and Portsolly home?

"You!"

Freya glanced up, startled. A fat young man of around her own age was glaring down. He was furious about something. About someone. Her.

"Who said you could tie up here?"

"Sorry, I thought this was the public wharf."

The man spoke over her with volume flicked to loud. "People like you. All the same—don't even read the regulations."

Though it galled Freya to retreat, she bent down to start the motor again. She kept her voice polite. "I didn't see any regulations. Can you tell me where I can tie up?"

"Nowhere. Clear off. Tourists!"

That did it. Freya straightened, gaff pole in her hand. It wasn't easy to balance against the swell, but at least she was on her feet and more this oaf's equal. "I'm not a tourist. I live on the island. If you can't tell me where to moor, I'll ask someone else."

"Don't bother." He snorted.

Not a pretty sight, Freya's assailant. Thick lips in a lard-pale face; the very fat nose encouraged comparison with a pig, *in so many ways,* Freya thought. She raised her voice. "I'd been told Portsolly's a friendly place. You'll be the exception that proves the rule."

"You tell him, lass."

The loudmouth swung round as Walter Boyne skewered him with a look. "Since when can't she moor her craft? You don't own the wharf."

"Clear off, Boyne," the bully said. But it was he who wheeled and stamped away.

Walter called after him. "An apology, Robert Buchan, would be in order."

The man's eyes bulged as he stopped, and his neck swelled.

Alarms went off in Freya's head; she said, hastily, "No harm done, Walter." Pork Person, by the look of him, might be on the way to a stroke.

"This incident *will* be reported. Regulations are there for a reason, Boyne." One last glare at Freya powered a pompous exit.

Walter muttered, "Oh, get over yourself."

The hull scraped against the wharf. Freya threw the mooring rope. "Catch," she said. She was shaking.

Walter tapped his skull as he slung the rope over a bollard. "You did well to stand up to the windy young fool." He pronounced it *full*.

Freya muttered, "Something got him going, that's for sure." She pulled on the backpack with unnecessary violence.

Walter grinned. Freya Dane, angry, was undeniably an impressive sight—her eyes flashing sparks like those of the welder in his workshop. "Lives in denial, that one. The Buchans were lairds here before the war, and better men than him lost the lot when he was a kid, including harbor rights. Never got over it, our Rob; thinks he's owed."

The girl grasped the offered hand as she scrambled up the steps. "Can I buy you a coffee, Walter?" There was a line of interested faces in the windows of the pub. They were enjoying the little drama.

Walter nodded. He said, slowly, "I've got a bit of time. Make it a beer."

He held the door open to the Angry Nun, but his eyes did not quite meet hers as she brushed past.

Freya relaxed. Walter knew what was coming.

6

Once, long ago, Portsolly had been a much bigger place—a burgh, a seat of government on this wild and remote coast, or so the tourist brochure said. But one glance out of the window and the grand past dissolved—this was just a village now: a long straggle of houses winding from the sea up to the coast road, high above the town.

Toward the end of the summer season, the backpackers would drift off and the owners of the bed-and-breakfasts would reclaim their houses with relief, shake out the duvets and wash the towels with extra disinfectant. For now, though, the pretty harbor was crowded with groups and knots of young people and families, even though a sudden shower was starting to thicken.

Standing at the bar, waiting to be served, Walter inspected the tide of humanity as it flowed past the windows and in through the door. He muttered, "A curse. Locusts, the lot of them."

"So, Walter, you and Robert. Cousins?" Freya's expression was innocent. "Thanks. On me." She nodded to the barman as he handed them both a pint.

Walter laughed. "Fair point. Still . . ." He led Freya to a table in a front window of the Nun. They were lucky to get it. The bar was filling up with pink-faced people—you didn't expect sunburn in Scotland, after all—and as more pushed in to get out of the rain, the place took on the reek of a wet dog.

"Tourists bring money, surely?"

Walter snorted. "A shirt and five pounds and don't change either. Looters, pillagers, always have been. English!" His voice cut through the babble, and people stared. Walter grinned amiably.

Freya choked back a laugh; the man was shameless.

Walter's smile faded. He turned his tankard to the other side for no particular reason and took a cautious sip.

Freya leaned closer. "Did you know my father well, Walter?"

He nodded. The long exhale of a sigh misted the glass. "I would call him my friend."

Freya said nothing.

Another gusty breath, then, "I thought it best, since we had but met, just to take you to the island. But it troubled me." He looked down into his beer. "I did not think it was my place to discuss his passing—not then, if you can understand, because—" He stopped.

So, more to the story. But Freya said, "It's okay." She didn't say she understood, because she did not. "But there was a clipping at the house, a newspaper article, and you were mentioned."

This time Walter looked her in the eyes. "We lost your dad and, very nearly—"

A baby howled, and there was pandemonium. He'd fallen from a high chair and, scooped up by his frightened mother, the child screamed louder.

Walter drained the pint in a swallow and stood. "Shall we?"

Freya was happy to go. The tables were too close for a private conversation.

Outside, the rain had stopped, but it had cleared the crowds from the quay, leaving the world a calmer place.

"Over here." Walter put his hand under Freya's elbow, guiding her toward a large stone shed at the other end of the wharf. A working building, it had its own slipway and stood a little apart. Closer, and she could read the sign. WALTER BOYNE & SON. SHIPWRIGHTS.

The place was well kept. There were no missing slates on the roof, and a pair of massive doors was painted copper red, as were the outer frames of the windows under the eaves. The inner frames were brilliant white—a pleasing contrast to the dark stone. From inside there came the tearing whine of power tools.

"Here you are." Walter opened a small door within one of the larger pair and stood aside, and Freya stepped past him over the threshold. The air inside was thick with resin and the hot cinnamon of sawn timber.

"We use a lot of oak and different kinds of pine. That's the smell. Other timbers as we need them." Walter was shouting.

Up close the noise from the equipment was huge, toothshakingly immense. Freya stuck fingers in both ears, nodding. She stared at the half-built boat that reared up toward the ceiling—it claimed most of the space in the center of the shed, and light from the high windows poured across ribs half-clad with overlapping lengths of timber. Walter Boyne & Son built wooden boats out of an ancient tradition; of course he'd been Michael's friend.

"Dan . . . turn it off. Dan!" Walter cupped hands to shout to a hunched figure at the other end of the workshop. He and another man were feeding a piece of timber through a benched power saw; both had ear protectors on, and both were oblivious to the newcomers.

"Excuse me, Freya." Walter strode the length of the shed, waving both arms. "Oi!" Finally, as the lumber completed its journey past the blade, one of the men signaled to the other and the power was switched off. As the howl died, the saw disk slowed and grew impressive teeth.

"I can see you, Dad."

Daniel Boyne was taller than his father. He took the ear protectors off and shoved safety glasses back on his head. Unshaven and dark-skinned with bright, cold eyes, he flicked a glance at Freya before he leaned down to speak to Walter. "What do you want? We've got a lot to get through."

Freya felt the impatience from forty feet. Walter said something in a low voice, and Freya looked away as Daniel Boyne glowered in her direction; the structure of the ship suddenly became fascinating. She wandered down the flank closest to the wall, running her fingers along the smooth wood. Someone loved this work.

"It's a long way from finished." Uttered like a warning.

Freya stood back, suddenly guilty, but she recognized the voice this time. Workshop Man. Of course. She forced a smile. Intense eyes, grayer than a cold sea, stared at her with no expression.

"Hello, I'm Freya. I think we might have spoken earlier? When I was trying to find Mr. Boyne. Walter, that is."

"Yes." Not even the ghost of an apology or a smile.

Freya's face stiffened.

This was news to Walter. "You should have let me know, Dan; it was Freya's first time on the island last night, I told you that. I was worried for her." He coughed and waved toward his son, the gesture some kind of apology. "He's not always like this."

Daniel Boyne cast Freya an unfriendly glance, then stared at his father. With an edge he said, "We're behind."

Freya blushed like a child. The hostility was hurtful and strange, and she felt her eyes well up. What was it with men in Portsolly?

Walter spoke sharply. "Freya's come a long way, a very long way. She deserves to know more about her father."

Daniel Boyne opened his mouth—and closed it with a snap. He moved rapidly away down the length of the workshop toward his assistant. "Denny, time for lunch."

It took Freya a shocked moment to register that Daniel was leaving, and then she saw he walked with a cane, compensation for an awkward, rolling limp.

Walter touched her arm. "Come to the office, child." He sighed. "You being here, I'd hoped that Dan . . ." Walter's face worked.

Freya linked an arm through his. "So it's not me, then, it's him." She found a smile. "I was starting to worry."

The office at the far end of the workshop was tiny, and Walter shoved the door hard. It opened protestingly. "A bit of a trick to it. In you come," he said and gestured to a wooden stool that stood between two elderly desks. One depressed office chair and a couple of dated computers completed the furnishings, though paper was strewn across every surface.

Perhaps Walter saw the room through Freya's eyes. He said defensively, "Put things on the floor when you can't find room on the desk—that's my system. Dan won't file, says it's not his job, and I keep forgetting." He looked away. "Sally used to do the books; place was tidy then. But I can still put my hand on what I need when I need it."

Freya smiled cautiously. "I shared a house with a girl once who dropped stuff out of the window—that was her filing system. True story. Drove the neighbors mad."

Walter filled a kettle from a sink in one corner. "Tea?" He splashed water everywhere. "Hold on, I'll just . . ." He mopped the puddle ineffectually. Freya resisted the urge to fix it for him.

"Tea would be nice."

There was a moment's awkward pause as mugs were rattled from a cupboard and the kettle burbled its way to a scream.

"Milk?"

Freya nodded, and Walter pulled a bar fridge open. He stared inside, perplexed. "I could have sworn . . ." He raised his voice above the kettle. "Sorry. No milk. There's sugar, though." He flipped the switch, and the howl sputtered to spitting silence.

"No worries. Black will be fine. No sugar."

Walter smiled faintly at the Australianism as he dunked tea bags. "Watching your weight? Never can understand why half of you go through life starving and the others, well . . ." He handed a mug to Freya, full to slopping over, and sat down heavily. He swallowed a mouthful of tea. "Dan's not a bad lad."

Freya might have smiled—the lad was certainly past thirty—but Walter was struggling. "I'm sure he's not; people don't like being interrupted."

"It's not that . . ." Walter's voice trailed away.

Freya sipped the scalding liquid.

Walter tried again. "I walked you into this, lass, and I am sorry for it. But I thought speaking with you about the night your father died"—he stumbled, getting that word out—"might help him. Dan's proud, you see, and he will not talk to me about it."

Freya said, softly, "Go on."

"He tried, he really tried to save your dad, and me as well, but the sea beat us all. He's the one left with the damage of it and not just what is physical. And now here you are." Walter shrugged, helpless. "You have a right to know what happened.

Sally, now . . ." A sad shadow passed across his face. "She was my wife, Dan's mum. Sally would know what to say to you and to him. She got on well with Dan—better than I do—but she died three years ago."

Freya murmured, "I'm sorry to hear it." She was; Walter's face had softened when he said his wife's name.

Walter turned the mug in his hand. "We say the wrong things to each other, you see. I try too hard; he thinks of it as prying." His smile was pained. "Fathers and sons."

Freya might have replied *Mothers and daughters,* but she didn't.

Walter stared out into the silent workshop. "He's been locked away since then, if you can understand."

"I know what you mean." It was true, she understood being emotionally locked away.

"And, after it happened . . ." Walter paused unhappily. "We were out there that night in *The Holy Isle,* as the paper said. Late, very late, coming back, but when the fish run in these times, you chase them even on New Year's Eve." He stared into the tea as if it could tell him what next to say. "I would have said I knew these waters, but that night the strait turned against us. The seas were high as this shed, and when the engine swamped, we were driven toward Findnar, toward the rock shoals at the end of your cove." Walter closed his eyes. *Mayday, Mayday. This is Holy Isle . . .* "But we could not raise the lifeboat service, and Dan begged me to let her go, take our chances with the inflatable, but I would not do it. I thought she would come through." He exhaled. "Michael heard us from the house, the signal got that far. He saw our lights too— red and green—so he knew we were straight ahead for the rocks. He tried to put out to help us. A foolish thing but brave." He shook his head. "It was my fault, all of it."

Freya was numb. This was why the letter had not been finished. "Go on. I want to know."

Walter grasped Freya's hands. "Be proud of your father, child, he did what few other men would or could have done that night.

He found us, and slung a line though the sea was wild. Daniel caught the rope right enough, and I thought—just for a moment—it would work, that Michael would pull us away from the rocks. But *The Holy Isle* took a broadside—you have to understand how huge that sea was—then she rolled." Walter was staring out into that night as the roar of the sea filled his head. "I was thrown free and came up, but hit my head. I blacked out. Daniel found me. He tried to get us to your father." He swallowed painfully. "The boy had Michael's rope still, and hand over hand he hauled us both. They got me onboard between them, and Michael tried to ride the surf back into the cove, Australian to the last." He smiled faintly. "The cruiser swamped. Daniel had hold of me, and tried to hang on to your dad, too, but your father would have none of it. He pushed Dan away to save me. That I do remember, then I was swept from them both." He dropped her hands. His eyes were bleak.

Freya's lips were stiff. It was hard to ask the question. "And?"

Walter blinked. "We two were lucky, if you can call it that. I was dumped on the beach, not the rocks, and Daniel was washed into the cave. He was alive. Barely. But one leg had a corkscrew break—as it turned out—all the way up through both long bones, and his hip was shattered. He was lucky to escape amputation, they told me later in the hospital. The inflatable from *The Holy Isle* cast up on the beach too—that's how I got him back to Port eventually." He grimaced. The longest night of his life.

Walter got up and put the mugs in the little sink. "Daniel cannot work as he used to—not at sea—and I'm getting too damn old. We're still rebuilding *The Holy Isle* eight months later. I should have let her go."

For just one second, Freya glimpsed the old man waiting beneath the skin of Walter Boyne, defeated by time and sorrow.

"We've got this, of course." He gestured at the shed. "It keeps us going, has to, now that we cannot seriously fish for our living. But it's a specialist market, wooden craft."

That must mean that times were lean. Freya asked, "What happened to my father?"

Walter spoke slowly, remembering. "I found his cruiser four days after we lost your dad. It was strange . . ."

Did she really want to know? Once told the truth, how would she banish the images in her head. Freya forced the question out. "What was?"

Walter was staring past her—a long, long way. "The cruiser was beached in the cove. Undamaged. And your father lay beside it." Walter Boyne, a private, proud man, was almost pleading as he said, "We had been searching all that time, and twice the Rescue from Ardleith wanted to call the search off because there's a current, a strong one, which runs out past the end of Findnar and sweeps north. They thought it had taken him, but I knew they were wrong because the wind, that night, was pushing us south. They would not listen—not until the sea gave him back to us."

Walter's voice roughened. "We are so sorry for your loss, child, me and Dan, so very sorry. But it comes out like anger with him because he thinks he failed your father, maybe that he deserves to be punished. Now here you are and he's ashamed—as if he had sinned in some way. His mother was religious, and it's in Dan's bones though he'll deny it. That was the only thing we fought about, Sally and me, what the priests put in that boy's head. My son has nothing to atone for. I do."

Freya clenched her jaw. "I'm glad you told me. Thank you, Walter." She stood, gathered her things, and walked away.

Walter called out behind her, "Have you somewhere to go now, lass?" He meant, *You should not be alone.*

She started to say *Please don't worry,* but the anxious kindness of his tone stopped the platitude, half-formed. "Is there a library in Portsolly?"

Walter allowed himself to exhale. The girl seemed composed. Did that ease the guilt? "Halfway between the harbor and the coast road, turn left into Tay Street. There's a B and B on the corner, Tay Cottage." He hurried in front of her to open the workshop door. "You'll find the library in the shopping square."

On impulse Freya leaned forward and kissed Walter's stubbled cheek. Surprised, he touched the spot.

"It's better to know, Walter. Thank you for all you both did."

Freya walked away quickly before he could see what she really felt. Desolation dug claws into the soft flesh of her heart.

CHAPTER 9

O N HER second day among the black-clad newcomers, Signy ran away and hid. It was not fear that made her hide, it was duty, for the customs of her people said a person must be buried as close to death as possible, and three days was too long. Signy was very frightened—an important obligation had been flouted, and that had consequences.

But, Cruach, it was not my fault. Please, please understand. Would the Sun listen? And by what power could she ensure he did not leave the world tonight before Laenna's soul was released and her body buried. If Cruach ignored her, Laenna would become a hungry ghost eternally unappeased. Another, unbearable tragedy.

Help me, Cruach, give me strength. And guide me, show me where she is. Signy did not dare to pray aloud, or stand up to find her bearings in the long grass. She must not be caught searching the meadow, for if the angry man found her, he would not understand; he might stop her making the correct offerings, and that would be a disaster.

And so Signy knelt, waiting for her prayer to be answered. Dutifully, she stared into Cruach's hot face until her eyes burned.

The morning was perfect and warm, and as her God climbed the sky, heat intensified, but still there was no sign. Signy grew dizzy; she had to close her eyes, for the power of the God was too strong. *Oh, please, please, you must help us, Cruach.* She knew the presumption was very great. One did not make demands of a God; it was dangerous.

But the wind dropped to nothing and the grass became completely still—Cruach had sent the sign. Signy could hear insects swarming, louder and louder, and there was a smell the wind had taken before—the sweet reek of flesh as it corrupted. Signy swallowed; how could she thank Cruach for this? But she must . . .

Signy could not look at the body—flies and ants had settled on Laenna wherever there was blood. Gasping tears away, the child covered her sister in a thick layer of grass and flowers—something, anything, to drive away the insects.

Laenna had never been still in all her life, and it was impossible to think they would never quarrel again, never cry together, never laugh. And yet, there was no one else to do what now must be done for this silent, unmoving body—no shaman, no mourners. No family. But still the funerary rites must be performed, that was her duty.

And so as Cruach tracked up and then down toward the long, pale evening, Signy toiled, grubbing at the hard summer ground with a part-burned piece of plank. Her sister must lie deep in the kind earth, too deep for animals to find her.

"Soon, Laenna, soon, I promise you will be warm and safe, and when I am home, our parents will hear that you have been properly honored." It helped to talk. "And I think the newcomers will leave Findnar soon. They cannot stay now, can they? This will be our island again, just as it was, and our family will return to you each summer. For you, Laenna, we will sacrifice honey; for you, eggs will be broken on the offering stone. Cruach will hear our prayers as He heard mine today, and He will shine down on your resting place. We shall not forget where you lie, I promise."

Offerings. Signy gulped back tears. She had nothing to pour on the earth of the grave—not even water—and there was no food to leave beside Laenna's body for the long journey her soul must make. But then Signy remembered—before the raiders came, she had left a large piece of comb honey wrapped in leaves on the offering stone. Would Cruach understand if she took His tribute?

She could gather gannets' eggs also—Laenna was owed the eggs. Honey and eggs might be enough.

The grave was finished, and Signy had decided.

As long twilight began to fade and Cruach declined into the west, the Wanderer rose. Far below, small as an ant, a child could be seen in that last light.

Closer, and the child was rolling another child's body into a hole.

Closer, and a small green packet was laid on the chest of the corpse with four speckled eggs as flowers and earth rained down, more and more, running through the hands of the living girl, falling like water as she called out her prayers.

The stars wavered and grew sharp. And faintly, from far away, they heard the child speak to her Gods. She implored blessings for her sister's soul passing now from one life through to the shadows of the next. At first the child's voice was strong, but then it faltered as all light left the world and there came the sound of weeping.

And if human grief is soon lost in the dark, the echo of Signy's suffering endured in the air as Laenna's grave was, at last, hallowed and her soul released.

Day and night had no meaning for the boy. There was only thirst, and pain, and not enough water. He craved water. But one morning, sun splashed him from the east and that was how he knew—for the first time—that water had a face. A small dark girl was sitting close, very close, beside him; she had something in her hand, a beaker. She touched his mouth on the side that did not hurt, and, surprised, he opened his mouth. And then there was water on his tongue.

The boy tasted the water. So sweet. He tried to reach up, he wanted more. He tried to speak. *Please! Let there be more water.*

The eyes in the face of the water girl—dark, very large, like those of a deer—seemed filled with light. She was smiling as water filled his mouth again. Nodding eagerly, she held the beaker as he gulped.

The girl glanced away. He heard her call someone—she used a word he did not know, *Goonhelder*. A name? He did not care. *More. Please. Let me drink.*

There was an old woman, and the boy remembered her face. Why? He frowned, trying to catch an image from the other side of the dark. The woman was smiling, too, and she had a skin bag in her hands. The girl stood. *No! Do not go. Do not take the water away . . .*

They both made soothing sounds, as if he were a dog or a horse. The girl knelt beside him again, and the beaker was full. He drank; that was all he cared about.

Gunnhilde sighed as she watched the boy swallow—it was a touching sight, and she wiped grateful tears from her cheeks. The little girl moved her too—she helped the boy to drink with such care, and perhaps that made him happy though it was hard to know. On so many levels, the boy's survival seemed a miracle; did she dare to hope that it was a sign of God's favor returning to Findnar? *Thank you, Lord, for guiding my hands. Your ways are wondrous to this, your humble servant.* Of course, she had never given up—not even for one day—but credit where it was due. Without the girl, this recovery might have taken a great deal more time.

"She might not know what I say, Brother, but she has an instinct for healing. The child understands suffering, and her devotion to this boy has been very clear. It is my belief the Lord is preparing the road for her to come to Him."

"Devotion?" Cuillin huffed. Every time he entered the shelter, the girl disappeared. He did not know why, but he was offended by her wariness. "I have never seen it."

"I assure you, Brother, it has been so. Will you hold this corner for me? I would like to beat the material." Gunnhilde held up a large piece of embroidered cloth. Shocking though it was, a woolen altar covering had been pressed into service as a coverlet, and she, Signy, and Idrun—the remaining novice—shared it at night. However, since the morning had continued sunny after the boy's dramatic recovery, the nun was determined to banish any lurking vermin.

Seventeen days had passed since that terrible day—the Apocalypse was Gunnhilde's name for it—and insect infestation would add to their torment in a way that seemed pointless given the larger catastrophe of their lives.

Cuillin thought comforting already-corrupted flesh useless, for God required that suffering be endured, yet in the end he did what Gunnhilde asked, if only to make the nun see sense. "The girl is a Pagan, Sister. It worries me you allow her to spend so much time with you and the boy."

Gunnhilde applied a stick to the wool, and dust enveloped them both. "They are both Pagans, Brother. Perhaps it is God's plan to bring them to Christ together and, before our Lord, I still say the girl has a good heart."

"If she has such a good heart, where is she now?" Cuillin peered into the shelter—the boy seemed to be sleeping, but the girl had disappeared.

"Thank you, Brother." Gunnhilde twitched the cloth from Cuillin's hands and folded it. "I said she might go after helping the boy to drink." Was there harm in such a small lie? "Do not concern yourself, she'll return when she's hungry."

Laenna's grave was only a small mound, but through the days since she'd buried her sister, Signy had slowly covered it with a blanket of white pebbles. She'd carried them back from the beach in the skirt of her tunic when the newcomers sent her down to guard the salt-making fire or to gather seaweed. But to mark the grave for all time, she'd rolled a small boulder to the head with much effort. This was her sister's pillow stone.

In the last of the warm season, the meadow flowers had begun to seed. Each day Signy plucked more of the seed heads and scattered them in a widening circle around where Laenna lay. Motherwort, hound's-tongue, sweet-smelling melilot, red valerian, and goldenrod. Digging the seeds in with a stick, she would often pray aloud, mostly to Cruach, but she invoked Tarannis, too, and, just to be sure, the Wanderer.

"Do you see us, me and my sister? In your names, I ask these flowers to grow for her, and I ask all that is good in creation to remember Laenna for all time and note well where she lies."

Had Laenna died, had all these people died because her clan had not known about the Wanderer and therefore not appeased the star? Signy would not make that mistake again; she might not like all of the newcomers, but she did not want anyone else to die, especially not the boy. He was awake much more now, and he'd smiled at her today; he even seemed pleased when she fed him or tended to his body, though they'd both been embarrassed when she'd cleaned him like a baby this morning. Still, Signy hoped he liked her even a little bit, because boys were more fun to play with than girls. Her brothers mostly had been kind, but Laenna often made trouble for Signy and they'd fought a great deal—and now she was gone.

Brother Cuillin shaded his eyes. He could see the native girl in the distance, and beyond her, the Pagan stones; it was a source of irritation, always, that they still stood, but other things were more important now.

"She's at that mound again."

He was working with Brother Simon and Brother Anselm. One by one they were collecting the stones of the chapel from where they lay among the grass.

Simon had more natural compassion than Cuillin. "She seems sorrowful each time she returns—perhaps someone she knows lies there. Help me, Brother."

Cuillin's back was aching, though it was yet early. Steeling himself, he bent to grasp the lintel stone. *For you, Lord. My pain is only a shadow of yours . . .*

Brother Anselm staggered past, his shoulders bowed beneath a yoke from which two buckets hung filled with stones. Tipping the load onto a growing pile, he trudged back toward the others.

Cuillin admired his brother's spirit—Anselm was patient, as stoic as a mule, though once he'd been the most accomplished illuminator in Findnar's Scriptorium.

"Two won't shift that"—Anselm gestured to the lintel—"let me help." He dropped the yoke from his shoulders.

Cuillin knew his brother was right; another back, another pair of arms might make the task possible. What difference did it make if the stones were large or small—this was all God's work. Gratefully, he intoned the sacred name. "Therefore in the name of Christ our Lord, one, two, heave!"

In a line, the three monks hoisted the stone to their shoulders. Their legs trembled beneath the weight, since all three had led sedentary lives in the Scriptorium lettering sacred manuscripts before the raiders came, and yet now they stumbled on together. For Christ their master.

"Here, drop it. Careful, carefully!" Cuillin took charge, and his brothers obeyed. He was troubled by this desire to lead, but he saw now that humility and obedience had always been hard for him. Even when he'd been sent north to Findnar from the Motherhouse at Whitby, Cuillin had dared to question his superiors. Why should he be ordered to this gull-haunted wilderness so many sea days away from the Motherhouse when there was so much to do in Whitby's Scriptorium? But the Abbot had commanded, and Cuillin had obeyed—of course. Now, though he prayed often on his faults, there were few men left on the island, and the monks—and their few sisters also—seemed to look to him as the most senior of the surviving brothers. And he found himself consulting Gunnhilde more and more; perhaps they were falling, naturally, into the roles of Abbot and Abbess since they both had the example of the Motherhouse to mimic. Cuillin banished that beguiling, prideful thought and crossed himself as the three trudged back to raise yet another piece of stone.

"Let us dedicate our labor to God, my brothers. With faith and His help we shall rebuild, together, His holy sanctuary on this island."

Brother Simon and Brother Anselm crossed themselves and nodded cautiously.

God's help was certainly required, for faith wilted at the thought of all the work to be done.

From a distance, Signy watched the men. She sat down in the long grass so that they would not see her, for she did not want to help them. It seemed a stupid thing to do, taking stone from *this* place and putting it down *there*—what was the sense in that?

She patted the pillow stone affectionately. "I think this God of theirs is very hard to please, Laenna. They should sacrifice something; then perhaps He'd help them a bit more." She laid her mouth close against the white pebbles covering her sister's chest and whispered, "But what should I do? Can you see me where you are? Tell me what to do. Please, Laenna, I want to go home."

"Signy, where are you?" Gunnhilde was calling.

"Should I go to her, Laenna?" A brisk wind rushed past, bending the tall flowers that hid where she lay. Signy's tunic fluttered, a flag in the grass.

The old woman called out more strongly, "I see you, Signy! Come, I need your help—the goat." She mimed milking.

Signy sat up and waved. She understood more of what the woman said now, for every day she tried to use new words. The language of the newcomers was ungainly and sounded ugly, but she knew enough now to call the old woman by her real name, *Goonhelda*. It was hard to say, and unmusical, but Signy had taught the old woman her name also. She now knew the name of the other girl too—*Eedrunn*. That was less difficult, a little. Even the boy could say *Signy* now, and he was closer to the right pronunciation, though he made her laugh when he tried to say other words in the clan language. But *Coolun*, the angry man, spoke to her only as *Gurl*. A sound like a growl. He did not try to say her real name. But time passed more quickly around the fire each evening now because Goonhelda liked to teach and Signy liked to learn. That is, when the newcomers were not chanting; they still did so much chanting it was hard to get to sleep sometimes.

"I'd better go, Laenna." Signy kissed the pillow stone and stood up, her arms full of the poppies. She sauntered toward Gunnhilde.

"Milk, Signy, yes?" Gunnhilde handed the child a leather bucket and pointed at the goat. Signy nodded—she didn't much like milking, but she'd rather do that than other things.

Their one surviving nanny was hobbled not far from the ruined chapel. She had an evil disposition, and it was clear she resented captivity after roaming free since the raid. A few days ago Signy had helped *Coolun* and *Ansuum* recapture the island's few domestic animals, including the goat. She knew she had proved her worth because she could run faster than any of them, animals or men. And it was she who had brought the nanny back to the ruined settlement. Now the goat, a pregnant sow, and one of a pair of plow bullocks—the other had been slaughtered and eaten by the raiders—must be brought into the temporary byre at the other end of their shelter each night. This was another of Signy's chores, and if Gunnhilde seemed not to like living so close to the animals because of the smell, Signy did not care; she was grateful for the extra warmth they brought.

"Shall I take those? They're pretty." Gunnhilde pointed at the poppies in Signy's arms; she mimed taking the flowers.

Signy backed away and shook her head. She seemed alarmed.

Gunnhilde smiled, determinedly. On some days communication was difficult. "When you've finished"—the nun mimed stripping teats again and picking up a full bucket—"come to me, please." She pointed at the girl and then toward the shelter where they all slept.

Signy nodded. She went over to the goat and sat down beside her. The nanny stared back and bleated. "Yes, I know. You don't like me; well, I can't help that. We just have to try to get on." Signy wiped her hands on the grass; she'd make the milking last as long as she could . . .

Some of the ceiling timbers of the nuns' dormitory had survived the raid unburned. Any wood was precious and must be protected from the weather, so Cuillin and the other monks had worked hard to patch the old roof with bundles of heather weighed down with stones. Of course the thatch leaked, but it was better than being outside when it was cold, especially at night. The men also filled holes in the walls with clay, straw, and animal manure. Gathering dung from the byre was Signy's morning work, and watching her expression as she worked the slop of mud, straw, and clay together with bare hands had been one of the boy's chief entertainments as he recovered day by day. He'd even chuckled when, trying to scratch her nose, Signy had smeared muck across her face. She'd stuck her tongue out at him, and they'd both laughed.

His face was a little better now. The green slime had bred maggots because Gunnhilde would not allow the old layer to be removed when she added more on top, and that horrified Signy. The boy hated the creatures moving on his skin, but Gunnhilde would not let Signy pick them off. Just today, the nun had finally wiped away the fermented poultice with all its squirming inhabitants.

Signy had been impressed. The maggots had eaten the burned flesh from the damaged side, and though the boy's face would never be perfect, there was new skin where the worst of the burns had been and some of the puckering was smoothed. She'd tried to tell the boy with smiles and gestures, and perhaps he understood—he'd smiled as if he did.

Signy, her head against the flank of the goat, thought about the boy; she knew his name now, for he'd told her. Pointing to his chest he'd whispered it: *Magni*. He had not told the others, just her. Goonhelda was kind, but he did not like the men, and they did not like him. Everyone knew it was dangerous to tell enemies your real name. Signy understood, and she was flattered he'd trusted her to use his name well. Yes, she should not have liked Magni, but she did. He made her laugh and he was brave; or perhaps she just missed her brothers. Signy stared over at the soot-dark hovel where Magni was lying. He had spent so much time there alone and in pain; Nid would have hated that.

A cold wind ruffled the poppies. Signy shivered. Winter was coming, and soon they would all be forced inside unless she could work out how to mend the coracle and run away back to her home. But the work would have to be done before the gales—if not, she would have to wait until spring. And where would she get the skins?

The goat stamped impatiently and tried to pull against the hobble. Signy said, wrathfully, "If you spill this, I swear I'll skin you."

The nanny tried to butt her. Sitting cross-legged on the ground, Signy rescued the precious bucket of milk, but only just.

"Oh, all right, you." Signy stood carefully. She had to juggle the milk and the flowers *and* prevent the nanny from running ahead to a patch of grass. "There, greedy one." Fixing the hobble, Signy watched the goat tear at the forage. She knew she could not put off going back for much longer but, shading her eyes, she stared toward the God stones. Could she risk stealing just a little of the milk? Only a small offering, in return for safe passage home, and she could take some of the poppies to the altar too. Gods liked red things, everyone knew that—they were the next best things to blood and fire.

"Signy." Gunnhilde was waving at her.

Signy waved without enthusiasm. *Too late.* She cradled the flowers as she trudged toward the old woman. The fire pit would have to do for the sacrifice. It was good to have Gods on your side, and they liked it if you were practical—if you tried to help yourself instead of just asking for favors all the time. She liked Brother Veedoor, the kitchen monk, because he was practical too. He had only the fire trench in the shelter to cook with, but he managed to make quite tasty food, and Signy admired that.

Since he was nice to her, Signy showed Veedoor how to make a bird net. Netting was much more efficient than Veedoor's method of spreading badly made birdlime around the buildings, hoping roosting birds would stick to it.

Flax grew near the rushes at the edge of the marsh; having picked and soaked a quantity for some days, Signy scraped the rotted matter away from the long fibers just as her mother had taught her. Twisted, the strong cords could be knotted into a net with small stones attached around the edge. Signy demonstrated how to make a throw, and Veedoor practiced diligently until he'd mastered the skill. He'd done well, too, smoking the first birds he caught. Plucked and gutted, they'd been hung in the rafters over the fire, and though they were tough, he'd saved a wing or two just for her, which Signy appreciated.

Tomorrow she'd get him some eggs in thanks—he'd worked out how to roast them in the coals without the shells exploding. Signy liked roasted eggs, they were much nicer than raw.

"There you are." Goonhelda took the milk. "Bear looks happy to see you." She nodded toward the boy; he was sitting up. "There is food if you will feed him, please." Veedoor at the fire trench held up flatbread—not all the barley had been burned in the fields.

Bear. Signy knew why the old woman called Magni by that

name. The skin jerkin he had worn, the only thing that survived from his past, was made from bearskin; he'd had woolen trousers, too, but they'd been charred, and the old woman had cut the rags off before she set the bones of his legs.

Perhaps, thought Signy, *it is better to be known by the name of a great and fierce animal—the spirit will help Magni. And I can call him that too. It will be safer.*

On impulse, before she gave him the bread, Signy put several poppies in Bear's hands. *For you.* She smiled and nodded, but he stared at her, confused.

You do not know, and I cannot tell you. Signy backed away. Tonight, when everyone was asleep, she would sacrifice the rest of the red flowers in the fire trench and, as well as praying for a safe return home, she would ask Cruach that Bear's healing might be complete and that he be given a happy life—perhaps even with his own family.

But they are murderers! That was another voice in her head, and it was true. Was Bear a killer too?

Bear did not understand Signy's strange smile when she gave him the flowers or why, suddenly, her eyes darkened when she looked at him, almost as if she was scared. But he hoped she knew the gift made him happy.

Seven times each day all of Findnar's inhabitants, including Signy, stopped what they were doing when Cuillin struck a metal cauldron. One side was cracked, and it was no substitute for the bell taken by the raiders, but the discordant clank was loud enough to be heard all over the island.

Clongk! Clongk! Clongk! It was the third summons of the day. *Tierce.* Was that what they called this one?

Signy bent her head and rapidly crossed her chest, mumbling anything she could think of—the names of flowers, of the colors of the sky, the fish in the sea. She knew now that the newcomers were praying, just as she prayed to her Gods, but they did it so *often,* and that wasted a great deal of time.

Standing together beside the now orderly piles of building stone, Cuillin and Gunnhilde finished reciting their prayers. The monk crossed himself and gestured toward the girl in the distance—the pose, at least, was pious. "So, Sister, do you think she prayed with us? Really prayed to our Lord?"

Gunnhilde smiled affectionately. "Of course not, Brother. She has no real idea what any of this means, yet."

Cuillin frowned heavily. "You know she'll run away the first chance she gets."

"But until we have another boat, there is no way to leave the island, Brother. Plainly it is God's wish that we live together here, in peace, until that time. All of us." Gunnhilde smiled at her brother. He was a most worthy man but utterly without humor or, it seemed, an understanding of natural human affection. She asked God to grace his heart with compassion.

At that moment, Signy looked up and smiled like any ordinary child. The nun waved cheerily, and she whispered, for Cuillin's benefit as much as hers, "You might be surprised, Brother. She will make the Lord proud one day, I'm sure of it. Bear as well."

The monk snorted but said nothing more. Gunnhilde was too partial. He, however, saw things clearly and had no time for the wavering mist of sentiment—it just confused things.

He stared at the girl as she drew closer. A trick of the light seemed to crown her head with the ring of distant stones, and he stiffened with distaste.

Heathens were like mongrel dogs, almost impossible to tame or train, and they always bit the hand that fed them when they had you fooled. Well, he was no fool, and he would not permit Gunnhilde to be savaged either.

CHAPTER 10

WALKING UP the steep street between white cottages, Freya recognized the small shopping area from the night of her arrival. There was a chemist, a hardware shop, an old-fashioned haberdasher, a butcher—charmingly described as "General Smallgoodsman and Purveyor of Quality Fare"—a fishmonger, and quite a large supermarket. That seemed a pity to Freya—so many old houses must have been cleared to make room.

And there, in front of her, was the library—all colonnaded front and gilded lettering. Once, to judge from the size of this building, books had been taken very seriously in Portsolly.

Briiiiiink! The bell on the library counter grated like that of an old-fashioned bicycle. A suitable noise, one to match ornate glass cabinets and oak tables laid out in rows. There were old-fashioned linoleum floor tiles, too, polished to a gleam, and signs saying SILENCE, IF YOU PLEASE written in the graphic style of another time. It felt eerily like the set of *The 39 Steps*.

"Can I help?"

Freya jumped. A woman with crisply bobbed hair had arrived behind the counter. Flat shoes and a tweed skirt, even a hand-knitted cardigan over a blouse with a Peter Pan collar—definitely a blouse, not a shirt—this was the librarian from central casting.

Freya coughed—it was that or giggle. "Yes, thank you." She smiled sweetly, and in her best I've-really-been-very-well-brought-up-please-ignore-the-scruffy-clothes voice, she said, "I'm on the hunt for some information."

A calm response but not warm. "Yes?"

"Er, yes. Compline House on Findnar Island? I'd like to research its history, and that of the ruins as well."

"The Abbey." A definitive statement.

"Possibly." Freya was becoming annoyed.

The woman's eyes were pale blue and cooler by the moment. "I think you will find the evidence points to that conclusion."

Freya's smile stretched only so far. "I live on Findnar, that's why I'm interested."

The librarian blinked. "Then you will be Michael Dane's daughter." A statement, not a question. She flicked a glance at the only other person in the room, a large woman trussed in too-tight tweed; she, too, was staring.

Fresh gossip in the town tonight, that's me. Freya hunched defensively. She dropped her voice. "Yes. I'm from Sydney. But I . . ." It was hard to put into words when it came to it. "As I said, I really just want to know more about Findnar—it's so interesting." *And that, Freya Dane, is a cop-out.*

The librarian's expression warmed by just the smallest amount. "Naturally, we have many books on the history of the whole area, including Findnar." She pointed at a corner where a glass cabinet was set slightly apart. "Please be careful, however; many of the books in that section are old and valuable—and fragile too. Some may not be borrowed, of course." It was said without emphasis; there was still that hint of disapproval.

Freya returned service. "And you are?"

The woman lifted her chin. "I am Katherine Wallace Mac-Allister, Portsolly's chief librarian. And I had the pleasure to count myself a friend of your father's for many years."

A friend of your father's. Someone who was a part of Michael's life here, the years in which Freya had had no presence.

Katherine MacAllister's expression softened at the distress Freya could not quite hide, and the girl saw the librarian was younger than she'd first thought. Close up, Katherine's skin was unlined, and there was only a little gray in her hair—it was the manner that made her seem middle-aged, and the clothes.

"Would you like, that is . . ." Katherine's tone was tentative.

She wants to tell me about him, but Freya could not tolerate the compassion in the woman's eyes. She spoke over the librarian. "Thank you for your help. I have all I need for the moment."

Freya's table had too many books on it. Geology, history, theology, biography—even short-story anthologies—and each volume related to the far Northeast of Scotland as well as Findnar. It would be the work of months to absorb even some of the facts, but facts took Freya away from confusion, for a while.

It all felt so familiar. Taking notes, organizing topics, grouping references for further study—she'd always liked research, liked grazing when she could not be sure what she wanted to find but trusted *something* to jump off the page.

The library was a solid building and, absorbed in her work, Freya had not heard the rattle of rain on the windows. She looked up from her notes only when the street door blew open and then shut with a crash. A rubbish basket fell over in the gust. It rolled into a leg of her desk, strewing its contents around her feet; surreptitiously Freya picked up an apple core from the floor. Hers, it had strayed from the upturned bin. You weren't supposed to eat in the library, several notices said so.

Rubbing her eyes, she bent to tidy the debris and registered the library clock. "Bugger!" It was close to seven. She didn't want to be caught on the open water of the strait at evening, not if more rough weather was on its way.

Freya shut down her laptop and unplugged her phone. She grabbed an armful of books. Hurrying to the counter, she hit the bell, and then again; a moment or so passed before the door to the back office opened.

"Miss Dane, I thought it might be you." A slight quirk of the lips.

Freya said breathlessly, "Sorry to trouble you, Miss Mac-Allister, but I have to go."

Katherine said, pleasantly, "It's very Australian, isn't it? *Bugger.* An expression of anything from outrage to mild disappointment, or so your father used to tell me."

Avoiding the invitation to offer a response, Freya made a stack of the books she'd chosen.

"I've only dipped into a few of these—so much fascinating material. Perhaps I might take a couple, though I don't have a library card, of course."

"I can make out a temporary slip, or you can join online. It will not be a problem; we know where you live." The librarian actually smiled as she moved the books to her side of the desk.

Perhaps she's only got so many smiles and doesn't like to use them up, thought Freya, but she chuckled politely. "You do. But there's a few too many to fit in the pack tonight—very hard to choose."

Katherine nodded briskly. "If I may advise . . ." She worked through the books Freya had selected, frowning slightly. "*Annotated Annals of the Parish of Portsolly and Perrin Bay,* by the Most Reverend Andrew Gibone, DD, MA Cantab. An interesting man." The book was impressively large and bound in sober calfskin, and Katherine was actually enthusiastic as she said, "Dr. Gibone had a passion for the ancient records of this region. He taught himself to read the runic inscriptions, of which we have a number in the area, and farther north, too, of course." *Lady, you don't know the half of it,* thought Freya.

"He posits a controversial theory as to the origins of Compline House, though nothing has ever been proven. Not even by your father—though he certainly tried. Dr. Gibone believed the building stands on pre-first-millennium foundations."

Freya said, politely, "That old? Fascinating." She leafed through the front of the book and saw the date of publication: 1842. The book had last been borrowed in September 2011; *Bet it was you, Dad.* She caught Katherine's glance, and they both stared at the date stamp; Freya resisted the urge to touch the page.

The librarian cleared her throat. "And this will be useful, *Early Religious Foundations of the Scottish Peoples*. Sir Neville Buchan, privately printed in 1903, as you see. Less elegant in style, but he was schooled by his mother, a redoubtable woman. They were the lairds of Findnar then, and in fact your father bought the island from his descendants. An extremely old family." Katherine brushed an invisible speck from the binding. "The Buchans owned much of Portsolly itself once as well as Findnar, though they are sadly declined now. The male line only has one childless descendant and, should he pass without issue, the original family will be extinct."

Freya touched the gilded title of the book; it must have been expensive to produce. "I think I've met him. He's certainly 'declined.' All the way to the lower primates, I'd say, maybe even the invertebrates."

Katherine raised her brows. "Robert Buchan?"

Freya opened the book so the librarian could scan the bar code. "Yes."

"Was he very rude to you?"

Freya nodded. "He was."

Katherine shook her head. "I am sorry for it. Young Robert has led a disappointed life, and some cope better than others with that, though that is no excuse for bad manners. There was always a strain of . . . shall we say, odd behavior in that family; too much intermarriage between cousins. Debt and death duties were a considerable problem—Robert's father died without a will—and selling the island became a necessity, or so I believe."

Katherine cleared her throat busily, picking up another of the books. "Now, I would also recommend *Island Life in Scotland: Recollections and Folk Memories from a Bygone Age* by Elspeth Arlott." She stroked the worn cloth as if it were a friend's hand. "Miss Arlott never married but retained each one of her faculties until a very advanced age. I remember meeting her when she was an old, old lady. She had great natural powers of observation and would have made a fine journalist. Of course it was not permissible for women of a certain class to have careers in those days, such a waste."

Giving the book a final affectionate pat, she passed it to Freya, who stowed it with the others. "Thank you, Miss MacAllister," Freya said. "I'd better be on my way."

Katherine smiled brightly. "Please call me Katherine. After all, I've heard so much about you, Miss Dane."

Freya felt her eyes filling and turned away. *If he talked to you, why didn't he talk to me?* She mumbled, "Freya. Please," and made a business of closing her pack.

The librarian made a final, hopeful bid. "And don't forget, you're free to charge your phone and laptop at any time—we were always happy to help Dr. Dane in that regard."

The library door stuttered and banged open. Katherine hurried to close it. "So very annoying. The council keeps promising to fix the catches and the locks before winter but . . ."

The air from outside smelled of rain. Freya extended her hand to the librarian. "Good-bye for now."

Katherine shook it and did not let it go. "Perhaps it is a little late to go back to the island tonight?" She seemed genuinely anxious. "I would not trust the strait on an evening like this." Quickly, as if she might wish to take each word back having used it once, Katherine said, "I should be pleased to offer you a bed." Perhaps Freya looked startled, because Katherine plunged on, though her color rose. "I'd enjoy to pass on my memories of your father while they are still fresh, if you would like that. The past is a fragile thing." The librarian's face was briefly undefended. She was lonely and proud—and dignified.

Freya was touched. She paused; was she ready for this? "You're sure it wouldn't trouble you?"

A minute adjustment of the Peter Pan collar and Katherine was back in control. "I should not have suggested such a thing if it were at all inconvenient. It is past time I closed anyway."

"Were you staying open just for me?"

Katherine broke in over Freya's confusion. She'd brightened up considerably. "I shall meet you at the street entrance—please be sure to leave nothing behind." Katherine Wallace MacAllister marched through to the back office, flicking off blocks of lights as she went, heels tapping on the linoleum.

Freya hurried out to the street, then she stopped; she hadn't brought a change of clothes, and after her exertions at Findnar and in the boat, she felt grubby, not to mention gritty.

"Is something wrong?" Katherine was unfurling an umbrella against the spatters of rain.

Freya shrugged on her pack. "No. Well, nothing serious, just that I'd kill for a shower and I don't have clean clothes."

The librarian laughed quite merrily. "Och, we shall find you something. But it will be a bath. Shower rooms, I'm afraid, are scarce in these parts. Come along."

Katherine stepped out briskly, and Freya hurried to catch up. She was soon concentrating so hard on not panting—as the gradient of the street got steeper and steeper—that she forgot to be concerned about spending the night in the house of a stranger, a stranger who knew her father better than she did.

CHAPTER 11

KEEL COTTAGE was the last house at the top of a narrow street and looked to the east. Katherine saw where Freya was looking. "Yes, there's your island—we used to wave to each other." Unaccustomed confidences, once voiced, are dangerous things, and the librarian laughed a little nervously. "Well, we said we did; just a silly joke. Much too far to see, of course."

The librarian unlocked her house in the milky evening light. She waved her guest ahead as she flicked the inside lights on.

"Why, hello, little mother. And how are your babies this evening?" A tabby cat with white feet and moss green eyes wound her way in and out of Katherine's legs, mewing. With a quick glance toward Freya, the cat led them toward the back of the cottage, tail in the air.

In a basket beside the Aga stove were four kittens. Ears still folded flat and eyes tightly closed, they were only a few days old. Their mother jumped in among them and began to lick each squeaking infant from nose to tail.

Katherine knelt beside the basket lined with plaid and stroked the kittens with one gentle finger. "Such a very clever girl. What handsome babies you have." The tenderness moved Freya sharply.

The librarian felt Freya's glance. She stood, brushing her knees vigorously. "I shall just get Ishbelle something to eat. Please, make yourself comfortable."

There was a table with two chairs. Freya sat. "She needs her strength, feeding babies," she observed.

The cat rubbed against Katherine, gazing into the face of her mistress as she tied on an apron. The muttering purr ramped up a notch. "Have patience, child. There." She placed a bowl beside the cat in which were heaped morsels of fresh fish. Both women watched with pleasure as Ishbelle devoured the food before a leap back into the center of the basket; she stepped around her squirming children and settled on one side, nudging her frantic kittens until each one found a nipple.

Katherine sighed and turned to her guest. "A sweet sight, though what I'm going to do when it comes time to give them away . . ." She shook her head, denying the thought. "The guest room is upstairs, and so is the bathroom. I shall run you a bath."

The two bedrooms in Keel Cottage were divided by a small, blindingly clean bathroom. Tucked beneath the roof, each room had its own dormer window, and the second bedroom was simple though stylish. A white-painted rectangle with curtains of sage green silk, it had a single bed made up with rose-sprigged linen and a white hand-hooked rug on the floor. An IKEA chest of birchwood drawers and an armchair covered in the same green silk as the curtains made up the rest of the furnishings.

Katherine pushed the casement open. She waved her guest forward, saying, "It's a pretty view."

Beneath, the village and the harbor were displayed like a naïve painting—all twisted streets and tiny houses bunched tight against each other, with toy boats clustered, bobbing, at the foot of Portsolly's great cliff.

"I try my best to get home for the sunset," Katherine said.

Freya looked out toward Findnar as the vault of the sky flushed gold with streaks of flamingo pink. "God's a good painter when He wants to be; bit gaudy sometimes, though," she said. The women shared a cautious smile.

Katherine waved toward the east. "And there's the comet—

Cuillin Ursus. It comes from the constellation of the Great Bear. I saw it for the first time the night before last."

"There's a comet?" Freya searched the sky. "Where?"

The librarian pointed.

Her guest squinted and saw, finally, the indistinct silver lozenge rising behind Findnar. "It's not very big," she said.

Katherine closed the window and twitched the curtains together. The silk made a hushing sound. "It will be. Around here they still think of it as a portent of disaster—nonsense, of course. It's a lump of rock and dirty ice with an erratic orbit." She smiled at her guest. "The natives—so superstitious." An edge of irony.

They were seated in matching armchairs, one on each side of Katherine's fake-log fire. The chairs were deep and the room warm—too warm—and Freya was fighting sleep since it was after dinner and they'd made inroads into a second bottle of Côtes du Rhône.

"How long will you stay on Findnar?" Katherine's inquiry was polite, possibly nothing more.

Freya considered the question. "I had thought . . ." She cleared her throat. "I have work to do, so a couple of months, I think." *That long?* Freya surprised herself.

Katherine murmured, "Of course. Your father made so many remarkable finds, and it will be a puzzle to know how best to deal with them—there are so many regulations these days."

How do you know about Dad's finds? But Freya did not voice the thought. "Well, yes, I'll have to decide what I need to do with his things, but I meant my own work. The isolation will be good for that—no traffic, no city white noise. Maybe the peace will help me think better on paper."

Katherine expressed surprise with a polite smile. "You are a writer?"

"Not ordinarily." Freya was uncomfortable; she'd managed to ignore the thought of work all day. "It's the thesis for my doctorate. Archaeology, of course." Relaxed by the wine, the two shared a smile, and Freya found she didn't mind. "It's my contention that common themes in church art during the early medieval period were much more influenced by their immediate cultural surroundings than is currently accepted; that's what I want to prove."

Katherine looked at her quizzically. "A comprehensive topic indeed."

Freya swirled the wine in her glass. "My problem is I can't tease out a proper linking thread, and I've been stalled for months, going round and round in circles. Detailed research from Australia can be tough in a field like this, and though my supervisor is understanding up to a point, I'm very late delivering. Sometimes I think I'm not meant to do this. Maybe Findnar's my last hope."

"But you'll be able to hop across to Europe from Aberdeen or go down to the London collections should you want to—that might help." Katherine seemed sincerely encouraging.

Freya brightened. "It would be so great to visit the sites I'm interested in. I need to *see* the work, the manuscripts, the statues, even the vestments, in their context." *Yes, Dad, validation.* "There's a collection of early copes in the Victoria and Albert, for instance; it's just not the same looking at things like that on the Net somehow."

"In that case, I have something to show you." Katherine rose and took a small silver box from the mantelpiece. "This is unique, I think, and very old, but it bears on your topic. It's from this area."

Inside, resting in cotton wool, was a crucifix half as long as Katherine's palm. The body of the cross was made from two pieces of black stone—*Jet?* wondered Freya—but it was the figure of the Christ that made the piece remarkable.

Carved from ivory that was dark with age, the body was not naturalistic, but each element of that tortured form added to its power—the ribs seemed to burst from the torso as if exploding, and the legs and arms were twisted in desperate agony.

Yet it was the face that was truly shocking. One side was ruined by pitiable scarring, and this was not the damage gouged by time or a plow blade; these marks had been a deliberate choice, each tiny detail exquisitely rendered by the anonymous artist.

Freya was mesmerized. Michael had written about a crucifix he'd given away. She glanced quickly at Katherine. "I think my father mentioned this—it was in his notes of a dig he did just before he died." The word was still hard to say.

"Yes, Michael gave it to me for Christmas." Katherine said it lightly, as if this were a matter of small importance, but her eyes were defensive.

Freya absorbed the words. The librarian had called her father Michael, and he had given this woman a present, a very important present, just before he died.

Freya touched the crucifix gently as she tried to absorb the feeling in the figure. "This is very early, primitive almost. But I've never seen a Christ with a face like this one—it would have been blasphemous to show the Son of God as less than perfect. A very brave artist, or foolish."

They both stared at the face of the man who'd been frozen in agony for more than a thousand years. Katherine said softly, "I never tire of looking at it—horrifying and moving. And if I'm drawn by the spirituality of organized religion, he reminds me of the price to be paid for certainty."

"I've been reading some of my dad's records. As you say, he found a great many artifacts on Findnar—early Christian material, but other objects as well, pre- and post-Viking era." She paused. She should give the crucifix back to Katherine, but holding it, she touched her father's hands.

"I learned so much, and we had so many debates." The librarian gazed at her guest. "You're like him, you know—you have all his passion. He was obsessed by his work on Findnar. But be careful, Freya, or you'll never leave; the island will claim you for its own as it did him."

The comparison to her father was kindly meant, a compliment, but the words punctured Freya's mood.

She put the crucifix in Katherine's hands. "Thank you. You've given me lots to think about." That was true.

The wind blew itself out through the night, and by dawn, the world was calm.

The girl in the white room half-opened her eyes to the radiant day and panicked.

Holy Mother! I've missed the bells!

From long training, her body responded, and the girl fell from the bed and onto her knees, crossing herself as she gabbled a desperate novena. *"Ave Maria, gratia plena, Dominus . . ."*

A sound cut through the prayer—knocking, then a voice.

"Would you like tea, Freya?"

As she crossed herself and fumbled for a rosary that did not exist, Freya Dane sat back on her heels. *Confused* did not begin to describe the feeling.

"Hello?"

The girl closed her eyes, screwed them up tight. "I'd love a cup, Katherine—down in a sec."

"No rush, your clothes are by the door."

Freya stood shakily. She was wearing a man's T-shirt lent by Katherine the night before. It was soft from much washing and old—the colors faded, so that the familiar image of the young Che could only just be made out. The image of a revolutionary seemed unlikely in Katherine's house, and Freya did not want to think about the implications, not now.

She rubbed her knees; they hurt from hitting the cold floor because instinctively she'd not knelt on the rug. *Sinful flesh must be mortified.*

Where did that come from? Freya stared at herself in a small mirror near the window. She looked the same, didn't she? Shivering, she sat on the bed. *Too much to drink?* She'd never suffered delusions before.

It was true she'd gone to a church school in Sydney, but it had been Anglican, not Catholic; perhaps—but it was a stretch—something in Portsolly had triggered . . . what? She'd never been remotely religious. There was the Abbey, of course, *but you can't catch hysteria from ruins.* Ridiculous! Too damn Jungian, and who believed any of that stuff anyway? *The shadow.* Nonsense. Yes. *Is it?*

Freya moved too quickly, and the room wavered. She was dizzy. At least she knew why that happened. She'd always had low blood pressure, especially in the morning, and this was a tangible, physical cause, the opposite of mystical visions.

Clothes, outside the door, Katherine had said—and there they were, a neat pile; jeans, underwear, T-shirt, and thermals all washed and, yes, ironed.

Freya folded Che carefully and put him neatly in the center of the pillow after she'd made the bed. At the door, dressed in her own clothes, she looked back—Michael's T-shirt, it had to be.

I had a right to him too, that was Katherine's message without one word spoken.

"Milk?" The kitchen was brilliant with morning light.

Freya blinked as she entered. "Thanks, yes." She was distracted watching Ishbelle and her kittens; the basket had been placed in a splash of sun by the back door, and the cat was a tough mother, washing each squeaking kitten with a tongue like pink sandpaper. Not so different from Elizabeth, really—Freya remembered bath time as a little girl, how vigorously her ears had been washed, how much she too had protested. She smiled ruefully.

"Sugar?"

Freya nodded; she didn't normally use sugar, but today was different.

Bright and fresh, Katherine deposited the cup in front of her guest before she sat down on the other side of the table.

Freya sipped the scalding liquid. "Maybe it was a strange bed, but something got to me last night. I had weird dreams." Here she was, sitting across a table where her father must, once, also have sat. How many times—that was the question. Perhaps Keel Cottage felt like home to Michael. Was that Che's message too?

Katherine cleared her throat nervously. "Your father . . ."

Freya jumped.

Katherine hurried on. "Has anyone told you where he's buried?"

Freya shook her head.

"Michael has become part of Portsolly's history."

Freya put her cup down carefully; they were near enough to touch. "How so?"

"The cemetery is part of the grounds of the church. It was deconsecrated and sold—declining congregation and all that upkeep, the usual story. Your father was the last person buried in the Portsolly cemetery." Katherine looked away.

Freya was uncertain what to do. Katherine was upset, and she should say something, but the librarian cleared her throat and said brightly, "Yes, indeed, the building's been bought by an architect from Ardleith, and so the church has been deconsecrated. He used to come here as a boy with his family, and now he's turning it into a summer home."

"What Dad would have called a shack." Freya tried to match the determinedly light tone, and her reward was Katherine's smile as she offered marmalade.

"Well, the church is a little large for a shack, I suppose, and there's the spire. Don't often get one of those, even in Australia. But perhaps it is an odd choice for a holiday house—I've always thought it a grim building." Katherine paused. "Perhaps you would like me to show you Michael's grave? The churchyard is actually rather lovely, and I could take you there on my way to work—I walk right past."

What to say to that? Freya crunched a bite from the toast. "This is delicious. Lemon and lime? Bet you made it yourself."

Katherine nodded; she seemed pleased. That helped. "I think I should get going back to Findnar, so another time. But thanks for the offer, Katherine. Very kind of you."

"Of course, I quite understand."

They both knew Freya would visit her father's grave alone.

Later, ghosts of truths unspoken wove around the polite fare-wells like smoke.

"You'd not like me to strip the bed? I'm more than happy to, Katherine."

"No, no, please don't bother. Be sure to drop in again to the library soon, Freya."

"I shall, certainly. Good-bye and thanks again."

After the spontaneity of last evening, morning had made Katherine MacAllister into the well-defended person she usually was. But Freya knew that she, too, was not the most forthcoming of people. They would have to take this slowly. She stepped into the shining morning with complex regrets—for so many things.

"Freya? Freya, wait!"

Halfway down Keel Street's hill, Freya stopped and looked back.

Katherine was hurrying toward her, waving; she was holding a shopping bag.

"For your work." A quick duck of the head, as if that were ex-planation enough, and Katherine strode away.

Freya watched her go before she peered inside the bag.

A package was wrapped in tissue paper, but she didn't have time to look; she wanted to see where her father was buried.

CHAPTER 12

SIGNY LAY on her back beside Laenna's grave. It was spring, warm enough to dream of happier times.

"Signy! Come quickly." Bear was calling, so agitated he spoke the raiders' tongue.

Signy bobbed up. The boy was running toward her, hair flopping and bouncing on his shoulders and, if anything would make her believe in the newcomers' God, this miracle would, for Bear ran fast on straight legs. She was so used to his face now she didn't see the scars.

"They have come for me."

Signy gaped. "What?"

The boy hopped from foot to foot. He tried again, this time in her words. "It's good, Signy. Come!" Bear hauled the girl to her feet and towed her toward the cliff path. His joy was powerful, more powerful than her fear. And she saw where he was pointing.

"Look!"

There was a boat running in to the cove. As they watched, its single sail bellied, and a final push from the wind drove the hull up the beach.

Signy's heart swelled. She could not breathe. She snatched her hand from Bear's and ran back up the path.

"Signy, wait. It's all right, we'll take you home." But the boy could not catch any part of her, not even the rags of her tunic as they flew out behind.

Signy stumbled through the meadow, streaming tears.

She reached Cuillin first and collapsed, sobbing, across his feet. As she reached up, painfully learned words deserted her. "Orwic, Orwic!" *Raiders!* But this was her language, not his.

The monk almost dropped the piece of dressed stone he'd been carrying—another step, a little more unbalanced, and he'd have crushed her skull. "You could have been killed!"

Signy gasped the word. "Raiders!"

Cuillin dumped the rock and clutched Signy's arm—he, who never touched female flesh—but she scrambled up, breaking his grip. "Goonhelda, I tell. Must!"

"Wait!"

Sobbing, Signy ran toward the living quarters. She burst through the sacking that divided the women from the men. The old nun was praying with Idrun.

"Raiders. We run. Now!"

Gunnhilde clutched the terrified novice as Cuillin stumbled in. "Hide!" He snatched up the cauldron and began to beat it—terror made the old iron ring.

Gunnhilde froze, for the sight of Cuillin's wild face shocked her. Then she and Idrun grasped Signy's hands, and they ran so fast Signy's feet skimmed the ground. They were all crying.

"Trees, hide good."

Gunnhilde managed to nod. A sheep track on the side of the combe led down to a thicket of trees, but the path was steep and narrow. Sweating, the three slowed their pace as, behind them, Cuillin beat out the warning.

Idrun was shaking. "Where are our brothers, Mother?" Gunnhilde did not say it. *Dead, they will all be dead.*

The three burst on toward the trees. There was only the noise of wild bees and their feet as they ran crashing toward the lowest part of the little valley.

Signy pointed. "Big, good!" She pulled the sisters toward the largest tree in the glen, an oak. The spring had been late after a hard winter, but it was fully in leaf and the canopy would hide them.

Gunnhilde pushed Idrun forward. "Quickly, child."

Idrun jumped, and one hand grasped a low branch—it held her weight. In a moment, she lay along its length.

"Idrun, help Signy! Your girdle."

Idrun nodded. The rope girdle had been wound around the novice's body several times, and she flung one end for her companion to grasp. Signy had climbed trees all her childhood, and she swarmed up the trunk. On that first thick branch, she pointed down at Gunnhilde.

"You." She mimed catching the end of the rope, but jump as she did, faster and higher every time, Gunnhilde still could not quite grasp what hung so close. Signy slipped her knees over the branch and dropped her arms down.

"I pull."

The girl's voice was muffled by her tunic. It had descended as she hung, exposing her skinny little body, but so frightened was Gunnhilde, she did not see Signy's nakedness. Catching at their hands, she did her best, and together the girls pulled Gunnhilde up to a low fork; another wrenching scramble hauled the nun higher.

All three rested for a moment. "Up." Signy pointed. "More up."

Gunnhilde was pale, but for the sake of the girls, she tried not to show how frightened she was. "Yes." She pointed to Signy and then to her own chest. "You show us, Signy; we'll follow."

And then Cuillin stopped beating the cauldron.

"Sisters? Can you hear me?" Signy could see him through the leaves—Brother Cuillin was standing at the top of the combe; he cupped his hands and tried again.

"Sister Gunnhilde, Idrun! Please come out, all is well."

Signy frowned. He'd ignored her as he always did. She was used to that, but she'd never seen Coolun happy before.

Gunnhilde's anxiety matched Signy's. What if her brother was a hostage? She was responsible for these two young souls, and though she was ready to meet her Savior—she'd lived more than fifty winters, a great age—she would not throw the lives of these children away. She shook her head, a finger to her lips.

Cuillin hurried down the sheep track. Behind him came other men, men they did not know.

Signy touched her eyes and pointed. *I see.*

Reluctantly, Gunnhilde nodded; she whispered, "Take care, child."

Signy said nothing—of course she would be careful, she did not wish to die. Descending from branch to branch, she dropped to the ground, soft as a leaf. Once Coolun and the men were among the trees, they would not see her, and she could scramble up the far side of the combe—she had to know the truth.

Cruach, help me now . . .

Signy knew where Bear would be, where he always was when not working: standing on the cliff looking out to sea, his damaged face turned into the salt wind as if it alone could heal him, restore what had been taken.

She was right, but instead of standing where he could be seen, he was hiding behind the young rowan at the top of the path. Even at this distance she could hear him—he was crying. Edging closer, she saw what he saw.

The vessel had not come to raid; this craft had no shields, and none of the men carried swords. Dressed in black robes tucked up into belts of rope, some were herding animals through the shallows, goats and several sheep, all bleating as their young were carried across the surf. There was even a bellowing cow in the boat, with a very young calf. She would not jump into the sea, abandoning her baby.

Because she was kind, Signy made a noisy approach, scuffing pebbles on the path. Bear heard her, and he turned away quickly, wiping his eyes with one dirty fist.

"Hello." Signy did not know what else to say.

Bear nodded, clearing his throat. He would not look at her but said, bitterly, "Just more of *them*. I was wrong."

"I am sorry, Bear." What was she saying—sorry these people were not raiders?

"You do not mean that." His fury seared her.

Signy shot back, "No, I was being nice." She folded her arms and turned her back on him.

Eventually Bear said, "They've brought an anvil." He pointed. "That means they're staying."

Signy peered past his hand. Yes, among the goods on the beach, an anvil had been unloaded, and Bear was probably right—setting up a smithy made these people settlers, not visitors. There were large wooden chests on the beach as well, and three women and a girl were carrying them, one by one, up above the tide line.

"More Christ-sisters?"

"Yes." Bear's glance was dark. "They greeted Cuillin like their own true brother when he arrived in the cove. He was smiling." He made a disgusted noise.

Signy beckoned urgently. "We should go, Bear; they'll see us."

The boy's eyes were bleak. "I do not care."

She ventured closer. "But I do. I don't want them to see us. They've brought a ship; you know what that means."

Bear turned and looked at her. "What do you mean?"

Signy swallowed. "We can take it, and we can both go home."

It was night, and the clinkered hull perched, canted, on the sand. She was starting to shift as the returning tide crept up, and very soon she'd ride the surface of the moon-calm water.

The body of the ship was wide and shallow and quite short, for she was designed for trade and service, not war. The boom was tied off at the top of the mast with ropes attached to the flanks of the vessel, and around it was lashed the sail. A hawser had been looped over the neck of the prow and was secured under a granite boulder high on the beach—this was the anchor.

Signy fought the sense that the vessel was waiting for them, as if this meeting was appointed; it was just a thing, this boat, a clumsy, wooden thing, inanimate, not like a horse or a bird, something you could talk to. And it was intimidating, too, now she stood at the water's edge. "The ship's too big for us, Bear. How will we sail her?"

The boy shook his head. The moon touched the white part of his eye, a little flare of light when he looked at his friend. "Once we're out past the headland, it will be easy. You will see."

Now that the time had really come to leave the island, Signy was frightened, and she felt guilty. The Christ-sisters and Christ-brothers had been kind to them both, and they were repaying that kindness with theft; she was leaving Laenna's grave behind too.

"What?" Bear sensed Signy's hesitation.

She turned away, pointing to the rock that pinned the line from the prow. "The mooring rope. Shall I throw it?"

"Not yet."

Bear hurried into the sea. Shivering, he stood beside the hull in the tide's returning surge, peering at the ship. Tapping along her length, he smelled the wood and flicked Signy a smile. "Well caulked and well made—there's sap in this timber—she's young and flexible still and won't let us down; she'll take us both home, Signy."

Home. Signy's eyes blurred. Perhaps Tarannis, God of Storms, would accept her tears as a sacrifice and they would be safe in his domain. But then she thought of Laenna; this island had taken much from her and from her family; perhaps it was time to trust the sea and not the land. "I am ready, Bear. Tell me what to do."

The tide, the rushing, full-moon tide, was higher on the beach with each volley of waves, and for the first time as he glanced at Signy—stick arms, stick legs, standing so uncertainly in the shallows—Bear felt doubt. He squashed it; too late now, they were committed. "Right," he said. "After I'm onboard, you free the rope when I say so. You'll have to climb up quick, but I'll hold her with the steering oar. Then we row—that'll get us out of the bay and into open water."

The prow of the ship tossed like a horse's head at the sea's nudging, but Bear judged the moment well. A bigger wave and the vessel was floating, free from the sand and, as she dipped, head pulled down by the mooring rope, Bear jumped for the neck and, with a scrambling swing, was over the side. Nearly winded as the prow reared up again, he pulled the rope taut while he hopped across the rowing benches.

"Now!" Bear had the tiller in both hands and began to pull in the direction opposite to the tide's drag. Muscles half the size of a man's held that flexing hull as Signy, straining hard, shoved and shoved, and burrowed beneath the rock to free the rope.

Bear yelled over the slap of waves, the clatter of shingle in the wash. "Signy, hurry!"

"I'm trying, I'm nearly . . . there!"

The rock tilted into the hole Signy had scrabbled, and freed the line. She grabbed the last hank as it snaked away, burning her palms. With her arms nearly jerked from delicate sockets, the power of the restive craft and the waves pulled the child at a stumbling run toward the sea.

"Jump. Now!"

Easy to say and much, much harder to do, Signy mistimed her leap and fell, belly-flat into the shallows. The shock of cold water closed her eyes and mouth, but grim strength, the power to hold on, hauled her body against the water's weight, and she surfaced, coughing.

So how did Signy do it? How did she climb the side of the bucking hull and find her way across the rowing benches to the stern?

Bear could only think about that afterward, and when he asked the question, she did not answer.

For now the girl jumped into his sight, more sea spirit than mortal, streaming water and seaweed, and joined him at the steering post. Holding the tiller, they heaved together, shivering, joints cracking, hauling to turn the ship toward the open sea.

The tide helped, and so did the wind, reversing off the land where before it had been rising from the strait.

Then Bear did a mad thing. "Hold the tiller. I'll row."

Signy nodded. Why would she question when there was nothing else to be done?

Swooping to a bench in the middle of the vessel, Bear found an oar and shipped it. Made from spruce, it was three times his length and more, though light.

He dropped the blade in the running sea, back bent and straining against the obstinate water. Years spent watching his brother and the war band told Bear what to do: dip and heave the blade back, dip and heave.

Teeth clenched as she tried to hold the hull, Signy saw what Bear was doing—he was pivoting the vessel, on one oar, and turning the prow toward the mouth of the bay. There was open water in front now as the beach fell away behind—receding, receding—and it began to seem possible. But how to steer and row at the same time, with just two?

Signy called out, "Calm water over there!"

Bear nodded, shouted back, "She'll wallow and we'll set the sail—just a bit more . . . not far."

Two exhausted children, but Tarannis was their friend, for perhaps it was he who guided them to flat water. And in that pool on the surface of the sea, the hull rocked like a cradle as Bear pulled in his oar and called, "Hold her steady. I'll manage the sail."

Hold her steady. Signy nodded and managed to do what was asked.

Bear looked up. The sail must be freed from the boom and then tied off to the sides of the hull, and he must judge exactly how much air should be allowed into the belly of the cloth—that was the tricky part. He wet one finger and held it up, turning his head toward the floating moon as it rose, and then to where the sun had left the world. "The wind remains offshore. Gods be praised for this, at least."

Signy nodded. Her arms trembled holding the tiller, and she could feel the ship swing away from her grasp; then she got the inspiration.

Leaving the oar—Bear saw and shouted at her, "Signy? Signy, go back!"—she returned with a coil of rope. Slipping a loop of walrus leather over the tiller's end, she pulled it taut and fed the other end through a metal ring, tying it off as tightly as she could. And then she scrambled toward the boy with the ruined face and the bright, bright eyes.

"It will work better with two."

Bear smiled at her, happy. "It always does."

Despite the fear, despite the pain, he was joyous. This was his proper place, a ship at sea. He climbed the mast as he would a tree, right to the boom—Signy gasped as he swayed above—and unlashed the sail, tie by tie.

It dropped cleanly, and Signy had caught the sheet on one side as he slid to the deck again. Bear grabbed the rope on the other and ran it through an iron ring.

By day the cloth would have been gaudy—brave red and yellow stripes—but the moon leached the color away. On this night, the red was black and the yellow gray, but the sail was so new—like the rest of the ship—there was no wear on it, not even one patch.

Signy smiled and gathered the sail sheet in her hand. She loved seeing Bear so happy.

He shouted out, "So on my word, we haul."

She nodded.

"Now!"

In unison, one on each side, the boy and the girl pulled in the sail. Air filled the cloth with a crack, and it curved out above in a glorious, pregnant curve—ells and ells of heavy, woven wool, still smelling of sheep's lanolin, strained in the wind, carrying them home.

"We'll see her fly now!" Bear had his lines caught and tied away in less than five breaths. He turned to help Signy, but she had done the same and was standing there, smiling.

"Yours are sea people too?"

She nodded happily. "But we never had anything as fine as this."

"Then we shall steer her together."

Signy looked up into the drum-skin sail and felt the power of the sea surge through the keel tree beneath their feet. While Bear took the tiller, she freed the steering oar and turned her face toward the island as it slipped away behind them.

"Sleep well, Laenna." She raised both arms in farewell to her sister.

Then she smiled and reached out her hand to Bear.

He took it. "Home?"

She nodded. "Home."

And they held the tiller together as they looked out toward the moon-road beyond the mouth of the bay.

CHAPTER 13

PORTSOLLY WAS a small place, and it had few obvious land-marks within the town, but one of them was the spire of the church. For centuries, fishing boats had navigated to har-bor safely once the spire appeared over the horizon. And at night, a lantern burned there to guide stragglers caught out at sea. For most of that time, too, the building had stood by itself and looked directly out to the strait, secure on its own spur of rising ground. But then, over the hundreds of years since it was consecrated, the village had crept closer until, at last, the church was locked tight among smaller buildings. Now it was the focal point, the center of a nest of narrow streets. Only the spire, a finger pointed directly at God, pierced the sky above the roofs like an admonition.

But of what? wondered Freya as she stood outside the somber building. Did she imagine the church had a secretive air? It was built from the same granite as Compline House. The local stone. And, though supremely hard, it was weathered by the salt wind. Some stones had flaked into curious patterns, too, as if granite had a grain, like timber.

"Frost damage."

Freya jumped. The voice came from above, and she looked up, shading her eyes.

A man was perched on the steeple, his harness fastened to the very top of the spire. He was enjoying her confusion. "The craz-ing of the stone, it's frost damage." He rappelled down and landed beside her with breezy efficiency.

The stranger had thick, rope-blond hair that curled well past his collar. Innocent brown eyes, a wide grin and white teeth were additional assets. "And, I know what you're thinking. How come there's frost, this close to the sea?"

Freya found she was smiling. The way he spoke was droll—and it wasn't just the beguiling Scots accent.

"That's not what I was thinking, actually."

"No?"

She shook her head. "I was wondering what you were doing." She gestured toward the steeple.

"Oh, just checking the structure and the cladding—there are stone tiles up there. They're not in bad shape, but some will need renewing." The man unclipped the harness and stepped out of the straps.

"Oh. You're a steeplejack?"

He grinned. "No. Guess again."

"Very Rumpelstiltskin. Anyway, I don't know anything about frost. I'm from Sydney."

"An Outlander! Excellent. It will be my privilege and pleasure to show you the sights, starting here. This kirk now, is an outstanding example of early Romanesque. My name's Simon, by the way, Simon Fettler. And you are?"

Slick as an otter fresh from the sea, Simon Fettler.

She laughed. "Freya Dane," she said and held out her hand.

He took it and held it and smilingly bowed. "I am pleased indeed to meet *you,* Freya Dane. But let me show you something you'll never have seen in Australia." Simon placed one light hand beneath Freya's elbow and, as if it were the most natural thing in the world, steered her toward the portico.

She let him sweep her along solely because he had such great timing—and he made her laugh.

"Now this is just my private theory, but having bought the place—"

Freya stopped. "*You* bought it?"

"Certainly. You seem confused. Do I not appear holy enough to dwell within the tabernacle of the Lord?" Simon allowed himself to look hurt.

She giggled. "I can't comment. Besides, I'd heard you were an architect, not a priest, and that the church had been deconsecrated."

"Well, so I am an architect. But do not mock or be so quick to judge, Freya Dane. They come in all shapes and sizes—so I am told—the clerical gentlemen. In here."

Simon ducked beneath the lintel of the porch. Like Freya's back door on Findnar, it had been built for shorter people. Pulling open an iron-bound door, he bowed her inside.

"I always liked this building, even as a kid. It's not especially large, and it will keep me more than poor with the work that needs doing, but I find the space handsome."

Freya did not, for the interior was grim, as Katherine had said, and dark. She said, politely, "It will certainly make an unusual house."

He nodded happily. "It will indeed—just needs more light, that's all. Glass was sparingly used in early churches, of course—the expense, and then the taxes. That's why there are so few windows."

They both looked up. A modest clerestory ran around the walls beneath the roof, and wan daylight struggled through, a cool green.

Like living under the sea, thought Freya. She shivered.

He strode ahead, chatting happily. "Perhaps I shall put a stone lantern into the roof like St. Paul's—but smaller, you get the idea."

He's right, Freya thought. *I shouldn't judge. He must be able to see the possibilities of this building.* She relaxed, content to listen as he ran on about his plans. She was never this at ease with strangers, and it was a nice feeling. He *was* attractive too—open and warm and funny—that was a change. Her last boyfriend had been a brooder and self-obsessed, not to mention passive-aggressive. And yes, there was a glint when he flicked her a glance. Freya decided she liked being glinted at.

Simon stopped; he was staring at her—plainly she was expected to comment. She said, quickly, "So, will your renovations be allowed through council?"

He shrugged. "Och, it is a listed building certainly, but the interior has been altered before, many times. No strangers, these stones, to being moved about a bit, and they don't care, they'll outlast us all." He patted a wall as if it were a restive horse. "You see, Freya—do you think me bold, appropriating your name?" That naughty glint again.

She waved airily; it was so good to lighten up. "Not at all—appropriate away."

Simon's grin widened, and he swept his arm in a generous arc. "Early buildings are a passion of mine, you see. And I know from research that some of the fabric of this church *is* authentic—and very old indeed—but how much? That's the question and a very good one. I've made a practice out of restoring old structures, some almost ruins. I enjoy the work. And it's always a challenge."

This time he smiled straight into her eyes.

Woah, lad, thought Freya. Simon was certainly intriguing, but then, of course he knew he was—*and he knows I know that too.* Men like that were a worry. *Who cares?*

They laughed simultaneously.

Standing together in what must, once, have been the nave of the church, they faced a dais set upon a flight of granite steps. Squat pillars, thick as tree trunks, lined up on either side.

Simon pointed toward a side aisle. "Over there was a lady chapel—it's long gone, but you can see where the screens were by the marks in the floor. The altar was up there"—he gestured to the dais—"under the rose window."

Freya stared at the delicate tracery of stone, which framed clear glass; it was the prettiest thing in the building. "That's really lovely, Simon," she said, "though it might be a bit later than the rest of the building."

He nodded and flashed her an approving glance. "At least the stone mullions survived. A genuine bit of Gothic that, and it must once have had colored glass. John Knox and his merry friends would have seen that off, of course, but though they de-Popeified Portsolly thoroughly and turned this building into a plain old kirk, they couldn't destroy everything, even if they tried. Come and see what I've found."

Simon ushered Freya to a side wall. "Do you see? Here, and here also . . ."

Old surface plaster had fallen off, exposing a painted surface underneath. A man's face peered out with bulging eyes. He was snarling, and for a moment Freya drew back, intimidated. She'd seen him before, or someone very like him.

Simon didn't sense the trepidation. "So refreshingly violent; the days before political correctness, obviously." He grinned. "I bet it was the elders who had him covered up, but how are the mighty fallen now? Barbarians, one; Elders, zero."

Freya resisted the urge to tell Simon about the carved panel in the undercroft of Compline House. She said, "It does seem quite old. I'm betting Norse. Quite a find."

Simon flicked her a glance. "I'm impressed. The official history of the church says that parts are supposed to have been built pre the turn of the first millennium, Common Era, but the text provides little real evidence, though I've been doing some work of my own. However, perhaps this gentleman goes some way to proving that theory if he can be dated." He paused, staring at the brutal little face approvingly. "Anyway, I've decided he's my protective deity. After all, he chose to emerge from the dark only after I bought the place."

Freya glanced at Simon. "He's a bit scary, isn't he, to be a protector?"

Simon laughed. "Not at all. Think of China—all those snarling lions and demons. Thailand too. I think he's either a demon or maybe a Viking, as you say—a raider from the sea. That's exciting if it's true, because though there's a lot of myth about Vikings in

Portsolly, I've found few actual records so far. I'm hoping there's a whole cycle of frescoes under the plaster—wouldn't that be great?"

"Yes, it would." Freya's enthusiasm was ignited by his own, and Simon sensed it.

"You're welcome to drop by and observe progress any time you're passing. It'll be a bit of a process turning this place into a house, but it's going to be great, just great."

It seemed churlish to disagree, but Freya found it odd to imagine eating, sleeping, washing, working on a computer—all the day-to-day banality of life—among such frowningly massive forms. She glanced at her watch. "You certainly do have a challenge here, as you said." She held out her hand again. "Thanks for the tour—very interesting."

Simon took her hand and shook it gently. His fingers were warm.

Freya held his gaze, slightly embarrassed, and asked, hesitantly, "Would you mind if I had a look in the churchyard? Does one need to get permission or . . . ?"

Simon shook his head. "Not from me."

There was a small self-conscious moment as Freya removed her hand from his.

"I don't own the graves; they're the property of the families, and the council is responsible for the graveyard, but I signed on as sexton—the title came with the building and it seemed the least I could do. So there you have it—I'm the official protector of those who lie here at peace."

Freya was surprised how moved she felt. "That's really nice to know."

Simon sensed the change. "Anyone special you want looked after? You have only to ask."

It was hard to say it. "Michael Dane. I've come to see his grave."

Simon nodded, his eyes compassionate. "Ah. He was your dad?"

She shrugged and looked away, conscious her eyes had filled.

He said, softly, "The Australian connection." He sighed. "People in Portsolly speak well of your father, though I never knew him. We stopped coming here for holidays before he bought the island. I am so sorry for your loss, Freya."

She managed to respond, "Not your fault, Simon, not anyone's fault." *Was that true?*

He nodded slowly. "But a sad business. Let's go and see him, shall we?" He picked up her hand, tucked it into his arm, and walked Freya toward the porch.

She let him. But why, if she had not wanted Katherine to come here with her, did she feel so comfortable with this man she had never met before?

Inside a high wall, the graveyard lay behind the church. Ancient and crowded, it allowed little space between graves, and many of the memorials were unreadable, the names consumed by centuries of Scottish rain and lichen. But Katherine had said it was beautiful, and Freya could see why; roses climbed everywhere, and there was the sound of bees in this sheltered place, busy among the flowers.

"Here you are." Simon squeezed Freya's hand gently, then walked back toward the church.

She appreciated his sensitivity, but now it seemed lonely to visit her father's grave by herself.

So much of Michael's life had been solitary. It had been his choice to exist here, on an outer edge of the world away from other people, and so it was in death, for he was buried in the least-used corner of the cemetery, beside an ancient yew tree.

Freya had expected to cry. She had tried to rehearse how she might feel, hoping that would help her through the actual moment. Now, standing on the raked gravel path, she began to murmur the Lord's Prayer, but she felt self-conscious. Theatrical. She'd never been religious, didn't believe in an afterlife—though she'd often wished she could—and there was no comfort to be found in words that were only words.

Freya bent to pick up a leaf that had fallen on the grave and saw that someone had arranged for an inscription. Who? Perhaps her father had left instructions for his lawyers, as he had about the letter she'd found in Compline's kitchen. Katherine, perhaps, could have taken charge? Or Walter.

Freya closed her eyes. She remembered Katherine's face this morning, when they'd talked about Michael's grave, remembered the undefended feeling in the other woman's eyes. She felt unkind excluding the librarian from this moment. Too late now.

Freya stepped closer to the grave—stainless-steel lettering was incised into the dark stone.

MICHAEL DANE
BORN SYDNEY, AUSTRALIA 01.08.1956
DIED PORTSOLLY, SCOTLAND 01.01.2012
SCHOLAR

Scholar. How could a life be summed up in just one word? He had been a father and a husband and, it seemed, a lover. A friend too.

But Freya remembered a man with large hands and small feet and a lopsided grin who had made her feel safe. She remembered, too, that her father was a good cook, where her mother was not, and that he had told her stories about the past. And the sense he had given her that each life, no matter how ordinary or obscure, was still a wonderful thing, that everyone had a history. That everyone was important.

No one else knew, now, that he felt like that.

There had been happy times, too, in her father's life. How do you carve happiness into a monument, or laughter? If Michael Dane had been an enigma, this piece of stone was mute about his complexity.

Freya turned away from her father's grave clear-eyed. His body might be buried here, but his work was all that remained of his voice; perhaps that was the way she could speak with him again.

At the cemetery gate, she stopped and looked back. She lifted her hand in salute. *Sleep well, Dad. I'll be back.*

No, she didn't believe in the afterlife, but she'd try to understand what he'd wanted her to do.

It turned out there was a shop that sold camping equipment in Portsolly, and even though Freya did not relish using her single credit card, she treated herself to a fleece-lined hat, two pairs of gloves, a gas-cartridge camping light, and an extralarge flashlight. Apples, a few oranges, six eggs (she'd forgotten them before), fresh bread, bacon, a head of lettuce, tomatoes, and washing powder from the supermarket, and she was ready to go back to the island.

Trapped by the lights where the main street of Portsolly joined the coast road, a line of small cars was not going anywhere. One or two interested glances were cast Freya's way as she hurried down the hill toward the harbor, but she was oblivious, focused on getting back to Findnar.

Nearly there now, nearly to where she'd left the little cruiser moored. The bright sea, the soft breeze with its tang, and the smell of kelp—all these real and natural things—filled Freya with relief after the complexity of the last twenty-four hours. She wanted to shout *Thank you!* when she saw the wharf, and just over there . . .

It was gone. Michael's cruiser wasn't there.

Freya stared. She must be mistaken—she must have just forgotten where she'd moored it. She hurried the length of the wharf, searching.

The harbor was busy with boats lining up behind the breakwater—small sailing craft, one or two bigger yachts, and even a three-masted ketch. The trawlers would have left at first light, but *her* boat was gone. Definitely. Confusion flashed to anger in one crisp second—the cruiser had been stolen.

There was a shout. "Freya!"

She turned. Walter was waving from the top of the workshop slipway.

She ran toward him. His expression changed as she got closer. "What's wrong, lass?"

"Dad's boat. It's gone."

He spoke over her. "Are you sure?" He craned to look past her shoulder.

"It's disappeared, Walter. Really it has. I looked just now; someone's taken it. Does Portsolly have a police station?"

Walter was as angry as she was. "It does, and we'll get this sorted, don't you worry."

He barreled through the workshop door, calling out, "Daniel! Get off the phone."

From the door of the office, Daniel stared at his father and then at Freya, a handset cradled between chin and shoulder.

"Hang on, won't be a moment," he said. The tone was cool.

Walter wasn't having any. "Give me that." He spoke into the phone as he snatched it from his son. "Call you back, Denny. Don't let them give you rubbish—backsawn oak, that's what we want." He pressed the disconnect.

"I was halfway through the order, Dad." Daniel spoke mildly, but he frowned at Freya.

She glowered right back—the nice girl had just taken a holiday.

Seeing the exchange, Walter quickly said, "Freya's boat's been stolen. Hello? Hello!"

He turned away. "I want to report a theft. Of a cruiser, *and* I've got a suspect for you . . . Right." He glanced at Freya. "Yes. The owner's with me now." He put his hand over the receiver. "They want a statement. I can take you to the cop shop."

She nodded. The bright day had just turned dark.

"I've had an idea." Walter pulled the door of the police station closed as he and Freya left.

Not really listening, Freya nodded politely. She was exasperated and feeling sad. All she wanted was to get back to Findnar.

"You want to go to the island, right?"

She stopped in the street. "Yes, I do, and, Walter, I've been thinking too. Could I hire a dinghy from you? Just until the cops deal with this."

But Walter spoke over her. "They'll find Michael's craft in a day or two, don't you worry about that—Portsolly's small. So we'll take you back today, and soon as the cops locate the cruiser, we'll tow it over. Meanwhile, when you want to come over to Port, just call; Boyne's water taxi. Simple."

Freya was torn. It was nice for the problem to be solved so easily, and she'd get a chance to talk to Walter, too, as they crossed the strait—maybe he could tell her more about Michael in his final months. But independence whispered a caution; she'd be beholden to the Boynes—more beholden. Did she want that?

"Never play poker, Freya." Walter laughed. "Just like your dad. You don't like favors. But this isn't; this is neighbors and friends."

Freya could feel the heat in her face. "You've been so good to me already and . . ." Embarrassed, she let the words die.

Walter chivied her on, pulling his phone from his pocket. "Morning's wasting. Step out, lass." He stabbed a number, and someone answered.

"Where are you? Good." A quick look at Freya. "Yes. Down in two."

The boats had thinned out by the time they walked to the working part of the harbor, and Freya saw, for the first time, the trawler that had caused Michael Dane's death.

The Holy Isle was large and fine and brave. A scarlet hull, fresh white paint; she might have been new except that she wasn't. She'd been a wreck, and they'd brought her back from the sea, brought her back to life. Freya's vision blurred. *It's just a boat. Don't be stupid.*

Walter did not see her distress as he surged ahead toward the wharf. "Dan, where are you?"

And there was Daniel Boyne, standing on the deck staring down. Surly.

Freya snapped her eyes out to sea. *Dear God, lend me patience.*

"Freya wants to get over to the island, so we'll use the run-about." Tethered to the stern of the trawler was a large clinker-built dinghy, and the serious outboard motor said the craft was all about work.

Walter took charge; he bustled back to where Freya stood. "Let's get your stuff onboard."

More in command of herself, she surrendered the backpack gratefully; the weight of the books had carved trenches in her shoulders. "Thanks. I can manage the shopping."

As he busied himself with checking fuel, Walter called over his shoulder, "Dan, help the girl."

Daniel Boyne clambered down to stand beside Freya on the wharf. She tried not to notice how long it took.

He gestured at the bag from the camping store and the bags of groceries. "I'll take those."

Freya wanted to say, *Don't bother,* but she didn't. Silently, she allowed him to pick up the bags and watched as he limped toward the hull and stowed her possessions on the boards under the seats.

Walter was all focus. "Right. So, run Freya across the strait, Dan, and I'll call Denny back about the order."

"But I thought . . ." Freya started. *I'd rather chew my arm off!* Family training meant she couldn't do it, couldn't actually be rude. Not out loud.

Daniel seemed no happier than she felt. "Dad, there's a great deal to do and—"

"And I'll do it. See you in an hour." Walter stumped off without a glance back.

The silence was embarrassing.

Freya broke it without enthusiasm. "Where would you like me to sit?" *Scrupulously* polite; Elizabeth would have been proud.

Daniel mumbled something.

Freya did not ask him what he'd said. With a gracious bob of the head, she clambered down to sit amidships murmuring, "Thank you," trying to grease the wheels of politeness. The actual meaning of the word made no sense, for she felt no species of gratitude to Daniel Boyne.

The radiant day had turned sullen. As they powered out into the strait, the sky was layers of pewter descending to ominous dark in the east. Smooth as oil and powerful, the sea heaved and flexed beneath the dinghy—these were the sinews and muscles of the deep. *Building up strength for later,* thought Freya.

Dan opened the throttle wider, and noise extinguished the possibility of conversation unless one of them wanted to shout. Freya didn't, and neither, it seemed, did Dan. However, she felt the difference between this dinghy and her father's cruiser. Michael's boat was certainly serviceable, but this craft had a heft all its own for heading into the wind and, when she sneaked a glance at Dan, he seemed at ease steering the runabout. They crossed the open water without incident, though foam was beginning to blow from the wave caps.

Sweeping past the headland, Freya saw the cave mouth. She pointed and Dan nodded. Heading in, he choked the motor back until the dinghy wallowed in a trough between two large waves. He gestured for her to move aside. "I need to row us in. Safest way." He pointed to her current seat between the rowlocks.

"Of course."

With some difficulty, Freya clambered to the prow as Dan took her seat and shipped oars. The backpack was in the way and, impatient to catch the following sea, he picked it up to toss to her. "Here."

Freya leaned forward hastily. "Don't throw it." She almost

snatched it from his hands. "There are valuable books in here." *Oaf!*

Dan said nothing. Hauling hard, first one hand, then the other, he allowed the crest of the wave behind to push the dinghy toward the cave at an angle. It was a nicely judged maneuver, and the little boat slid beneath the arch as if on a rail. At that moment, the rain came after them like bullets bouncing across the sea.

Freya was jittery and close to tears. It would be torture to wait out the weather in the cave with this man. She wanted to be warm and secure in the house, preferably locked in, but veils of gray were sweeping in from the open water, and she could see them lined up in rows as far as the horizon; there'd be no respite for some time.

Freya mustered her manners. "Thanks, Dan, very kind. I'll put my stuff in the cart and be off."

He shrugged. "You'll get wet." One oar feathered, and the dinghy nudged up to the quay. "Tie her up."

That nettled Freya. "I was just going to."

To show him that boats were her natural territory as much as his, she jumped to the quay, a neat hop. Tying the prow line securely, she turned to reach down for her things.

The dinghy rocked beneath Dan as he stood up with her pack.

"Careful!" And, of course, Freya wished she hadn't said that.

He was offended. "I won't drop it." He held it up.

Freya took the pack with a tight smile. The flap was loose, and she could see Katherine's present lying on top of the books. Fearful the bag had been splashed with seawater, she knelt and took the package out; inside the shopping bag were layers of tissue and a wadding of cotton wool, she peeled that back carefully.

Black stone stark in its white nest, the bone of Christ's body was stained by the earth it had lain in—Katherine's crucifix. There was no note.

Freya picked it up very carefully. That contorted body, this ruined face, was tragedy given form. So much pain. Her father had brought it out of the earth, but now Katherine had given it to her. How much this gift must have cost her. Freya's eyes filled.

Putting the last bags on the quay, Dan tried not to see Freya's distress. "That's the last of them."

She managed a nod as she fumbled rewrapping the crucifix.

Dan's eyes softened, and he said mildly, "Here, let me."

Freya snapped. She grabbed his hand just as it touched the bone figure.

And something happened.

Flames shone in his eyes, the reflection from some great burning. Screams. A monstrous howling. Agony. Terror. Somewhere a bell clamored.

There was a woman. Hair wild, face streaked with tears and blood, dressed in a ripped brown tunic, she struggled to hold a massive book above her head, as if to ward off a blow. A man stepped close; his sword had a red edge.

Freya clutched the crucifix. Physical pressure at the top of her skull, an immense pain, made her gasp. The air was charged; she could smell ozone, as if lightning had hit them both. She had to look at him. "Did you see?"

Dan stared at her. He shook his head.

"But . . ." Freya knew he was lying, his green face told her that. She was astonished. Not even angry.

Dan stood straighter, unraveled his spine joint by joint. "I'll get back," he said. He climbed into the stern of the dinghy and fired the outboard. He raised a hand but did not look back as he took the boat out into the strait.

Freya wanted him to go. When he waved, it felt like a hive of wasps moved into her head; it stung to think and it was hard to stand, but something lanced through the dark behind her eyes, the buzzing, burning shadow. *Twice.* Twice in one day she'd been . . . somewhere.

And now Daniel Boyne had been there too. *Why?*

CHAPTER 14

S HE WAS a very well-made boat, and she had good manners.
As Signy scrambled from one side of the deck to the
other on Bear's orders, constantly pulling on the lines while
he steered, the keel rode easily over a running sea. The moon had
reached its zenith, and the silver road laid out before the prow was
brighter than any beacon calling them home.

"I can see it. My village! Ow!" Signy fell between two rowing
benches.

"Signy! Where are you?"

The child struggled up, smiling, and wiped blood from a cut
over one eye. "Here I am."

The moon caught her bright teeth, her happy grin, as she
swayed and hopped over the obstacles toward him. But then she
peered at the narrow mouth into her clan's harbor.

"How shall we bring her in, Bear?"

The boy glanced at Signy's worried face. He was calm, for her.
"We'll drop the sail off a bit—we only need enough belly to steer
her by. It will be nice to sleep in a proper house tonight, won't it?"

She grinned. "Oh, it will. My own bed, after a heap of rot-
ten straw. It's close to the fire too. My father built it for us, and
it's stuffed deep with heather and sheepskins. Me and Laenna, we
share . . ."

Signy gulped. Her sister had another bed now. What would she
tell their mother?

"Let out the sail." Bear pointed. "A bit at a time."

She nodded and darted to one side of the boat. Unlashed, the rope that held the sail ran across her palm, hot as fire.

"Good. Now the other side." He did his best to sound confident.

But Signy knew Bear well after this last sorrowful year. He was anxious and trying not to show it. She caught the line quickly.

"Pull it in! More . . . That's enough."

But maybe it was not. The hull was still running hard, planing toward the harbor opening with an active following sea as Signy stared ahead. She swallowed. If they made it through, there was another obstacle, for rocks lay on either side. Easy enough to avoid in the day, night and moonlight changed everything. Something huge and black—the jagged tooth of a sea monster, wet and shining—reared up. "There!"

Bear saw what she saw.

"Steer!" He scrambled over the benches toward the taut sail. How much time did they have? The boat plunged toward the harbor's entrance, and Bear could not loose the sail lines quickly enough.

"Laenna, help us!" Signy tried to hold the ship. She could hear Bear cursing, then flapping and snapping; the sail was loose.

But the sea carried them on.

Bear was beside her again, and it was enough, just, that they held the tiller on the steering oar together.

"How steep is the beach?" He spoke softly, transfixed by the land rushing toward them out of the dark—the zone where the earth met sea.

Signy shook her head. "It changes each winter. I don't know . . ."

Now they did. The keel tree grounded with a shuddering wallop, and the hull was flung sideways. Signy lost her hold, and the world swung away, out of her control.

"No!" Bear tried to catch Signy, tried to grab her as she fell, but he was not fast enough. He could only plunge after, trying to control his own descent into the black water.

"Bear!" She thought she'd said his name, but the sea filled her mouth and then the stern swung.

The steering oar, loosed from control, clipped Signy's head, and dark swallowed her whole.

The moon found her because air was trapped in the folds of her tunic. Buoyed up, she was held half-suspended between the moving surface of the sea and its floor, fathoms deep.

The moon tracked over the floating girl, and Bear saw her face—white against black. He went down again, down to get her, like a cormorant. And grasped her wrist.

And though his own body was mortally weak, something—enough—was left of the strength that had held the ship. Lungs collapsing, blood in his mouth, he hauled her skyward, starward.

His head burst through to the air, and hers followed. If he could just get her to the shore, if he could only squeeze the sea from her chest, if . . .

Signy lay open-eyed on the surface of the water.

"Help her!" What God would hear him in the surf's roar?

Time ceased. There were only the stars to see his despair as Bear struggled to the beach. Half-sitting in the shallows, he held Signy from behind, his arms clamped around that frail chest. He'd seen it done like this when men were hauled from the sea having fallen from one of Reimer's ships.

Signy was too young to have breasts, but as Bear compressed her chest, he could feel ribs like little sticks beneath the skin.

"Breathe for me, Signy!" He was shouting at her, blind to everything but that calm, indifferent face.

Nothing. There was nothing.

Sobbing, Bear dragged Signy from the shallows and laid her on the hard sand, away from the waves. All he had was his own breath. Gasping air, he sealed his mouth over hers and blew. And again. Once more. Her mouth was soft and slack, her teeth a hard little barrier, but he would empty his life into her body if he exploded his own lungs to do it.

"Signy!" Bear's breath pushed her own name deep, and that was, finally, the thing that called her back. He felt her move beneath him. Life! Terrified that gossamer thread would break, Bear inhaled again and blew as if he were each of the four winds.

Signy struggled, found the strength to push him aside. The vomit when it came was clear water, no blood, no foam.

White as driftwood, they sprawled beached at the high-water mark near the hull, abandoned by the sea, and soon it was cold. This night might ice their bones yet.

Bear floundered to his feet. On the sand, the girl lay within touching distance of the steering oar, which had nearly claimed her life. But the boom had dislodged when the ship struck the beach. It had collapsed down the mast, spilling the loosened sail like a curtain over the side; cubits and cubits of woolen material lay on the sand, and it was largely dry.

"Don't fight me, Signy."

"What?" Her voice was a thread.

Signy's body left a pathetically shallow trail in the sand when he dragged her closer to the hull, but that was a good thing—any heavier and he couldn't have managed it.

"Now, I have to do this." Bear ripped at her wet clothes so that she was exposed to the night, naked and twitching with cold. "You'll be warm soon, then I can find your parents," he told her.

She was too cold to speak.

Tucking one edge of the sail under her body, Bear turned Signy over and over in the material until she lay imprisoned within its stiff cocoon. The wool was coarse and scratched her skin, but she had no surface feeling.

Surrendering to the dark, Signy closed her eyes. Fugitive warmth became her beloved companion. She slept.

Tell her parents. Tell them she's alive.

The words ran through his head like a chant, but Bear was exhausted and very cold. If he did not find them soon, he, too, might die; but he had to do this. For her.

There were only a few buildings in the clan's settlement. On a natural stone terrace above the beach, three or four round huts were grouped around a low, log-built house thatched with reeds. The cliff that protected their backs towered against the sky, a black-cut shape against the setting moon.

Bear felt nothing, but he knew he still had a body because he watched his feet as they trod over rocks beside the landing beach and found the wooden trackway. In the black and white of night, they left dark smears behind.

Blood? It was an effort to remember it was dangerous to bleed. It would be too easy, now, to float away from his collapsing body, except for Signy. She needed him.

Bear fell down by the God stone at the door of the largest building. He felt that, for the pain in his knees was so sharp he whimpered like a small child. On his belly, he shunted closer to the door, banged on it with a closed fist. Again. There was no movement, no stirring from the other side.

"Friend, help!" He used what words he had of the clan tongue.

A voice in the night is to be feared, but his had not yet broken, and he heard himself. He sounded like a girl. Who would be frightened of a girl?

"Please, Signy here. Please . . ."

He used their daughter's name so that the family inside would understand.

There was a rock close to Bear's hand, water-smoothed, a big gray egg. Last strength closed his hand around it, last strength picked it up.

He hit the door, and the sound was enormous. He heard the crash as it rolled around inside the house unobstructed, unabsorbed.

Using the God stone beside the door, Bear pulled himself

upright. He was slow because his legs were weak. He stood and listened. Nothing. No sound at all.

His fingers convulsed again around the rock in his hand. Leaning forward, he shoved the blank face of the door with his chest and a shoulder. It moved. And stopped. There was something in the way.

Bear pushed again, expecting, at any moment, to hear a voice raised in anger or confusion.

He made an opening big enough to slide through, but the dark behind the door seemed wrong. Where was the glow from the fire pit? Ashes would have been banked high last night—enough for some light to remain.

But there was no light. Instead, faint radiance from the stars spilled through a hole above his head.

The place yawned, deserted. No one slept beside the fire pit; the box beds by the wall were empty, and the sanded floor puddled with water. A broken bench told the same story as the clay cooking pot, shattered on the floor. The hall had been looted, the clan was long gone.

Where? Who could say?

At least there were no rotting bodies. Signy would be grateful for that. And perhaps there was hope that her family had escaped and were still alive. Somewhere.

As the night waned, Bear crept in beside the sleeping girl, burrowing beneath the sail. He lay along the length of her, hoping that his body warmth would reach her or hers him, even through the layer of coarse wool. At least they were still alive.

Then he slept.

Signy touched the God stone at the door from habit—there was a dimple like a navel where many fingers from the clan had rested. There had been just enough light to see that, and the open door. No door is left open all night.

And so Signy did not call the names of her family. She knew there was no point. As she had run from the beach toward the houses, not even a dog had barked. No loving voice would ever welcome her home. They had all gone. The clan settlement was empty.

But still, she must show respect; then perhaps her family's Gods would offer protection, for this hall had been their dwelling place. That was why the stone stood by the door.

She said, softly, "I ask permission to enter this place. I am the daughter of the Shaman Odhrahn, son of Alhrahn, son of Ehrwald. This is our hearth-home." Her throat seized, but still she continued. "I must tell you what I know, so that it can be recorded in the stories of our people in this place."

Signy stood by the fire pit gazing up toward the hole in the roof. She avoided the sight of the empty bed her father had built. She would never sleep there again.

"I have nothing to offer, except this."

In one hand Signy had an oyster shell—she'd picked it up from the midden beside the trackway. She closed her eyes and slashed the shell's edge across her right wrist. It raised a welt, but nothing more. Teeth pinched her lower lip as Signy tried again, but it took several attempts before she achieved the sacrifice. Blood, her blood, dropped onto the cold ashes of the fire pit. It was joined by her tears.

"Mother, Father, I ask help from you now even if we shall not meet again. I need a knife and clothes for me and for my friend. Show me."

Faith was something Signy did not question in her family's hearth-home. The sacrifice had been made, she would be given what was asked for. To stop the blood, she clamped her other hand across the cut and opened her eyes.

Nothing seemed to be different, but then, her injured arm freed itself and rose in the air. This was the sign she'd expected. Signy relaxed and watched her right arm as it swung around; her hand was pointing toward the back of the room.

She waited for the summons. It came. The blood stopped flowing.

Signy walked forward, carefully watching her hand and arm as they floated ahead of her.

Just before she reached the blank back wall, her feet stopped and her arm dropped. Now it lay quietly at her side, and there was no sense, as there had been just now, that it was separate from her body.

"I thank you, Mother and Father."

Signy managed the words in a strong voice before she looked for her gift. They had helped her, and that meant they must be dead, their spirits with the ancestors in the clan haven in the sky.

Whoever had sacked this place, when they came, had missed the small box. Careless, perhaps, or in a hurry; it might have looked too humble to contain anything of value. But Signy knew what she'd been given, and she removed the lid with clumsy fingers. Inside something flared red, the same color as her blood, and that almost defeated her. But she leaned forward and reached inside; something soft was there. Cloth. Garments. Two tunics—one red, one brown—and two shirts of soft linen.

They were men's clothes—these would be her mother's work made for her father, or perhaps for Nid or another of her brothers. Swampingly large on her own body and on Bear's, they would at least be warm and, too, there were belts. One was of plaited leather with worked silver ends, another had an iron buckle.

Best of all, there were leggings and straps to bind them— enough for her and for him—and one pair of men's leather shoes. She would still go barefoot—but that was best at sea. Bear could have the shoes.

At the bottom of the chest were further riches, for a dagger lay there. Coated in pig fat—only a little rancid—it was still inside its leather scabbard. Signy remembered. She had seen it in her father's hand, often; that it had been left behind confirmed much.

She would not think of that now. No, from this time on, her

father's knife would hang from her own belt. This would be her knife—his gift to her.

It took no time to dress. Bear would need her now even though he would not know that—because she had the knife. With it, they could gut fish and strike fire. She would give him the silver-ended belt; men, too, liked pretty things.

As she left, Signy turned back one last time, at the God stone.

"I thank you for my gifts. As a child of this clan, I ask your help as I go into the world. May you, my father, and you, my mother, be safe, and all of my brothers. If you are in our haven in the sky, may you find rest and good food and deep sleep. And may we meet again."

Signy pulled the door closed.

CHAPTER 15

WHEN BEAR woke, he was alone.

His clothes had dried on his body, and the morning was fine enough to treasure though the sun's light was, as yet, weak and pale.

"Signy?"

Shaking sand from his hair, Bear sat up. His panicked glance swept the empty beach; then he saw the line of small prints leading toward the trackway and the huts.

"Ah . . ." Bear was angry with himself, suddenly furious. She'd gone there alone, but as he ran across the beach, he saw her walking toward him, a little figure rimmed by rising light. She was carrying something.

He ran, waving vigorously, calling out, "I'm here! Here I am, Signy."

She stopped and waited for him to reach her.

Bear was breathless. "I'm sorry, truly sorry. I wanted to be there when . . ." He saw the red tunic she was wearing.

She held up her hand—*Don't speak*—and dropped the bundle at his feet. "These are for you. The shoes too."

Bear bent down. He picked up the shirt and the tunic—even he could see how well they'd been made. He swallowed. "Are you sure?"

She nodded. "Yes. A gift from my family." She was only a little girl, and her dignity was heartbreaking. "They've gone, Bear, and I think they are dead."

He blinked tears away. *No one should suffer like this.* The boy held out his arms.

That broke Signy's courage. With a sob she fled to him, and he held that fragile body against his own thin chest, trying to breathe her pain.

"I have to go back, Bear."

It was hard to understand what Signy said, the words sobbed out between great gasping breaths.

"But . . ."

She nodded, wiped her eyes fiercely, hiccuping. "I wanted to come home, yes." She stepped back from him. "But there is no home for me. And now I must tell Laenna. She should know."

Bear said the wrong thing. "But she's dead, Signy."

"Yes, she is dead. The raiders killed her. Just like my parents."

Those dark eyes, awls to score Bear's soul. He shook his head, pleading. "They may have gone somewhere else and we will find them."

She yelled at him. "No. You came with them. You sacked the island with them, and then they did this. You're just like them."

"No, I'm not. Not anymore." Bear shrugged the thought away, the treacherous thought, *Yes, I am.*

He tried to take her hand and flinched when he saw the gash across her wrist. "Come to my home, Signy. Live with my family. Please. My mother will welcome you as her daughter—she only has sons. Just a few days' sailing, that is all—we can float the ship again and travel on."

Unwillingly Signy looked to where the hull lay, canted on the sand. It was true, the sea was returning.

"Laenna is all that remains of my true family on this earth, and I will not leave her. Not after this." She pointed toward the semi-ruined buildings. Fire had done its work—it was easier to see that in daylight.

"Take the ship, Bear. You need it more than me." Signy hitched up her tunic and ran toward a cove between high rocks.

White legs flashing, she was a red blur against black crags and the pale sky.

Bear called out. "Come back."

But he had no choice. He ran after her, and the boy with the ruined face cried as he ran.

You would not have seen the coracle unless you knew where to look. Wedged upright at some distance from the high-water mark, it was the same color as the rocks, but Signy did not have the strength to pull it out, try as she might.

Bear wiped his face when he got close. He did not want her to see. "I can help."

"Get away!" She bared her teeth, a small ferocious animal.

Bear reached up to grasp the odd little craft.

Signy bit his wrist. She drew blood.

Shocked, he dropped his hand. "Signy!"

"Leave me alone. I don't need your help."

"Oh, Signy . . ." Bear slumped. She meant what she said. He stared out toward the strait; now he did not care if she saw his tears.

Perhaps his sorrow shook her resolve. She licked one of her own bloody knuckles and after a moment sat beside him.

Poor Bear. It was a reflex action to put his arm around her bony shoulders. "We're both hungry. Come on; we can sort this out later."

Signy said nothing, but she allowed him to pull her up. Hand in hand they walked along the beach. There were oysters and whelks on the rocks and fish trapped in rock pools; food was there for the taking and driftwood, too, with mounds of seaweed cast up above the high-tide line.

Bear pointed. "If we can make fire, I can broil a fish or two."

Signy pulled out her father's knife. "All we need is something to strike against."

Bear stared at the blade and grinned. "Maybe the Christ-brothers left tools onboard the ship; anything iron will do." He trotted away toward the vessel and then stopped. Looking back, he called out, "You know it, don't you?"

"What?" Signy was gathering driftwood.

"We're good together, you and me. Us against the world." He waved and ran off.

She watched him go. *Against the world.* How big was the world anyway . . .

CHAPTER 16

FREYA WAS trudging away from the cave in the rain pulling the cart. The journey back to the house was a repeat of the first but worse, much worse. Her mind seethed with images and sounds—and fear.

Walking time is thinking time—Michael always said that—and as Freya plodded on, her thoughts became calmer; logic is a wonderful thing sometimes.

The praying in Latin this morning, for instance; that had to be some kind of really, *really* vivid nightmare brought on by reading—and some of the material she'd dipped into at the library had been about early religious life in Scotland. Those monasteries must have been grim and cold, and blighted by an unforgiving code that had terror at its very heart. For a scholar, she was plainly far too imaginative—too much right brain, not enough left.

But there was the crucifix. That was trickier.

Freya reran the images in her mind. She'd been taking it out of its wrapping and peeling the cotton wool back when Daniel reached over to help. She'd tried to take it back, and they'd touched it together. *Boom.* She stopped, oblivious to the rain pricking her face, and stared at the strait. Storm or no storm, Daniel Boyne was already halfway back to Port in the sturdy little dinghy. He'd be wet by now. She hoped he was soaked.

Freya stared at her hands, held them up. The wallop when he'd touched her—*No, touched the crucifix*—had been like sticking fingers in a power socket, but there were no marks on her skin, no aftermath. Daniel had gone white, though, and then green, as if he wanted to be sick. Then he'd flat-out lied.

They *had* both seen it—destruction, terror. It had felt like the end of the world.

She yelled at the sea. "Why did you run? Can you hear me?" *Of course he can't, idiot.*

Trembling, Freya wiped water from her face. She *knew* the world to be a solid place—well, at the nonmolecular level. (*So, not very solid at all, really.*)

But this cliff was real rock; the rain was very cold and it was wet. She looked down. There were pebbles on the path, and pebbles were actual *things,* here-and-now things. *But what you saw and he saw was just as real; it wasn't a movie or something on the Net, some fantasy. And it wasn't a dream.*

Freya stared up toward the house. "Was this what you meant by 'visions,' Dad?"

Above, the path climbed away. If she wanted to be warm and safe inside Compline, if she wanted to know more—because she was convinced there was more to know—she had to do this. She started forward—and stopped. Her legs didn't want to work like legs; they didn't want to hold her up. Freya groaned; it was too hard, all of it.

"Come on, you can do this. Jesus!" Blasphemy—she tested herself, tested whatever had made her pray this morning.

Count. Count the steps. Freya nodded: Elizabeth. When you can't face the thought of something, walk toward it and count the steps—enough steps and you forget what you're frightened of. And what was she actually frightened of here? Insanity? She was pretty sure, really fairly positive, that she was not insane. But she took a step and began to count. "One, two . . .

". . . and four hundred and thirty-seven. Thank you, God, whoever you are."

Freya stumbled around the last curve, past the twisted old rowan. Pausing to let her breathing settle, she hitched the pack higher and flexed her right arm—stiff from pulling the cart. There was the house, cold and dark and empty. Forlorn; that made two of them.

A bath. Whisky! Who cared if it wasn't even lunchtime; she didn't. Only a few steps now, *four hundred and thirty-eight, nine, four hundred and forty. . . . So, Dad, I need to find where the crucifix came from. You have to help me, you owe me that—at least. Four hundred and forty-one, two, three . . .*

She hurried into the house from the rain. What a relief it was to wipe her face and put her burdens down. She'd take out the books and . . . her present, later.

Now, if she wanted that bath, she had to make the stove fire up. Paper, dry heather, peat, flame—simple things, simple tasks, the remedy for confusion.

It was quiet inside Compline. Thick walls stopped most sound, and there was only the rain—fingers on the glass, *pat, pat, pat*— as Freya struck a match and the paper caught. Soon the firebox would heat up, and so would the kitchen. She pumped water to fill the pipes at the back of the range. Something was working, and that was a relief. Now for the whisky.

Freya put the empty glass on a stool beside the bath, but it wasn't until she'd eased herself very, very slowly into the scalding water— gasping as her body flushed scarlet from toes to collarbones—that she saw why her father had bothered to build the dais that supported the tub. Fully relaxed, she leaned back and found her face at the perfect angle, the perfect height, to inspect the green mound that stood like a sentinel behind the house.

The hill—smooth, flat-topped, and symmetrical—was gracefully framed within a deep, single window set in the thickness of the wall. Rain blurred the image but only in the pleasing way of an Impressionist painting seen too close.

Natural optimism bobbed up as Freya soaped the length of her body. All the nonsense she'd experienced had to have a reasonable explanation, and she was definitely going to find it. The things around her—the bath, the soap, the water, this house—were all just as real as the cliff; the rest, the visions, had to be about the work of an overwrought imagination and jet lag; sometimes that lasted for a week, and she'd been here only a couple of days. What other explanation could there be?

Humming, Freya pulled the plug, stood up, and saw the side of a building through the glass. She'd not noticed it before. Was that a bell tower? Curious, she slung a leg over the side of the bath and padded toward the window. The rain was heavier, streaming down the pane, when she got there, and whatever she'd seen the moment before was no longer visible.

Freya was perplexed. The only structures on the island were the house, the barn behind it, and the ruins. There was nothing else. Was there? Her feet were getting cold on the slate floor and, looking down, she glimpsed her own nakedness. Nauseated with a sense of sin solid as a blow, Freya wrenched a towel from a chair and covered her torso, her thighs, with trembling hands.

Mortal sin! To uncover nakedness, even one's own, was to slip into the Devil's waiting hands. She would need penance, much penance, to expunge this evil. Holy Mary, help me! Dress and hurry—no, run—to the church. *And she would eat nothing until she had been confessed of this heinous breach of her vows. It would be little enough to offer to God in apology for offending Him.*

Freya opened her eyes. She was lying on the floor of the bathroom. Naked. Shivering.

She sat up. Stood. And though her heart squeezed against her ribs like something captive, anger spread from her gut to her head so fast, sweat burst out on her face.

Snatching up clothes, Freya pulled them on so fast she ripped the neck of the T-shirt.

"No more jokes!"

She slammed the bathroom door with a crash and marched to

the kitchen. She was angry because she was frightened; she understood that, of course. Schizophrenics experienced delusions, saw visions, saw God, thought they *were* God, didn't they? Was that it? Was she becoming schizoid? Schizophrenia occurred less rarely in women, especially past the teens, but late onset did happen, didn't it?

Abruptly Freya dragged a chair close to the stove. Hands between her knees, she rocked back and forth, back and forth. Maybe she should ring home, see if anyone else in the family had had to deal with this stuff—with bipolar or whatever. Was that why he'd left them? Had Michael been mentally ill all those years ago?

She stared at her watch. It was the wrong time in the Southern Hemisphere—she'd completely freak Elizabeth if she rang in the middle of the night.

Why, Mum? Oh, you know, just 'cos I'm seeing things at the moment. Was Dad crazy by the way?

They did say, whoever *they* might be, that mental illness was the great undiagnosed epidemic in society. Was this what it felt like to be mad?

"Oh, how would I know? Time to work!"

It was past midday, that's what the hands on the old wall clock said. Seated at Michael's desk in the big room as rain battered the windows, Freya stared at the crucifix. She'd been reluctant to touch it again—had left it in the cotton wool nest—but that didn't mean she couldn't look.

"Who made you?" The Christ stared back at her across the void of time, mute.

"And you, what about you?" She opened the small lead box and . . . nothing happened. Freya grimaced. As if they had a voice, the manuscript pages begged to be translated. "I know, I know, but I'd be at it for years." *Katherine.* Would the librarian help her? She'd be bound to know who read Latin in Portsolly.

Freya shifted restlessly. It would be logical—and sensible—to invite Katherine to the island to at least look at the manuscript and give her opinion. And she might know about it anyway, since Michael had given her the crucifix. So many questions. Was she, Freya, brave enough to ask Katherine some of them? And did she really want the answers? Now that was the *real* question.

She dropped her head into her hands. In the last hour, she'd assembled all the reference cards she could find that mentioned the dig in the stone circle, and she'd located site plans and photographs, especially of the crucifix—to compare to the original. But the more she'd read, the more perplexed she'd become. Just as her father had been. "But it would have been blasphemous, surely, to carve a likeness of Christ that was not perfect in every respect?" *It would indeed, Dad.* Staring out toward Portsolly, she consciously defocused, waiting for inspiration. Nothing.

The new gas camping light was excellent on a dark day. Nothing so romantic as a pretty glass shade, but the white glow showed a whole lot more detail in the cavernous space of the undercroft.

Judging by its iconography, the crucifix was very old. Perhaps there were Byzantine influences in the work, but her father had not thought so; he'd placed it as much older—Celtic, perhaps.

Freya shook her head. *Not Celtic, Dad.* But what? Pictish? And yet those enigmatic early inhabitants of this part of the world certainly weren't Christians. Why would they carve a crucifix?

Freya examined the surface of the timber panel propped against the wall. Was there really a family resemblance between the popping eyes, the bared teeth of these carved warriors and the face on the wall of Simon's church? She tapped the surface of the wood very gently. This at least was very, *very* Pagan.

So. Christian objects and Pagan artifacts—and all on Findnar. She nodded companionably at the ferocious little men. "Charming, the lot of you. I'm not scared, by the way—just remember that." And she wasn't, not of them, anyway.

It was an interesting piece, though, and Elizabeth would like it. Her mother had a collection of tribal art and votive objects from all over the world on one wall of her living room—this would look well among them.

Freya laughed. Here she was standing in front of quite possibly one of the more important pieces of carved wood to have survived the very early Middle Ages, and she was thinking about the thing as a design statement!

She flexed her neck and her back; she was stiff from sitting after the walk up the hill path. She had a choice—continue to study Michael's notes or go outside and try to locate where he'd found the crucifix. Physical work to take her mind away from her thoughts.

She peered at the windows in the front wall of the undercroft. The rain had stopped.

No contest. Dig.

The sky had cleared, and the sun, a little past its zenith, shone down untroubled by cloud.

Freya was whistling—a cheerful sound in the same key as the soft breeze from the south—as she set off over the meadow behind the house toward the rising ground. She had loaded up the wheelbarrow with her father's tools from the barn—a shovel, a spade with a narrow blade, several big wooden sieves, paintbrushes small and large, and an assortment of scrapers and digging implements. She also had several of Michael's red and white ranging poles in various lengths, and two folded PVC tents to protect work in progress. And, since she meant to document everything as meticulously as Michael always had, a digital camera was slung around her neck. Finally there was a thermos of hot tea and sandwiches. Archaeology, like an army, always marched on its stomach, and she was planning on staying outside as long as she could.

Green and voluptuously smooth, the hill loomed closer as she walked. Freya put the handles of the barrow down and shaded her eyes. Scanning the area slowly, she tried to understand the lay of the land, tried to visualize, so far as she could, what it must have looked like in times past. She didn't know much about ancient tree cover or historical climate in Northeast Scotland, and until she did some serious research, the nature of past settlement on the island—except for the few pieces of information she'd gathered so far in Katherine's library—could only be guessed at. Michael had said the ruins were ecclesiastical, and Katherine had called them "the Abbey," but how old they truly were and from what actual era, she could not say. And Freya didn't want to consciously speculate because that brought her close, far too close, to the strange visions. But she would not acknowledge the dread, she was here to *work*, so . . .

Locating the exact place where someone else has already dug is generally a frustrating process. Freya knew she was lucky that various landmarks—the largest ruins, the house, the hill, and the standing stones—had been noted on Michael's plans of the area, yet even triangulating between points on these structures, she would be left with a dauntingly wide area in which to dig.

Archaeology, Michael used to say, was about strong backs, sensitive hands, and good boots. Freya had not done fieldwork for a while—recently, her time had been taken up by writing *about* fieldwork—but as she trudged off toward the circle, she started to feel excited.

She absolutely *was not* a treasure hunter. She was about legitimate research based on her father's careful notes—research that, if she were clever, would bear directly on the meat of her thesis. *Regional Iconography*—well, the form of the crucifix was certainly regional, not to say so local that she'd never seen anything like it in any of the artifacts she could remember—*And neither had you, Dad; you said that.*

She badly needed other comparable examples from the island, and to be able to place them in their correct time context too. Then she could begin to build her case based on original research into these previously unknown objects—provided she could prove that their form was influenced by the society on Findnar at that time, as opposed to more standard Christian iconography in other societies around the same time.

Certainly, and you'd like a unicorn with that?

"Ow!" Because she was not paying attention, Freya's foot had gone down a hole, and she pitched over the top of the barrow, banging her head on a white stone half-sunk in the surface of the meadow.

Laugh or cry? Sitting up, she touched her skull gently; already a fat lump was growing under the skin, but her fingers came away clean—no blood.

Archaeology—dangerous work. *Not usually.*

But what had tripped her up? "There you are." It was quite a large hole, but made by what, exactly? Too big for a rabbit, it might have been a badger, but Freya had no idea if they liked being this far north. "A fox?" Unlikely, considering the number of nesting birds there seemed to be on Findnar.

Freya knelt down and peered into the opening in the turf. About the size of a child's head, it was close to the stone and just a bit off to one side. She slid one of the ranging poles inside—it went down more than half a meter until it struck earth; quite a deep hole, then.

Time was wasting. But as Freya began to get up, the pole slipped from her fingers. Cursing, she reached down into the hole and found it, but when she moved, the pole knocked against something. Not stone, not wood—something else.

Intrigued, Freya extended her arm into the void and felt around carefully. Something smooth, the shape of an inverted bowl. *The cranium of a skull?*

She'd not expected to turn up a skull in the middle of the meadow, but that's what happened when she enlarged the burrow—and there was more than just a skull.

As she carefully peeled back damp turf and dug into the ground beneath, it became clear that an entire skeleton lay in the earth. Complete except for the skull, which had been dragged aside by whatever creature had made the burrow, it was small, but not that of a child, since the pelvis suggested an adolescent and the sutures on the top of the skull were still clear. So, a teenager?

Freya took a set of photographs—close-ups of the front of the skull and wider shots of its position near the rest of the skeleton. Carefully, so as not to disturb the sides of the hole she'd dug, she eased down to squat beside the bones. Lifting the skull gently, she examined the back. "Wow—what happened to you?" There was massive damage there, and some of the bone was missing. Without proper analysis, Freya could not tell how old the skeleton was, but judging from the color—the bone stained almost ocher—it had lain in the sandy earth here for some time. Unlikely, then, to be from a contemporary person—something of a relief; Freya was spooked enough without contemplating a murderer loose on Findnar.

Examining the skull closely, she decided these might be the remains of a girl, since there were no prominent brow ridges; however, there was no dating evidence visible and no grave goods. And nothing to say what the status of this person might have been.

"Were you Christian?" Freya was not convinced; the layout of the grave was wrong, for Christian graves faced east, invariably, and this one did not.

Clambering out, she crouched beside the pit. It was then she noticed something odd. She'd peeled back quite a lot of turf from the site and laid it to one side, and now she saw there was a layer of water-smoothed pebbles in cross section on all sides of the pit. Once the little grave had had a covering of stones just like a white blanket, and she found that touching. The pebbles could only have come from the cove, and that meant a lot of trips up and down the cliff to decorate the resting place of this nameless person.

On impulse Freya picked an armful of meadow flowers and scattered them around the lip of the excavation. And though she could not replace the covering of pebbles, at least she could mark where the small skeleton lay and cover it with the PVC tent until she returned to gather the bones.

Standing back to contemplate her work, Freya pulled the thermos out of the barrow and poured a cup of tea. A surprise is always a good beginning, and that was the lure, of course, the anticipation, the hope, that other finds lay waiting for her.

She threw the dregs of the tea onto the grass. Time for the real task of the day—just what *was* the best way to approach the site within the ring of standing stones?

Since the afternoon was fine now, Freya enjoyed the stroll toward the outer circle of stones across the rising ground. In their shadows she put the wheelbarrow down and stared. Close up, the monoliths bulked larger than she'd imagined, and though they were severely weathered, the enigma of their presence was still powerful. "I'm one of the mayfly folk, aren't I? You've seen us come and go for so many, many years—just little blurs in time."

She didn't have to count them. Michael's notes had told her already that there were the remains of thirteen standing stones in the outer circle with an inner ring of eight uprights.

A significant depression at the very center of the two rings showed, Michael thought, that at least one large stone had been removed, and another lay half heeled over, leaning against its neighbor. There appeared to be no altar stone or central offering table.

"How old are you?" Freya stood in the center of the inner ring. Who knew? Who could ever tell? Some of these monuments, all over Europe and Russia and Ireland, were thousands and thousands and *thousands* of years old, and she was so privileged to be the temporary custodian of such a site. These stones must have taken much effort, and many, many people, to erect, so it was clear Findnar had been very important once, a sacred island.

Freya flung her arms wide. "Where did your builders come from? Can you tell me?" *Because you didn't tell my dad . . .* Ah,

Findnar—talking to the stones seemed somehow normal, a definite worry.

But she was here to dig—the crucifix site, that was her real target.

Owl-light had settled on the meadow before Freya stopped. Weary, she clambered out of the third test trench and groaned. It was torture to stretch her back; still, it felt good to be a physical being again.

She'd enjoyed this afternoon. Time had disappeared because the excitement of discovery was always a profound drug—no good pretending she wasn't addicted. But the first two trenches in the center of the circle had yielded only animal bones—a lamb, probably, and a rabbit. The finds had been properly bagged and noted for future study, but she'd filled the pits in again.

The third test trench, however, had become interesting. Freya had dug into the depression where something big had once lain. The earth had been rich and loamy and almost black, and she might have missed the pieces of pottery, except for that first flash of terra-cotta red in the soil. The shards she uncovered had incised lines—Samian ware perhaps? If it was, that meant long-distance trade routes, and if the pot wasn't from Roman Britain, it might have come from ancient Gaul or even beyond.

Freya had enjoyed teasing the soil away from the shards—it was nice to feel she still had some skill at such delicate work. Gradually, too, she was able to see some hint of the shape of the find from the way the pieces lay together. It seemed to be a wide, shallow bowl, and after photographing and measuring what she had exposed, she coaxed each piece from the earth and bagged them individually—there might even be enough to attempt some kind of reconstruction. Could she have found an offering bowl? That seemed possible in a place of Pagan worship but, in itself, it didn't help to explain why a crucifix had been found at this same site, or the intriguing little lead box with its pages of Latin manuscript.

With almost no light in the sky, Freya unpacked the last PVC field tent and spread it out. Unfolded, it was big enough to cover the excavation, and she sent up the archaeologist's prayer to the Gods of the Earth and Sky. *Please don't let it rain tonight. Please!*

Something white drifted past, silently disturbing the air beside her face. Freya jumped.

It was the owl—the one she'd seen on the night of her arrival. She watched it swoop high and then drop to the meadow; a moment later it was in the air again, a mouse in its talons. Freya heard the little thing squeak, but it was doomed, destined to become tomorrow's owl cast. Was it a shock to be reminded that existence was pitiless?

And then the image she'd avoided thinking about for the whole day returned. Flames reflected in a man's eyes—Daniel's eyes; flames from an inferno that did not exist.

Soon it would be night, and she would be alone with her thoughts.

CHAPTER 17

THERE'S PLENTY more, Dan. I made enough spuds for dinner and lunch tomorrow. Lots of meat too."

"That's fine, Dad." Dan covered his plate as Walter tried to put yet more slices of pork into the lake of gravy. Walter couldn't cook, not in the formal sense, but roasts were simple, and that's what they had most nights. Unless Dan, desperate for a change, got pizza or cooked eggs.

"I thought you liked pork?" Walter was worried.

Dan put his fork down. "I do, Dad, just not very hungry tonight." It was the smell. He'd smelled meat roasting this morning on the island—no, meat *burning*—and he'd been terrified, as if he, like the woman he'd seen, had been about to die. *What was that?*

Walter cut into his food. He was pleased; for once he'd got the crackling right. "Weekend coming up. Any plans?"

Dan shook his head. "Pass the salt."

Walter mumbled through his food. "You don't need more salt."

Dan bit back a sharp response. He said, patiently, "What, are you the food police now?"

"We all eat too much salt."

Dan rolled his eyes.

Walter said, stubborn, "Don't look at me like that. Got to take care of yourself, Dan. We want to make old bones, you and me."

Dan said nothing. He picked up a forkful of meat, and chewed and swallowed—somehow.

"I've been wondering . . ." Walter cleared his throat; this was delicate territory. "Would it help to see someone?"

Dan ate faster; this was winding up to something. "What sort of someone? Animal, vegetable, or mineral?"

"Very funny. What I meant was, would a doctor help?"

Dan lined the knife and fork up on the plate, covering some of the food. "I've seen all the doctors I want, thanks."

"I didn't mean a *doctor*-doctor, though now I think of it, you haven't been doing the physio, have you?"

"No." Dan was short.

"It won't work unless you do it, they said that."

Dan shot his father a dark look.

Walter's hands went up. "Okay, okay. So . . . we should try someone else."

Dan slapped his leg. "Useless. Don't need anyone else telling me that all over again."

Walter leaned over the table. "This is different, Dan. It's about your head, not your leg."

"My head." Dan repeated the phrase. "You want me to see someone about my head."

"I don't think you're coping. You're punishing yourself for some reason, and there's no need. There, said it." Walter looked at his son—he was pleading.

Dan pushed back his chair. He got up with some effort and, limping to the sink, scraped the uneaten food into a bin.

Walter tried again. "Dan, I think you're depressed. It's not surprising . . ."

"Are you depressed, Dad?" Dan's voice rose. He skewered his father with a look.

Walter swallowed. "Well, no, but . . ."

"He was your friend, Michael Dane, not mine. Why should *I* be depressed?" He started for the door of the kitchen.

"Dan." Walter rose.

His son turned back.

"Look at yourself. You can't live the rest of your life like a volcano waiting to explode. You need to get better. You need to enjoy yourself again."

Dan spoke over his dad. "I'm going to the pub; don't wait up." He pulled down a weather jacket from the hooks beside the back door.

Walter called after him, "Not every girl is like Alice, Dan. Not everyone walks when life gets a bit tough."

Hand on the latch, Dan said, patiently, "I know, Dad."

Walter hurried on—*in for a penny.* "She didn't mean what she said. Women get themselves upset and say things. You've got to give yourself a chance; smile more, it's a good habit. You know what they say, 'Smile and the world smiles with you.' "

That made Dan smile—a bit. His voice softened. "It's okay, Dad. I'll think about what you've said."

"You will? You really will?"

Dan pulled the door open and nodded. "But I'm not going to a shrink. Nothing wrong with my head. There, I've thought about it." The door closed. He was gone.

Nothing wrong with my head. Sturdy defiance. But there was, and Dan knew it. Not just the darkness of the last months and the anger—no, make that fury. After this morning, he had to face more than that.

He stopped in the quiet street. No sound but the sea, close by, but if he closed his eyes he could smell that inferno, and hear it. The screaming. The bell. Drifting smoke, blood all over the grass, these had been real things. And the man with the sword—a *sword*—he'd been real too. An image of Walter slicing the roast intruded—dizzy, Dan clutched at a lamppost. They'd think he was drunk, if anyone saw him.

But the village was deserted. Behind curtains, TVs flickered, and he heard the whoop and clamor of a studio audience. Normal life was inside those rooms, people sitting together, tranquilized by images from far, far away. Was that what had happened at the island?

Dan wiped the sweat from his face. No. It wasn't some kind of movie, or flashback to something he'd seen somewhere. He had been in another *time,* and not just as an observer. There was so much he did not understand. Most of it.

All of it.

To ward off the dark, Dan began to walk. If he warmed up a bit, maybe the pain in his hip and leg would lessen, and exercise did make a difference, that at least was true, but he so rarely bothered. It hurt too much at the beginning.

But there was the pub. Alcohol drowned the aches—or, at least, took them somewhere he didn't have to be for a while, comfort and oblivion all in one. And at the Nun, he was away from Walter's anxious eyes. He could talk there, too, even if he was less welcome than he'd once been.

Aggression—that's what the publican said. *You're upsetting everyone, Dan. You pick fights for no reason.* He'd not been aggressive before when he drank; he'd thought of himself as a happy drunk, good company.

Laughter burst from a cottage close by. Was he the cause? But the guffaws were recorded, not real. *Paranoid, too, are you?* Things were lurching out of control, he could feel it. Walter was right—*can't go on like this.*

Dan walked on, staring at the harbor. Streetlights lit the boats with an orange glow, intense as any apocalypse, but nothing, nothing to compare to what he'd seen on the old wharf at Findnar. *What did that mean?* Delusions? Brilliant. As if there wasn't enough going on.

Women said they forgot the pain of childbirth, but his dad was right. Dan could not erase the pain of Michael Dane's death—not mental, not physical. And it was etched in his bones now, in his damaged body and in the despair and terror and personal sense of failure—and the guilt. He just wanted it all to go away.

Did he have the guts to top himself? He'd thought about it quite often, especially after Alice walked away. His fault, of course—he'd not been able to ask for help and retired into a black night of his own making. Too much whisky, too much work to prove that he could, still, work—even if it wasn't at sea—and Alice had got tired of the moods. Very tired of him too.

And now, there was Freya Dane. Dan stopped, staring out toward the island. A light burned there, just one, in the house on the other side of the water.

Maybe Freya was a nice woman, maybe she was not, but she frightened him. He'd never been scared by a woman before. Humiliated, yes. Scared? Not before this morning.

Dan breathed deep and took another step and then another. He welcomed the pain—it was potent, and it stopped the mad roiling in his head. Maybe he would go to the pub after all. He could see it up ahead, light streaming from the windows and music too—muffled but still insistent. He sighed. Why was there always a price to be paid for company, and why were songs always about love?

He half-turned, staring back toward their house. Walter would not sleep until he heard Dan's key in the door, but he was thirty-one, not sixteen. Time to move on—if he could find a way to do that—time for a different life.

Ignoring the click and grind of his hip, Dan walked faster. Only a few steps now, not many (but who was counting?).

He stopped. Part of him had registered the tide was up, and the boats beside the quay were riding high at anchor. Most were familiar craft. He backed up a pace; Michael's cruiser was tied to a bollard.

Dan stared. The phone in his pocket chirped. A text. He thumbed the icon; it'd be Walter—*Just worried about you*, or some such message.

But Dan was wrong, and his face changed as he read the words. *I can see you Daniel Boyne. Be careful how you pick your friends.* The number of the sender had been blocked.

CHAPTER 18

BEAR HAD managed to lash the boom back to the mast and now the trading vessel rode easily on the water secured by two separate lines to the beach. Each hide rope was anchored beneath a stone, the biggest Signy and Bear had found. It had taken them a morning, after they'd eaten the fish he cooked over the fire she'd made, to roll the boulders above the high-water mark. Now the ropes flexed as the ship swung on the tide, but they were good lines, well cured, flexible, and very strong.

"You are certain?" Bear hadn't been able to change Signy's mind in a morning of arguing. He glanced at the coracle. He'd carried it from the cove, and now it lay on the sand waiting for her to take it. His heart spoke, not his head. "It's a long way to paddle alone."

She did not look at him. "I've done it before." That was a lie. She'd traveled with her siblings or her parents in the old days.

Signy ran toward the hide bowl, and Bear hurried to help her drag it to the water's edge.

The boy stood in the surf, careless of his new clothes, and held the little craft steady. The coracle would buck and tip Signy out if the moment was not well judged, but she rolled over its edge and into the middle with practiced ease.

"Good-bye, Bear."

He heard the tears in her voice. At the last moment, she reached up to kiss the good side of his face, and he felt her lips brush the soft bristle along his jaw.

"I hope we meet again in this life, Signy. You have been kind to me, and I will not forget that."

How to cover desolation? Speak up, speak loudly. He raised his hand. "The tide will drop soon. Journey well, my friend." He did not say, *This is madness.* She already knew he thought that.

Signy ducked her head and picked up the paddle as she settled her seat in the boat; balance was everything. She had little emotional strength left. "Push me, Bear, a good, strong push."

With his help, the coracle bobbed over the crest of a small wave. As it slid down the back, Bear watched Signy dig the broad blade of the paddle into the sea. It was hard work, and she was tentative at first, but she began to find the looping, sweeping rhythm, and the little craft progressed slowly toward the harbor's mouth. Soon, too soon, she would be on the open water of the strait, and Bear knew she would not look back.

"Signy!"

She did not acknowledge his shout.

"Signy, wait. Wait!" Bear could not control his voice; the shout became a plea.

That Signy heard. She slewed around, the coracle answering the movement.

Bear stood waist-deep in the tide. "You don't need to do this. We'll go back together in the big boat."

Together. The word rang like a bell.

Signy stared at him. She dropped the paddle and cupped her hands around her mouth. "You mean it?" The boy shouted back, "Yes." How sad he looked. She let the waves sweep her back to where he stood but he said nothing as she scrambled over the side of the coracle and into the shallows. "I'm glad you changed your mind, Bear." Signy touched his arm as they dragged the craft onto the beach. "Truly. It is better this way. The Christ people will have cursed us for taking their ship, I think. And perhaps the curse would have followed you. It needs to be lifted."

"Doesn't frighten me. They don't have the power." Bear spat into the tide. "They live on seaweed."

Signy was shocked. "You can't say that." A curse was serious business and not to be mocked.

Bear took both her hands in his. "Signy, we'll take the boat back because you want to and for no other reason."

The girl stared toward the ruined clan settlement. "This place has been cursed too. By the blood of my family. Nothing will prosper here until that is atoned for also." She did not mention Bear's name. She did not have to.

After the terrors and privations of the previous year, the Christians on Findnar had been crushed to discover the new vessel, a replacement for the ones the raiders had taken, was missing. For Gunnhilde this had been a double loss because Bear and Signy had disappeared, too, and she felt personally betrayed.

Without the vessel, another want-filled winter loomed but with yet more bellies to be filled on the island. Gunnhilde, with great remorse, had prayed many private hours, seeking forgiveness for her part in the catastrophe, and if her knees burned, she knew she deserved the pain and bore the self-imposed penance gladly.

It was the guilt that shamed her most, and the disobedience of her heart. She had deliberately ignored Brother Cuillin's warnings about the Pagan children, and the whole community was paying for their duplicity. She should have seen the Devil nesting in their souls, and yet it still seemed hardly credible that two such scraps could have stolen the ship.

"Sister, Sister, they've come back!"

Stretched prone before the altar in the part-built chapel, Gunnhilde did not, for a moment, make sense of Idrun's words.

"Come back?"

"Signy and the boy."

The two nuns hurried to the cliff path. It was true, the ship *had* returned, sailed boldly into the bay by Signy and Bear as if they had merely gone fishing. Gunnhilde could see them smaller than beetles below, securing the craft to the shore.

"Deo gratias," the words were a bemused prayer of thanks. "Dear Lord, we thank you for bringing Signy and Bear back to us. This is a miracle."

"We do indeed, Sister. Well may you thank our Lord, but gratitude is not enough. A theft was committed."

Cuillin, the newly elected Abbot of Findnar, had arrived behind the women. "Sister, I ask that you bring the children to me in the chapel."

Both nuns knelt in the pose of penitents. Gunnhilde crossed herself and said deferentially, "Of course, Brother Abbot," and, as was proper, she did not look up, but she struggled with obedience to this man. She was still surprised by Cuillin's sudden elevation—elected by the community in Chapter only yesterday—and absorbing the hurt of not even being proposed as Abbess of the nuns (and coleader of their double monastery). Perhaps the defection of the children had cost her this as well. Findnar might be a much smaller foundation than the Motherhouse at Whitby but with new members arriving so recently, it was clear their little community could be expected to grow. Many felt a calling to preach in the wilderness as the early fathers of the Church had done and perhaps one day, Findnar might be an important Christian center on this remote coast. Poor Gunnhilde. She burned to be allowed to contribute to a greater degree, if only to expiate sins and misjudgments of the past.

But Cuillin waved an impatient hand over her bent head. "Get up, Sister. I will await you in the chapel." His shoulders slumped as he strode away. Though it was his clear duty to discipline the children, he knew it would be difficult imposing his will on Gunnhilde. On the one hand, she was too soft to be in charge of any of their young people—and it was for that reason he'd successfully argued against her becoming his coruler—but on the other,

Gunnhilde's belief in the rightness of her own opinions was most unsuitable for any nun. And today there was proof—if he'd ever needed it—for later she dared to argue with him on the matter of penance.

"God is love, Brother. These two children cannot endure the privation of a long fast. See how thin they are." Perhaps the brutal raid of last year gave the nun courage, for more suffering seemed pointless. "And the scourge. Please, Brother Abbot, not the scourge. The boy has not long recovered from his previous wounds, and Signy is just too little to withstand it."

Cuillin, appearances to the contrary, was not without pity, and yet he hardened his heart. *For you, Lord, only for you is the stray lamb brought back to the fold with diligence.* With manful effort, he achieved a reasonable tone. "No, dear Sister, you are wrong. Bear and Signy knew what they were doing. The boy, as the elder, might have led her astray, but they chose this evil path willingly. And if they were strong enough to take that ship . . ."

Signy edged closer to Bear. Her understanding was not so good that she grasped the meaning of each word, but *fast* she knew, and also *scourge*. Big-eyed, she trembled as she knelt beside her friend. Bear saw the effect of Cuillin's words on Signy, and he began to tremble also—with rage.

"But, Brother, they *returned* the ship. They thought better of what they did and brought her back to us. And they came willingly, knowing they would be punished, when they could just have continued on. Surely that counts for something?"

God's warrior tried not to waver. "Perhaps our actions will seem cruel now, Sister, yet we are responsible for the souls of these children in all eternity. Through too much kindness, too much indulgence"—his gaze was implacable—"Satan came close to seizing them both. God's intentions are clear, and by our chastisement of their bodies, the Evil One shall be banished from their hearts."

Cuillin bent to pull Signy to her feet, but Bear knocked the monk's hand aside. Glaring into Cuillin's eyes, he thrust his body in front of Signy. "I kill you." Rage bloodied his voice, but his eyes were blank and wide—the stare of a man, not a boy.

Cuillin recoiled; he signed a cross between himself and the minion of Satan he now saw. "Child of Hell!"

"Brother. Brother!" Gunnhilde hurried forward. "They are just frightened and hungry and cold. Our Lord said, 'Suffer the little children to come unto me'; He wants us to show them His light, not destroy it forever in their hearts." She knew Cuillin would not forgive her, but she had to try.

The Abbot was not, ordinarily, a cruel man, and in that moment he was given enough Grace to see the truth.

Standing over the terrified girl, his fingers held like claws—the only weapons he had—Bear was just an exhausted boy protecting someone he cared for, and she was only a starving child.

It was true, also, that they *had* returned the ship when they might, it seemed, so easily have sailed away forever. Had God, then, worked within them? Was this His message here?

Cuillin took a step back. He hated administration, it was his own particular cross to bear, but that, too, was the Lord's will, and last night, to defeat worldly pride in his elevation, he had flayed his back with the scourge to such a degree that he'd hardly slept. Dizzy with exhaustion, he pressed a hand to his eyes. "Very well, Sister, I shall pray that God guides me further in this matter. But you must know that the Lord's instructions *will* be carried forward when it pleases Him to further enlighten me."

Gunnhilde snatched the monk's hand and kissed it. "Bless you, dear Abbot Cuillin. Compassion is the quality of Christ—you walk in His sweet shadow with your mercy."

Cuillin waved his hand, dismissing them all. If he was to salvage any dignity from this fiasco, he must pray in solitude and ask God's forgiveness for the weakness of his will.

Whispering, the nun chivied the pair from the chapel. "Quickly, children, we must not disturb the Abbot's prayers."

Signy did not really know what had happened, but her legs trembled and she was very frightened. Bear grabbed her hand. "I will not let him hurt you, Signy." She had no time to reply as they were swept on toward the shelter.

"Now, child, you cannot wear those clothes." Gunnhilde pointed at the blood-red tunic—in itself an appalling color—for it exposed the girl's arms. "Our new brothers and sisters have brought clothing with them, and there must be something . . ." Bending, she riffled the contents of a coffer and pulled out a black kirtle. "Let me see if this is too big."

"But, Sister, my mother made this." Signy did not surrender her tunic easily, batting aside the old woman's hands. But the nun managed to hold the black kirtle against the girl's body. "Signy, you must stand still. The Abbot will be angry if he sees you improperly dressed."

The child's eyes filled. There was no escape; this was what returning to Findnar meant. She managed to say, "If I may not wear them, will you look after my clothes? Please, Sister. They are all I have of my mother."

Gunnhilde sighed, but she understood. "Very well, I shall keep them among the habits. Do not look, boy."

Signy removed her red tunic as slowly as she could; she glanced at Bear as he turned his back—he had given up so much because she would not leave Laenna.

But as the nun fussed, Bear dared to smile over his shoulder. It was a brave smile, one of absolution.

Signy mouthed, "Thank you."

He nodded.

But for Signy and for Bear, the comfort they truly sought, the love of a family, a place by the fire at the heart of their clans, was missing.

And that night in separate places, huddled among the snoring members of their own sexes, both sobbed until they slept at last.

"It still seems very strange to me, Laenna, the things they believe."

Signy rolled over, sucking a stem of grass. She was supposed to be herding the goats away from the cliff, but she'd hobbled the nannies close by, and their kids did not stray far from their mothers. It was hard to find time to talk to her sister among so many chores.

"Take the Mass." Seven seasons had passed since her return to the island, and it was spring again. Signy knew much more about the Christians now—she no longer called them newcomers—but she was still confused by some of the things they did each day. "You know, the sisters and brothers really do think they eat His flesh and drink His blood. The Jesus. It's supposed to be magic, because all we see is bread and ale. What I want to know is why they can't just put honey on the altar like everyone else?"

It was a rhetorical question, and Signy knew why, because Gunnhilde had told her the story many times. And yet she still felt queasy when she thought of the way their God-person died. It seemed barbaric and odd that they liked to hear how much He had suffered.

"But you don't have to worry about any of that." Signy patted her sister's headstone. "I should get the goats back. I'll come again tomorrow, when I can sneak off."

She stood up. She felt dizzy, and her belly griped. It was similar to the pain of eating too many hard apples, similar—but different.

Signy looked down. She'd made herself a nest in the grass beside the grave, and there was blood where she'd been sitting—not much, but enough to tell her that childhood, today, had ended.

It was a shock. She knew about the moontide, of course, everyone did, but there were always ceremonies, for in her family, and her clan, the first moontide of a girl was important.

Light-headed, Signy slumped to her knees. "Laenna, I wish you were here—we could go to the stones together. You remember, don't you? Our mother was so proud when it was your time."

Laenna's first moontide had happened in the year before the disastrous raid, and all the women from their clan, and the female members of their own family, had rowed to Findnar with her to celebrate at the stones.

That gathering had caused great trouble with the Christians, for they'd been angry about the nature of the Women's Mysteries and rudely interrupted before Laenna's ceremony was properly finished. If the men of the clan had been there, perhaps blood would truly have been spilled rather than celebrated. It was after that incident that clan members began to visit Findnar surreptitiously.

"What should I do, Laenna?" Signy was being deferential to her older sister because she knew what must be done. At the rising of the next new moon, prayer should be offered at the stones, asking for long life and fertility. Something important needed to be sacrificed too—something red. It was the wrong season for berries, and even if she'd been able to find any, they would not have been enough. Perhaps she should take the red tunic back and offer it to Cruach, though it upset her to think of giving the work of her mother's hands to the stones.

"And there will be no one to do the chants with me." Loss stabbed Signy—this would have been such joyous news to give her mother, her aunts, and her female cousins.

Tears dropped down Signy's cheeks as she doubled over her tender belly. She must remember that the pain she felt was good, that it had a purpose.

Signy raised her arms toward the sky. "I have lived nearly fourteen summers, and today I am a woman. I claim my place in the clan, a child no longer."

She dropped her arms and sniffed. Perhaps Gunnhilde would understand—she had no one else to talk to.

᧒

The old woman looked anxious. "You are sure, Signy?"

Signy nodded patiently. "Yes, Sister. I have my first moon-tide."

Gunnhilde's eyes widened. "Hush! We do not speak of such things." She hurried to a coffer against one wall of the nuns' dormitory. "You will need these." She offered Signy a bundle of rags. "You put them between your legs and then tie them around your waist—like a belt." Embarrassed, the old woman fumbled the cloth into an approximate shape.

The girl stared at her. "Thank you, Sister, but I wanted to ask about the pain and—" She stopped. Gunnhilde had placed a hand firmly across her mouth.

"Signy, you cannot have been paying attention. I told you the story of Eve; it will answer all your questions."

"But the pain—I don't remember that bit." Signy was bewildered.

Gunnhilde tried not to speak of such things, since the body was too easily the plaything of the Devil, but it was her duty as Novice Mistress to put her own feelings aside when she counseled her girls. "Let me remind you of what happened, Signy. Satan, in the guise of a serpent, tempted Eve with apples from the tree of knowledge. God had forbidden only this one thing to Adam and Eve, but Satan was very wily. He knew that our first mother as a woman was weak and foolish, and he convinced her to give in to temptation—and so she ate the apple. Then Eve persuaded Adam to eat the fruit, too, and God saw this disobedience. The pair, man and woman, were cast from the garden of Paradise together, and as punishment God decreed that women should bring forth their children in pain and suffering as penance." Agitated, the old woman pointed at the rags in Signy's hands. "Bleeding each month reminds us of the sin of all women. We must bear the pain in silence and subjection, for we betrayed mankind."

Signy frowned. "But, Sister, I am not Eve, and I have betrayed no one. The moontide is a good thing—it means I will have babies."

"Hush!" Gunnhilde glanced around the dormitory. It was empty—the other nuns would be assembling for Tierce. "I must go to the chapel." As she spoke, the bell began. "I shall pray for you, child, and I shall ask our Lord that you gain a proper understanding, but you must not come to the church while you are bleeding, nor must you help in the kitchen. This time each month you are unclean." The old nun signed a cross over Signy's head and hurried away.

Signy stared after Gunnhilde—living among the Christians was so strange, sometimes. What would have happened if she and Bear had journeyed on? Would her life have been happier? Whatever he said, his family might not have accepted her. On Findnar she was a servant and generally kindly treated; with his people she might have become a slave and still been a stranger among people who believed different things—other different things, it was true, but the raiders were fierce and violent. The Christians were not fierce, just severe.

Laenna, you have to help. I'm so confused.

Bear did not sleep among the brothers anymore. His living quarters were a crude hut he'd been permitted to construct next to the new animal byre. It was there, after Compline, that he spent his evenings in solitude, banished from the company of the monks. It was presumed that Bear slept the hours away in sloth, but that presumption was wrong.

The winter after he and Signy returned to Findnar, the youth had found a whale rib on the sands of the cove. Cast up after a storm, it was almost twice as long as he was, and Bear covered it with sea wrack until he could remove it unseen.

In a night of thick rain, when none of the brothers or sisters was outside the Abbey buildings, he'd hauled it back to his hut. There he'd slit the neck of a stolen cockerel in thanks; the blood sacrifice was to Loki the Shape Shifter, so that he would not be seen by Christ's men.

Bear felt guilty about the bird—the poultry were Signy's responsibility—but he asked the help of the God of Fire here too. *Let them not know about the chicken; let Signy be safe from their malice.*

Perhaps it was Loki who inspired Bear that night for, as reparation, he decided to make her a gift.

It was the labor of all that winter and three seasons of the following year, but length by length Bear worked the whale bone into useful things, and some objects he made for their beauty alone.

In that first year as a maker, his fingers were clumsy. Unused to such delicate work, they had a hard time creating the forms he saw in his head. His tools, too, were crude—scrapers of flint he chipped to an edge, a knife blade stolen from the refectory—but gradually his shape-making skill increased.

The only light to work by was the small fire in his hut, and there were many failures from his first attempts, but the handle for a knife—a sea otter—at last pleased him. Soon other creatures hiding in the bone emerged—horses, hunting dogs, a bull. Smoothing them with sand hour by hour, he marveled at the beauty of the whale ivory, its translucence when he worked it, its purity.

And toward the end of the second year, when he thought his skill was adequate, he fashioned the tiny image of a ship in full sail—this was his gift to Signy, and as yet he had not given it to her. Rigidly enforced divisions between men and women on the island meant that they spoke little, and he did not want to bring trouble to his friend. Soon, however, he would find her. Soon. When the time was right.

☾

"Signy. Over here!"

She was on her knees in the herb garden behind the kitchen picking comfrey for the Infirmarian.

Panicked, she looked around. "You should not be here, Bear. You know that."

The boy grinned engagingly. "No one to see—I checked. They're all still praying."

Signy stood. Cruach was at her back, and light picked out the edges and folds of the black kirtle.

Bear paused; he did not like to see Signy dressed in black—she was not one of them and, besides, black was the color of the carrion crow's plumage. But he smoothed his expression and sauntered toward her, not too fast, not too slow, his heart rising in his chest. In these last months his beard had grown, and he could feel that the soft bristles covered some of his scars. That gave him confidence.

"It is good to see you, Signy."

"Hello, Bear." She glanced at him shyly. "Should you not be plowing?" It was summer. The barley stubble had been burned in the fields, and seed would soon be sown for the winter crop.

Bear shook his head. "Finished. Bullock's fed and watered too—I started early. They have nothing to reproach me with."

Signy rearranged the leaves she'd gathered in her apron. She was nervous; so was he.

Bear held out his hand, fingers closed over the palm. "I've brought you something. A present."

"For me?" Signy's eyes shone, but she put her own hands behind her back as if to resist temptation.

Bear glanced away. Signy had grown up, and it hurt him to look at her. He wanted to touch her skin.

In the silence they could hear bees.

Bear swallowed. "Shall I show you?"

Hesitantly, Signy moved toward him. "If you like."

They were standing so close he could smell her, lavender and fresh grass, and Bear was suddenly terrified. She might not like what he had made. "It's not much." The words came out rough, as if he were angry.

Signy's eyes widened. She seemed hurt—and confused.

So was Bear. His heart jolted, but he opened his fingers, and on his palm lay the little ship, jaunty and full of spirit.

"You can use it for a cloak clasp or a brooch."

Lightly, by accident, her fingers touched his palm as she turned the ship over; a slender pin fitted into a keeper on the reverse.

"I tried to write your name, too, but I don't know all the runes." He held the piece close to her eyes so she could see the detail.

Signy stared silently at what he had made.

"You do not like it." Bear was shamed. He turned away.

Signy touched his wrist. "You are wrong. It is . . ." She paused. With great reverence she picked the little carving up.

"This is . . . It is the most beautiful thing I have ever seen, and you made it for me."

Relief was hope. Bear said, eagerly, "I made her to remind you. One day, we will leave this place again together."

They were staring at each other. Bear's throat and his gut were drum-tight, for he had said what was in his heart before he had known it.

Signy's eyes clouded. She stepped away from him, a formal, graceful movement.

"I must finish my work. Thank you for the present, Bear. It shall be my treasure."

"Wait! I want to show you this too." Hastily he removed the knife from a small scabbard on his belt.

Signy's eyes were always candid, and now they widened with awe. "This is just like a real otter. You are so clever, Bear. You really are." She touched the edge of the blade. "But where did you get the iron?"

Anywhere else and Bear would have shouted out loud for the

pleasure of her compliment. In Signy's presence, he shrugged. "From a candle sconce." He grinned. "There was a flurry when they missed it, but no one suspected me." Why would they? To the Christians, he was the Pagan, a brute with little feeling, just like an ox or a mule. "Brother Simon in the smithy helped me—he's my friend; the haft is whale ivory, too, from the same piece that made the ship."

Signy was troubled by this easy confession of a sin, but Bear trusted her. She would tell no one.

"Both pieces are very fine. Truly, Bear, you should be proud."

Bear colored but said, impulsively, "This winter Simon will teach me to make charcoal too. The forge will burn hotter, and then we can make stronger iron. One day I will make swords— good ones that hold a proper edge."

Signy touched the knife blade again, testing the edge. Her eyes were serious. "Why would you want a sword on Findnar? This is a place of peace."

A place of peace? Bear wanted to laugh, but that would upset his friend. Instead, he held the knife toward her. "Hold it, Signy, it's very well balanced."

She glanced at him, but did as he asked. Bear stood behind her, guiding her fingers along the otter's body.

"The secret is the grip. See? Like this." He rested the haft in the length of her palm and closed her fingers around the belly of the carving, guiding her thumb along the back. "It helps you to stab—the thumb held straight."

She grinned. "Here we are in a monastery, and you're telling me how to kill?" She laughed. She couldn't help it. So did he.

The laughter died. Signy dropped her eyes from his.

Bear stood closer. "You might need to know one day."

She did not immediately move away. "You should go, Bear. I have suffered too much penance already this month." She half-smiled. "I try, I do, but Gunnhilde says I do not know how truly willful I am."

Bear spat into a patch of garlic. "Willful? Strong-minded is what you are, and that saved you when we took the ship. Don't let them twist the life out of you with their words, Signy. They will if you let them."

She did not reply. She knelt again among the herbs.

He tried one last time. "You were not always like this—remember that, Signy. You are not one of them."

She bent to her work with only a little wave as Bear strode from the infirmary garden.

But she followed him with her eyes, and the comfrey, forgotten, spilled out of her apron.

Bear troubled her, unsettled her dreams; she thought about him a great deal. Having had three sons, her mother would have understood, for she was wise in the ways of young men. But Signy could not talk to her mother, nor could she ask Gunnhilde's advice, or even Idrun's. They would both be shocked—nuns were always shocked about something.

But she could talk to her sister.

Sometimes, when Signy asked a question, Laenna answered not with a voice but with omens, or a sudden breeze, or the smell of flowers in winter. And there was the white owl. Signy sometimes asked the owl important questions if no one else answered her. He seemed to protect Laenna's grave.

"Yes, I will ask for your advice, Sister, but what will you say to me?"

CHAPTER 19

*S*HE WAS *running, fast as she could. He saw her! Hard to breathe. Gaining. He was gaining. She dodged. Gasped. He was close, breath on her neck.*

She feinted. Not wide enough. His hand. Hard. Cold. Grabbed her arm. He laughed. The man laughed. Ax high. Flash and drop. Her head, he hit her . . .

A whistle. High pitched. Someone must have left it on—the kettle.

No. It wasn't the kettle. Someone was screaming. She was.

Freya sat up in one convulsive movement. Fingers pressed over her mouth. Chest heaving, she tried to stop the images.

"Freya?" A man's voice, downstairs. "Are you all right?"

A sharp rap, and a rattle. The latch on the back door—it always shook. Another rap.

Freya reached over to the table beside the bed. Where was her watch? Where *was* it! *Christ! Past ten!*

The knock again, less heavy. "Hello?"

Of course, *of course,* he knew she was in the house, he'd have heard the scream. But she'd locked the door. *Had she locked the door?*

Disoriented, Freya put a hand to the back of her head. It hurt. Not *hurt,* blazed with pain. *Please, God, let this just be a headache . . .* She expected blood and broken bone because she *knew,* knew what had caused the cold-hot, black-red *agony.* Her mind flinched.

"Can you hear me?" His voice again.

"Who's there?" She knew who it was. Why was he here?

Cold, plank floor, no socks; sweater on over pajamas. Shivering. That would stop soon; maybe the pain would too. Freya fumbled down the stairs.

"It's me. Dan."

"Just a minute."

A deep breath. One more. And another. No shivers—just pain, a bit less. Still there though.

The back door was not locked, but he'd waited for an invitation. That was good. Polite. Why had she been so scared? Dan wasn't an enemy. Was he?

"Hi, come in." Freya held the door open.

He saw the pajamas and switched his glance to a point just beyond her left shoulder. He wasn't embarrassed, but she might be. "I'll not stop."

Before she could ask, he hurried on. "I've brought your father's cruiser back. Someone moored it in the harbor last night; it's not been damaged. Good morning to you."

"Wait." Freya stepped closer; he stepped away. She did it again; so did he. It was comical, but not funny. "I'm not contagious, Dan."

He stared at her. "Pardon me?"

She expelled a sigh. "Tea. You're welcome to a cup, and you can tell me more." She padded down the steps. He'd follow or he wouldn't. Perhaps she cared. Actually, she did—he distracted her, and that was good.

Freya shoved the kettle beneath the spout. Six pumps, seven, eight. Why was she so weak? She clattered the kettle on top of the gas and twitched her hand away as if the sound hurt her fingers. The pain was still there at the back of her head. "Sorry I didn't hear you at first. Thick walls, I suppose." Hard to make polite conversation.

Dan was looking at her strangely. Of course. She sounded odd, but he sat down anyway at the far side of the table. Freya joined him on the opposite side as they waited for the kettle.

"I'll get the milk." She half-rose again.

He said, hastily, "No need. I drink it black." He coughed.

"I'm very grateful to you for bringing the cruiser over. I could run you back to port."

He almost looked panicked. "No need. I towed the runabout."

Freya cleared her throat; words flowed like treacle between them. "So, do you have any idea who?"

"Brought her back? No. Reckon it was kids on a joyride. I'll tell the cops she's been found if you like." Dan said nothing about the text—he was still trying to work out what it meant.

"Thanks, that would be good." It was hard to imagine someone taking the portly little cruiser for a joyride. Freya blinked the thought away and fought not to close her eyes. She was tired, very tired.

The kettle tried to yelp, sputtered and screamed, higher and higher. Freya leaped—anything to stop it—so did Dan. She fumbled the kettle from the hob, grabbed the teapot. To help her, he did too. The pot hit the slates. Red shards scattered.

Hulls. Silent. Out of the dark. Rocking on oars. Shields. Ax edge, then another. More. Silver. Caught by the moon. Too many men. Soon they would land. The gate! Chanting. Prayers on the wind. Death. Too close.

Sweating, they stared at each other. There was no getting used to this.

Freya tried to stand. And failed. Tried again, staggering like a drunk. "Did you . . ."

Dan went to help her—and stopped. He did not touch Freya; instead he bent and picked shattered china from the floor. "Dangerous. Where's your rubbish?"

She managed to point at the bin. Now she understood what *reeling* truly meant, for the room swung and pitched as she clutched the back of a chair.

Dan dumped the shards in the bin. "I've left your dad's boat at the mooring. I'd best be going."

Freya said nothing, and Dan swallowed, a slow grating of the larynx, as if he wanted to say more. Climbing the stairs to the back door took time. He paused, lifted the latch with care, and closed the door once he was outside.

Could she have stopped him? Freya did not know. She felt ashamed, as if she'd done something wrong.

And that's absurd! Filling a mug with scalding water, she jerked a tea bag up and down, then slumped into Michael's chair, rubber-legged. Her hands shook as she dumped sugar, lots of sugar, into the tea, and the clamor of terror grew faint, fainter, as she drank.

And then Freya noticed—the pain had gone. She touched the back of her skull. Nothing.

And now?

Now she had the cruiser back. She'd take flowers to Michael's grave today. Then she'd ask questions.

Motoring past the breakwater and into Portsolly's harbor on water clear as glass, Freya tied the cruiser extra well to a bollard on the wharf. She resisted the urge to pat the superstructure; it was good to have her back, it really was.

Portsolly was busy today, pulsing with a small rush of tourists. Like seagulls, they were eating well ahead of the journey south and squabbling, too, as they bought fish and chips and ice cream on the quay.

Freya climbed the wharf steps and nodded at the blow-ins like a Portsolly native. She carried a bunch of meadow flowers picked on the island while the dew was still on the petals—they were pretty though she didn't know their names. Pink, white, blue, and scarlet. On the top step she paused and just lightly touched the crucifix—it was hanging under her shirt. It seemed right, now, that she wore it. She did not know why.

Beside the harbor, kids and gulls shrieked, competing with boat engines and the slap of water, but as Freya walked the steep streets heading toward the church, the babble of human existence faded and the lanes narrowed into empty silence.

It was still a surprise, the church, even a second time—such a big building among the village houses. This time she skirted the portico and continued around to the cemetery at the back. The cliff reared above, catching the glint of a cool sun; it was a presence, that cliff, brooding and powerful.

The gate to the graveyard screeched, and squealed again as she closed it. She crunched across the gravel toward Michael's grave—and stopped. This was seriously annoying; she'd forgotten to bring a vase. Simon might have something, but they'd met only once and she'd never found it easy to impose, as Elizabeth would say. Besides, he might think this was a way to meet him again, and she didn't want that; easier to walk to the shops and buy something.

"Freya?" It was Simon. Standing on the far side of the gate, he seemed genuinely pleased to see her. "I heard the gate. Every time it opens, day or night, it howls like a soul in torment. That might be appropriate, but it drives me nuts." He held up a can of lubricant. "Scream banishment."

Freya succumbed to the synchronicity. She said, lightly, "Who comes here at night, Simon the Sexton?"

He chuckled. "You'd be surprised—bit of a lovers' lane, this place. There's others, too—drug dealers, their clients." He sprayed the hinges as he talked, opening and closing the gate several times, sprayed some more. "Excellent—no more creak."

Freya glanced toward the clustered, pretty houses. "Drugs. Really? Portsolly seems so peaceful, sequestered from the problems of the world somehow."

Simon wiped away some grease. "Oh, kids get bored with nothing to do at night, and it's hard to hide from prying eyes in a village if you don't have a car—except here."

Freya could see what he meant; the graveyard *was* discreet, tucked away behind the convenient screen of its yew trees.

"Simon, can I ask a favor? I didn't want to bother you but, since you're here . . ." She held up the flowers. "I need a vase; jam jar, anything would do."

"Follow me, Miss Dane." Simon wheeled toward the church, and Freya tagged along, ignoring the shiver of dislike as she entered the building.

Simon had camped in the nave on a blow-up mattress. His bedding was neatly folded, and he'd rigged up a one-pot camping stove. "Put the kettle on. I'll just duck into the vestry and consult with the moderator." He wiggled his eyebrows goofily.

Freya giggled and became aware of how tense she really was. She called after him. "Thanks. No tea for me though, if you don't mind—things to do."

"Suit yourself, fair maiden. I shall return." Simon made a flourish as if he had a cloak and an imaginary mustache—a pantomime villain—before disappearing through a door near the altar dais.

Freya's phone warbled—the message tone—she'd turned it on at the harbor. Thumbing the voice-mail key, she heard her mother's voice. *Hello, darling. Won't use up your battery. Ring when you can. Love a chat. Been thinking of you.*

Freya sighed. *Me too, Mum. Me too . . .*

"Australia calling?"

Freya jumped.

Simon was standing beside her. "Sorry. Didn't mean to startle you."

She managed a strained smile. "Just a message from my mum."

"Which one would she like, then?" Simon waggled two vases, one of white porcelain, the other of brass. "These were shoved in a cupboard when the kirk packed up its panoply and departed."

"Er, the white one."

"White it shall be. By the way, I heard you got the cruiser back."

Freya was startled. "How did you know?"

Simon said, cheerfully, "The newsagent. You're a person of

interest, being new and from so very far away." He pronounced it *verra*. "But now, for the hire of this peerless object, there's a price to be paid." He offered her the vase.

Freya smiled uncertainly. "Oh?"

"A bargain, I promise you. After all, you are his daughter, and I'm sure he'd approve." Respectfully, he waved toward the west door. "I've found something in the crypt. If I am right—and perhaps you can tell me—it kicks the dates back a long way. Only take a moment to look-see, I promise."

The strange feeling of a moment ago dispelled, and Freya was intrigued. She put the flowers down. "You said that little of the fabric of the church is original?"

Ushering her toward a side aisle, Simon nodded. "As I said, lots of alterations over the centuries, and the church is supposed to have burned, partially, twice. Once when the whole town was sacked—the Frasers, I believe, out and about spring raiding—and once when the rector got drunk one Hogmanay Eve a long, long time ago." Simon opened a low door. "It's just down here."

"Sacked?" Freya stepped through into a passage not much wider than her shoulders. The ceiling was a long way above her head and the space badly lit; her heart lurched unpleasantly.

Simon flicked on a light. "Oh, probably just a legend. Everyone claims to have been sacked around here, for the tourists. I loved all the legends as a kid, couldn't get enough of men with swords and axes, all that stuff. Watch your step, by the way; there's a short staircase just ahead." The fluorescent lights cast shadows down Simon's face; his eyes were deep holes and his mouth cruel. For one panicked moment, Freya was frightened.

Simon touched her arm. Close up, the illusion vanished. His expression was anxious. "Are you okay?"

She managed a deep breath. "I don't much like tight spaces, or the dark. Claustrophobia, I suppose. It's just recent; it never worried me before." *Before I came to Findnar.*

Simon was contrite, his eyes big and soft. "I am so sorry, Freya.

No need to be brave." He picked up her hand to lead her back to the church.

Freya said, quickly, "Oh, we've come this far; besides, I'm curious."

"Only if you're sure?"

She nodded. Simon visibly relaxed. "It's a much bigger space in the crypt, and there's plenty of light, I promise." He shuffled past her, but the passage was narrow and his body brushed against hers; there was a frisson of something, a definite frisson, but so different from what she experienced with Dan. This was actually pleasant.

"Here, as advertised—bigger and better. What do you think?" The space before them seemed about the same size as the crossing of the church above, and much of it was roofed by intersecting vaults, massively groined. A number of dusty tenants remained in residence, including the effigy of a knight lying on a slab raised not much higher than the floor. He was clutching a shield and a sword, with a dog at his feet, but his face had been damaged. There were niche tombs from a later time lining the walls, and they, too, had been vandalized, much of the elaborate stone detail broken away.

Simon shrugged. "Protestant reformers. Busy lads—they must have enjoyed their work. I just love fanatics, don't you?" A shared grim laugh. "With the exception of our lone Crusader, you'll see that none of the other graves is earlier than the fifteenth or sixteenth century—Buchans mostly. Local lairds."

Freya nodded, engrossed, as he rattled on. "But over here there's something earlier, a good deal earlier, I suspect."

He was leading her toward the back of the crypt, and here the space was narrower and lower, the vaulted ceiling of the later period missing. Her breathing quickened.

"It's directly under the altar, so this was the place of greatest prestige in the crypt—to be buried, I mean. Have a look."

Simon was pointing at a stone box about the size of a packing case for a wall oven. "There's no inscription on the exterior, but if you look inside . . ." He pushed against one side of the lid.

Freya hurried to help him, and the top began to slide away. As it did, she saw bones among dust.

Simon grunted with the effort. "Built to last."

The compression in Freya's head was growing and grew tighter, but curiosity pushed discomfort away. She said slowly, "It looks like an ossuary. Not so surprising in a Christian church, I suppose, if a bit archaic."

Simon nodded as he reached down into the grave. "But then there's this. Quite surprising, I think, considering where we are." He held up a small bowl of age-green bronze.

Freya stared. "Grave goods; that's odd."

Simon nodded. "And this was with it." He proffered an elaborately worked enamel and glass lozenge on his palm.

Freya peered at the object. "Decoration from a weapon? It's very fine—very high status."

Simon offered the little jewel to Freya as he reached into the ossuary again. "And, most important of all . . ." Something small lay in the palm of his other hand, something that glinted.

Freya blinked. "Well, well." Inside her skull, an image wrapped in mist clamored for attention.

Simon's expression was mischievous. "My thoughts exactly. Thor's hammer, and it's made of gold. Curious and curiouser, but a clue and a puzzle at the same time."

Freya nodded brightly. The mist was gone, but her head was beginning to buzz as pain settled behind her eyes.

Simon, intent on displaying his finds, was less observant than he had been. "As they say on TV, 'But wait, there's more.' Look at this."

He was pointing toward a collection of bones—the remains of the occupant of the grave. Immediately behind the skull, there were lines scored into the stone.

Freya stared at Simon. "Runes."

"Can you read them?"

She exhaled slowly. "No, I wish I could. But the grave objects and these"—she gestured at the scratches—"are Pagan."

"And they're in a grave which occupies the place of honor in a Christian church." Simon's grin was crooked. "Why? you ask. My question exactly."

"Hello, Dad." Wind tried to stir the branches of the yews. They creaked, unwilling to move.

Freya was alone. In the open air again, her head felt better. Companionably, she sat on a corner of the raised grave, as if it had been her father's bed. She murmured, "I've brought these for you—from Findnar."

She leaned forward and placed the vase just below the inscription on a little plinth. In white set against black, the color of the flowers seemed almost too vivid.

"I wish you could talk to me, Dad." She faltered. "I don't know what to do." It was true. Did speaking the truth help?

Freya stared at the lettering on the grave as if it could give her an answer. Nothing came—nothing. She closed her eyes, squeezed the lids tight shut.

"But I don't think I can leave the island, not until I know." She groped for the crucifix. "I'll try, Dad, I really will, to get some answers to what's happening, but someone has to help me."

She looked expectantly at the headstone, where his name was written.

And felt embarrassed despair. Had she really thought this would be a dialogue?

Loneliness. Aloneness. It played tricks on your mind.

Caught by the wind, the door closed with a snap, and that made the two people in the library look up. Neither of them was Katherine. One was a tragically pimpled teenager at a computer terminal; the other was an old man with a peak of milk-pale hair and the stoop of incipient osteoporosis. He nodded encouragingly to Freya. "Can I help you?" He seemed to mean it.

She hurried forward. "I'm looking for Katherine MacAllister."

"Miss MacAllister does not work on Saturdays. I am Alexander Callaghan, assistant librarian." He pronounced it *Callachhaaaan,* and his nose, large and very pointed, pecked the air as he bowed. Freya tried not to giggle, for Mr. Callaghan resembled nothing so much as a wading bird, even to the feathery plumes of his head.

The girl glowered in her corner and sniffed; it was a contemptuous sniff. *Perhaps good manners offend her,* thought Freya as, ignoring the surly child, she said warmly, "Thank you very much, but it's actually a personal matter. You don't know where I might find Miss MacAllister this morning?"

"Certainly I do." Alexander tenderly laid a book down, as if the binding might bruise. "Come with me."

The square outside the library was clumped with dense rows of market stalls. Aimed at tourists mostly—wandering in small throngs, looking and touching—there was the usual collection of food and drink, cheap Indian and Chinese clothes, detritus from garages and attics mislabeled "antiques," and fruit and vegetables marked "organic." *Yeah, right,* thought the cynical Freya. There were also several book stalls, and Alexander pointed to one at the far corner of the square. Shaded by a large umbrella, it had prime position near one of the exits to the square, and a sign announced, K. MACALLISTER, ANTIQUARIAN & SECONDHAND BOOKS. COLLECTIBLE EDITIONS.

Leaving the assistant librarian to his one grumpy customer, Freya tracked across the square, dodging runaway children, feral girls with dreadlocks, and older couples slung about with cameras.

"Katherine?"

The librarian was seated behind a long trestle table. At the rear, display cases were filled with bound books, and the front of the table had lines of paperbacks in neat rows.

"How nice to see you, Freya. So, your boat was found back on its mooring?"

Freya's eyes crinkled. "Yes." A stack of Saturday papers lay beside Katherine's chair—the newsagent. It was high time to introduce herself, get in a preemptive gossip strike; he, or she, might even know who'd taken the cruiser.

"But I wanted to ask if you'd have time for a chat later?"

Katherine's look was alert. "Is there something wrong?"

Freya shook her head, then half-nodded. And shrugged. "I was wondering if you'd like to come over to the island, because it might be good to go through some of my father's stuff. Together. Maybe later today?" The last words rushed from her mouth, unedited.

The librarian was unused to quick decisions or, at least, acknowledging them. "Saturday is always busy, as you see." Freya's shoulders slumped. Katherine changed gear smoothly. "However, I haven't been on Findnar for some months. Yes, I should like to come. Two conditions, however, and one of them is onerous, I warn you."

Freya said eagerly, "I'm sure I can help, whatever it is."

Katherine held up a finger. "One, you help me pack my stall away this afternoon—that's the onerous bit; and, two—is there something you want to tell me?"

Freya dropped her eyes. "Perhaps." She added hastily, "It may be nothing." How much she ached to say more.

Katherine smiled pleasantly. "Of course."

"Hello? Anyone home?"

Freya knocked at a black front door. Solid, respectable, it was a clear and definite contrast to the white walls of the house, as were the red geraniums in the window box.

There was no answer. Adrenaline, raised when she'd let the knocker drop, fizzed in Freya's blood. She tried again, and this time the crash of the little Viking ship had real force. "Hello?"

No signs of life, not even the bark of a dog. Maybe she'd misunderstood the newsagent's directions, but she'd described the house, right down to the window boxes.

Freya glanced at her watch. Nearly two o'clock, and she had a couple of hours to fill; what to do? She eased the straps on her backpack and put the bags of groceries down, flexing her fingers. She'd tried to shop as lightly as she could for her guest tonight, but there was still quite a bit to carry.

Staring toward the harbor, Freya shaded her eyes. Maybe she'd find Walter in the bar of the pub; she was hungry, and they might still be serving lunch.

Mentally debating the allure of hot chips against a sensible sandwich, she began to walk away. She almost didn't hear the voice call out. "They're not in."

She turned. A woman stood in the opened door of the next house down from Walter's.

"They've gone out." She had a flat face, the Boynes' neighbor, and her arms were folded tight over a meager chest.

"Oh, yes. I worked that out." Freya tried a friendly smile. "But would you know where?"

Never a beauty, Julie Tyler was somewhere anonymous between forty and fifty and felt it personally. She didn't like pretty girls, never having been one herself. "Try the fleet pool." Her eyes raked Freya up and down.

Freya nodded. "Thanks." *For not much.*

Julie Tyler watched with bright, hard eyes as Freya hoisted her bags. "You're that girl from the island—Michael Dane's daughter. The Australian."

Freya smiled over her shoulder but started walking. "Yes. Thanks again."

The woman called out, "You should watch yourself over there. Word gets around; a girl alone." Some kind of duty done, she went back into her house with a decisive sniff.

And lovely to meet you too, thought Freya. She picked up pace, refusing to think about the woman's last remark.

Not two hundred meters away was the harbor wall and, squinting against the sun, she could see a man. He was limping along the deck of a large fishing vessel—*The Holy Isle,* there it was. And there *he* was.

What would she say?

Freya walked toward the dock. Daylight disinfects fear—it had worked for her, and she hoped it'd worked for Dan as well.

"Hello." She kept her voice neutral. Dan nodded. He was sorting drill bits on the engine housing.

Freya cleared her throat. "I didn't really get a chance to thank you this morning, Dan—not properly—for bringing Dad's boat back." *Words, words, words.*

Dan stood, unbending his long body, but a cramp in the damaged leg made him clumsy and he dropped a large drill bit. They both winced at the rolling clang as it clashed across metal and bounced to the deck.

Half-hunched, Dan turned away from Freya when he bent to retrieve it. She could see the embarrassment.

She said, brightly, "I wanted to ask," but it was quite hard to go on talking inanities. Her mouth made disobedient shapes. "If Walter's around?"

After a pause, Dan shook his head; he nodded past the stern of *The Holy Isle.* "Had trouble this morning when I got back. Dad's at the workshop trying to get parts."

"I heard. The engine. That's a shame." Freya smiled cheerily and felt like an idiot.

Dan stared at her appraisingly but this time she did not look away. He said nothing, and that direct inspection was intimidating.

Freya said, finally, "Dan, I think we need to talk." Stricken, she thought, *Idiot!* She'd meant to work up to it more slowly.

But Dan caught his breath and started to cough. He couldn't control the hacking explosions—he'd been bullied at school; this was the legacy.

"Are you okay?" Concerned, Freya started toward the ship's ladder.

"What does it look like?" The words tore from his chest.

Freya opened her mouth. And closed it. And backed away. *This is stupid.*

She picked up her bags. "I'll find Walter."

Dan almost let her go. "Stop." Not an apology.

Freya hesitated.

He said, "I agree. I agree with you. We should talk." He pointed at the ladder. "You'd better come up, Freya Dane." He used her name as if it was another language.

As she stared into his eyes, the seconds paraded by so slowly, Freya didn't know what to do.

The glimmer of a smile. "I am not a dog, and I do not bite. Well, only so often."

Freya made up her mind. She dropped the bags on the quay and put her foot on the first rung of the ladder, but the vessel moved on the tide and she almost fell between the dock and the side of *The Holy Isle*. Dan flung forward. He captured her wrist in one hand and thrust the other toward her. "Take it!" Freya's fingers grabbed his.

It was sound this time. A girl. Laughing.

CHAPTER 20

Y OU'RE JUST my friend, that is all." Signy was lying, or
perhaps she did not know. She was laughing as she ran.

Bear made a huge effort. He launched himself at
Signy's back but, feinting, she dodged and fled.

Bear fell hard, with nothing in his hands. "Signy!"

She stopped and looked back, panting.

The boy beat his chest, then lay still.

"Oh, Bear . . ."

Signy flung herself toward him, heart in pain. That huddled
shape in the grass . . .

"Caught!" Bear's arms whipped around her knees, and he
pulled her down. But if he was strong, she was wily.

Kicking, half-laughing, half-gasping, Signy bit those grasping
fingers.

"Ow! Not fair."

She jumped up and fled again. "Life is not fair, Bear!"

Propped on an elbow, Bear shaded his eyes. He watched Signy
sprint toward the stones and smiled. This was a game he liked.

Licking his hand, Bear sauntered after his quarry. Uncertain of
so much in his life, he was certain of this—Signy's heart was not
in escape.

Will he come? Do I want him to come? Fit as she was, Signy
was panting as she ran toward the circle stones. She knew where
to hide—a small, Signy-size crevice had been created when the
brothers first tried to push the stones over in the inner ring. Like

trees half-fallen in the forest, two of the taller monoliths leaned against each other and toward a third, shorter stone. From some angles, the smallest stone concealed the hiding place.

Flat on her belly, Signy wriggled inside the earth-smelling shadow and refused to think. But that was impossible.

Why had she allowed Bear to kiss her after the goat escaped? She should not have. Abbot Cuillin preached regular, hours-long sermons on Sins of the Flesh, and despite that, she had somehow agreed to play this dangerous game.

It had happened so quickly. Between one instant and the next, after Bear ran the goat down and she joined him, there had been a moment of . . . what?

She had thanked him. Of course. But the nanny, outraged at being kept from a patch of new bracken, was twisting and bucking, and Signy could not hold her, so Bear wound his hand through the rope.

As if it were natural, he'd leaned across the animal's back and his mouth had touched hers. She'd not known what to do, but he'd laughed, and she'd giggled too. Then he'd let the goat go—and taken Signy's face between his hands and kissed her again. Lingeringly. And she had let him.

He murmured, "You see, it's nice." His breath had been sweet and warm.

Unheeded, the nanny had escaped to the bracken, and viewed from a distance it might have seemed then as if Signy was running after her wayward charge. But she was not—she was running from Bear—and herself.

Lately Bear's image filled her dreams with heat; more and more, she wanted to look at him, to talk to him. To touch him.

To have him touch her.

Be honest, she thought. She was happy Bear had chased her, but that frightened Signy profoundly. This must mean the Devil was setting a snare—since her first moontide, Gunnhilde had told her so constantly. *Temptation, Signy, is his weapon. You must guard against him, challenge him. You must keep yourself pure, for God desires purity above all things.*

Yes, but what *was* purity?

"I know you're there, Signy."

The girl opened her eyes.

Bear was standing in the center of the circle. Slowly, he turned, his eyes raking each standing monolith. "Talk to me." His voice caught. Bear had not expected this, playfulness consumed by yearning. "Please do not be scared, Signy. I would never hurt you."

Signy edged forward a little. She remembered again, how well, the depth of her own loneliness and his. Once, they had been closer than sister and brother.

She called softly, "I'm here, Bear."

The boy stopped. The damaged side of his face was half in shadow; sun and dappled light lent him beauty.

Signy exhaled a long breath. "You can find me if you try."

But Bear did not move; he held out his arms. "Come to me, Signy."

After a moment, she squirmed from her hiding place. She stared at Bear across the fallen stones. Would she do as he asked? Her blood rushed and whispered, and it was hard to hear the sounds of the world.

Bear dropped his arms.

Signy walked toward him—slowly, at first, and then she ran and he gathered her up as if she were a precious thing.

Time—the past and the future—had them in its grasp, and they chose surrender. To each other. Soon, her black kirtle, his old tunic, lay entangled and discarded.

"Signy!" One word, shouted to the sky. A cry, a blessing. There had been so much death, but now, Bear and Signy enfolded each other—man to woman, woman to man—for the first time, and life sought itself in each of their bodies as Bear's hands found and lingered on the contours of this sweet, unfamiliar landscape.

His touch was hot, and Signy gasped, for her skin was not her own now—it was his, too, as their bodies slid against each other. The muscles in Bear's arms and chest were so hard she clung to him, but not for comfort, this was more urgent. She squirmed and molded herself around his legs, against his hips; pliant and soft, she kissed him, breathing his breath.

Bear slipped his thigh between hers. She pressed against him, allowed him higher, opening herself to him. He groaned; it was hard to savor this girl as he wanted to, for Signy was ripe and she was perfect. What he had imagined in his fantasies had been smoke. This, *she,* was real. His mind abandoned him. Now there was only fierce, red desire. He pushed her thighs apart, spearing down.

Signy welcomed Bear, took him deep inside her body. Now it was she, half-sobbing, who lay beside the stones, a man above her, her body for him, he for hers. She had watched, secretly, as other girls cried out, long ago, at the long-day summer gathering, and now it was her time. And if there was pain, like theirs, it was brief.

Intent, drowning in each other, the world and the past did not exist. There was skin, and hands, and eyes, and exquisite agony, almost more than could be borne.

And after the suffering, after the blood and fire of their child-hood, this first coupling, this uniting of flesh, brought strength to their bruised souls, brought blazing light and heat and sweetness. And peace.

Enfolded, naked, they lay together in the moving shadows of the afternoon, and the whale-ivory ship, hanging from a thong around her neck, rode between Signy's small breasts. Slowly she traced the line of Bear's jaw with one finger and kissed the scars on his face.

The boy caught her hand in his own. "We belong to each other now, Signy. I to you, you to me. Deeper and nearer than blood, while I have breath in my body."

As he said the words, faces came to Signy from the dark and the past.

She began to chant. "Laenna, hear me. This is my beloved. Mother, Father, you have another son. Odhrahn, Nid, here is your brother Magni, the great Bear. Welcome him, my family, since we have joined together here, in this sacred place."

Bear held Signy against his chest as her breathing slowed.

"You are my clan, Signy. You are all the friends of my childhood. You are my brother, Grimor; my mother and my father too. While I live, there will never be another woman at my side, only you. I have waited for you, and the Gods, here, have given you to me, as I give myself to you."

Bear knelt beside Signy, and his eyes traveled each part of that slender body, whiter than whale ivory. The flowers of late spring were closing their petals, but he plucked them from the grass and scattered red clover and pink comfrey, tawny primrose and white primrose over her skin, a breathing garment of color. He laughed, and so did she because they were happy. An unfamiliar feeling.

"After such glory, it's a pity we have only these to wear." He picked up his tunic. It was colorless with age, and her black kirtle was a reproach to the bright afternoon.

Signy grimaced as he helped her pull on the dress. She stroked his chest drowsily, trailing her fingers along the muscles in his arms, savoring his skin and his smell.

But she dropped her hand. And stepped a pace away. She had never seen a man naked before and was too aware, suddenly, of his eyes on her body. Adam and Eve, before or after the fall?

Signy's eyes filled with tears. Suddenly, right—so clear a moment ago—seemed wrong. "Have we sinned?"

Bear was devastated by her misery. He grasped her shoulders. "Look at me!" He tipped Signy's face up and wiped the tears away. More gently he said, "They are fools to make their lives so barren, and we are not like them. You are all that keeps me alive."

She brushed grass from her tunic, defiantly. "I do not want to believe this *is* sin, no matter what the Abbot says." She would not think of that now. "This place is sacred—just as sacred."

She stared around the circle of stones. Yes, this was holy ground.

A twig snapped, and there was bleating close by. "The goat!"

Bear grinned. "I'll get the nanny. You can say she led you a chase. As you did me."

"*That* I shall keep to myself."

But Signy's smile faded as she watched Bear go. *Father, Mother, help your daughter . . . bless us.* She closed her eyes to hear and see better.

Distantly, the bell at the Abbey tolled.

That summer was golden. After the upheavals of the last years, contentment settled over Findnar, and for the first time there was more than enough food to eat, even with continuing new arrivals from the Motherhouse in the South.

Each long, warm day the brothers and sisters marveled at the swelling grain and exclaimed at the quantity of milk given by the cows and the goats. Even the size of the eggs and the number of piglets born were cause for grateful comment on God's blessings.

Signy knew better. This new abundance had a specific cause. Her moontide had stopped—the sacred coupling in that holy place had brought fecundity to the island.

She was ravenous all the time. Sneaking new milk direct from the cow was not enough—she begged extra food from Brother Vidor and ate early mushrooms as they sprang in the fields. And she dreamed, waking and sleeping, of Bear and of the next time they could be together. But she would not tell him about the baby until the third moon had passed, just to be sure.

Perhaps, at last, the time had come. The time when she would truly say good-bye to Laenna and go with Bear into the future. They would found their own family now. Her sister would understand.

᠖

The service of Prime, on a cold, dark morning. Summer had fled and the warmth of early autumn was a memory as the bleak day began with a homily from Abbot Cuillin.

"Brothers and Sisters, as was said by St. Gregory the Great, there are seven cardinal sins. You know of pride and greed. We wrestle with these each day and moment of our lives. But today, I shall speak of lust. As the apostle James says, 'Then when desire has conceived, it gives birth to sin; and sin, when it is full-grown, brings forth death . . .' "

At the back of the chapel, Signy heard Cuillin's words as if each was new-made and meant for her.

"Tremble when I speak of lust! Fornicators, even in thought, will burn for eternity in a lake of fire. And they will be torn apart by ravening beasts as they burn, symbols of the appetites of the body uncontrolled in life."

Was it Signy's imagination, or was Cuillin's glance sweeping the congregation to seek her out? Trembling, she wrapped arms around her belly as the Abbot's voice dropped. The monks and nuns strained forward to hear what he said.

"Oh, my brothers, oh, my sisters, how little defense we have against such horror. The sin of Eve—offering temptation against the will of God at the bidding of the Evil One—stains us still. And the sin of Adam—helpless against the wiles of that woman, all women—is that he succumbed. Oh, weakness. Oh, abomination! We are all as they were. From this horror, the urgings of our flesh, only the Lord can protect us, strengthen us, preserve our purity of thought and body . . ."

A rigor shook Signy. She could *see* flames and smell flesh as it blackened in the fire, and yet, what dwelled inside her body was *not* sin made flesh. Was it? No! This child had been created in love and by love; it and she were not evil. Bear was not evil.

But Cuillin's words rolled over her and filled up her head with clamor. Signy grew more and more anxious, and then came pain. It ripped her, gripped her, as if a dog or a wolf had her in its teeth. And she could not think or pray it away.

Signy was the last of the lay servants to leave as the religious processed from the chapel after the service.

Gunnhilde had been waiting for her. She beckoned. "Are you well, child?" The nun was worried. Signy had seemed almost joyous in these last weeks, a considerable change, but this morning she was pale and sweating. As one of the most senior nuns, and mother of the novices, Gunnhilde was bound to watch for signs of disease among the women, especially since winter was coming and they would all be living so close to one another.

"Thank you, Sister, I need nothing," Signy answered. But her pace increased as she hurried toward the women's sleeping quarters.

Gunnhilde frowned. "Child, wait."

A direct order must be obeyed; Signy stopped.

Panting a little, the nun joined her. "Walk with me, dear child. Let us admire the work of our diligent brothers." Gunnhilde waved toward the half-roofed cloister being constructed along an outer wall of the expanded chapel.

"I am sure our Lord is grateful, as we are, for all that is done to beautify this Abbey in His honor." Gunnhilde smiled at Signy, but her eyes were watchful.

The girl tried to respond, but the pain in her belly pulsed to the beat of her heart.

Gunnhilde was alarmed by Signy's pallor. "You are not well." She put her hand on the girl's forehead. "No fever, that is something, but do you know the nature of your affliction, daughter?"

Signy swallowed painfully; her mouth was dry. "No, Sister, but I am frightened." Perhaps this was not a complete lie. Her mind, and now her body, was tormented.

The nun nodded. "I see how it is—your spirit quails after

Abbot Cuillin's homily." Signy flinched. Gunnhilde nodded and clasped the girl's cold hand. "To overcome our own nature is God's test. Draw on His love, have faith that He *will* answer your prayers and bring you safe home to His sweet Presence after this time of trial."

Home. Signy shook her head. Her voice cracked. "No. He could not love me, I am not deserving."

Gunnhilde said earnestly, "But this is the burden we all carry. He knows we are imperfect, but as a loving Father, He strengthens us so that we may do our best to avoid temptation."

Temptation. The word opened like a wound in Signy's heart. "You do not understand, Sister." She broke away and almost ran from the cloister.

Gunnhilde let the girl go. She sighed. For some, herself included, the journey toward God's Grace was a very hard road.

"Are you there, Signy?"

The evening was troubled by sharp rain as the light died, but Bear did not care. He had hurried to the stones, hoping to find Signy. If she did not come, he would leave two black pebbles inside her hiding place—a private signal, one to say he had been there and one to ask if they could try to meet again tomorrow evening— the second day of the week after the Sabbath. The stone circle was the safest place on the island to meet, for the religious thought it cursed and would not willingly go there.

"Signy?"

Bear stood still, peering through the gloom. He shivered. The wind was annoying, and soon it would be night. He had so hoped that this evening . . .

Somewhere close by, he heard keening; the hair on Bear's forearms stood up as he moved closer to the sound, for he did not know if it was human.

He found Signy huddled behind the offering stone, out of the wind. She made a small bundle with arms clasped around her knees, and she had been crying for so long her eyes were swollen to slits. He knelt beside her. Rage filled his chest with red bile; someone had caused Signy to suffer. That person would pay, richly. "What have they done to you?"

"No!" She pulled away from him.

Bear sat back. "No?" He was puzzled. It was almost, in that moment, as if she hated him; his heart began to speed.

He tried again. "Tell me."

But Signy shook her head. She moved away from his touch. She did not want him.

In that moment Bear might have howled like a wolf, but he did not. He was a man now; she had made him that.

"Would you like me to go?" His voice, at least, was steady.

"Yes," a fierce whisper.

Ice touched Bear's heart. He would not plead. He was halfway across the inner circle of stones before he heard her call.

"Bear, come back."

He kept walking.

"Please. Wait, Bear." Like a night spirit, Signy ran, a darker shape in the gloom. She reached him before he had quite left the stones. She knew she must draw him back. "Come into the circle." Signy did not touch Bear, instead she beckoned. Scarlet-eyed from grief, her face was chalk pale.

Bear yearned to reach forward, yearned to enfold and comfort her, but he said, with stiff pride, "If that is what you want."

Wearily, Signy nodded. "I am sorry. Will you return with me?"

He swallowed. "Signy, I do not know what is wrong but . . ."

She ignored the plea he had not meant to utter. Head down, she walked to the offering stone. Her step was heavy.

The moon had slid up from beneath the world. It was rising through a wrack of wind-driven cloud, and there was enough light to see Signy place her hand on the offering stone. "Put your hand on mine."

Bear did as she had bidden. He was chilled by her expression.

"Do you swear to me that we are one?" Her eyes were dark holes.

He tried again. "Oh, Signy, you do not have to ask."

"Swear!" Signy seemed much taller, her head against the driven moon.

And Bear remembered she was a shaman's daughter. He said, slowly, "Yes. I swear; in the eyes of my Gods and yours, we are one."

Signy's cold hand trembled beneath his. "Give me your knife."

The reek of strangeness was sudden and powerful. Bear knew what was coming, and terror gripped his chest, but he observed his hand, the one not covering Signy's, remove the otter-handled blade from its pouch and watched as she took it from him.

"This is what we must do. First I will cut your wrist, then you will cut mine." Signy held the blade to the sky and made three circles around the moon; then she pointed the knife at his eyes.

"I shall tie our wrists together, and we shall see which Gods have the most power on Findnar." Her voice was calm and her face serene. And blank as a mask.

Bear forced himself to speak. "I think you are ill."

But Signy shook her head and spoke to him patiently. "We need to do this, Bear. Hold out your arm."

He had honed the blade and did not fear to be cut with it; if Signy was quick there would be little pain. But the thought of slicing her tender skin brought acid to his throat. He hesitated.

"Your arm!" The voice of a priestess. Was that where Signy's new power came from?

Bear did as she bid him, and felt nothing as the edge was drawn across his wrist, not even when the line of dark blood began to drip.

She offered her wrist to him. "Do it."

And so he did. A clean cut even though the stars wheeled above his head.

Blood, their mingled blood, dripped on the offering stone as Signy bound Bear's wrist to hers with the belt from her kirtle. She was humming from deep in her chest, a sound that built in power, a sound he could feel in the stone beneath their hands, and then her chant began.

Bear did not know all of the meaning, but he understood one thing, Signy was waiting for judgment.

And then the words changed; she was reciting the Paternoster in the Christian language.

"What are you doing?" He was spooked. The night wind had risen, but it seemed to blow outside the circle of stone, and they were at the center of an unseen force.

"I am asking the question." Signy was sweating. Her eyes were lightless.

"What question?" The skin beneath the hair on his scalp puckered.

"Which God will save our child."

"Child." Bear faltered. "Our child."

"Yes." A breath that was almost a howl.

"But . . . this is good. For us both. Oh, Signy, don't you see? We must leave Findnar. You cannot stay here, not carrying a baby. The rest is bad dreams, that is all. You are frightened." His wrist, streaming blood, had begun to hurt badly.

Signy said nothing. Eyes closed, she was praying to Mary now, muttering the name over and over. Suddenly she convulsed. Falling to her knees, Signy sobbed from the pit of her being. "The child of our sin will not stay in my body. Mary has abandoned me; they have all abandoned me."

Bear unbound their wrists, ripping at the bonds. He pulled the distraught girl into his arms.

"Fight this, Signy. Please fight this."

But blood flowed from Signy's body, and in bitter pain the legacy of Eve, their daughter, was lost.

CHAPTER 21

GULLS WHEELED and called, lost and plaintive. Dan's fingers clamped to Freya's as if they had fused, though she pulled, trying to take her hands away.

A surge slapped *The Holy Isle* and fled along her flanks—the tide was turning.

Freya chanced a glance at Dan. His eyes were undefended. She knew that look—he'd been seared, flayed by feeling. She swallowed. "Come to the island, Dan. Tonight."

The invitation shocked them both.

Freya hurried on. "We need to be there, on Findnar, for any of this to make sense, I truly believe that. And Katherine MacAllister's coming over too—she was my father's friend. More than that." Freya hardly noticed that acknowledgment. "You'll be quite safe, I promise." *Why trivialize this?* She willed her breathing to slow.

Dan let Freya's hands go, first one and then the other. "A chaperone?" The beginning of a smile. He grabbed a corner of the engine housing and hauled himself up, favoring his twisted leg.

Freya did not try to help, but she stood also. "I have to go." She clambered down the ladder, more careful this time.

As she hurried away, he called out, "Why?"

"Katherine's got a stall; I said I'd help pack up. Cruiser's moored back at the public quay." Freya didn't repeat the invitation. If he wanted to come to Findnar, he'd be there on the dock.

G

Michael's boat rocked gently at its mooring as Katherine and Freya arrived. *He's not here.*

"What time did you say we would go, Freya?"

Freya stared at her watch; she'd been so certain. "Around now."

"Hello." Dan—he'd sauntered up behind them. "Where shall I put this?" He eased the pack off his shoulders.

A jolt hit Freya. If Dan got in the cruiser, there was no going back to normal, not ever. *Whatever normal is.* She was sure he knew it, too, for all the self-possession. "In the locker if it'll fit. Maybe you'd take us over there, Dan? You know the strait better than I do."

He nodded and handed Freya's shopping bags down as she climbed into the hull.

Katherine said, brightly, "Maybe this will fit too." She held out an overnight bag. "I'll cast off, shall I?"

Freya could feel the heat as she blushed. "I am so sorry, Katherine. Do you two know each other?"

The librarian smiled kindly. "Of course we do."

Dan actually grinned when he caught Freya's eye.

"Should have guessed—not even three degrees of separation in Portsolly." Freya stood to one side as Dan made his awkward way to the cabin and fired the motor.

The journey across Fuil Bay was peaceful. As the day began its long decline, the sky turned from topaz to shining pink, and silver clouds sailed out of the west like vast swans. Conversation was spasmodic but cheerful over the noise of the motor, and even Dan seemed relaxed.

"After September, the sea will hold you on the island as it pleases. Much safer you winter in Portsolly." Dan raised his voice as the hull slammed into a wave.

"Who says I like safe?" Freya grinned over her shoulder, but Dan was staring at her, willing her to hear him. Glib words died in her mouth. No one had ever looked at her like that—he wanted to protect her. She tried to smile. *It's okay. I'm scared enough for both of us.* And yet, as they drew closer to her father's island, her island, she had never felt so alive. As if her life had become almost unbearably vivid, each sense peeled back and utterly open. If she could only reach out, she might see into the heart of . . . what?

A moving shaft of light touched the stone circle. One by one, the monoliths shone against the darkening sky as the cruiser sliced through the sea. How long had the stones stood there? How many people had seen what she saw now?

Katherine pointed. "A fine sight. I have missed the island."

Freya did not take her eyes from the stones. "I can understand why."

The note of the engine changed as Dan eased the boat around, setting her on a long, curved course toward Findnar's cove. He knew the grain of this water, knew when to fight the current and when to use it, but sometimes, even on a calm night, the sea lay in wait. *Because it has no mercy.* "And no conscience." Perhaps he said the words aloud, he did not know.

Freya glanced at Dan's rigid profile. He'd muttered something she'd not quite heard. "What do you reckon, good night for a barbie or what? I even remembered the beer." Two six-packs of Stella Artois bumped against her feet in the bilge.

Dan lined the prow up on the opening of the sea cave. He was sweating. *None of this is real. It can't be,* he thought.

Katherine said helpfully, "Australian for barbecue."

"I did not think Freya meant the doll." Dan dropped the revs, and the hull lost momentum as it idled through a trough; he waited for the swell to build.

Freya needled him gently. "If you get this wrong, we'll be fish food."

Dan did not remove his eyes from the cave mouth. "Supportive. Not."

Behind the boat a gathering crest began to push the hull forward and, coupled with a spurt from the motor, the weight of the sea carried them under the rock arch and all the way up to the quay.

"Oops—nearly took the prow off." But Freya smiled as she climbed out of the wallowing cruiser and caught the rope Dan threw.

He shut down the motor and watched as Freya loaded her backpack—beer first, sausages next, then tried to stuff more groceries on top. "You'll not get any more in." He knew Freya was worried about his leg. He picked up a loaf of bread, butter, and several cheeses, and relieved her of the vegetables, too, though he managed not to touch her hands.

Katherine hoisted her bag. "We've both been on Findnar before, Freya. You don't have to worry."

"Okay then, off we go." Along the beach, Freya paced herself to Dan's uneven stride, though she hoped it wasn't obvious. As the climb up the cliff path began, she caught Katherine's eye. The librarian wasn't remotely short of breath, though Freya was panting already. She did not look at Dan.

As the top of the path wound into sight, Freya edged past him. "I'll just light the lamps. Excuse me."

There was room for two people, but an accidental touch, her jacket hushing against his, gave them both a jolt. Freya stumbled, and Dan flung a hand toward her. "Careful!"

She saved herself but cannoned back against the cliff face; their hands did not touch.

Bemused by the strange performance, Katherine called out, "Are you all right?"

Freya mumbled, "Fine. Take your time." With a shake she strode away.

The kitchen yawned its usual dark challenge to the open door, but Freya hurried down the steps with much more confidence than even a day ago, and groped for the pack of matches on the table. Moments later, lamp held high, she stood beside the back door. "Welcome to you both."

Dan paused. *Freya—she was a Goddess too.* Half-smiling, he drew back to allow Katherine to enter first. *A Norse Goddess in wet-weather gear.*

The librarian ducked beneath the lintel, navigating the kitchen steps one by one. "Thank you," she said.

Freya watched with approval. "They caught you too, the steps?"

"Only once." Katherine's voice was wistful.

Dan hobbled toward the basket of peat beside the stove. "A fire, then. Where shall it be?"

Freya rattled the latch down behind her guests. "At the front of the house—on the turf—there's a great view on a calm night. We shall light a beacon." *But beacons are warning fires . . .*

Katherine was standing at the kitchen table, beside the captain's chair. "While Dan gets the barbecue going, we could organize the beds," Freya said to the librarian. "I'll have to break it to him gently, but he gets the couch." She did not say, *And you can show me where you used to sleep.*

Katherine glanced toward the top of the stairs. "I'll get the sheets, shall I?"

So, you know where they're kept. "Thanks, that would be great."

So much unsaid.

An untethered silver balloon, the moon sailed higher as they watched.

"Another beer?" Freya waved a long-necked bottle. "Drink them while they're cold. No refrigeration on Findnar." She was sitting with Katherine beside the fire in front of the house and hadn't felt so relaxed in a long time.

Katherine smiled, and they clinked bottles. Firelight suited the librarian, flattered her bright eyes and pretty skin. "I like beer, by the way. Michael taught me how to drink it."

She looks lovely tonight, Dad, your dear friend. Freya poked at the embers, and sparks flew up into the dark. She called out, "Fire's nearly ready, Dan."

Exiting Compline via the front steps, Dan put a bowl of salad, knives and forks, and a plate of buttered bread on the turf beside the two women. Freya held up a bottle of beer, and he leaned down to take it. "I heard you talking about refrigeration, Freya. Put the meat and milk in the shed—as the year grows old they'll freeze, if that's what you want."

She waved airily. "Ah, but this is summer. Hot, hot, hot." A flirty leer. Horrified, she paused. *That came out wrong.*

Dan arranged sausages on an iron rack filched from the kitchen range. He seemed engrossed.

Katherine stared into the heart of the flame. "There's something about watching a fire. A sense of connection, I suppose, to all those who've been here before." She pulled her jacket tighter.

Freya muttered, "Good friend, bad enemy where I come from."

"Bushfires." Dan turned the sausages one by one, head cocked away from the smoke. "Not a problem here—very few trees—and then there's always the rain." He grinned and stood back from the heat, his face gilded by flame. "Scotland was covered in forest once. The Vikings are supposed to have cut the trees down. Or that's the legend."

Freya sat up. She asked, "Do you think Findnar was forested?"

Dan half-closed his eyes, staring into the dark. "Maybe, though it's more exposed here than the mainland."

"But it does make sense that there were trees here once. Below the stones on the eastern side there's a sheltered little valley. A couple of big oaks and conifers grow there, plus a fair bit of scrubby stuff—bog willow and such. I thought it must just be a protected microclimate down there, but maybe not." Freya got to her feet. "Can I help, Dan?"

"I can just about manage sausages." Deadpan.

She grinned. "My apologies. You're a natural." She started toward the house. "I'll get the sauce. Can't have a barbie without tomato sauce."

"Here." Dan slung Freya a flashlight. She caught it on the run and took the front steps two at a time.

He called after her. "Be quick. They'll burn."

Who will? Freya shrank from the thought. It wasn't funny.

"It's a bit basic." Freya placed the lamp on the bedside table. "But I hope you'll be comfortable. I haven't had time to get started on the house, making it feel more like my place, I mean."

Katherine stared around the little room. The iron-framed bed filled much of the space. "It's perfect just as it is."

"I'm glad you came." Impulsively, Freya kissed Katherine on the cheek; Katherine returned the gesture with a stiff little hug.

An awkward pause. Freya cleared her throat. "I hope one hot water bottle in the bed's enough? It's cold up here." It was, this late in the night—close to midnight—and the wind had backed to the east.

"A cool room is best for sleeping in. Good night, Freya." Katherine turned away bravely. The bed would seem very empty. Both of them knew that.

"By the way, I've got something to show you tomorrow—very interesting. Do you read Latin?"

Katherine's look was quizzical. "I do."

"Well, that's good. See you in the morning." Freya grinned.

"But . . ."

"It's a surprise—something Dad found. Sweet dreams."

Closing the door softly, Freya padded down to the kitchen. She was wearing football socks and a jacket over thermals, and waiting for her in the still-warm room was Daniel. How did she feel about that?

"Cocoa?" He held up a mug.

Freya sat at the massive table. They both knew the time for small talk was done. "Thank you, but I'll sleep well anyway tonight with both of you here."

That passed without comment.

Dan lifted a saucepan of hot milk off the gas ring, and Freya realized she liked watching him. Fine hands, economy in all that he did.

He caught her glance. "Sugar?"

She shook her head and wrapped both hands around the mug as it was offered. The surface of the cocoa trembled slightly.

Dan sat down on the other side of the table.

If she reached out, she could touch him.

They drank in silence until he said, "So. Where do we begin?"

Freya got up from the table and added more milk to her cocoa—the physical distance made it easier to think, but only slightly.

"A bit of background. There's something I want to show you tomorrow, and I need your help too. I've got a dig going—something I'm searching for—and it will happen faster with more than one pair of hands. It's important because there are things . . ." Freya, uncertain, tried again. "My father found some artifacts, you see. Significant objects. This crucifix was one of them." She lifted it out from beneath her clothes so Dan could see. "Dad was looking for a particular grave and, I don't know, but everything odd that's happened here—and to you and me"—she felt heat rise in her chest and her throat—"well, I'm certain it's connected with what he was doing and even with this. I just feel that."

Dan raised his eyebrows at her fervent tone.

Calm down, Freya. "Look, I've been trying to say—oh, I don't know, but this—whatever this is—it's all leading somewhere."

The kitchen was shadowed, and the old stove hissed gently, its belly full of peat—a big, metal cat. The house was chattering, too, windows flexing behind drawn curtains, doors shifting a little as the air came and went around the building.

Dan spoke cautiously. "What else did your father find?"

"A lot of things. Believe me, an enormous number of artifacts, some of them very valuable—the kinds of things you see in the best museum collections."

"Really?" He looked surprised. "But doesn't the government usually get involved?"

Freya nodded. She tried not to show how anxious she felt. "Yes. There's all sorts of regulation about troves and hoards, and I'll have to do something about that, but at the moment . . ." Her voice trailed away. She went to the kitchen dresser and pulled out a drawer. "He thought this was important, though—it was found with the crucifix." She held out the small lead box.

Dan took it from her carefully. Their hands did not touch.

"Open it if you like. It's quite the surprise packet."

He glanced at Freya and with supreme delicacy prized up the lid. "But this is . . ."

She opened the stove with unnecessary vigor and pushed more peat into the firebox. "Yes. It's a manuscript. A very small one. I'm hoping Katherine will be able to read it; my Latin, such as it is, isn't up to the task."

Dan closed the little box with care, and Freya hesitated before she sat down again. "Look, I know it seems inconsistent, but each time it happens"—she paused, and gathered herself—"these . . . visions—I don't know what else to call them—grow stronger. More vivid. I see and hear more; more detail, that is."

Dan answered the implied question with a nod, though he did not speak.

She leaned forward. "And they happen either when I'm here alone or if I touch you. Or when you touch me, but not always." She inspected her hands. *Slow down.* "It doesn't work with anyone else, Dan. Not your father, not Katherine—just with you." She muttered the last words to her fingers before she looked up.

He was staring at her. She couldn't read his expression.

"I feel like an idiot, trying to put this stuff into words. They can't just be hallucinations. You see them too." She heard herself pleading.

Dan sighed, a long exhale. "It is hard to understand, certainly, or even believe, but I came willingly to this house, did I not?" The ghost of a smile.

He was making her work for this conversation, but Freya was more practiced talking about feelings than Dan was; perhaps that was fair. She said, pensively, "I thought I was going crazy. I was going to ring my mum and ask if we had schizophrenics in the family."

"Hmmm. Always a possibility, I suppose." Was he amused? Freya could not tell.

"We should deal with this systematically, eliminate unlikely explanations one by one." Sturdy Scots reductionism—a way of denying his own fears about insanity.

Freya shifted in her chair. "How? It's *all* so unlikely."

Dan said carefully, "Well, we should experiment. Find out what makes it happen. For instance . . ."

He pushed his chair back and walked around the perimeter of the table until he was standing beside her. "If I do this . . ." He picked up one of Freya's hands—she did not resist as he turned it over—and the tingle was a clamor *inside* her head now, but nowhere else.

"Do you see anything, Freya?"

She shook her head. "You?"

Dan frowned. "No. Give me your other hand."

Freya did what he asked.

"Stand up." He helped her to her feet with a slight tug. She stood in front of him. Dan was a head taller than she, and one part of her, that small part that remained detached, saw tension as the muscles moved in the column of his throat.

"It's waiting for something." Her words were a nervous blurt.

Dan dropped Freya's hands and rocked back a step. "For what?"

She rubbed her eyes. "Oh, I don't know. It's just . . . a sense. But what's *it*, anyhow?"

He said, lightly, "Tomorrow is another day, there's no hurry. I'll away to my couch of dreams." He gave her a rueful smile with a bit of mischief in it, and the severe lines on his face were transformed. He looked young suddenly.

Freya tried not to stare. *So, you are human and quite nice when you want to be.* "Good night, Dan. No nightmares now."

He shook his head. "The couch and I shall keep them at bay by main force. We're famous for it, we Scots. Wrestling with the Boggart."

They both laughed. That was a first.

CHAPTER 22

A<small>ND THIS</small> was with the crucifix?" Katherine would not acknowledge the little spurt of jealousy.

"Yes—that's what Dad's notes say."

The lead box lay open between them on Michael's desk.

Katherine extracted the little packet of vellum. "This certainly is a surprise."

"But interesting. Dad didn't have time to translate the manuscript and—"

The librarian interrupted. "It's in Latin."

"Yes. Not my forte, I'm sorry to say, and I was hoping that you . . ."

Katherine's expression changed. She looked much more cheerful. "You'd like me to translate it?"

Freya nodded. "If you can. Only if it's not too much trouble."

Not too much trouble. Katherine eyed the little manuscript. "I can, and I'd be delighted—thank you for trusting me." Her eyes filmed abruptly.

Freya was uncertain what to do. She put a hand on Katherine's shoulder; after a moment, the librarian covered it with her own and sniffed. "Silly of me." Awkwardly she patted Freya's hand. "Coffee, I think you said, then I'll get started."

It was the perfect day for digging, radiant and warm but not hot. A soft wind set the seed heads nodding as Freya led Dan toward the girl's grave site.

The tent she'd rigged was still securely pegged and, as she lifted up one side, Dan's eyes widened. *"Blunt force trauma,* as they say in the crime shows." He pointed at the skull.

Freya nodded. "Yes, poor girl—well, I think it's a girl. A violent death, but I don't think it's contemporary." A slightly breathless laugh.

"Did you put the flowers around the grave?" Dan looked at Freya curiously.

"Yes. Unprofessional, I know." She climbed down into the excavation. "I hope you don't mind, but I want to bag up the bones so I can take them back to the house for study later. Can you pass the ziplock bags and the bucket of brushes down?"

"Happy to help."

She smiled at him, shading her eyes as he passed the tools down. "All right, that would be great. The skull will be tricky to lift. We could start with that if you like."

Dan smiled his crooked smile. "If I am to be of use, I shall need your hand."

Freya saw what he meant—a big admission.

"Okay." Expecting the thunderbolt, she still reached up to brace Dan while he half-slid, half-scrambled to the bottom of the trench. They were both breathless as he found a steady place to stand.

"Daniel, I've worked it out." The morning sun was a corona for Freya's head.

He squinted, trying to see her in the dazzle of light. "What?"

"It doesn't happen when we're relaxed." She'd been about to say, *When we're happy.*

After a moment, he nodded. Very deliberately he held out his hand. "Let's test the theory."

She gave him a paintbrush, smiling.

The delicate work of bagging up the skeleton had taken a while. The skull was in worse condition than the other bones, and that made it tricky to lift, but Freya was finally satisfied that they'd cleared the grave of all the bones that still existed. And she'd been pleased to find a few scattered beads behind the top of the spinal column. Amber was not as good as coins with an actual date, or pottery, but at least they were contemporaneous to the burial.

"So, what now?" It was definitely easier to talk to each other this morning, and Dan even accepted Freya's help to pull him out of the trench without comment.

"We can come back for her later. She'll be quite safe here." Freya placed the bags of bones under the plastic sheeting and carefully repegged the edges of the tent. "I want to show you something else. I've been digging up there." She pointed toward the ring stones.

"Where the crucifix was found?"

"Yes." Freya sauntered beside him at an easy pace.

Dan was not sure if he was grateful for her consideration. People said you felt an amputated arm or leg long after it was gone; he felt, all the time, the shape of his amputated independence.

She paused at the edge of the outer ring of stones. "They're something, aren't they?" She patted the nearest monolith. "But why won't you talk to me?"

"You'd not understand their jokes."

Freya wheeled. "How do you know?" But she smiled at him. "Dad dug here, and he wrote about looking for an important grave site in this area. He thought it was linked to what he was seeing."

"Seeing?" Dan's tone sharpened.

She faced him. "From the time he found the crucifix, he saw them too."

Dan frowned. "Them? What them?"

Freya said softly, "The people we see, Dan. We've never really talked about that, not properly: if you and I see the same things?"

Unconsciously, he backed away just a step or two. "What do you want me to do, Freya?"

"Try to tune in. I don't know—follow your instincts."

"Ah." That fugitive smile. "And what shall you do?"

"I, Daniel Boyne, shall continue to dig." She pointed to her trench. "I found pottery shards here the other day—high-status ware. Might even be Roman."

He looked dubious. "A long way from home."

She laughed. "I meant Roman Era, though it's a puzzle why it would be north of Hadrian's Wall. But it could be an offering vessel, and there might be more material to find. Why don't you just look around—get a sense of the place."

"I've never been good at sensing things."

"*Things* have changed, Dan. Just . . . try." Freya nodded and clambered down into her trench. Soon she was absorbed. More shards, perhaps a different pot with higher sides and . . .

"Freya, come and have a look."

Her head popped up.

At the other side of the inner circle of stones, Dan was standing on a patch of ground where the grass was different—shorter, much less dense.

"It might be nothing." His tone was neutral.

She brushed soil from her knees and hurried over. Dan was holding a long metal spike. He offered it to her. "Push down—the earth's quite soft."

Freya sank the spike into the soil. It went down easily, as if through fudge, then the metal hit something. "Stone."

He nodded. "Feels like it."

"Could just be stone-stone?"

"Maybe, but it's big. I've tested quite an area with the spike. I think the object's long but not so wide." Dan swept his arms out to indicate dimensions. "You asked me to trust my instincts." He grinned.

She flashed a wary smile. *Two speeds this one, stop and go.*

It took more than an hour to fully uncover the stone. A rough oblong, the slab was more than two meters long, less broad, and at least three handspans thick. But it was worked stone—the marks of tools were still visible on the edges.

Dan leaned on a shovel at the bottom of the pit they'd dug and stared at the earth they'd shifted—it was piled up on the edges of the trench. "Maybe it's from the Abbey buildings."

"What's it doing here, then?" Freya stared gloomily at what they'd found; stone, after all, was just stone. "Hang on." She brushed an edge and stared up the nearest monolith. "Does this look like similar material to you—to the uprights, I mean?"

Dan glanced around the inner circle. "Maybe, but I'm a ship-wright, not a stonemason."

"But could this be one of the stones? The monks might have pushed it over and . . ."

"It's not long enough to be one of the uprights." Dan's tone was reasonable.

Freya's enthusiasm flickered out. "You're right." She scrambled out of the trench and stared again at the circle. "You know, the odd thing is there's no offering stone. Dad noticed that."

"No offering stone?" Dan was weary—aching from all the digging and muscles long unused.

"No altar, if you like."

He pointed to a corner of the stone block, then brushed away the remaining soil. "Have a look at this."

Freya stared at the shallow carving. "An equal-armed cross inside a circle." She sat back. "Christian."

He nodded. "But it's the same symbol."

She was confused. "As what?"

"The lead box. Does that not have the same device on its lid?"

"So maybe this is just a spare bit of stone the monks used for practice." She was trying to be pragmatic.

"You said it yourself. If it's from the Abbey, how come it's all the way out here? A long way to carry something this big." Dan grimaced. He could feel the stone's mass in his muscles. "I'd not have liked to try, that's for sure."

"Hmmm. Why *would* you go to the trouble of carting it so far?" Freya sighed. "So many unanswered questions, who'd be an archaeologist?" She wiped her face with the tail of her shirt, smearing sweat and dirt across her cheeks.

Dan grinned.

"What?" Freya was suspicious.

"Nothing. You were saying?"

She stretched her back, a bit deflated. "It would be so great to lift the slab, see if there's anything underneath, but not today. I need to document while we still have light." She'd have to take Katherine and Dan back to Portsolly in the morning—they both had jobs—and she couldn't move such a massive stone without help.

Dan tried to recapture their earlier, positive tone. "Should it be covered when you're finished?"

Freya nodded. She picked up the bundle of ranging poles and slung the digital camera around her neck. "This won't take long. Then we can see if Dad had any more field tents—or a tarp, if we're desperate . . ."

There was smoke coming from the kitchen chimney as Freya and Dan trudged back toward the house.

"Katherine must have lit the stove; that's nice of her."

Dan nodded. "A bath—now there's a thought."

Freya said, dreamily, "Seconded, and that first beer won't touch the sides."

Dan nodded. They both sped up.

Freya was quite merry as she opened the door and clattered down the stairs. "Hello. Anyone home?"

Katherine called out from the big room at the front. "In here."

"You have first go at the bath, Dan." Freya headed across the kitchen as her guest negotiated the stairs behind her.

"I could start looking for a tarp if you like? Have a bath after that," he replied.

"Okay, thanks. I don't think there's anything else in the barn, but you could see if I've missed anything, I guess."

Dan, having reached the bottom, stifled a sigh and began the trudge back up.

Sitting at Michael's desk, Katherine was waiting. She was wearing white cotton gloves, and arranged around her, in small piles, were leaves from the tiny manuscript.

"Hello, Freya." Her face was faintly flushed.

"You've found something." Freya knew, she just *knew*.

Katherine nodded. Her voice quavered the smallest amount. "When your father began to dig the grounds of the Abbey methodically, he would often ask me to research particular details of religious life for him. That was some years after we first met, of course." She did not look at Freya. "There was so much that was interesting in the old monastic chronicles—the histories of the times in which the writers lived, the rules that governed monastic life, all sorts of things—and I was always delighted to help. In fact, the work became a passion of mine. However, the marginalia, the little personal comments in the margins of the manuscripts, were most compelling of all to me. Real voices, personal opinions of actual people, and all so long ago—many of them frank and quite touchingly direct. And, too, with practice I found I could identify the broad time frame of a particular writer by the style and form of what was on the manuscript page—the way the letters were formed, for instance, whether the text was large or small." She paused, then said, cautiously, "On that basis I am inclined to believe that this manuscript might be placed from around the end of the eighth century to mid–ninth century, Common Era. And it was not written by a monk."

Freya frowned. "Who, then? A layperson?"

Katherine shook her head decisively. She tapped one of the little piles. "This was written by a nun, and it's a diary of sorts."

"But . . ." Freya pulled a chair up beside Katherine. "The diary form wasn't invented in the West until hundreds and hundreds of years afterward—if you're right about the date."

The librarian handed her a single page. "Yes. And only men wrote diaries even then, because they were more likely to be literate and women were not. This is as far as I've got. My notes are in brackets."

"What lovely writing you have."

Katherine colored with pleasure. "A lost art."

But Freya hardly heard the librarian's answer, for rising off the page, like smoke, like mist, was the essence of a voice not heard for more than a thousand years.

FEAST OF PRISCA [JANUARY. VIRGIN
MARTYR OF THE EARLY CHURCH.]

Cold today. Ink frozen again. Many ill with flux and lying in caldarium but no meat to eat—this is a bad winter. I have chilblains, and Brother Abbot says it is punishment from God for my rebellious [disobedient?] *heart. I am ordered to confess my sin in Chapter before my brothers and sisters.* [Double monastery? Celtic Church, therefore?] *I will do your penance gladly, Lord, but would be grateful for warm hands, for it is hard to grind the colors with cold fingers. I have the curse of Eve today, my belly gripes, and there is very little linen.* [The writer must be a young woman and unusually frank.]

Freya met Katherine's glance. They were both breathing rapidly.

FRIDAY FAST.

Most dear God, may I serve you better. I do not like
herring, but it is your bounty, and I am unworthy. Still
cold in Scriptorium, but today I have learned to make
a good green from salts of copper. Perhaps that will
please my brothers. [Why was a woman permitted in
a scriptorium, in company with monks?]

Why indeed? wondered Freya.

PURIFICATION OF THE VIRGIN.

Coarse wool is hard to bear, but I have no shift—penance.
Mother——[name hard to read] *says acceptance of my*
faults is an important task for me. She helps me pray,
and we ask for strength so that I may withstand my own
nature. Gathered oysters for Brother Vidor. Shells shall be
used to mix colors for God's work here. My feet still numb
from wading in the cove at dawn. Sea very cold. I saw my
friend. We did not speak.

Freya put the page down. She was pale.

Katherine leaned forward. "Do you agree she's a nun?"

Freya gazed at her unseeing. "Yes, I think she must be—except
for the reference to 'my friend.' Nuns aren't supposed to have personal relationships, are they? But this is the first time I've heard,
or anyone's heard, a woman's authentic voice emerge this early
from a convent. That's just . . ." The word was hard to find. "It's
eerie."

Katherine nodded. "And, if this is a double foundation, it's
most likely a pre-Conquest monastery of the Celtic Church. The
symbol on the lead box may therefore be roughly contemporaneous with the manuscript."

Freya paced the room but stopped with a jolt. "Would you like to take the manuscript back to Portsolly tomorrow, Katherine? You could translate the rest of it during the week."

"Would I like to?" Katherine's smile was fervent. "It's a privilege. An honor."

Freya said quickly, "And maybe you could come over here again next weekend? Would that be enough time?"

"Certainly, I should like that. And I can do more in the next hour or so too."

"Excellent. I just need to cover the dig at the stones. Dan's looking for a tarp."

Katherine was already absorbed as she reached for the next tiny piece of vellum. She said absently, "Try the undercroft. Michael stored most things there . . ."

The beam from Dan's flashlight splayed over the surface of the monolith. "Runes?"

"Yes, but I can't read them. Frustrating."

Dan grinned. "You hide it well. But what about the other symbols?"

Freya lifted a shoulder irritably. "I don't know. No one does if they're Pictish." She was standing quite close to Dan; he smelled comfortably sweaty, and she must have as well. He didn't seem to mind. "Their language has never been deciphered, though some symbols crop up all over the place in this part of the world. Serpents, double disks"—she pointed—"and one I find really odd—a hand mirror." She smiled. "Ah, vanity; human nature doesn't seem to change much."

Dan stared at the enigmatic stone pillar. "I agree. We're them, they're us."

Freya held her lamp higher and turned a full circle. "What I don't understand—among so many things—is why the monks would allow this thing to stay here. A Pagan monument." She held her lamp higher. "Findnar is full of mysteries, that's what Dad said."

Dan eyed the Compactus. Beside it, beneath the windows, was a bank of low cupboards. Gray-painted metal, they were anonymous, in the style of locker rooms all over the world. "Might solve a small one if we look over there. The tarps?"

"Okay." Freya strode to the first cupboard. It was unlocked, and on the shelves were neat coils of rope, aluminum tent pegs and, best of all, several groundsheets with rings inserted in the edges.

"Yes!" She hauled out a folded piece of plasticized cloth and gathered armfuls of pegs. "This looks big enough. I'll rig it over the stone in case it rains tonight." She took the staircase at a run.

Dan called after her, "Stone melts, does it?"

From the kitchen he heard her shout, "No, but if there's anything underneath, water percolates and . . ."

A moment later, and her abashed face appeared around the door upstairs. "Sorry, Dan, that was rude. Take your time."

He did not answer.

Spooked, Freya hurried down the stairs. "Dan?"

"Here I am."

Freya could see his light now, swaying and bobbing as he limped toward her.

"Just wanted to explore a bit more. Have you seen the wall, by the way?"

"What wall?"

Dan waved the flashlight. "Come and have a look." He was leading her away from the stairs into the dark. "It may be nothing, but . . ." He pointed the light. "This bit is different from . . ." He swiped the beam in an arc. "From this. See?"

Perhaps it was the way the flashlight played with the plastered surface, perhaps she imagined it, but there seemed to be a bulge in the wall. Freya nodded slowly. "Something's been blocked up."

Fear congealed in her chest. "I'd better do the tarp while there's still light, though. Have that bath, Dan. Back soon." She waved cheerily this time as she hurried away.

But Dan wasn't fooled. Before he climbed the stairs, he turned and looked back. Freya had asked him to follow his instincts, and he had. Twice. Down here there was something. But what?

The owl was hunting again. As Freya trudged back across the meadow, she watched it quarter the ground beneath its wings.

She didn't know if she liked the owl—there was something alien in those great unblinking eyes, that golden, vacant stare.

She stopped. The bird was behaving strangely—it seemed to be flying backward and forward in a regular pattern.

Squinting in the half-light, Freya watched as the owl fluttered down and landed on the apex of the field tent. Wings neatly folded, it turned its head all the way around to stare at her.

Freya called out. "Impressive—very *Exorcist*."

The owl ignored her. It launched into the air, heading toward the rookery. *That's right. Go rob a nest. Knock yourself out.*

Freya sighed and walked on. She was weary, and the ring stones were farther away than they looked—everything always was on Findnar. She wasn't enjoying the thought of rigging a large tarpaulin single-handed in a rising wind either, but once she arrived beside the pit, training took over. With a fair bit of swearing, she finally outmaneuvered the flapping plastic and pinned it to the earth.

Arms in the air, Freya shouted, "Thank you!" Then, on impulse, she bowed to the stones before she marched off toward Compline. "See you all soon. Be good." *Each step, and I'm closer to hot, hot water . . .*

As she reached the site of the girl's grave, Freya stopped to collect the bagged skeleton and strike the tent. The sun was sinking into a furnace of scarlet and gold on the western horizon, and she paused to admire the dying of the day, turning for one last look at the ring stones.

Something moved in the inner circle. Fluttered. A figure.

This time there was no mist and no ambiguity. This time, someone really *was* standing there—a woman—and it wasn't Katherine. This person wore a dress of some kind—a dull red color. No. Not a dress, a tunic. That's what fluttered.

"Hello." Freya started forward. "Hi." The stranger was too far away to hear. Freya waved.

The girl—if it really was a girl—was standing close to the center of the inner ring.

She was standing right beside the excavation.

Freya began to run toward the stones.

CHAPTER 23

BEAR WATCHED from a distance. He always watched from a distance now.

Being a lay servant, he stood at the back of the church, but he could see Signy lying facedown before the altar with the other girls.

He had not been able to change her mind. Now, in the blustering spring weather, as drafts rushed through the cold church, it would be accomplished. Today Signy would take vows. She would become a postulant and then, in time, she would be made a nun.

As the moon had waned last night, there had been one final, pointless conversation.

"You know why I am doing this, Bear." She had been patient with him, as if he were a stubborn child. "I did not resist temptation. The life of our baby was taken to show me the sin of what happened between us—and that the Gods in the stones are false. It is for me to make amends now and serve my brothers and sisters, and the Lord, as faithfully as I can."

At first he had tried to reason with her. "But what will you serve, Signy? A tortured man dying slowly so that you can drink his blood, eat his flesh?" His voice had risen. "We are not savages." He'd grabbed her wrist when she tried to turn away. "Look at this scar. We two are joined by blood—our own and that of our child. Please. *Please.* This place just wants slaves, willing fools who cannot see the truth."

Signy had shaken her head. Dark circles under her eyes told of deep suffering. "I will pray for you at the vigil tonight, Bear, and

I shall pray, also, that you may be healed and find peace—as I pray for the soul of our daughter." Her voice had cracked. That was something, some indication that she still felt emotion. His Signy.

But the girl in the black kirtle who lay before the altar today was no longer his Signy.

Last night, though, his Signy had faltered when she said, "I must give back your gifts, Bear. I can take nothing that is not sacred into the convent." And she had handed him the little ship, then the knife.

Neither could speak. At last he'd said, "But this they cannot take from you." He'd marked the little lead box with a cross.

So many weeks of winter work with only a rushlight to see by, but he'd made the box and the crucifix that lay inside. Jet from the cliff formed the body of the cross, smoothed and burnished with sand and pinned with a tiny nail of copper, and the crucifix was small enough to hang between Signy's breasts. Something of him would go with her, if she would allow it.

Hesitant, she'd taken his present in her hands.

Bear groaned, and some of the monks turned. They frowned at him, but he did not care. *That girl, the one on the end, she's mine, not yours.* That was what he wanted to say. But it was not true. Not now, for last night he'd destroyed their last moment together.

As he tied the crucifix around Signy's neck, he'd taken her face between his hands. "I brought you back from the dark kingdom, once. I gave you life. Do not take mine away."

"No!"

Signy had pushed him, and he'd fallen hard against the wall of the church. A heap of rags on the cold earth, he'd watched her run.

Perhaps she had heard him. Perhaps, as she lay there before the altar, his words were in her head still. "You are not a nun, Signy. You'll never be a real nun. Don't lie to yourself."

He'd pulled himself up against the rigid wall, the chilled, cut stone. Fury swamped sorrow as he remembered. This building was the symbol of all that had been taken from him, and yet this

Christ, the ghost they all worshipped here, had been only a man—they all said that. How could he also be a God?

One by one, the postulants to be were commanded to stand before Abbot Cuillin. Gunnhilde stepped forward to attend them, emotional as any bride's mother. In the sisters' dormitory, Bear knew their worldly clothing would be stripped away and their hair cut to stubble. Rerobed in postulants' habits, the four would be dedicated to a God none of them would ever see, and Signy would never, willingly, look at him again.

Waiting for the girls to return, Abbot Cuillin censed the altar. All his brethren knelt, heads bowed, and beat their chests in accusation of sin.

Bear snorted. How much iniquity could be accomplished on a gruel of oats, barley, and seaweed? He would not watch what was to come, he could not.

Emerging from the church like a badger from its hole, Bear blinked in the cool spring light. He knew what he'd left behind. Darkness. The church was lit only by lamps of seal oil and odorous tallow candles, and this was the frightened, haunted world that Signy, the bright, sweet friend of his youth, would now inhabit willingly.

Bear ran toward the meadow where the barley was a green fuzz of urgent life. The rising swell of voices followed him, and then the bell began; the service of consecration was finished.

He leaned on his staff. It was done. Signy was lost to him.

Bear turned and stared at the circle of stones. They had buried their daughter there, and now he would make her soul an offering, the ship he had made for her mother.

CHAPTER 24

I N THE two years since her profession as a novice, much had changed for Signy, and that was because she had been singled out by Brother Anselm, the monk who ran the Scriptorium.

One evening in the Abbey kitchen, after she had finished pounding dried fish for tomorrow's break-fast, she was told to rake the ash and reset the fire for the morning.

But Signy found a piece of good charcoal among the spent coals, and sinfully, she hoarded it. Every day between Vespers and Compline, a little personal time was permitted, and this particular evening Signy decided she would draw just to vary the tedium of prayers, work, and sleep. She liked to draw when no one was watching.

In the nuns' chamber, her sisters were bent over sewing and handwork at a table. Signy withdrew to the end of the room, farthest from the lamps, and faced the wall. There she prostrated herself as if in private contemplation. From the back, in this dim corner, it would look as if she was telling the rosary, but surreptitiously she had begun to sketch on the flagged floor, her face against the stone.

After a time, she knelt to inspect what she had drawn.

"Now, what are you doing here, Sister?" Brother Anselm had been made the chaplain of the novices recently, and it was his habit to join his charges just before the final service of the day.

"Nothing, Father." Signy scrambled up and tried to move one foot surreptitiously beneath the skirts of her habit to scuff the images she'd made.

Anselm signed a cross over Signy's bent head. As was proper, the novice was discomforted at being directly addressed, yet he had known her since she was just a small, lost heathen. His heart had been warmed to see her slowly turn from paganism to the one true God.

"Nothing? But you are always so industrious." The monk waved the girl aside, expecting to see a work of piety from her busy fingers.

There were faces sketched on the stone flags. A likeness of Sister Gunnhilde, her age and kindness captured in just a few quick lines, the features of the youngest of the novices, Witlaef, tenderly displayed as the shy child she was.

"But . . . these are secular images." Brother Anselm's confusion turned to concern. "Rub them out, Sister. Quickly. You are not to speak of this." Anselm stood in front of the novice as Signy swiped the images away with the hem of her habit. He raised his voice and addressed the others to distract them. "Sisters, it is time to join your brothers in the chapel. The bell will shortly ring for Compline."

Processing out behind the nuns and the other novices, Signy reflected on her luck at being discovered only by Anselm, and also on her perverse instinct for implicit disobedience.

Much was risked by drawing what she saw, the world of everyday monastery activity. But some small flicker of defiance still burned in her heart, try though she might to smother it. It was hard to be mindlessly, gratefully obedient hour after hour, but on the day she had miscarried her child, she had turned away from her previous life. By this act she had accepted the power of Christ and His mother into her life, and with that came the obligation to atone for her sin with Bear. Yet sometimes it was hard, and sorrow for all she had lost made the old life beguiling. Signy struggled to fight such thoughts, struggled to banish Bear's image from her mind, and that of the tiny, perfectly formed baby who had never breathed. Her nameless daughter.

Perhaps, one day, God would tell her when she had suffered enough for what had been done.

"In the Scriptorium, you will work behind this screen." Anselm pointed to several large panels of woven bog willow. In one corner of the copying hall between two unshuttered windows, a tiny room within the greater space had been created.

It was four days since Anselm had discovered her drawings, and even now, Signy found it hard to believe what he said to her. "Our blessed Abbot has agreed that you will be the Scriptorium servant. In silence and by my instruction, you will learn to prepare ink and colors for the valuable work that your brothers perform. And, too, if your progress is satisfactory, I shall teach you the preparation of vellum."

Signy had stared at the monk. The words scarcely penetrated. "Me, Father?" Her voice had been a strangled squeak.

Anselm had nodded. What he did not tell the awestruck girl was that, in time, she might also be trained as a copyist.

The Abbot had only reluctantly agreed to Anselm's unusual request, but both men knew there was little real talent among the Scriptorium monks. And they were ambitious. If Findnar was to become the seat of learning they believed it should be, holy books must be copied and a library created. Skill, therefore, must be identified and fostered in the Abbey. However, to consider that a girl, a postulant, might be trained for such tasks was daring and radical, and a potential cause for scandal.

"Our Abbot was naturally most concerned that the work of the Scriptorium might be disturbed by your presence here. With God's help, we shall guard against that by all means in our power."

Signy had nodded vigorously. "Oh, of course, Father. I would never willingly do such a thing. In Christ's name, I shall do my best, unworthy though that be. I am so grateful; it cannot have been easy to convince our beloved Abbot to allow me this honor." Her eyes had been troubled.

The monk had been moved, for this reply was evidence of genuine humility, but he held up his hand. "You are correct, Sister. It has cost him, and me, many hours of anxious prayer, and so, for a time, you will be in the Scriptorium on sufferance as we continue to pray for the Lord's blessing on this work."

"For how long?" Signy had winced. "Forgive me, dearest Brother, I spoke without thought. I humbly await knowledge of the Lord's will." She had clasped her hands in a tight knot and murmured the apology, properly, to the floor.

Ah, youth. With some nostalgia, Anselm had remembered the impetuosity of that fleeting season. "Our beloved Abbot will inform us both. Meanwhile he has laid down other conditions. Mark them well."

Reverently, Signy had crossed herself and knelt. "Yes, Father. I humbly await his holy instruction."

Anselm had attempted severity. "First, you are never to speak unless addressed by me, or the Abbot himself."

Signy had nodded diligently.

"There is to be no coughing or sneezing—even if you are unwell. The needs of nature must be ignored. Attend to them before entering the writing chamber. You will be at your place immediately after the break-fast, before your brothers, and you may depart only after they have finished and when you have swept and cleaned the copy chamber. The Abbot has most strictly decreed that you will not, at any time, be seen by your brothers here. Or heard."

"Of course, Father. And thank you. I will not let you down." For the chance that was offered, the chance to learn, Signy would have agreed to anything, sacrificed anything.

And at first she was the most menial of assistants.

Gathering oysters so that the shells could be used as paint receptacles, she also dug clay to be dried and ground for earth color and picked plants from which to extract dyes. Then with egg whites, honey, and soot begged from the kitchen, she learned to make ink. The greatest trial was making quills, for Signy was to harvest feathers from living geese—and though they pecked her and beat her with their wings, she became adept at drying and cutting the quills so well that there had never been better writing instruments on Findnar.

Gradually, she was permitted to take on increasing responsibility, including the preparation of vellum from calfskins and goatskins. Signy grew to hate this process, for the lye burned her hands and scraping the hides was tedious and smelly. But the result, once the dried skins had been well burnished, was magical: soft, supple, and fine-surfaced, Signy's vellum was greatly appreciated in the Scriptorium, and Anselm was well pleased. As he had thought, this girl was quick to learn and diligent. And with good reports, Cuillin permitted Signy to continue with her work.

And now there came a remarkable day.

After diligent prayer, Anselm decided to instruct Signy in the formation of letters in the Roman alphabet. If she was ever trusted with copying any part of the holy books, she must learn an acceptable scholar's hand, though he did not expect her to read, just to mimic what she was shown.

Anselm had no idea if Signy could actually master writing. A woman's mind was certainly not the equal of a man's and never would be, but he was curious to pursue the experiment, for he had never had the teaching of a clever girl before. For practice, he supplied her with a piece of slate on which he had written the letters of the Roman alphabet, and he began to instruct her on how to form them.

Once begun on this road, Signy stole all the time she could from her usual chores, and then she had an epiphany. One evening when the monks finished work, she secretly began to search among their manuscripts for the individual letters she now knew, for she was hungry to know how letters became words.

First she worked out the name of Mary, and then Jesus, and

then God. Saying the names out loud, she fixed the images of the letters to the sounds. With growing excitement, she painfully spelled out a series of words; then she composed her first sentence: *Praise God, Jesus, and Mary.*

Over the following months, Signy began to write more and more. Slowly copying prayers at first, and comparing the Latin to its meaning in the Christian language she now spoke, very gradually she began to make sense of both. And as she had once drawn the world around her, she haltingly began to write of what she saw and felt on scraps of vellum in her cubicle. And on one slow day, when Anselm had sent Signy to beg leaves from the Infirmarian's woad plants to make more blue pigment, she dared to visit Laenna's grave.

Signy had not talked to her sister in a long time. Since she was a postulant, every minute of her day was accounted for, and an absence brought trouble. Today, though, she had the luxury of a little time. "I have missed you, Laenna," she said. "I know personal affection is a sin and must be guarded against, but I thought you would like to know that I can read now and write too."

Signy held a scrap of vellum up to the pillow stone; it was covered with her tiny, careful script. "Would you like to know what it says? I wrote it yesterday." She cleared her throat. "Feast of St. Marinus and St. Asterius. Rain since Matins. Very cold. With God's help I found a small patch of chalk in the meadow. Brother Anselm is pleased. He has shown me how to make white pigment for my brothers. After Tierce, I was sent to ask for cabbage and parsley to make green dye. In the garden, I saw my old friend. I did not look at him, but he tried to talk to me. I must confess this. My thoughts led me to sin."

Signy's voice faltered. She stopped reading. "Laenna, do you ever wonder what it would have been like, being a mother? If we were still at home, we might both have our own households now. And babies." She picked at the new weeds among the white pebbles. "If I become a nun, I will never know what that is like.

Not properly." She closed her eyes. That was a lie. She knew what it was like to be a mother, even if so briefly.

"I had better go—they will ring for Sext soon. Next time, it will not be so long, I promise."

Later that day, Anselm put down his brush with a sigh. He had just applied the last morsel of gilding to the final illustration of Luke's Gospel, the Ascension of Christ into Heaven. His task was complete.

Anselm guarded zealously against worldly pride and, for that reason, none had yet seen this work. Brother Abbot would be the first audience for the manuscript, the latest to come from Findnar's Scriptorium, but Anselm felt tired and flat. The ending of something was so often an anticlimax—and a loss.

"Brother Anselm, I must ask your advice." The master of the Scriptorium jumped; the Abbot had arrived, unheralded.

Anselm cleared his throat. "Abbot, I shall give it to you gladly, if that is the will of God." He stood quickly. Was this a good moment to show Abbot Cuillin what he had accomplished?

But Cuillin was staring at the restless sea beyond the windows. He said, absently, "Amen, Brother, to that." The view was obscured by a fleece of mist on the water—only if he squinted could the Abbot see to the far side of the strait.

He was worried. A visitor from the mainland was expected today, a rich merchant from the township that was growing up on the site of the old Pagan settlement. This man had sent a messenger in an impressive ship several days ago. It seemed that the no doubt self-styled Lord Solwaer wished to visit Findnar, but what did he want?

Cuillin sighed. His gaze focused on the top of the cliff where the path to the cove began. At least the new work there—work that he had insisted on and that had involved every able-bodied man on the island—gave him some comfort. A great gate and palisade now shut off the path so that the way down to the cove—and up—might be controlled by the Abbey. Last summer, rumors had reached

Findnar of raiders returning to the North. It had therefore become prudent to arrange protection.

Anselm coughed discreetly, and Cuillin remembered why he was in the Scriptorium. "Brother, glorifying our Lord is our chief task, as you know. And it is in this, particularly, that I need your expert advice. Ten years, forty seasons, will shortly have passed since the raiders burned this island, though Christ's mercy has kept us safe in the time since the comet. Having prayed on the matter most earnestly, I seek your guidance as to how best to mark this anniversary."

Brother Anselm bowed his head reverently. This was an important matter, and St. Luke must wait. "A great honor it is, Abbot Cuillin, to be consulted by you in this way. Have you considered a cross for the church, perhaps? A large and noble one, graced by a likeness of the body of our Lord? Or, perhaps, a Christ in Glory could be created on the wall behind the altar? In Rome, I have heard that holy pictures—very large ones—are made by cutting up myriad tiny pieces of stone, of different colors. Perhaps we might attempt something in that manner? It would certainly be novel."

On such confidential business the men were speaking softly, but Signy had excellent hearing, and the pair were no farther away than the length of her arm. She knew she could be punished for listening to a private conversation, and so, clutching Bear's crucifix, she closed her eyes and began to pray, petitioning God's mother to prevent the words from reaching her ears.

"My thoughts have been similar, Brother. Prayer has told me that such, or similar things, would be acceptable to our Savior, but I am troubled. Who among us has the skill to create such works?"

Signy opened her eyes. Prayer, today, was ineffective. To distract herself, she put her most recent writings in the little lead box and slipped it into a drawstring bag. She looped it to her belt and tried to concentrate on mixing more ink.

Anselm looked grave. He fiddled with the ratty end of the beard that rested on his belly—that was a habit in times of worry and explained why the hair was matted and yet wispy. He worried a lot.

"Our brothers labor diligently; however, their skills are . . ." He said no more as the monks contemplated each of the men in the Scriptorium.

The Abbot ventured a name. "Brother Nicodemus?" Anselm gazed with dispassion on his brother—a ratlike man with a red nose that dripped miserably, even in summer. The Scriptorium Master strove hard to remove unsafe, uncharitable, and possibly personal feelings from the faculties of rational judgment. He shook his head, regretfully. "Brother Nicodemus works hard, it is true. Perhaps, one day, the Lord will place His gracious hand upon our brother's head and vest in him the abilities required for such a project. But until that time . . ."

Cuillin nodded. "Until that time, indeed . . ." With a shared conspiratorial glance, both acknowledged that their brother, though solid, was also stolid. This was a task that required actual talent.

"Brother Paul?" Anselm shook his head.

"Brother Jude?" Again, the veto.

"Brother Martin?" A vigorous and decisive shake this time. Brother Martin, incontestably, was clumsy, and oxlike good nature was not enough. That left only the harried novice who had taken over some of Signy's duties as she was given more responsibility. Peter was just a child, however, and could not be considered.

Cuillin closed his eyes, fingering the beads that hung at his waist. He had hoped God would show him the correct way forward, but that was not to be today. "We shall speak of this more, Brother. I have much to do." Sketching a cross in the cool air, a general-purpose blessing, Cuillin strode away.

Anselm could only bow; there was not time for more.

"Father, may I speak?" A soft voice came from behind the screen. Signy never spoke unbidden—it was as if a spirit had whispered in his ear.

Anselm said, severely, "You have broken a condition of your work, Sister."

Signy murmured, "I know, Brother." Her tone was utterly humble. If Anselm privately reflected that he was far too lenient with this girl, he still sighed. "Very well. In the name of God, Sister, I give you permission."

Signy cleared her throat. "Brother Anselm, I most humbly apologize, but I heard your conversation with Abbot Cuillin. Perhaps I should have told you—"

"Brothers, continue with your work." Anselm knew the monks would listen to this exchange with keen attention. In the distance the mist was breaking up, and he saw a sail on the water. A large ship was beating toward Findnar—the Pagan visitor was near; he had been talked of last night during the personal hour, and there had been a great deal of speculation. Anselm crossed himself. *Lord, defend your flock from evil.* "You may speak, Sister. Quietly and quickly. I am very busy."

Signy lowered her voice so much Anselm had to bend close to hear her. "Father, I know of a person who has the skill you seek. He is a carver, and his work is very beautiful."

Anselm's eyebrows ascended. "I am astonished, Sister. A craftsman, you say?"

The girl swallowed. "Yes, Father. He makes animals, mostly. Seals and birds, horses and dogs too. From whalebone. I have seen them."

Anselm was shocked. Surely one of his monks would not be so profane? "Dear Sister, think carefully of what you are saying. Animals are God's creatures, it is true, but they are without souls and not suitable subjects, therefore, for a man of God. The work of our hands is dedicated to our Lord and what He might require of us, not to luxurious or prideful idleness."

There was silence behind the screen; then a hand appeared, an object hidden in the palm. The fingers uncurled, and there, displayed like a treasure, was a crucifix.

Anselm stared at the object with painful intensity. And then gasped; Christ's face!

"Who made this . . ." Speech deserted him. He wanted to say *abomination*. "Speak." Unwittingly, Anselm raised his voice—and regretted it. Behind him was a sudden perfect silence.

Signy hesitated. She was frightened by the monk's tone. She said, in a whisper, "He is not a monk, Father."

Anselm closed his eyes in pain. This was more than serious for the novice. He said, urgently, "For the good of your soul, name this person."

There was a confused pause. "Bear. It is Bear, Father. He carved the crucifix and gave it to me when I took my first vows."

Anselm hissed a stricken breath. A heathen. Not only had his sister accepted a personal object before consecration to Christ but she was seriously proposing this Pagan, an animal herder who had *already* carved a blasphemous likeness of Christ using his own face, as the creator of an image for their church—a thing that would be sanctified.

There must have been illicit contact between the pair. Anselm was aghast at the images that rushed into his mind. His pretty little protégée now seemed a wanton temptress—Satan's creature—and he had fostered her pride through the vanity of the work he had given her.

Anselm reproached himself bitterly. He must tell the Abbot immediately all that he knew. If Signy's soul was to be saved, that was his clear duty. Penance must be done, severe penance, by both the miscreants—the heathen for omission, his sister for commission. Anselm pulled the screen aside in one violent movement. "Leave the Scriptorium. Go!"

Signy shrank back against the wall; she was terrified. Her once kindly teacher seemed a man possessed by fury as he thrust his face close and hissed, "Pray. Immediately. You and he and that . . ." With horror, he gestured at the crucifix. He would not touch the blasphemous thing. "This is sin. Meeting in secret.

Illicit, *criminal* conversation between you." Anselm would not name the boy and, oblivious to the effect he had on Signy, he was shouting at her now.

The world she had worked so hard to belong to collapsed on Signy's head like an emptied sack of stones. Dazed and shamed, she stood. Every eye in the Scriptorium was on her, and she had the craziest desire to laugh. Shock. The brothers, and she, were stunned by the drama of the moment.

Signy collapsed to her knees; she whispered, "Father, forgive my presumption. I meant no sin against our Lord. I seek to glorify Him as you do and as you have taught me to."

Anselm flinched and his face flushed, a sweating red. She had said the wrong thing, Signy saw that. She said, quickly, "Bear has always been a carver. Just little things, but they come from his love of all of God's creation. I believe his talent is holy, not sinful, and I have not knowingly spoken to him since I was consecrated to our Lord. The crucifix was a gift, that is all, a symbol of holiness, to help guide me on my new path."

"Sister, how can you not know . . ." Words deserted Anselm. He heard the honesty in Signy's voice and saw it in her eyes—it was clear the girl had no idea the carving was blasphemous. *Once a Pagan* . . . But there was nothing to be done. His duty was clear.

He waved toward the Scriptorium door; he would not speak with her. He could not.

In that moment, it felt as if she had been turned to rock. A story she'd heard as a child floated through the roiling chaos; thirteen girls once danced in the light spring air, flouting their parents and the Gods. Unless it was midsummer, nothing danced but the waves or fire. The Sky God and the Sea God punished the blasphemous friends, and they were turned to stone. It was they who stood, black and rigid—God stones now—on the highest part of Findnar. Would she join them today, another outcast who had offended the Gods?

A hardly voiced titter swelled behind Signy as she stumbled

from the Scriptorium, swallowed words breathed out in half-whispers. She heard a smothered laugh, and turning, Signy saw her brothers stare, hands over their mouths, yet their eyes were bright. They were enjoying her abject fall from favor.

Strength flowed back, and Signy raised her head, dropping the leather thong over it. The Christ with Bear's face hung once more between her breasts. She was white as the limed walls, but fury kept her strong as she walked away.

CHAPTER 25

THE EVENING had stretched and mellowed beside the fire in the big room. After dinner—fettuccine with leftover sausage, chili, garlic, and tomatoes, plus the last of the beer—Katherine retrieved a sheet of paper from the desk. "More translation," she said. "Shall I read it?"

Freya poked the fire energetically. Staring into the flames, she nodded.

Katherine settled into Michael's chair. She'd carried it from the kitchen into the big room.

Dan glanced from one blank face to the other. Where had the tension come from?

Katherine cleared her throat. "So, as before, I've arranged the statements according to the feast days the writer mentions. The Annunciation of the Virgin falls at the end of March, and this is what the writer says.

" '*My sisters are jealous. Except for Mother Gunnhilde, none speak to me now, even in the personal hour. I am lonely, but I assist with materials for the new manuscript that is being prepared, the Book of Revelation, or the Apocalypse, which tells of the end-times.*'

"The next is about a month later. 'Mark the Evangelist'; the entries become quite short now. '*I saw my friend in the field after Tierce. He was with the sheep. He waved, but I did not wave back. He looks so unhappy.*' "

Dan flashed a dry glance at Freya. "A nun, you say?" She shrugged uneasily.

Katherine looked over her glasses. "And this is the last for today, only a few lines. St. Breaca; that falls at the beginning of June. *'I showed my teacher the crucifix. I will be.'* The next word is obscured. *Punished*, perhaps?" Katherine hoped the word was *punished*, and not something worse. "It continues: *'The Abbot has ordered it.'* "

Dan might have made a joke, but he did not.

"The vellum is damaged here, but then the text continues: *'Why is this God so cruel?'*" In the uncertain light, Katherine's eyes were dark. "I think there must have been a tragedy."

Dan glanced at Freya. "And we'll never know what happened." She nodded absently, sipping the last of her beer. Dan said, lightly, "What did they do to naughty nuns in those days?"

Freya shivered. Katherine looked at her sharply. "Are you cold?"

Dan stood. "Take my chair. You'll be warmer by the fire."

Freya clamped both arms to her sides, but that did not stop the tremors. "I'm okay. Truly."

Katherine paused, then said, "Time for bed, I think. I'll leave you both to the fire."

Freya forced a yawn. "I'd forgotten about digging muscles." She got up, gathered plates and glasses. "Night, Dan. Hope you sleep better tonight."

He half-rose. "I could give you a hand with the washing up."

Freya hesitated. *Would it help to tell him?* But Dan was eyeing the couch. She twitched a smile. "No need. Won't take a minute in the morning. Good night, and thanks for your help today—we accomplished a lot."

Dan stretched. "Surprisingly, I enjoyed the digging, I really did. But after that I won't move, trust me. Nice to sleep by the fire."

Light seeped through the uncurtained window, and Freya woke with a start. Lying in the narrow bed, heart running like a stag, she listened to the voices in her head.

You hardly know this man or her. Katherine. Be careful—there's much of value on Findnar. She will know about the treasures; maybe he does too.

Why is he here, really? Just because you asked him? He wants something, something he's not telling you. Another kind of time on Findnar? How stupid is that. Hectoring, even vicious.

"But it's true. Something's going on here!" Why was she suddenly so frightened? She had thought it would be better with people in the house. Was it the numb anguish of the last diary entry? That hit like a hammer, still.

Freya swung her legs from under the duvet. Something moved behind her; she felt the air displaced. She whipped around. Nothing. *Breathe. Just breathe.*

She fumbled for clothes in the half-dark. They were on the floor somewhere—she'd been too tired to put them on the chair last night and dropped them where she stood. T-shirt, jeans, hooded top. That was enough.

Monday had become a cold, gray day. Behind the controls of the cruiser as they crossed the strait, Freya could not think and, it seemed, could not feel, but she could sense it: darkness, coming closer, moving faster. And tonight she would be alone, with a whole week to wait before she had company on the island again.

The craft bumped over the bones of the waves. "Sorry!" Freya called over her shoulder.

Katherine and Dan were sitting together in the body of the little vessel, prey to the flying water.

Why hadn't she talked to Dan about the girl she'd seen? *Concentrate.*

Freya throttled the engine back, ready to motor past the breakwater. Soon they'd enter the harbor, and the waking world would claim them. Normal life. Hers had been normal once, too, only last week.

She nudged the cruiser toward the quay. This bit, at least, was easy.

"There you are." Walter was waiting for them. "I was starting to worry." He was overjovial.

"Catch the rope, Dad."

With effort, Dan stood up to help Katherine. "Careful, it's slippery."

"I can manage, Dan. Thanks very much for inviting me, Freya." The delivery was light as Katherine clambered from the boat. "I'll let you know how I get on with the rest of the diary. Looking forward to next weekend already." A friendly smile, and she strode away.

Dan tried not to look surprised.

Freya said, too quickly, "I was meaning to ask, but forgot. Would you like to come back, too, Dan? I can pick you both up same time, same place next Saturday. I'd really appreciate your help again."

Dan nodded. "Fine," he said, with no expression.

Walter looked from face to face. Freya, usually so vivid, seemed drained of life. Dan, of course, was much as he always was. Taciturn. No change there. He smothered a sigh.

As Freya pulled her pack on, Dan gestured. "Like a hand?"

She shook her head. "I can manage. Thanks." Edging around him, she went to step over the fish guts left by an untidy fisherman on the wharf steps. The stench hit her. *Like a corpse.* Shocked, she stumbled.

Dan reached to help. "Careful!"

She avoided his hands just as Walter nudged the guts into the water. "Very bad manners—you nearly slipped," he said.

"But I didn't." Freya arranged her face into a smile as she raised a hand. "Thanks, though."

Father and son watched her stride away among the crowds on the quay. Walter waved, Dan did not.

Walter turned to his silent son. "So, good weekend?"

CHAPTER 26

BROTHER ABBOT?"

Anselm knocked timidly on the door of Cuillin's cell. It was, he knew, as sparse as his own.

"In the name of God, enter."

A prie-dieu was set beneath the unshuttered window, for Cuillin was known to spend much of each night in prayer assisted by use of the discipline. Anselm's back twitched at that thought. A bitter east wind blew most nights in spring; couple that with self-inflicted injury and he could only wonder at his brother's stoic piety.

"Yes, Brother?" Cuillin suppressed impatience. He did not relish being disturbed, and in the refectory below waited Solwaer, the visitor from the mainland, with a numerous entourage. On his instructions, they had all been provided with mead, barley bread, and cheeses, and told the Abbot would join them shortly. In his very bones, Cuillin suspected the man wanted something he could not, in all conscience, supply. Why else would he have come? Politics did not come naturally to the Abbot of Findnar.

"Brother Cuillin, I would not disturb you except that"—Anselm swallowed—"something most serious has occurred."

Familiar pain began to throb behind Cuillin's eyes. *Lord, bless me with fortitude.* "What concerns you, Brother?"

Anselm's doom-laden expression deepened. "Sin, Brother Abbot. Of the flesh. Congress between a novice and a lay servant of the Abbey and, most heinous of all, blasphemy."

249

Cuillin was astonished. "Brother, these are most serious charges. Whom do they concern?"

"The novice Signy, Brother."

Cuillin closed his eyes. It seemed he had been waiting for this day, with dread, for years. "And with whom was this sin committed?" he asked. There could be only one answer.

"Bear, Lord Abbot."

The weight of the silence that followed was tangible. It oppressed them both.

"And the blasphemy?"

Anselm struggled the words out. "A crucifix. The man carved it for her, a present, she said. He used his own face as the model of our Lord's. I would have brought it to you, but I did not like to touch so profane an object."

"His own face?" Cuillin blanched. Christ with a scarred face. A horror, demonic. He waved dismissal. "The girl is to go to the chapel and stay there. Send Gunnhilde. Our sister must watch that the girl does not run away." He could not bring himself to say the name of the sinner.

Anselm crossed himself. "It shall be done." He hesitated. "Before God, I feel responsible."

Cuillin's eyes were bleak. "And so you are. She, that . . . Pagan"—he mouthed the word as if it were a curse—"was in your care."

Miserably, the monk bowed his head. The Abbot was right. Anselm knew that his flesh was very weak and that the penance he deserved would be severe—he dreaded that—but he did not dare imagine what might happen to Signy. He cared about the child still, and that was double suffering.

The door closed softly.

Cuillin knelt at the prie-dieu. Despairing, he asked, "Why, Lord, did you send us the heathen children? They have brought nothing but upset and confusion to this holy place and to your servant. Tell me what to do, I beg." He sank his face in his hands.

Sometimes, in darkness, there was a voice of comfort to be heard, but now there was only silence. Had he been deserted, like Christ, in his own hour of trial?

So, he was alone. And he still had Solwaer to contend with.

It was deep night within the church, but the world outside was close to dawn, close to the time of Matins. Signy was cold. And terrified. And furious.

Barefoot and alone, she knelt on the hard floor just as she had done through the night. Her postulant's habit had been taken away, and she was clothed in the tunic she'd found in her parents' house. Sleeveless, it was no barrier to the frigid air, and she was shamed by its color, remembering how shocked Gunnhilde had been when she'd first seen it. The tunic was also very short on her now, leaving her knees and calves naked.

It had hurt her, very much, that Gunnhilde had disrobed her. Terrified of being shunned, Signy had pleaded with the nun, begged her to leave the habit even if the veil was taken.

But human feeling was a snare of the Devil, this Gunnhilde now truly understood. Too many times she had defended the girl, to the great cost of her community.

And so, Signy ceased to struggle as she was stripped—veil, habit, shift, rope belt, even her sandals were removed, until the novice no longer existed. In her place was a bareheaded savage dressed in red, the color of dried blood, a visible outsider—a Pagan. And this was what the Findnar community would see at Matins this morning. Gunnhilde, deaf to her pleas, had even taken the crucifix and the little lead box. Signy would never see either again.

She heard a rooster crow—night was ending, and it could not be long now. She'd endured the penance meted out by Cuillin but, exhausted and weakened without food, without water, she did not know why. Obedience? That had been one of her vows, and she had accepted it, said the words that bound her gladly, hoping she would please the great and powerful God to whom she had promised herself. In the same spirit, she'd worn the black habit, since that was what He demanded in return for all the rewards she would be given after this life of suffering was ended.

Abbot Cuillin's words echoed in her head. Was it only yesterday she'd lain prostrate before him in front of this same altar? He had said, coldly, that humiliation of the earthly body led the penitent, even such a sinner as she, to God.

In the cold and dark, as she'd gone over his words again and again, Signy had begun to understand something—the truth that lay behind the pious statements.

The Abbot wanted to break her, not for God or for the good of her soul, but because she frightened him. She always had. She'd been born a Pagan and a woman; he did not know how to control her.

"Don't do this, Signy, do not let him win." He was so close, warm breath touched the nape of her neck. Bear. A dark column above her, his face a lighter blur, but she could smell him. Warm, of the earth, of his animals, not the sour, cold reek of the monks in their unwashed wool.

"You must not speak to me, Bear. You must not use my name, for I have given it to God."

"But it is your name, your clan name, called out by your blood father when you were born so that all in your family would know and acknowledge you. These people are not your family or even your clan. What family treats a daughter as they have done?"

Signy was proud, but she was close to breaking. It was true, her parents would ache to see her so crushed.

"Come with me. Now. We can leave together, just as we did all those years ago. I've built a coracle; it's small, but it was made for us, you and me, and they don't know about it."

Was it so easy, then, to run away?

One of his hands found hers. Signy allowed him to help her

stand, but the blood fizzed in her legs after all the time kneeling. It was agony. If he had not held her up, she would have fallen.

"Signy!"

Gunnhilde was standing in the doorway that led to the robing room. She had a full habit draped across her arms: Signy's clothes.

Bear grabbed Signy's wrist. He pulled her toward the west door, the door that led out of the church.

"Wait!" Gunnhilde hobbled after the pair. She was frantic. "I am to help you dress, Sister. Our Abbot has decided he will not further scandalize the community. This is a great mercy, an act of compassion." She held the robes forward with shaking hands. "But if you go with this man, you will prove his worst suspicions true. You will be outcast from our community."

Signy's vision blurred, she swayed.

Bear pulled her against his chest as she crumpled. "Do not listen."

Gunnhilde gasped. "How could you have done this, Bear? After all the kindness of the past."

"Kindness?" Bear laughed. A harsh bray. He shouted at Gunnhilde, shouted at the altar. "You people with your dying God and your stunted lives. Holy? All you see is filth. This is my woman, bound by blood, hers and mine—and ours." His eyes lanced Signy's. He was implacable. "Tell her."

The world spun. Signy did not raise her head. "I will not speak of such things, Bear. I cannot."

Taking her by the shoulders, Bear said urgently. "Real people do speak of such things. Tell the old woman."

Gunnhilde did not know what to do. Very soon the community would enter the church; they might even have heard the shouting, though, mercifully, the walls were very thick. "Signy? Dearest daughter—"

"I am not your daughter." The girl spoke in a whisper; she raised her head. "Bear is right. We are bound by blood—the blood of our daughter."

Gunnhilde wailed. She clamped Signy's habit to her chest. "Have you forgotten all your vows?"

Bear loomed over the old woman. "Not the ones that count."

"What is this? What is this noise?"

Gunnhilde gasped. She darted to Signy. "Kneel. Please!"

"No!" Bear wrenched Signy away.

The Abbot had entered the church. "Sister Gunnhilde?" Cuillin gaped. Shock. Anger came later.

The monk wheeled quickly and bowed to his guest, trying to block the man's view and that of his attendants. He gestured toward the east door.

"Forgive me, Lord Solwaer. Perhaps it will be best if you return to the refectory. We can pray together a little later."

Lord was a courtesy title. If he was seeking conversion for himself and his people—the professed reason for his visit—then Solwaer could be very important to the future of the Abbey. A Christian community on the mainland would help keep Findnar safe, and it would also be a source of wealth, for tithes, in return for spiritual oversight, were always welcome. Of course, Cuillin, having heard Solwaer's self-gilded history, knew that his guest was an opportunist and most likely a liar—a formerly footloose rover who by energy and ruthlessness now dominated a part of the mainland coast. But God called all kinds and conditions of men to His service; perhaps this near brigand could be made a faithful servant of the Church through Cuillin's teaching. A powerful thought.

Solwaer—tough, broad, and the shrewd survivor of a hard life that had already lasted far longer than was deserved—shook his head at the invitation to leave the church. An amiable smile split that brown face. "Abbot, I seek to know more of your ways and the ways of your God. Perhaps I should observe how you rule this island in His name, for you have much to teach me, I think."

There are some men whom it is hard to deny, and Solwaer was one.

Cuillin frowned. To argue would be to diminish his authority;

so be it. Breathing hard, he strode the full length of the nave and, placing his hand on the altar, he glared at the trio before him.

Bear held the Abbot's gaze, eyes wide and empty.

"Novice Mistress, explain what has happened here." With effort, Cuillin spoke quite softly. Bear he ignored. To tell the truth, the gathering rage emanating from the larger, younger man intimidated the Abbot.

Solwaer observed this will-battle with interest.

Trying to force Signy to her knees, Gunnhilde quavered. "Abbot Cuillin, my erring sister has—"

Bear exploded past the old woman and took the altar steps in a leap. He shoved his face into Cuillin's. "You do not own Signy, Monk. She comes with me."

The Abbot picked up the altar cross in both hands. It was heavy, but he held it high, skinny arms twitching with effort. "You are a demon, a curse to this place, and always have been. The novice you speak of has given herself to Christ—you have no rights here."

Solwaer pointed to Bear, and four of his followers leapt; the youth was brought down in a heaving melee.

"Bear!" Signy struggled from Gunnhilde's grasp, but the old woman grabbed her tunic.

The sound of cloth as it rips is very loud in a nearly empty space, and Gunnhilde wailed as the fabric tore; as it fell from Signy's shoulders, the girl's chest was exposed.

Shocked silence was filled by a man's laughter.

It was Solwaer.

Clapping, he strolled forward. "Truly, Abbot, I do not know when I was last so well entertained." He stood over the huddled novice. Perhaps he was trying to assist with the tunic, but Signy knocked his hands away, sobbing.

Solwaer gazed at her benevolently. "It seems, Abbot, that you have troubles with your young people just as I do."

The girl crouched on the floor, cradled by Gunnhilde.

Solwaer sighed. "It's the same everywhere, isn't it? How to keep girls from misbehaving when ungelded bucks sniff around."

Bear, pinioned, growled and spat. Part of his tunic now served as a gag.

Cuillin gathered what rags of composure remained to him. "You have shamed us all!" he bellowed at Signy. "And you . . ." He hissed at Bear, tried to stare him down—at least the girl was crying, that was something—"you are banished from this place and—"

Too late, Gunnhilde saw Bear heave his captors aside and grasp the candle stand beside the altar.

Signy screamed as they both saw the long spike connect with the side of the Abbot's head. Perhaps the tallow lessened the blow, but Cuillin was still swept sideways and down the altar steps. His head hit the floor as he rolled away, the sound between a *pop* and a *thock*.

Solwaer jumped forward and grabbed Bear, the knife in his fist pressed against the young man's windpipe—so hard that a fat, swelling thread of blood appeared.

As Bear struggled, he dropped the candle stand. It fell beside the prostrate body of the Abbot with an outrageous crash just as the door behind creaked open and the community streamed in half-asleep. The first of the monks nearly fell as they tried to avoid Gunnhilde and Signy, kneeling in their path.

Solwaer's men swarmed over Bear as their leader stood back, knife in hand. "Sister, I shall rid you of the Demon—tell the Abbot, when he wakes—but I shall return and will be delighted to receive more instruction then."

"Bear!" Signy's long wail was swallowed as the west door closed behind Solwaer's back.

Pandemonium broke out in the church. How could God permit such things to be?

For Bear, the journey from the island to Portsol—the old settlement had a new name now, one that increased the Chieftain's
standing in the scattered settlements of the western shore—was
passed in a pain-fog. He floated in and out of consciousness, in and
out, and heard bits of what was said. "Not worth a ransom, is he?"
and "He'll be gelded. Too much fight in this one." And ". . . goes
there, empty-handed, comes back with a free slave. That's Solwaer. Monks better count their fingers next time."

Bear drifted on the laughter. He remembered things from long
ago. He remembered the sound and feel of a keel driven up on
the shingle of Signy's clan settlement. He remembered, too, the
wooden trackway from the beach to the houses.

This time he was dragged because he could not walk; he still
left a trail of blood. Some things don't change.

Bear opened blackened eyes. The round huts were gone. Now,
banked around the base of the great cliff, there were many buildings, some made of stone. Some huts had even begun to straggle
away from the main settlement, as if to escape before they were
noticed.

And, jutting into the dangerous, narrow channel, was the
greatest change of all. Cutting out from the land, a long arm of
black rock rose above the water. Solwaer was indeed a powerful
man if he could cause such things to be. Many slaves had dragged
those stones into place. Bear closed his eyes. He would not become one of them.

"Here." They pushed him through a low door, and he collapsed.
Falling, falling down. He knew nothing more than blank dark.

It was evening. Far away, someone was screaming at him,
taunting. Bear woke thirsty, his belly griped and hollow. No food
for a very long time, that was it.

The voice howled insults as it called him from the dark. *Filth,
Monks' whore.* Something hit him, slicing and vicious, across the
shoulders. A whip thong, it bit hard, gouged flesh to the bone.

Bellowing, Bear leapt up and struck out blindly, but the whip caught him again. Across the face, his damaged face. That horror destroyed any ability Bear might have had to think.

Solwaer's foolish servant had not thought to find a berserker in the hut, and soon he lay dying, one eye gouged from his head. When the man did not return, several others were sent, but howls from inside the prison slowed their approach. It was only the final scream of their companion that made them rush the door. It took all four to hold the captive and still they could not pry him away from the corpse until he had pounded Whip Man's head into a mush of blood and brains.

He woke quickly this time, came back from wherever their blows had sent him, and shook his head to clear blood dripping into his eyes. He would stay awake, first, and then, he would remain alive.

Bear sat up. Pulled by two sinewy slaves, the cart he sat in was jolting down a narrow street that stank of shit. People of the settlement pressed back against the house walls as they passed. Solwaer ruled with fear, it seemed. But the blood had stopped, and Bear could see their destination if he blinked hard. There was a clear space among the huts, and men stood in groups, some holding torches that flared and guttered. They were waiting for something. For someone. Him.

The cart rocked and stopped in front of a hall. Constructed from fir logs and the same black rock as the breakwater, it was, at best, functional. Bear remembered Signy's home. The carcass of that first building existed here, but it had been swamped by this ugly structure. *But ugly is powerful.*

Bear was comforted by that thought. He looked down at his fingers—bound so tightly they were turning blue; there was blood beneath his nails. He'd killed a stranger with nothing more than these hands. Cuillin had been right to fear him. The Abbot had sensed what Bear had not known for so long. He understood himself in a new way now. He was dangerous.

A spear nudged between the slats of the cart. It pricked Bear cautiously between the shoulder blades, a goad. From a safe distance, men taunted him with drawn swords. They were taking no chances. "Up!"

Solwaer's men did not know Bear understood a good part of their language. Many of the words they used were Signy's local dialect, and this was an advantage Bear would guard as long as he could.

"*Up!*" The word was bellowed, but one of the guards gestured also, waving his sword arm toward the sky. "*Up, slave. Lump. Stupid ox!*" The man's voice said he was nervous.

Bear nearly smiled. Never presume your enemy is stupid. He stood, as if he had just understood. The cart rocked. He was pleased to see how much bigger he was than Solwaer's men; living on Findnar had been hard, but he'd stolen food for years and gathered a lot more from the cliffs, the sea, and the meadows; he'd eaten better than the monks and was taller than any of them, and so it was here. His escort edged back farther when they saw the true size of Solwaer's new slave.

Bear raised his bound arms. He did his best to look amiable and dull-witted, but his escort saw a demonic giant with the face of a bloodied monster. The biggest of Solwaer's men gestured and pointed. "In there."

Bear was happy to hear the quaver in his voice.

Inside, the hall was dim with smoke. Torches flared and spat burning resin around the perimeter, but for all the flame and crackle, light fought to penetrate gloom. Hanging from tie beams in the roof were wheels with oil lamps of red clay on the rims. These fared little better. The one bright glow came from the fire pit, and it was toward this that Bear was prodded. Women drew back into the shadows, clutching children as he passed, and men muttered. Bear saw fear in their eyes.

Perhaps I am a demon. Perhaps that is good. He bared his teeth suddenly, a flash of white, and hissed. A frightened *waaaaaah* came from the women. Several of Solwaer's men rushed forward, spears and swords held high.

"Our Lord takes his seat!"

There was a raised dais beyond the fire pit. On it stood a large wooden stool draped with rich pelts of fox and wolf and white winter hare. A man was standing beside the empty honor seat, and he held up one hand, announcing again, in a strong voice, "Lord Solwaer is in his hall."

Curtains of ocher red hung over a doorway behind the dais. The man, Fiachna—Solwaer's chief housecarl—pulled the hanging back, and Bear had his first sight of Solwaer since the violent blur in the Abbey church.

Since they were separated by a considerable space, Bear thought Solwaer must be a young man, but as the Chieftain sat, and Bear was shoved forward by the guard, he saw deep lines etched into Solwaer's face and white streaks in his hair.

So, not young, not old.

Fiachna spoke again. "Solwaer, our Lord, sits in judgment on this man, who has murdered one of our comrades."

Portsol's Chieftain stared down at Bear. "You may think it is good that you are still alive here, in this hall. But I can promise that soon"—he smiled quite kindly, and those around the dais drew back; Solwaer famously smiled often but was no man's friend—"soon, you will not think that breath in your chest, blood in your veins is good. To breathe will be pain, and your blood will find another home besides your heart. The floor beneath my feet." Mothers covered the eyes of their excited children, and some left with the very youngest.

Solwaer paused as the crowd settled again. "But why do I waste my breath with this savage? An ignorant, dumb brute. An animal herder. And like an animal, he will be butchered when that is useful to his masters."

Solwaer laughed loudly at his own joke, and merriment swept the hall. This was what they liked, a good show on a cold night.

Bear nodded, completely calm; he even chuckled with the crowd. "Lord? Perhaps I may speak?"

Silence preceded a rising babble. A good death, even of a slave, was a thing to be appreciated. This man had courage.

Solwaer held up his hand for silence. "Perhaps you understand what I say, but that will not help you. Speak, if you like—it will be the last exercise your tongue will have. With words, that is." Another guffaw, happily echoed.

Bear did not acknowledge the taunt, and he did not blink as he stared at Solwaer.

The guard stirred uneasily. Though the slave was well bound, he had the air of a man preparing himself.

"And I say that I will meet death, when it comes, on my feet with my hands unbound. And my death will not be tonight." This had the air of prophecy, and an interested ripple passed through the crowd. Perhaps the man was a shaman?

Solwaer frowned. "You are stupid after all. I shall choose the time and place of your extinction, not you, slave."

Bear expanded his chest and raised his battered head. He loomed taller than Fiachna, even though the man stood on the dais. "I am a freeman, not a slave. I have a lineage, and you are not my lord."

A collective gasp, like a wave up the beach that would not be stopped.

The Chieftain gestured at the ropes binding Bear's hands. Fiachna shot his lord a glance, would have spoken, but a hand was raised. "Do it. He will not be a trouble to us much longer, this Demon."

Reluctantly, one of the guards stepped forward with a dagger in his fist; another stood close with a raised sword.

"You may recite your lineage, poor though it will undoubtedly be, and then you will die as you have lived. Like a dog." Solwaer's tone was soft, but the sneer was audible.

The rope fell from Bear's hands. He flexed his fingers and then his arms. The guards gripped their weapons; they would not have unbound the Demon, but then, none of them was Solwaer.

Bear's breath was deep, as if to plunge into the winter sea. He said, loudly, "My father's name was Ragnar, son of Iarl, son of Othere, son of Britwulf Ironhand. I am full brother to Grimor."

Solwaer leaned forward, but only a little. Perhaps he was interested, perhaps he was uncomfortable on the stool.

"At my birth I was named Magni for the son of Thor, though now I am called Bear. When I was young, I was among Reimer's band, which burned this coast and the island."

The watchers exchanged astonished glances, and a gathering roar ripped the gloom like wind.

Bear was unmoved as shouting men drew swords and waved them, feinting toward where he stood.

The Chieftain ignored the howling mob. He raised a hand to Fiachna. Stepping forward to the front of the dais, the chief carl roared, "Silence! Silence for Lord Solwaer."

Like a brook in high summer, sound settled to a mutter.

Bear stared around the hall. Unblinking, he searched the faces of each man, each woman, and even the children. He would remember them should they meet again.

Solwaer waved an impatient hand. "Continue."

Bear nodded. "When Findnar was burned, forty seasons ago, I was left behind." He touched the raised scars on his bloodied face. "This was my legacy. Perhaps it was my punishment; that is what the people of Christ said, though they healed me, mended my legs. They even tried to save my pretty face." He laughed.

None in the hall responded. It was sobering to see a man who had been part of such destruction, even if it had been so many years ago.

"Believe me, the face you see here is an improvement, though some have called me Demon." He smiled, blank-eyed. "Then there came a time when I tried to leave the island. I was still a child. We stole a ship, and the woman you saw in the Abbey church was a child then, too, Lord Solwaer, but she was brave, and this place, Portsol, was the home of her clan. We sailed the ship here, Signy and I."

The hall was silent as Bear stared at Solwaer. "Nine summers ago the houses here were deserted. Some were burned. Perhaps Reimer had sacked this place, perhaps another band had been here. There was no one left to tell us what had happened and, because we had stolen a vessel and her clan home lay ruined, Signy said we must return the craft to the people of Christ or we would be cursed. As this place had been cursed and devastated."

Solwaer stared hard at Bear. "There is no curse, animal herder. Portsol prospers because I am its lord."

Bear bowed his head, a small acknowledgment. His teeth glinted, caught in the glow of the fire pit. "And so we went back to the island. In time Signy promised to marry the Christian God, for that is one of the things they do, and she felt compelled to atone." Perhaps, in the end, he was economical with the truth.

There were jeers from some of the men in the hall.

Bear glanced at the most insulting, and they fell silent. "Yes, I was an animal herder. I plowed their land and sowed their crops, and I became a smith for them, and a carver." They had not found the knife in his leggings. Bear bent, and held his arm high. The blade flashed.

Fiachna would have jumped from the dais, but men close to Bear drew back. An armed demon was a different matter.

Bear saw them shuffle away. He laughed.

Solwaer's eyes narrowed; now he did lean forward. "You made this?"

"I did, great Lord. Forged this blade, carved the hilt." Bear stepped a pace closer and, for a moment, the men locked glances. Never taking his eyes from Solwaer's, Bear placed the knife at the other man's feet and stepped away. "My gift to you."

A sigh swept the crowd. Carvers were sorcerers, that was well known: they took the soul of what they copied and put that into the work so the object became magical, imbued with the power of the original. Smiths, too, could not be trusted—they dealt with earth magic, iron made from fire.

Solwaer nodded, slowly and deliberately. "I accept this gift, but it will not save you, Demon. Perhaps it will take your liver." The Chieftain gestured to Fiachna. The chief carl picked up the dagger and handed it to his lord; perhaps the otter pleased him, for Solwaer waved to Bear almost cordially. "And?"

Bear turned to the crowd. "This was the price I paid. I, son of Ragnar, son of Iarl, son of Othere, son of Britwulf Ironhand, became a herder. I learned much, and I have not come here to die." He whirled around and pointed at the man on the dais. "Solwaer, I will serve you usefully, for a time, but as a free man."

The Chieftain stood. He flicked a plaid shawl around his shoulders and faced the hall, firelight gilding the bleak planes of his face. "Yet, Demon, there is blood debt for the man you killed." His eyes flared as coals crumbled into the fire pit—the tone was a taunt.

Bear raised his hand. Swords around him flinched forward, but he smiled. "I will pay it. I shall carve for you and smith for you, as I did for the monks. What great chief ever has enough war weapons or things of value for his hall, or for himself?"

Solwaer did not respond.

Bear half-smiled and said, politely, "And perhaps in time I shall take up the trade I was trained for. A seaborne fighter. Then I may be more useful still."

Solwaer grunted. The people began to mutter and shift as he settled himself in the honor seat once more. "What do you want?"

"Only that which is mine and your help to take it back."

The girl. Solwaer blinked. He waved a hand dismissively. "Put him back where you got him. I shall think on this."

He could have fought them, but Bear, after bowing to the Chieftain, allowed himself to be prodded from the hall at spearpoint.

"One last thing . . ."

At the open door of the hall, Bear turned.

Solwaer stared at him, eyes bright as those of a black crow. He spoke slowly and clearly. "If you harm any of my people, I will have you flayed and cast, living, into the fire pit. Do not forget."

Bear met his glance. "Fire is not my friend, Lord Solwaer. I will not forget."

CHAPTER 27

As SHE walked up the high street, Freya turned her phone on. No messages. Not one. What'd happened to her mates, all those friends who said how much they'd miss her? She might have dropped off the edge of the earth.

She stopped. Adrenaline and paranoia, had they always been her drugs of choice? She so wanted comfort—a familiar voice, someone from home, someone normal. Elizabeth. She needed to be lectured, needed to be told not to be so silly.

Freya found the number and tapped it in. *Pick up, Mum. Please . . .* But the phone at the other end kept ringing. She let it go all the way, just in case.

And then she heard Elizabeth's voice cut in. *I can't come to the phone right now, but if you leave a message I'll return your—*

"Call. Yes, I know, Mum, but I was hoping for a chat. If you get this"—Freya looked at her watch; it was early evening in Sydney—"can you call me back? It's Monday morning my time here, and I'll keep my phone on. There's lots to talk about, believe me. Love you."

Elizabeth would sense it, though she'd tried to be breezy; her mother could always tell when Freya was upset.

But could she tell her why?

Freya, an unhappy huddle on a seat in the cemetery, was staring at her father's grave. Something was missing—the bunch of flowers she'd left only a couple of days ago was gone.

"You wouldn't think they'd do it, would you?" said Simon. He was leaning over the gate, smiling at her pleasantly.

"What?"

"Take flowers from a grave."

There was nothing to say to that. So much about life made Freya feel helpless now, and this was just one more small blow. "I hope they bring someone pleasure. Maybe they're better with the living." Embarrassed by sudden tears, she looked away.

The gate opened, and she heard Simon crunching up the gravel path. Uninvited, he sat beside her. "Anything I can do?"

Feeling stupid, she shook her head. She hated this fragility; she'd never been like this before, if you didn't count childhood misery.

"He can't help you now"—Simon nodded at the grave—"but I can."

Freya attempted a watery smile. "Oh?"

"Yes. Think about the good things."

She couldn't avoid a caustic edge. "It's that simple."

"Certainly." Simon's tone was bracing. *Next best thing to Mum,* thought Freya, quite surprised.

"For starters, how many girls own an island?"

"Islands are trouble. Capital T." A gloomy mutter.

"What, Findnar? Surely not." He was droll and warm, and charming.

"Easy for you to say." Just a brief glance in his direction, an acknowledgment he was being kind, but Freya sighed. "Oh, it's the different way of life, I suppose. And there's no power at the house either."

"Really? Your dad didn't fix that?"

She stared at Simon. "You know about the power."

He shrugged. "My family were friends with the Buchans—the people who owned the island then. The house was empty and locked up, hadn't been lived in for a long time, but we'd go over for a few days each summer and sleep in tents. All good, clean, primitive fun, parents and kids mucking in together." His face softened. "The long midsummer days of childhood. In a way, I think that's why I came back to Portsolly."

Freya nodded. She, too, understood the allure of holiday memories from long ago—the happy ones.

Simon continued, "Findnar was used for grazing sheep back then, but there were no other human inhabitants—not even a shepherd."

Freya sat up. "I knew it! Just seems so sensible not to waste all the grass. And I pump water in the house—there's primitive for you, but good exercise. That, and the cliff path."

Simon said thoughtfully, "Well, we can't do anything about that path, but power and water are an easy fix, with a bit of cash, that is. And if it's all too hard, you'll get a nice price if you decide to sell for the legends alone."

"Legends?"

"The last, lost hoard of pirate gold, me hearties."

Freya's mood finally lifted; she even giggled at the pirate impersonation. "Dire, Simon Fettler, just dire. Can I counsel against giving up the day job?"

He grinned. "That's better, but it might be true. There's a rumor, more than a rumor actually, that treasure is buried on the island. Lots of people have searched for it over the years, including us kids, of course, back then. Never found anything."

Freya shifted uneasily. "Everywhere has myths."

"Of course, and children love legends. It's a classic thing, a quest. Hours of fun ferreting in the ruins and telling ghost stories around the campfire at night." He fell silent, staring at Michael Dane's grave.

"Not just kids." Freya stole a glance at his profile. "Simon, you're an architect."

He nodded solemnly. "Last time I looked." He smiled at her warmly.

"I need a big piece of stone moved—a really big bit."

"On the island?"

She nodded.

"Well, you could do worse than what they did here, building this church. When they had to raise blocks of stone—big ones—they'd have built a crane on the spot." He waved toward the steeple. "Very efficient when you look at something like that."

"If I was going to make one—a crane, I mean—what would I need?"

Simon said, promptly, "Timber poles—sturdy, straight grain—and rope. And, let's see . . . pulley blocks, a couple of slings too. Depends how big the stone is. And a bunch of good strong bolts to hold it all together. Not hard."

Freya pointed at the cover on her father's grave. "But the stone I want to move is around that big. Well, longer—and wider. Thick too; quite a bit thicker, actually." She demonstrated, holding her hands apart. Bigger, smaller, "Something like this."

Simon nodded patiently. Women and dimensions. "Granite?"

She frowned. "Not sure. Would it be very expensive to make the crane?"

Simon didn't know Freya's financial situation, but he could guess—those references to being a student. "Well, there's a good hardware shop in Ardleith, a real one—and a timber merchant. Not forgetting the Chandlery, too, for the ropes and pulleys, though we might go for stainless-steel cable, on second thought. I'm not sure what it would all cost, but I'll bet we can negotiate a deal. What's the worst they're going to do—say no? And if it's still too much, we can think of another way; that's what I do. I've got a car, by the way—like me to drive you to Ardleith? Happy to."

Freya looked away. "You're very kind, Simon. But . . ."

"Ah, there's a *but* . . ." His smile glinted.

Here was an offer of help, a real offer. What was wrong with her? The gray lifted from Freya's heart. "I shall say yes then, and thank you, on one condition."

"And that is?" Simon stretched his arms along the back of the seat. He looked at her expectantly.

He really is very attractive, thought Freya. "I pay for your time, a professional consultation. You could come over and have a look at what's needed before we buy anything. Just so I have an idea of cost. And while you're on the island, you could give me advice about power and, oh, lots of things." The words came out of her mouth so easily, but when they were said, she understood. The decision had been made. She could not leave Findnar now or she'd wonder all her life. "When would be convenient?"

"Let me think, let me construe, let me not jump in without proper consideration." Simon pantomimed pondering deeply. She laughed at his silliness, a delighted giggle.

"Would today be too soon? It would be great to see the island again—apart from anything else."

Was she taken aback by his eagerness? "But aren't you busy? I've interrupted your work."

"Ah, but I'm on summer break. My time's my own until autumn, and it's a lovely day." His smile was winning.

Light had broken through the ceiling of white cloud, and there were ever-growing patches of blue behind the rips. It *was* a lovely day, and as the errant sun shone down on her father's grave, Freya could feel warmth gather in the black stone. Would he approve of her taking Simon to Findnar?

Oh, grow up. Take responsibility! "Thank you, Simon. It's a deal. Let's agree on a price for your advice, though. Just to keep this on the level?"

He stood. "I have standard hourly charges, but the first consultation's free, of course. Tell you what—let's get over there and I'll work out two time lines and two costings. One for raising the stone, one for evaluating what could be done with your house. I'll break both down into modules, and you can commission me for as much or as little as you please. Done?" He reached out a hand.

A moment's hesitation, and Freya shook it. "Done deal." Much

easier shaking his hand than Dan's. No second agenda. *Go on,
admit it. You're happy. You won't need to be alone.* "Today."

"Only today? We'll have to work fast, then."

Freya stammered, "I didn't mean, that is . . ."

Simon swept her up from the seat. "Time's a-wasting. Let's
look at your island, Freya Dane."

Breathless, Freya allowed him to chivy her from the churchyard. It was comforting not having to make all the decisions for
once.

CHAPTER 28

I'M SO sorry." Rain hit Compline's windows as if sprayed from a hose. "This is such a waste of your time, Simon. Not exactly strolling-around weather."

The architect stood behind Freya's shoulder as they stared out toward the stone circle through veils of falling water. "Wait five minutes and it's bound to stop," he told her.

"I'll confess the crossing got my hopes up—it was actually warm on the water for a minute." Though Freya joked, she felt oddly self-conscious. Yesterday Dan had been here in the kitchen, and talking to Simon alone, oddly, seemed like some kind of betrayal.

"Would you mind if I looked around while we're waiting? The house was boarded up all those years ago, so I never got to see inside."

"Of course not." Freya gestured toward the staircase. "Shall we start up there?"

Simon climbed the stairs behind her, and there was that intimate feeling of his eyes on her back. Did she like being so closely inspected?

On the narrow landing, there were three identical doors. "It's quite a small space up here—only two bedrooms and this." The third door led into a linen cupboard.

Simon pulled it open. "Quite a large space. Good for hot-water storage, or even—at a pinch—a shower room."

"Good storage-storage too."

Simon grinned. "Old houses. Never enough places to put things. But we can fix that, we can fix anything."

I'll bet you can. "Who's this *we*?"

Tousled hair, black clothes, striking, lean—Simon really was a treat to look at, and it occurred to Freya that she couldn't remember the last time she'd been so struck by the sheer physical presence of a man. But she smiled as she looked away. After all, it was rude to stare.

"So, this is mine." She opened the door to her bedroom. "Small, but I have everything I need. Cozy, really—a bonus on a cold night—and the chimney flue from below goes up the wall. That helps take the edge off." Seen with a stranger's eye, the single bed in the white room seemed very chaste and narrow. Too narrow for . . . *Stop that! Concentrate.*

She preceded Simon to the next door. "And this was Dad's. The bed's a bit too big for the room—doesn't leave much space. Lord knows how he got it up here."

"Just like Goldilocks. One bed too small, one too big . . ." Simon grinned, definitely a naughty grin, and Freya couldn't help responding. *Too fast.* She instructed her face and eyes into neutral gear. That worked until he said, "Pity there's no third to be just right." Simon winked. "But let's see what you've got here." He paced out the dimensions of the room, all business.

Freya let him. She wasn't ordinarily passive, so that was an interesting response. *He likes to control things.* She half-muttered, "Oh, shut up, Mum."

"What did you say?" Simon glanced toward her.

"Nothing." *Liar.* She added, hastily, "So what do you think?"

"Well, it won't be hard to rationalize the space up here." He tapped along the wall to where she stood. "Lath and plaster. Very easy to take down, and you might even be able to squeeze a bathroom between the two reconfigured bedrooms—if you let me colonize the linen cupboard. Then you could use some of the space in that massive bathroom downstairs as a laundry and for storage too."

"Not a bad idea." *Too expensive, of course.* Freya led her guest back to the kitchen. Money. *She'd always got by on so little. You could sell something, though, it's all yours. You'd have fun working on this house.* The gold torque glittered in its nest of cotton wool. *No!* Freya shook the thought away. All those government regulations hovered, just waiting for her to raise her head above the parapet.

Simon roamed the kitchen. "So, tell me what you'd like to do in here."

"I haven't really thought about it, not properly."

He lifted the pump handle and said, solemnly, "I have late-breaking news. The twenty-first century has all kinds of cool things—taps, for instance. And genuine running water, hot *or* cold, your choice." He grinned.

Freya folded her arms, and unfolded them. What was there to be defensive about? "Dad must have liked things the way they were."

Simon looked at her curiously. "Do you?"

"It's more work but . . ." Yes, it was more work, but she was getting used to the way things were on the island.

Pumping water sucks, be honest.

Simon's eyes crinkled at Freya's rueful expression. "No rush. If you do decide to sort out power and water for the house, it certainly can be done. Maybe you could consider a small wind generator with solar panels on the roof. You'd hardly ever need the backup though. I remember it was quite breezy here sometimes, a rich resource for power."

Freya laughed. "An understatement."

Simon sauntered over and stood beside her.

She fought the urge to move away. Just slightly. She'd always valued personal space.

His lips quirked. "This is how people keep warm in Scotland, Freya."

"Really?" She fought natural suspicion.

"Yes. Propinquity." The rolled *rrrrrrrr* made her laugh, and his grin was wicked. "Seriously, reliable warmth is important if the winter is not to get you down. SAD: seasonal affective disorder is real in this part of the world. More daylight in the house would help if you're vulnerable."

"I'm not sure. There was always too much sun in Sydney to know." They really were standing very close to one another. And there was that moment, that delicious feeling of hanging in space as it seemed he would bend down and . . .

Why did Freya do it? She moved away a step and said, recklessly, half-sorry, "I did wonder about a glass roof over the kitchen. Now that'd do great things on a dark day." *Timing. Always been my problem.*

But Simon didn't seem to be offended by her skittishness. He said, lightly, "Not just a pretty face, Miss Dane. Do you have paper?"

"Paper?" She was thrown by the non sequitur.

He said, patiently, "Yes. I could draw something—see if I can put your idea into pictures."

Freya opened the door to the big room quite quickly. "Sure. In here." A natural excuse to move away.

Simon paused in the threshold. "Well, well. Your father had a great eye—this is a lovely room." He ambled to the windows. "Bet the view's brilliant too."

Freya half-closed her eyes. What an elegant body Simon had: broad, straight shoulders, muscular back, long—very long—legs. And his hair. She wanted to touch his hair, feel its texture. "When you can see it. All of the western sky."

Simon turned back. Perhaps he'd felt her eyes on him this time. He pointed to Michael's desk. "May I use this?"

She hurried over. "Of course. I'll just make room." She stacked her father's card files on the nearest windowsill.

"Please don't worry. Paper is all I need." Simon sat without fuss.

"Is this okay?" She held out a wad of copy paper.

"Grand. I'd kill for a cuppa though. Always work better with a cuppa." A glinting smile.

"Sure." Freya felt the need to clatter about the kitchen as she pumped the kettle full and fired up the gas ring.

"Milk's in the barn—that's my version of a fridge. Won't be a moment."

Simon called out, "It's pouring out there. Happy with black."

"Wouldn't think of it. Besides, I like milk in mine." *And similar froth and babble* . . . Freya cursed herself as she ran back from the barn; she really was bad at flirting these days. *Note to self: stop trying so hard.*

The kettle was singing as Freya hurried back into the house, damp curls all over her face. She grabbed a dry sweatshirt from the bathroom, dragged her hair into a ponytail, and ran to pull the kettle from the gas ring.

In the doorway of the big room, she paused to settle her breathing. She carried a tray with the best of the mugs, and there was even a small silver jug for the milk. It might be tarnished, but Simon would appreciate the pretty form. "As advertised, tea with milk—and a surprise. Tim Tams, the best chocolate biscuits in the world. I smuggled my own from Sydney."

Simon was leaning against the window, shoulders back against the glass. He seemed completely at ease. "Have a look." He pointed to a sketch on the desk. "Just first thoughts, of course." He strolled toward her. "You've changed your clothes."

Self-conscious, Freya put the tray down and smoothed her top. It was as if they were speaking a different language to each other, the English conversation an irrelevance. "You were right. It was wet out there." She leaned over the desk. "You do work fast."

Simon had scrawled an impression of the back of the house with an airy structure attached. There was even a girl sitting at the table in the redesigned kitchen. Just a suggestive line or so, but she was looking straight back at Freya, waving. A little figure wearing a scribble of red.

Freya tensed. And then her brow cleared. Of course, the sweater she'd been wearing before was red. She'd pulled it on at the last minute before going over to Portsolly, just to make herself feel better.

Simon tapped the sketch. "There are lots of possibilities for Compline, depending on budget. We could make the kitchen work really well, and the rest of the house too."

Freya scanned the sheet carefully. "Looks great." *It really does,* she thought wistfully.

"The roof would be glass, as you suggested, but tempered. Tougher than a tank and traps heat really well." Standing behind her shoulder, Simon removed the sketch from Freya's fingers, but very gently. "I've modeled this on a conservatory."

"Conservatory?" Freya swallowed as she turned toward him. There was very little room.

Simon nodded. He said, gravely, "You can grow things under glass, even in this climate. Tomatoes, lettuces, herbs. Fresh food in winter." He tipped her chin up with one finger. She could not avoid his eyes when he bent down, just a little. And kissed her.

She said, breathlessly, "The weather here. Quite entertaining."

He murmured, "Especially when you have to stay inside." He drew her closer, kissed her again, and she did not resist. In fact, she enjoyed what he was doing, kissed him back languorously, her eyes half-closed.

Yet something hovered. Simon was waiting for something, waiting for her to *say* something. As if, by inviting him to Findnar, she'd somehow called down this storm and contrived that they'd be forced together and, being sequestered from the world, that she would . . . *Stop it, Freya!*

He released her, as if it was the most natural thing in the world. Freya swayed. She smiled at him uncertainly. "Tea?" He nodded. She could see he was amused.

"With milk too. After all your trouble, that seems only fair."

"Coming up." She tried not to spill the tea as she filled his mug. Not the easiest thing in the world. Perhaps Simon thought her awkward, even childish, but Freya thought how nice it would be to get to know him slowly—just as a friend—and then see what happened. But maybe they'd crossed a line, though she had to take responsibility for that too. She could have avoided kissing him. Possibly. *Really?*

Freya cleared her throat. "So . . . will it be much more expensive doing alterations over here? If that's what I do." From somewhere else, the embarrassed place she'd gone to, she noted that her voice was calm, the tone faintly wry. She admired herself for that.

Companionably, Simon beckoned Freya to sit beside him on the couch. "Getting the materials over the strait and up to the house will cost you a bit. But after that, it's all about being clever and not in a hurry." He stifled a yawn. The stove in the kitchen was roaring, and transferred heat made the big room cozy.

"Keeping you up, are we? Must be time to go home."

"Not at all." His smile was beguiling. "I like being here." His voice was a low, warm rumble, almost a purr.

There was something of the cat in Simon Fettler, Freya decided. A big tomcat blinking in the warmth. "Thanks for the sketch, Simon. I appreciate it, excellent food for thought." She peered toward the rain-swept strait. *Where is it?* But there was no sign of the sun as fleets of clouds were driven across the horizon. *Why am I so on edge?* But she knew why. The kiss remained wrong in some way. Enjoyable, yes. But wrong.

"Tell you what . . ."

"What?" Freya swung around. The response was sharp.

He said, mildly, "Are you okay?"

Her face flamed. She bumbled, hastily. "Of course. What was the what?" *Lighten up! He'll think you're an idiot.*

"Well, this house is intriguing."

Freya forgot to be nervous for a moment. "It really is. I went looking for information"—she pointed to the pile of library books—"but haven't been able to get to it yet. Quite a few theories, apparently."

Simon interrupted politely. "I have online access to the Faculty of Architecture library in Ardleith—it's a fantastic resource. Unique aspects to this structure were mentioned when I did a bit of research after I met you." He grinned. "Couldn't resist. And not that you'd know it up here but . . . the undercroft?"

"The undercroft." Freya echoed the word. Why was she reluctant suddenly to talk about Compline?

Simon nodded. "I'd love to see it. Just thinking about similarities to my church." He smiled at her expectantly.

"Oh, your building is much older than my cellar." She deliberately used the modern word. "That's Gothic or even later." She didn't want to make the offer; she wanted time to think. But in a normal world, the one other people, like Simon, inhabited, it would have been rude not to. "So, would you like to see it?" She twitched a smile back.

A low whistle. "But this is fantastic. Astonishing." It wasn't the vaulted ceiling Simon was struck by, it was the stone pillar at the bottom of the stairs. "Can I use the lantern?"

"Sure." Freya handed him the camping light. In the bright blue-white, the enigmatic symbols stood out etched in shadow. She was getting used to the reaction now—Compline's tour guide.

Simon peered at the surface. "I haven't seen anything like these symbols."

"Perhaps it's Pictish work—some of the carvings suggest that." Freya was deliberately low-key.

"Picts. That would make this really old." Simon stood back, and the light spilled into the space around them. He blinked. "This place is huge! Hang on . . ."

He strode over to the side wall. "You didn't tell me about this,

Freya. Bad girl." He said it merrily. They both stared at the carved panel.

Why *hadn't* she told him?

"Do you think this could be related to my little guy?"

Freya tried to sound enthusiastic. "Quite possibly, if both are local work. An artisan of the time could have been multiskilled. Of course, the wood needs dendrochronology for a date and—"

She stopped herself. It occurred to her that she didn't want to offer an easy way of making comparison between the panel and the angry little man Simon had showed her. What she wanted, most, was to be in daylight again.

He nodded toward the Compactus. "Lot of storage down here. Useful. Must have been hell to get up that path."

Freya managed a smile. "My thoughts exactly."

"Your dad built these?" Her guest wandered toward the cupboards.

Freya tensed. She hurried toward the deep-set windows. "I think the rain's stopping. Truly. We should seize the chance if you want to see anything of the island again."

"Hmm?" Staring at the anonymous steel cupboards, Simon seemed distracted.

"Yes. I'd like to show you where I need the crane. Can't afford to keep you here all day, can I?" She strode to the bottom of the stairs. "Coming?"

"Of course. Though I'm really not in a hurry to get back. Mate's rates apply to you." Simon ambled after her, smiling gently. "So long as I'm not outwearing my welcome."

"They're still huge. I was expecting them to look smaller, somehow. Less impressive."

"Why?" Now that they were standing in front of the double ring of stones, possessiveness crept up on Freya.

"Oh, you know. Kids. Everything seems enormous when you're

seven. We didn't come up here very much, though, when we were on the island. Off-limits—all the kids were warned off—really the only part of Findnar the Buchans seemed to want to keep to themselves."

Freya led Simon toward the inner ring of stones. "Maybe they were worried about damage."

He peered closely at a patch of lichen on one of the monoliths. "No, that wasn't it."

Why did she want to know? "So what was the problem?"

Simon paused, remembering. "I think this is where they thought it was, and they didn't want anyone else to find it."

"*It* meaning a hoard?"

He nodded. "Archaeologists don't approve of treasure hunts, do they?"

"No, not generally." *Except when it suits them.*

"Scholarship is all—of course, dear Dr. Dane." Simon bowed gracefully and flourished an imaginary hat off his head.

That drew a smile as Freya pointed toward the trench. "Not a doctor yet, but over there's where the crane is needed."

Simon paused and pointed back toward the Abbey ruins. "Quite a bit of monastic ware turned up over the years apparently—broken pots and suchlike. Nothing of much importance. They did find a bell, though—bronze, I believe, and marked with the cross inside a circle: Celtic Church. By the way, Ardleith Museum has a small exhibit of finds from Findnar. The Buchans donated material over the years."

"A bell—you've seen it?" She searched his face. *I've heard it.*

"Yes, I was at Ardleith last weekend. The museum was open, and it's the best thing in the exhibit, I thought. Does that interest you?"

Freya busied herself lifting the tarpaulin. "You mentioned a Celtic cross. Did it look like this?" She pointed to the symbol carved in the stone. At least the surface of the slab was dry. That was great after all the rain.

Simon squatted. "Yes."

She crouched beside him. "I want to know if there's anything under there."

Simon surged to his feet.

Startled by the sudden movement, Freya blinked. "So, what do you think?" A dazzle of sun, clearing from behind cloud, flared into her eyes. It was hard to see his face. "Will it be difficult to raise?"

"Not especially."

Perhaps it was her imagination, but he seemed tense. Freya got up; her jeans were muddy from kneeling. "Good to know. I'll just cover this again, if you don't mind waiting."

"Not at all. I'll have a look around, see what else I remember. Won't go far." He gestured toward the meadow and strolled away.

It didn't take long for Freya to stretch the tarpaulin and peg it down securely. Simon joined her as she finished, and they set out for the house together.

"I'm starved. What about a sandwich? Least I can do." She projected light and bright.

"I thought you'd never ask." He responded just as breezily. But that was forced too.

It was during the last part of the still, humid afternoon that Freya took Simon back to Portsolly. The sea was the color of pewter and moved with a swollen, dangerous roll.

He squinted toward the horizon. "It's glowering out there. You'd better be careful on the return trip; crazy weather, but that's Scotland for you."

"It's dry at least." She peered toward the little town. "Thanks for all the advice, Simon. You've given me lots to think about."

He grinned. "My pleasure entirely. Just remember. It needn't be as scary as you think—the money, I mean."

Freya said, drily, "That's good. Money and me—always a dysfunctional relationship."

He glinted a smile. "Better find that hoard, then."

She throttled back, and the cruiser lost momentum, idling down to a respectable approach speed. "Please don't forget the costings, Simon. You said you'd let me know."

He laughed. "So proud, Freya Dane. Of course. But designing the crane—that's just pure pleasure and I like the challenge. Gratis, free, and for nothing. A housewarming present."

Freya flicked a glance at her passenger. He seemed so light-hearted, and she liked his droll way with words; she liked the curve of his mouth too.

Their eyes met. He smiled at her. That conversation, again. The one without words.

She upped the throttle. "That's kind. Thank you, Simon." She hadn't meant to sound so formal. *Ah, Freya. So hard for you to be beholden.* Finn, her last serious boyfriend, had said that. He was right.

She nudged the cruiser to the wharf. The tide had risen, and she could see the pub. It was doing brisk business as the day closed in. "Here you are. If you don't mind, I'll drop you and run." She waved toward the sky. "Don't want to get caught on the strait."

Simon stepped neatly to the stern as Freya cut the motor and grabbed a ring hammered into the wharf. "It's been a pleasure— I really mean that."

He stepped ashore and fended the cruiser off as she upped the throttle, turning for home. She looked back briefly.

Robert Buchan was standing outside the pub, a pint glass in his hand. He was watching her.

Simon waved, and Freya waved back. It was only a moment, but before she returned her attention to the sea, she saw Simon raise a hand to Robert, acknowledged by a nod.

She hadn't thought of that. They knew each other.

CHAPTER 29

S HE WAS imprisoned in a windowless granary, musty with the ghosts of grain and old mold. For nine days and nine nights Signy had tracked time by the Abbey bell as it sounded canonical hours. Distantly, she heard voices. Her brothers and sisters—praying, singing, working—the sound coming and going like the wash of the faraway sea. But she was alone and perhaps would soon be forgotten. No one came if she called out, so she stopped. Gunnhilde would have called that pride.

There was no opening in those cold walls except the door—it was bolted on the outside—and there was no light. Signy slept, when she could, on the earth floor, but every night was cold, and if the hard-stamped mud was warmer than stone, anger was her only defense against the bitter air. That did not last. Despair soon drove her to curl up, knees to chin in one of the corners, wedged like an animal in a burrow.

Once each day, just after Tierce, she was given food, barley bread mostly, though green herbs were sometimes provided, and a skin of water. It was the only time that Signy saw daylight through the part-opened door.

But no one spoke to her as food was pushed in and the bucket of excrement removed. Solitude and silence and cold were the kindest parts of this penance; her own mind supplied the torture. Where was Bear? Was he alive?

On the first day, as the bell sounded, Signy began to pray. Mouthing the remembered responses, she called on Mary— begging for help from the mother of God, begging for justice—but there was nothing to sense, nothing to touch in the dark, no sheltering arms and no comfort.

Time lost its meaning, and slowly, very slowly, her will grew stronger. She heard her sister whispering. Laenna's voice was soft at first, but it was distinct and, in the silence between the bells, Laenna began to show Signy pictures—as if they were both invisible observers of life in the Abbey.

They watched the Abbot pray in his cell. Signy heard him ask God for her salvation, but his eyes were hard, his words dry husks blowing from the window into the night. Her brothers in the Scriptorium too. They pointed at where the screens had been and nudged each other. When Anselm was distracted, one drew a crude little figure, a girl, kneeling, her breasts exposed. This monk thrust his hips back and forth, his eyes bright and salacious.

And there was Gunnhilde. The skin of the old woman's face had collapsed into folds and shadows. Her eyes were haunted, and she alone of all the Abbey people stared toward Signy's prison and wept.

Laenna showed Signy that there would be no justice from the Christians and, in her sister's dreams, Laenna wiped Signy's tears away, her eyes full of compassion. And she whispered that it was time; Signy must leave Findnar and find Bear. He was waiting for her over the water.

On the tenth day the door scraped back. It caught on the uneven floor, and Signy threw her hands over her eyes, the light sharp as a sword. She was confused, for it was early, not long after Prime. As usual her belly clenched against hunger, but she would not show that, not to these people.

"Signy?" Gunnhilde said.

Signy did not answer. She shrugged back into her corner. She trusted no one.

The old woman pulled the door open as wide as she could.

Signy sniffed; the air smelled of the sea and other clean things.

"Oh, child." Gunnhilde's voice shook. The sight of Signy filthy as any wild creature upset her deeply. "I bring news. Good news."

"He will let me go?" Signy tried to be proud, tried to be strong.

Gunnhilde nodded joyfully. "You are very lucky."

Signy tried to stand, but she was weak and slumped to the floor. "The Abbot will let me leave Findnar."

The nun hesitated. "What do you mean?"

Signy faltered at Gunnhilde's expression. "But you said he would release me. My sister told me I must go to Bear."

The nun quickly crossed herself. "Now, Signy, I know your penance has been severe, but she cannot have spoken to you. Your sister is dead." If Signy thought she communed with spirits, things were most serious—the girl could be burned for such fantasies.

"But Laenna did speak to me, and she showed me pictures. I saw you praying for me; you were the only one."

Gunnhilde gasped. "Signy, stop! You *must* not speak of this. Your soul is in grave peril."

Signy turned her face away. "You are wrong."

The nun was at a loss. "Please, child, please listen to me. I bear the words of the Abbot." She swallowed. "He has decided. You are no longer a postulant. You will serve the Abbey as you did before."

Signy covered her face with her hands. "Bear said it was so— that I was a slave—and I did not believe him." She sobbed, a great wrench of sound that shook her frail body.

Poor Gunnhilde. Proper attention to the Rule fled as she pulled the grieving girl into her arms. "You have been given a chance to earn redemption. If your behavior proves trustworthy, perhaps, one day . . ."

Signy pulled away. "You do not understand. I will never be a nun."

Signy winced.

"Stay still, child." Gunnhilde was shaving her head.

"It hurts."

Gunnhilde sighed. It was true that the knife was blunt. "I am sorry, but most blades lack edge . . ." She stopped herself.

"Since Bear has gone." Signy finished the sentence.

"We make the best of the situation; that is our duty."

Signy closed her eyes. If this was her only choice, she would not agree, but neither would she oppose Cuillin. She would be silent and she would wait.

Gunnhilde said, earnestly, "The Abbot will be very pleased when I speak of your humility." She turned away to wipe the knife on her skirts. Signy had become an intractable problem for Abbot Cuillin, and in that Gunnhilde had seen an opportunity.

To some in the convent Signy was a martyr. There was the matter of the crucifix, of course, but during the days of her incarceration no other evidence had been found that Signy *had* betrayed her postulant's vows with Bear. Even the girl's detractors, jealous or scandalized or both, told Cuillin little he actually believed.

How grateful Gunnhilde had been when the Abbot summoned her. "Very well, I agree to release her. But know, Sister, that this girl is now your responsibility. She will labor as an Abbey servant and sleep in the byre loft. She will not be veiled, and her head will be shaved—let the community see that she is not among the professed. Only you may speak to her during this time, for I will not have others infected with her pride. And that is an end to this sorry matter until it pleases the Lord to instruct me otherwise."

Signy flinched as Gunnhilde wiped blood from her scalp.

The nun's eyes filled. "You are a frail creature, child, as we all are, but your loving Father understands."

"Loving Father?" Signy stared at the Novice Mistress, her eyes lightless. "Tell me, Mother, how can we marry our Father? If God and the Holy Spirit and the Lord Jesus are one being, is that not incest?"

Gunnhilde hesitated. What should she say? "It is not seemly for a woman to be a sophist." Anselm had much to answer for.

Where else would Signy have got such ideas? She went to a coffer and raised the lid. "I have found a kirtle for you; it is serviceable and will keep you warm." Gunnhilde held out the old garment. Earth brown and patched, the cloth was coarse, but there was a shift also. "And these are yours." Gunnhilde prayed the sandals would not bring her trouble. Only the novices and the fully professed were permitted shoes.

Signy fingered the rough garment. "So, no habit or wimple." She laughed. "But that is good. Let them see me as I am." She stared at the nun defiantly. "I am a Pagan, Gunnhilde. I always have been."

Defeated, the old nun shook her head. "Get dressed, Signy. Please." She offered a bowl of water and a cloth.

"You asked me to be grateful. I *am* grateful—most grateful to you for all your kindness, for this water, even for the clothes. And I am sorry we can no longer agree." Signy took the bowl.

Gunnhilde tried to speak, but her lips trembled. She whispered, "I shall pray for you, my sister and my daughter, for so you are to me. I shall ask that you find peace and a way back to God and to the community, which longs to welcome you home."

"Home? I think, now, that I have no home. And Bear was my true family."

Gunnhilde ached for the dignity with which Signy faced the lonely void in her heart. It was then she took a most dangerous decision. She went to the box in which was stored her spare habit and shifts and lifted them aside. "I have kept these safe for you." She offered the crucifix and the small lead box.

Signy could not speak. She stared at the cross. Slowly, tenderly, she raised it to her mouth. And kissed that suffering face.

CHAPTER 30

F OR A time, it seemed the ceremony might not go ahead.
Storms, one after another, swept in from the strait in dark
battalions as the morning aged, but then, as all later acknowledged, Cuillin called down a miracle.

For an hour, surrounded by his followers, he held the cross
from the Abbey church above his head and blessed the waves,
calling on them to calm. For a time there seemed little result, but
toward Tierce, the winds abated and the rain ceased, *but not
everywhere.* Like when Moses parted the Red Sea, perhaps prayers
had found a way for Solwaer's ships to sail to Findnar over a sea
road that gently rolled, while all around, outside the strait, the
waters raged.

For months this day had been planned, the very day when all
the adult men of Portsol would be baptized in the Christian faith.
Having accepted Christ, Solwaer's men, too, would be brought to
God. And he, Cuillin, would soon become the conduit whereby
Salvation descended upon a great mass of unbelievers. This was
a profound mystery to him still. Was Faith, then, a form of holy
contagion—a fever for His divine presence spread by the Lord
Himself? Cuillin shook his head with wonder at the thought. He
was unworthy to be the vessel, if that's what he was, of such glory.

And yet he could not suppress just a little earthly pride, for it
was with the satisfaction of a job well done that the Abbot of Findnar surveyed the island's cove today. Wherever he looked, men
knelt, staring at the great cross in his hands. He nodded to a novice
and said, loudly, "With God's Grace, let us begin."

As instructed, the boy hurried to hold back the fluttering silk of Cuillin's cope. The Abbot tried not to shiver as he signed a cross over the multitude and raised his voice against the sound of the waves, powerful competition on this chill, windy day. "As Christ suffered and died for our sins, so you, Lord Solwaer, and all your followers here today, will shortly die and be reborn into His blessed Grace. Beloved of God, children of Faith . . ."

The men of Portsol did not understand the Latin, but they watched Solwaer shuffle from foot to foot. Their leader was definitely nervous. The men muttered; something was not right.

Sensing unrest, Abbot Cuillin spoke faster and cast drops of holy water toward the chief convert.

Solwaer stepped back a pace. It had been explained to him that "dying" was purely metaphorical, but he still glanced toward the ships drawn up in the cove. If he had to run, how long would it take?

Cuillin gathered himself. With all the force in his lungs, he bellowed, "In the name of Christ our Lord, accept baptism in the Holy Spirit and the living word of God!"

Two of the larger monks appeared beside Solwaer. They hurried him to the stream that flowed from the cliff and cast aside his cloak. A sound like a disturbed hive came from the crowd. Solwaer was naked. He made a powerful sight, muscled and scarred.

A nod from Cuillin, and the brothers seized the visitor, pushing him under the water. Shocked by the cold, Solwaer struggled to raise his head, but they shoved him down again.

The men of Portsol stampeded. Sprouting knives and swords, roaring vengeance, they bludgeoned a path to their leader. Among the mayhem, Cuillin knelt on the stream bank. "God! Protect your servants."

"Stop! *Stop!*" Solwaer's bellow prevented a massacre. Just. "I am unharmed."

Burning with cold, the Chieftain of Portsol clambered to the bank. He shouted at his men, "You've shamed me!" Shivering, he turned to the Abbot. "Brother Cuillin, it seems my followers will need instruction before they, too, receive the Holy Spirit."

Cuillin nodded vigorously. Under these trying circumstances, he would not attempt mass baptism. Besides, since their leader was now fully Christian, the men of Portsol were, notionally, consecrated to Christ already. Immersion could wait.

Solwaer had never been so cold in his life. He muttered to Fiachna, "I'm freezing my bollocks off."

A panicked glance, and the chief carl saw the truth. His lord's testicles were certainly shriveled and white, his prick retracted to the length of a baby's finger. Sorcery!

Fiachna glared at the whey-faced Abbot. Protectively, he pulled a long linen shirt over his master's trembling body, followed by a red silk tunic. This was a precious object, befitting such a man, and it covered Solwaer to the knees. Silently watched by all on the beach, Solwaer pulled up russet wool trews, and Fiachna bound his legs with leather leggings.

"Belt!" Solwaer was starting to feel better, or at least warmer.

Fiachna bowed and held the object to his master. Broad and polished as a new chestnut, the leather was closed with a silver buckle.

"Cloak!"

With an evil look, Fiachna snatched it from one of the attendant monks, unnerving the man greatly. The cloak clasp was worked gold and very valuable also, as was the plaid cloak itself, lined with winter marten. Finally there were the shoes, bright yellow-green and very soft.

"Much better. Give me the torque."

The chief carl had kept this last object hidden in a rabbit-skin pouch. Bear had made it—a reason, perhaps, why the man remained alive. Reverently, he placed the worked gold around Solwaer's throat; fully arrayed, his master was kingly.

Solwaer nodded to the Abbot. "I am ready."

But Cuillin was not—shock still gripped his body from the near disaster, and he sent up a fervent prayer. *Help me, Lord. Lend me your strength.* Turning toward the men massed on the beach, he intoned, "Dear friends in Christ, this is a joyous day." His voice shook, and he cleared his throat. "Please join our community in a Mass of thanksgiving." The words were steadier, and he took that as the signal for the procession to begin.

A shivering novice led the gathering toward the path. He swung a silver censer—a baptismal gift to Findnar from Solwaer—as the monks formed up in pairs to conduct the converts to the Abbey.

Solwaer had not told Cuillin the censer's provenance. This holy item had been looted from another monastery and had found its way to him, along with a gold platter embossed with equal-armed crosses. He had purchased both objects with a well-grown girl he'd fathered on one of his slaves plus an excellent bull of good size. He'd been sad to see the animal, renowned for its potency, go. The censer he'd brought to the Abbey this morning; the gold platter had been melted down weeks ago by Bear and reworked into the torque. Solwaer liked to think of all the gold crosses melting into this other form—it seemed appropriate, somehow.

At the Abbey, it took some time to gather the press of men into Findnar's church, since the building had not accommodated so great a gathering before.

Anxious to make a good impression, Solwaer glared at any of his followers who spat on the floor—the monks frowned on such behavior. If he was honest, though, the gloom depressed him. The church stank of old, cold sweat and tallow. It was dank, too, as well as dark. Still, it was necessary that he do this, necessary to gain the trust of Cuillin and his monks—and nuns. Solwaer looked around. Where were the nuns?

As Cuillin had earlier explained, after the regrettable occasion of the previous year, separation of the sexes was now strictly enforced, with the exception of confession. A long screen had been installed along one side of the nave, and Solwaer could hear a certain amount of coughing and whispering behind it.

The regrettable occasion. Solwaer's attention drifted as the Mass began. Was the cause of that scandal behind the screen with her sisters? He remembered the girl kneeling in this very place only so few months ago. Solwaer fingered the torque. He owed the girl thanks, for unwittingly, by her actions, she had provided him with a useful follower. Perhaps he should tell her so, personally.

Bored by the endless prayers, the nasal chanting of the brothers, Solwaer stared toward the meadow through a part-open door. There were sheep and cows in the distance, and something human moved among them.

It was her, the pretty novice. She'd been hard to see at first, dressed in a dirt-colored kirtle. He narrowed his eyes. *They've shaved her head!* The barbarity shocked him.

He returned his attention to the Mass with an effort. Bear would not be pleased when he heard—*if* he heard.

The Abbey had lost one slave, it seemed, and gained another.

CHAPTER 31

SOLWAER SAT alone on the honor seat, brooding. Perhaps it was a mistake being baptized. He'd entered a pact with a God more powerful than he'd thought, for after the Mass, Fiachna told him of Cuillin's miracle with the sea. Such a deity would have expectations . . .

The door to the hall hurled back, almost broken from its post. Bear, wetter than a seal, came in from the howling black, and he brought the storm behind him. So violent was the gale, rain was blown as far as the fire pit, and the coals threw a geyser of steam and smoke into the roof void.

"Close it!" Fiachna stood behind his master, pointing. He didn't name Bear, he would not acknowledge the man, but others rushed to wrestle the door back against the night. No one told the Demon what to do.

Bear, oblivious to the fuss, advanced through the hall, a sword in one hand, an ax in the other. He walked easily, as untroubled as any animal when it's the largest in the pack.

"You cannot come armed into the hall. Put your weapons away." Solwaer was irritated by Bear's lack of manners.

Imperturbable, the Demon dropped the sword into the leather scabbard on his back and leaned on the ax shaft. "Let's talk about the island," he said.

Solwaer rolled his eyes. "Is this about the girl?"

"You didn't tell me what they did. Time to teach them a lesson."

Solwaer shifted irritably in his seat. Lately he'd been troubled by piles, which itched and stung—it was like sitting on hornets sometimes. "The Lord Abbot administers his own domain, as do I. Besides, I am a Christian now, and I must listen for Jesus to speak in my heart so that I know what is right."

Bear's guffaw bent the candle flames. Fiachna started forward, a sword in one hand. Bear turned. An efficient twist and the weapon was twitched from the chief carl's fingers. The crowd in the hall surged forward, anxious to see the fight.

Solwaer bellowed, "Enough!" He peeled Bear with a glance that might have stripped skin from an apple. Fiachna stepped back first; he was breathing hard. Bear was not.

"You"—Solwaer pointed at Bear—"in there." He waved his hand toward the hangings. "Fiachna!"

Fiachna swept the curtain aside to allow Solwaer to pass. As Bear prowled after him, the carl muttered, "One day. One day soon . . ."

"It will be my day and your head." Bear did not have to sneer. This was simple fact.

"What is this nonsense?"

The two men were in the Chieftain's quarters. A substantial chamber behind the hall, it was constructed from logs and hung with cattle hides.

"You know, don't lie. The island, that's what you want, and we can take it."

Solwaer shrugged. "Why should I do such a thing?"

"It commands the strait from the other side. To control this coast properly, you need Findnar and Portsol. You've built this place from ruins; if we burn the Christians out, you can do the same over there."

"Are you deaf? I am baptized in Christ and I am a man of peace." Solwaer deliberately crossed himself.

Bear snorted.

Solwaer kicked a log into the fire pit. Sparks flew up in a billow of smoke. He coughed, spat, and sat heavily on a stool; even here, in his private quarters, it stood on a low dais. He said, pleasantly, "With the palisade, even monks can hold Findnar now, and there's nowhere to land except that cove. The monastery is safe from raiders, safe from you too. Deo gratias."

Bear swayed forward, one foot planted on the riser. "What if I said there was another way to get onto Findnar?"

Solwaer frowned. "If so, that is a serious matter, and Abbot Cuillin must be informed. You will tell me, I shall tell him, and our Lord in Heaven will bless you."

"You lie. There is no *Lord*." Bear bellowed like a bull.

Solwaer was annoyed by the histrionics. "I have promised to build a church in Portsol in His name; that is not a lie." He held up a hand for a horn of ale, and a girl—quite pretty and young, though bruised—scuttled from the shadows. Solwaer was hard on slaves.

Raising the horn, he pointed at Bear. The girl hesitated. "He won't bite unless you annoy him. Careful now, demons like girl flesh." Trembling, the child offered the monster a horn.

Solwaer waved toward the door. "Outside. Do not listen." He settled himself on the stool as the girl ran. "Why do you hate them so much?" He leaned back, his face in shadow.

"You know why."

"My feared demon, and here you are months later still hankering after a scrawny nun." Solwaer's laugh was hard. "This does no good for your reputation, sword maker. Plenty more girls to be had by my smith, even with that face. I'll tell them to close their eyes." This time the guffaw came from his belly.

Bear glowered. "She's not a nun. They just think she is."

Solwaer sputtered. Ale shot into the fire, which spat back. "They just *think* she is. Oh, that's good." He happily wiped tears from his eyes. "But, my demon, she is scrawny. I saw. Small breasts. Not even a handful."

Bear glared at Solwaer. Red danced in his eyes.

Solwaer sighed. "The problem with you is, you're never satisfied. I freed you from those monks."

Bear glared. "To become your slave."

Solwaer continued, unperturbed. "Are you a slave now? No. I took you in, gave you a place of honor beside my fire."

Bear stood straighter. "Honor? Night and day I work in your interest. Weapons, jewelry, carvings such as no one else makes on this coast."

Solwaer waved a dismissive hand. "*And* what do you do? You frighten the children, and the women, and disturb the peace of my hall."

Bear laughed derisively. "Listen to me, old man."

The goad was successful. Now Solwaer glowered.

Bear raised his voice. "I know what you are, and I know what you want. You're building this little empire very cleverly, but you're a trader, not a fighter. Guile is your natural game, but your followers are fishers and farmers; war is not their calling. But, of course, you're a Christian." Bear smiled like a dog. "You don't want to take the place yourself, though you'd like to have it. And this is not a lie." Perhaps the truth was dangerous.

The Lord of Portsol smoothed all expression from his face. "Speak on, Bear, if you wish to seem more foolish than you are. But not for too long." He looked Bear in the eyes and yawned.

"Given men who know what they're doing, I'll take that island for you. And I want a third of it." Bear stared back at Solwaer, that unsettling look, wide and blank.

The older man's scalp shifted. He'd spared this maniac's life. In the end, might that prove to be a mistake? "So tell me. If you were me, would *you* trust a demon?"

A smile split Bear's face. "If we come to terms, I will swear an oath, and I am not an oath breaker. If you will not do this, perhaps another may. I repeat. My price is a third."

Solwaer grunted. "Girl!"

Skittish as a hare, the slave peered out from behind the skin of a large, black cow. "Yes, Lord?" It was almost a squeak.

"More."

The slave hurried toward her master, cradling the swollen ale sack like a baby. She poured, trying not to look at the demon on the far side of the fire pit.

Solwaer pointed at the discarded horn. "Fill it." As the slave scuttled from the room, he stared into the flames. "So, what is this other way you speak of?"

Bear grinned. "Terms first, Solwaer. When those are sworn, you will know." He held up the horn, and Solwaer raised his own.

CHAPTER 32

Turn it off." Walter spoke into his son's ear. Dan was planing timber, and the workshop rang with howling cacophony.

Dan took his time. Only when the board had gone the distance did he hit the Off button and pull the ear protectors from his head. "What did you say?"

"Time to lock up." Walter pointed at his watch. "Fourteen-hour days are all very well, but you have to sleep sometime."

Dan hoisted the plank and placed it on a small stack beside the bench.

Walter asked, "Have you heard from Freya?"

"Not expecting to." Dan put the ear protectors on again.

As casually as he could, Walter said, "You still expecting to go to the island this weekend?" His words were obliterated by the scream of the planer. Walter rolled his eyes. For impenetrable, perfectly honed obstinacy, there was no one like Daniel Boyne— except himself.

He yelled, "Maybe you should call the girl. Confirm you'll come." The planer whined and died. Walter was suddenly conscious of the silence.

Dan slung chains around the bundle of planks. Moving them with an overhead gantry, he lined them up above a larger stack and released the slings. The timber dropped with a crack like a shot.

Walter gave up. He set off toward the office.

Dan called after him, "There's no point ringing. She turns her phone off."

Walter nodded. "Still and all, you said she needed help over there." He tried to pretend there were no stakes in any of this.

Dan clambered into the forklift. The engine whirred. "She's pretty self-sufficient, Dad." He set off toward a stack of rough-sawn timber.

Was it an opening? Walter followed his son, waited until he hoisted another load of wood and dropped it near the bench. "This girl is different, Dan."

Patiently Dan said, "I'm not thirteen, Dad. I'm past needing advice." He climbed down.

Before Dan could avoid it, Walter pulled his son into his arms, held him as he would have long ago, when his boy needed comfort. "Look, Freya Dane might talk like she's different, but she wants what they all want. A man strong enough to stand beside her through the hard times. She might not know that, but she does." He smiled. "Get in the boat, Son. Not life and death, is it?"

Dan gazed at his father.

Walter thought the boy was coming to his senses. "Go on." He gave Dan a bit of a push.

Dan stared at the workshop door as if expecting it to open. His eyes snapped back to Walter's. *Life and death.* "And time." He smiled.

"Time?" Walter was confused, but he hadn't seen his son happy in a while. That was enough for him.

"You left out time." Dan dropped the ear protectors on the bench. "See you later."

It was two days since she'd taken Simon back to Portsolly, and nothing at all had happened. Of course. She'd even managed dreamless sleep two nights in a row—that was a first on Findnar.

Freya straightened her back. She was stiff from all the digging, and discouraged. Three more trenches in the center of the stones, and precisely zilch result, not even pottery shards.

"So? Tell me. Come on." She stared at the stones severely. "Where should I dig?"

"Maybe I can help."

Freya swung around. "Dan!" She hadn't heard him approach. "What are you doing here? I mean, um, . . ." *That went well.*

Dan laughed. "And lovely to see you, too, Freya." He limped toward her.

"You're smiling." It was almost an accusation. *And that came out wrong too.* Freya leaned on her shovel in the trench. "Let's start again."

He was only a pace or two away. His eyes were brilliant; there were points of light deep in the gray. "Why not? It's what we do."

Freya choked back a laugh. "Hello, Daniel Boyne. How nice you dropped over."

"Very good—almost a welcome. Hello, Freya Dane. Dad sent me."

"Now, why would he do that?"

"He's into advice at the moment—told me to get over here and help out." Dan smiled disarmingly. "What was I to do?"

"He's right. I do need you." Freya's eyes flew wide. "That is, oh . . . I just can't get this right, can I?" She started to scramble out of the shallow trench.

"Like a hand?" Dan leaned down.

She hesitated. "Why not?"

"Up you come."

Dan pulled, and Freya found herself on the edge of the trench. Only three days and she'd forgotten how strong he was. "Oops. Nearly trod on your foot." Self-conscious, she brushed her jeans. "Blimey, I'm filthy."

Dan grinned. "I've seen worse. You're frequently worse."

How different he seemed—open, almost carefree. And such a contrast from Simon. Was that good? A neat wriggle and she moved past him. "I've been thinking." She strode toward the groundsheet covering the stone slab.

"A good start." He limped after her.

"Very funny. Anyway, you found this almost as soon as you started looking—the stone slab. I've had nearly three stupid days, killing myself, and I've found precisely nothing. You're a human dowsing rod, Dan. You are, really. That's why I need you." She tried to keep it light.

"If that's a compliment, I accept."

"What I mean is, I know—I just know—there's something here." Freya waved her arms around, a wide, jittery sweep. "But I can't make it land—whatever it is. You, though . . ." She looked at him hopefully.

Dan went to say something and frowned. His eyes traveled from stone to stone, and then back to Freya.

"What is it?"

"Come here." He held out a hand. His voice was low, and his eyes had changed. They were distant.

Freya hesitated, but she stepped closer, linked her fingers through his. Her palm tingled. "Do you see something?" She spoke very softly.

He looked away and lifted his head. He was listening.

Freya tried to match Dan breath for breath, tried to slow the lurch of her heart.

His eyes swung back to hers, the pupils huge and dark. He offered his other hand. "Yes. I see them."

Freya linked her fingers through his, and then she saw what he saw.

A naked girl and a naked man. The girl was small, with wild, dark hair falling down her back. Eyes wide, she was laughing, teasing her lover, her red mouth stubbornly closed under the man's insistence. But then she opened her lips and gasped, writhing against his body, one small hand caressing the nape of his neck, the other twisted deep into the mass of his hair.

The man was magnificent. The broad muscles of his back moved beneath the skin as he eased himself between the girl's knees. She opened her legs, helping him inside her body, and, almost growling, the man thrust his head back against the sky, his powerful throat exposed. One side of his face was perfect, but the other . . .

"No!" Freya broke Dan's grip. She stumbled back a pace, her face hot.

"What did you see?" They were both embarrassed, but Dan still asked the question.

"A girl. And a man." Freya swallowed. "They were here. Making love."

Dan nodded. "She was dark. Smaller than him. His face was scarred."

"Yes." She didn't have to say it. The man they had seen was the model for the Christ. "But the circle looked different." Freya gestured. "There was an offering stone." She pointed to two stones leaning against each other. "On top of the smaller ones, there. But it's odd."

"What is?"

It was hard to be clinical about the images that crowded behind her eyes—the erotic charge still lingered, and Freya's breathing was slightly ragged. "Well, you saw them first this time."

Perhaps it was safe. She turned to look at Dan and really saw him, his face. His eyes. And his mouth. She tingled as his eyes roamed her face.

He walked those few, final steps. He stopped. Very gently, he cupped Freya's chin with one hand. He stared into her eyes, searching.

"I wanted to tell you, the other day. I saw something, here." *Don't point. Your hands will shake.*

He shook his head. "I don't care, Freya."

Freya could not move; as if she had been turned to stone, she could not even speak. She watched her hands, first one, then the other, find their way to Dan's shoulders. He was lean, but the muscles were whipcord tight.

"What are you doing, Freya Dane?" He seemed amused.

That broke the spell. "Don't you dare!" She dropped her hands.

Dan's eyes changed. "Dare what?" Without touching her, he bent and kissed the base of her throat. His lips brushed her skin so lightly, Freya shivered.

"Don't mock me. I couldn't bear that." She closed her eyes as his lips traveled closer to her mouth. She was trembling. This was nothing, *nothing,* like kissing Simon.

"I would never mock you." Dan spoke into her mouth, whispering, "Closer." The word buzzed on her lips.

Something broke. Reserve. Self-protection. Freya molded her torso to his and kissed him back. Delirious, sweet dark engulfed her as they crumpled to the turf in something like slow motion, each moment, each movement heady and distinct. Then Freya remembered. Her eyes flew open. "But I have to tell you, Dan. I'm sure it's important."

"Later. Tell me later."

"Does this worry you?" Freya sat up suddenly. "I mean . . ." Strange, though, that Dan's face—here, now—obliterated Simon's so easily.

"We hardly know each other. Is that it?" He propped himself on an elbow.

"Yes." She was sincerely worried. "Here we are, necking like two teenagers, just after we saw them . . . not necking. Does this feel real to you, or is it just this place? I mean, it's not exactly typical behavior for me to throw myself at someone I hardly know." *It can be. Not exactly a nun, are you?* Sincerely embarrassed, Freya pinched her eyes shut in case he picked up the half-truth. He was smiling happily when she opened them again. "You're laughing at me." She zipped her jacket testily.

Dan dropped back on the turf, one arm behind his head. "You're getting better at picking it though."

"Says you." She hesitated, gave in, and wriggled down beside him. *Don't think.*

Dan pushed a wisp of Freya's wild hair behind an ear and kissed her gently, then harder. "This was my choice. I want this. I like touching you." Slowly, he unzipped the jacket again. There was no bra under Freya's T-shirt. His hand cupped one of her breasts. "You have really lovely skin." He touched a nipple, pinched it gently.

Freya swallowed a breath. "That's nice. My skin, the compliment I mean."

"I know what you mean, Freya." They stared at each other.

"Are you surprised?" She caressed the side of his face, and her fingers found their way to his mouth. He bit them softly.

"So many questions." Dan moved. He pulled her on top of him. "I'm not surprised, but maybe I can't believe it either."

Freya put her hands on either side of his head and stared down at him. "Why?"

"And that's—"

"Another question. Yes. I know." But she smiled at him, a shy smile. "Sorry."

He put his hands into her hair and pulled her down. He felt her heart against his ribs and whispered, "Never be sorry, not with me." His eyes closed as they kissed. Deeply. Deeper. Until the world spun.

Freya gasped a breath. She rolled to lie beside him, her chest rising and falling as if she'd run a race.

Dan stared at her profile. He traced the line of her forehead, her nose, her mouth. His finger stopped. "We have time." He half-laughed. "And that's an irony; it's the nature of this place that time surprises us both."

"It's just . . ."

"Ah . . . just."

"I've never been much good at relationships." Freya swallowed. "There. Said it." She tried to laugh. Bravely, she turned to look at him. "I thought I should tell you. Perhaps I'm just impossible or fickle, or too picky." Simon's face swung into her mind; she'd definitely been attracted to him. "And I've been accused of all three—often at the same time." Half a grimace, but there was a catch in her voice.

"Does it seem to you that I am concerned, Freya Dane?" Another man would have laughed. Dan did not; he held her glance. "And you are not impossible. Just"—he smiled—"unusual. And a little lost. But you are perfect. I thought that when you first walked through the door."

She hit him on the shoulder, but her eyes filled with tears. "You did not, you were horrible. I thought you hated me, and I felt like such an outsider."

"I hide things; so do you. And your father stood between us."

She stroked his face tenderly. "If I could wish one thing, it would be that you could absolve yourself. My father died, but you did not. Perhaps, if he'd had a choice, that's what he would have wanted."

"Why would you say that?"

"Because," she said slowly, "his death brought me here—and I have met you. He always wanted me to be happy." She caught her breath. This was true, she knew that now.

Dan knelt and pulled her up. On their knees, they faced each other. "Welcome home, Freya Dane. Welcome home."

Kissing him, she leaned her full weight against his chest, and they tumbled sideways together.

"Oh! Are you all right? Dan?" *Why? Why am I so clumsy?*

He lay on the grass with eyes closed. "Dan? Come on, please." She crouched beside him, suddenly frantic.

One eye opened. "Impetuous too. Good to know." He rubbed the back of his head. "Might get me into trouble one day, if not immediately."

She said, semidefiantly, "Never said I wasn't, Daniel Boyne."

He looked behind his shoulder. "I hit something—that's what hurt."

There was a swelling in the turf. Dan stared at it intently.

"A stone, maybe. We have quite a lot on Findnar."

"No, it's not a stone." He was picking at the grass, pulling it up with his fingers. "Have you a trowel—and maybe a brush?"

Freya was on her feet and back to Dan in less than three neat seconds. "A trowel, the man says, and my best brush." She handed Dan the tools and watched, intrigued. He scalped the grass from the lump, and as the soil was scraped away, a straight gray edge revealed itself. Delicately, Dan knocked with the wooden handle of the brush. "This is metal."

"Wait. Let me get the camera." She arrived at his side, panting. "You've got the knack, Dan, you really have." She fired off a few quick shots from different angles. "Keep going, let's see how big it is."

"Don't you know?"

Freya stared at him. A long, measuring glance. "Let's see."

It was a careful process. As if he had been doing the work all his life, Dan teased soil away. Slowly and patiently, he uncovered a small oblong, not much bigger than the palm of his hand.

"A box." Freya breathed out.

Dan nodded, brushing soil from each side. "The twin of the other one, but there's no cross."

"It's the unicorn. I asked for one."

Dan stared at Freya. "What?"

It was evening, the lamps were lit, and Dan and Freya were in the kitchen. She'd had a bath—it felt so good to be clean, and it was good, too, that he was here. It really was.

"So, shall we open it?" Her eyes shone in the soft light.

Dan reached across and stroked her cheek. "You should always wear blue—your own, unfair advantage in a cruel, cruel world."

Freya blushed a healthy rose. "And here's me thinking you a man of few words."

"I am that. Mostly." Dan pulled on a pair of Michael's cotton gloves and picked up the little box. "Ready?"

She nodded. She did not say *Be careful,* she knew he would be.

He held the box to the light, so that each surface was exposed in turn. "I think, in fact I'm sure, that the lid works the same way."

"Has to be the same maker, just has to be." Freya breathed the words like a prayer.

Dan went to work with a dental scraper, easing soil, crumb by crumb, from the hinge. He said, absently, "If wishes were horses, beggars would ride; one of Walter's favorite sayings. Something for the earth if you please, Nurse." Freya grinned as she passed him a watercolor brush.

He worked the soft bristles along the hinge line. "It's not damaged, so far as I can tell. The hinge, I mean."

"So close to the surface all this time, just amazing." Freya watched him work with pleasure. Dan was so deft and so patient. She was devoutly grateful they were easy with each other now. That was trust, faith too; she believed in Daniel Boyne, his instinct for this work, his born talent. She just did not understand the why of it.

As if he could read her mind, Dan looked up, full into Freya's eyes. "Happy?"

The room seemed to shift. "Yes." He made her breathless, he really did.

"Right, here we go." He worked his thumbnails under the overlapping edge of the lid. "I . . . just . . . do . . . not . . . want . . . to force it."

There was a faint sigh. "Air." *From a thousand years ago.* Freya had to remember to breathe.

Dan eased the lid up; it stuck partway open.

"What can you see?" She crowded close.

"You're in the light, Miss Dane."

"Sorry." She leaned back. "Anything in there, though?"

Dan held the box closer to the light and peered inside. He said softly, "There is." He handed her the box. "You try. Your fingers are smaller."

She caught the glimmer of a pale shape. After she dragged on a pair of cotton gloves, her fingers felt the size of hammers, but Freya eased the forefinger of her right hand through the opening and hooked it around something—something small and hard.

"Can you get it out?"

Eyes half-closed to feel what she was doing, she eased the object closer, closer. "Here it is!" She brought it out into the light. "Oh, just look at her."

A tiny ship lay in her palm, a Viking ship—jaunty, spirited. "It's not a unicorn, though it's lovely." Was she disappointed this was a Pagan object? No, not at all.

He leaned closer. "You'll have to explain that one day. Is it ivory?"

"Whale ivory." Freya said it at the same time. "Snap!"

The same material as the crucifix?

CHAPTER 33

D AN WAS in the kitchen, opening and closing cupboard doors. He called out, "I'll make an omelet. Got any herbs?"

"I'm not hungry." In the big room, Freya just wanted to ransack Michael's card files again; there must be clues somewhere that would help with the ivory ship. "You said you couldn't cook."

"I've seen it done. Cooking shows."

Freya slewed around in the chair. "You watch cooking shows?"

Dan limped toward the gas ring and clattered a pan down. "Once or twice, not a hanging offense. Herbs?"

"Try the bottom of the dresser. There's dried thyme, I think. Might be a bit old." She pulled the light closer as she opened the first box. *Come on, Dad, time to step up. Show me where to look.* The lamp gilded Freya with a line of soft gold.

"Dong, dong, dong."

Dan stood in the doorway. "Food's ready. That was my dinner gong impersonation, by the way."

"Hmmm?"

He snorted. She was hardly in the same room, *or the same time period, probably.* He marched to the desk. "Time to eat, Freya Dane."

"The thing is." She got up reluctantly, and only because he dragged her chair half out. "There's nothing. Nothing I can find reference to that seems similar to our ship in any way except for the original box and the crucifix."

"But that's a start." Dan towed her to the kitchen. "Sit. Chew."

Absently, she picked up a fork. "I know the chances are slim, really I do, but there's so much material to go through. Reams and reams of it, and I should search the stored material properly too." A surprised look crossed her face. "This is good."

He grinned. "I'm verra pleased to hear you say that."

She looked at him fondly. "Say it again."

Dan chewed and swallowed. "Which bit?"

"*Verra.* Go on, just for me."

"Verra. *Verra.*" Dan put the fork down. He leaned across and took her free hand. "Verrrrraaaa." A low growl.

Freya giggled, then sobered. "You make me tipsy, Daniel Boyne."

He kissed her hand. "A giddy girl, but one who needs to work."

She looked guilty. "Am I so obvious?"

"You certainly are." But he said it with a lilt. "Besides, I have something to think about as well."

"You do?"

"Of course."

Freya stared at him expectantly. "And?"

He said, "We need to shift that slab."

She could not quite mask her disappointment. Dan grinned. "And you, of course. I shall think about you, now, that's a given."

"Thank you for saying that, Dan." She leaned across and kissed him softly.

"And very nice you do taste. Egg, a bit of thyme, butter."

She laughed. "Compliments to the chef."

Dan leaned his elbows on the tabletop. "But how to hoist that stone out of the ground, that's the thing."

Freya ate busily. "Question without notice. Do you mind me working?"

"No. We both want answers. Besides . . ." He looked at her seriously.

The hairs of instinct stood up on her neck. "Besides?"

"We shall savor the wooing if it is slow."

Freya stared at him, and her eyes filled. "Why did we not meet a long, long time ago, Daniel Boyne?"

"Who is to say we did not?" He flashed her a cheeky smile. "Finish the omelet. I might not be able to do it again."

"I think you've found your cooking mojo." She mopped up bits of egg with bread. "Delicious, truly."

"Just tapped into instinct—something else I never suspected." Dan took the plates to the sink.

Freya lazed in her chair and contemplated this utterly unexpected man. "But you're a creature of instinct, Dan. You just didn't listen to it before."

"BF, you mean. Before Freya."

She laughed delightedly. "Oh, let this all be true. Let this not dissolve like mist in the morning."

"It will not dissolve, and neither will your piece of stone. And I shall come back to prove it to you."

"You're going over to Port?"

He held out his arms. "I am. It is a fair night, and you'll get nothing done if I stay. Trust me."

How intoxicating it was to kiss . . .

It was the dead time between deep night and dawn, and the house was quiet. At Michael's desk, Freya rubbed her eyes. Dan had left hours ago, and she'd finished, finally, reading all her father's card files. It was well past time to sleep, and she'd see him soon. Dan had said that. Ah, sweet anticipation. Perhaps she'd dream of him when she slept. How fast things changed. *BF*, he'd said. For her, it was BD.

And this time, *this* time, she would allow things to just be. She would not overthink or overplan or over-anything. She'd let him lead—he seemed that kind of a man, so different from any of the others. One day at a time, dear Lord. Just one day . . .

Freya stood and stretched luxuriously. She smiled at her reflection.

There was no answering smile. This was not her face.

Freya gasped.

Another girl stared at her from beyond the black glass—long hair, dark eyes, red mouth. *The girl they had seen among the stones.*

The girl moved closer to the window. The image disappeared. Blinked out. And Freya saw her own face. White. Stunned.

She gripped the edge of the desk. Like an accident, like an emergency, time froze and she gulped air like a fish.

And snatched up the camping light. And ran.

Katherine sat up in the dark. She flicked on the light. Another night of broken sleep, and her heart was racing as she'd deliberately woken from a bad dream—made herself escape the formless thing that chased her. This, too, was familiar.

Katherine fumbled for her glasses. There was a writing pad on the little table, and she'd left a pen beside it. If there was one benefit of broken sleep, it was clarity of mind when she woke. She liked to make notes about things as the world slept; it was always a good time to organize the day to come.

But though the phantom had been willed away, Katherine felt uneasy as she picked up the pen. She'd finished the translation of the diary last night—a cause for celebration—but the last entry had been strange if the writer was indeed a nun. Freya would want to know. Should she try to ring tomorrow—today, rather?

And if Freya does not answer? Katherine threw the covers back, suddenly hot. Perhaps she should go over to the island. She could not banish the certainty, the *necessity* of telling the girl what she'd read. Katherine's long-banished Catholic childhood stirred as she named the thing; she had performed a sin of omission, and that must be remedied if her relationship with Freya was to be an honest one.

Loving Michael Dane, finding in him her intellectual equal, had given Katherine more than a technical understanding of archaeology. It had peeled time open. Passion for him had ignited another passion in her—for the past, and for Findnar's past as well. He had shown her how to see, how to look, how to find meaning in the evidence of people's lives from long ago. That had been a comfort when he'd died, as if, in her own small way, she carried his work further. But there are many ways of seeing, and Michael had shown her that too. And some of the things he'd told her were as if he was using metaphors, or symbols, to tell the truth in a different way.

But now there was Freya, and she was so much Michael's daughter. Looking at the girl in the last days, Katherine had begun to wonder what it would have been like to have a child.

Katherine knew she was not an emotionally open person, too disciplined—or timid—for that, but with Michael she had experienced unconditional love for the first time in her life. And he had allowed her to be brave, to take risks. He lived again, in some ways, in his daughter. It was delicate, but Katherine longed for her and Freya to be close.

"Michael, tell me what to do. Should I tell her?" Perhaps, if she put out the light, she'd sleep and he would provide the answer by the morning.

"Good night, my dear love. I so wish you were here. Your daughter needs you. Perhaps, though, I shall have to do in your place."

Katherine yawned. She felt better sharing her anxiety with the empty air. She flicked the light off and lay in the dark with open eyes, listening. She still did not believe, not truly, that she would never again hear his step on her staircase. She sighed, and her eyes closed.

The night was windless. Breathless.

Abruptly, light spilled across Compline's front windows, blue-white. It tracked back and forth, erratic scribbles over the grass, toward the cliffs, into an immense night sky.

"Where are you?" Freya put the light down and wiped her face. She was sweating. She'd run as far as the stones and all around the Abbey ruins, trying to find the girl. "I saw you. I did see you."

Freya sagged. She huddled on the top step at the front of the house. "You were here."

As her heart stilled and her breathing slowed, she heard the night. The sound of the sea, below, came back, and something else. A soft *pat-pat*. She looked down. A large moth was battering at the glass of the camping light.

Behind her, the front door creaked and opened softly with a click, as if a careful hand had eased the latch.

Light jumped among the shapes inside the big room, traveled over the desk, spilled across the floor as Freya ran inside.

The room was empty.

Freya stopped.

She could hear herself breathe; she could feel the blood in her veins. Her heart squeezed and then ran fast as fire.

The door to the kitchen was open; she'd closed it earlier.

One foot in front of the other. *Count the steps.* "One, two, three, four." Shadows bled into corners when she raised the light high. The kitchen was empty.

But the undercroft door was ajar.

She had to do this. "Five, six, seven, eight . . ."

Freya placed her feet so carefully on the treads going down, and stopped at the bottom. "Hello?"

She stood in a circle of light, but all around was dense black. If she moved, *if* she moved, what would she see?

She swung the lantern in a slow, wide arc. The light passed over the walls—nothing. It traveled across the carved panel; the faces stood out stark—white against black trenches in the wood.

Freya walked forward—just a few paces. Then more—toward

the back wall. She was rigid, muscles corded with tension, as the light bounced and jerked.

There were footprints in the dust. A man's boots; Dan's. Her work boots as well, from the other day. But there were also other prints—delicate naked feet, the shape of the arch a pronounced indentation.

Freya was shaking, her whole body vibrating.

The small footprints led to the back wall.

And they did not return.

CHAPTER 34

THE STONES were Signy's refuge now, and on this warm morning, she drove the animals toward them. As the sheep and goats scattered to graze the slopes below, she approached the offering stone with a beaker of new milk.

Pouring the libation, Signy bowed. "Great Cruach, I beg that you hear me. And that my ancestors hear me." She clapped her hands three times and stared up at the God in the sky for as long as she could.

Cruach's power was too strong. Unwillingly, Signy squeezed her eyes shut, and it was a moment before she could see to place Bear's gifts on the offering stone. She kissed that tragic face one final time; this was a very great sacrifice.

Though she tried not to show it, Signy was frightened, for it was a long time since she had made the proper observances. She bowed to the stone three times and each time felt Cruach's warmth, like a hand, on her head; this, at least, was a good omen. Opening the lead box, she drew out a small piece of vellum covered in her own writing. It had been hard to make ink without the resources of the Scriptorium, but with soot and the white of a stolen egg, she had finally succeeded. Last night, beside her small fire, she had tried to make each word of the prayer perfect.

Throwing her arms high, Signy began to chant. "By the strength of the wind, by the height of the sky, by the might of the sea—by the power of all these things—I ask that you hear your daughter, Great Cruach." She laid the prayer on the stone and knelt, her hands held out in supplication. "This is what I ask. May

Bear find strength and courage and guile to defeat his enemies. Stretch out your hand against those who would do him harm. Guard and protect Bear so that he returns to me. And protect me also, great Cruach. My father was once your servant, and though I am all that is left of my family, I shall serve you in their names."

Signy lowered her arms. She was sweating. Would Cruach listen to her? She had deserted his service for a long time—he might not think her worthy.

She picked up a digging stick. "This is the last part of my offering and my prayer. I bring gifts." She placed the crucifix on top of the lead box. "I give these to the earth—your sister and my mother. They are precious; may they lie safe in her embrace. And when time is accomplished and all is well, may they be returned to me, and may I meet my daughter again in the land of the sky."

The day was bright and, for the moment, windless.

Gunnhilde shaded her eyes as she hobbled across the meadow. She truly must be growing old, for walking pained her now. In the distance, scattered across the hillside, the Abbey flock grazed peacefully. These were the animals that wintered over in the byre, and it pleased Gunnhilde to see the new calves and lambs. The herds were increasing again—that must be part of God's plan for their community.

Gunnhilde stopped, puzzled. She cupped her hands around her mouth and called "Signy!" The hobbled goats looked up, and a few sheep stumbled away, winter's fleece a burden when they tried to run.

She tried again. "Signy?" Turning, she surveyed the plow land and the meadows. And then she saw the girl. Signy had walked out from among the ring of stones.

Gunnhilde's heart lurched in her chest. This was a Pagan figure, a girl crowned with red berries and new green leaves.

A staff of hornbeam in her hand, Signy watched impassively as the nun labored toward her. She had woven the new rowan and last autumn's rose hips among her growing curls, the old year and the new. To perform the ceremony correctly, that had been necessary, but Gunnhilde would be shocked.

"Signy, what are you doing!" The nun arrived short of breath. These days, with increasing pain in her hands and her body, she did little physical work and was less fit than she had been.

"The tasks I have been given by Brother Abbot." Signy's tone was flat.

"But *this* is not God's work." The nun pointed to the garland.

Signy did not move. She was framed by two of the larger monoliths, and behind her was the Pagan altar.

The nun swallowed—this was a heathen priestess guarding her temple. "You should not come here, Signy. It is a cursed place, and these stones were raised by the Devil. I think they have bewitched you."

Signy stared at Gunnhilde quizzically. "The circle has been here longer than your church, Sister. To my people it is sacred. My father was a holy man. He was our clan's shaman—did I tell you that?"

Signy's lack of shame confused Gunnhilde. "But this is the past, Signy, the bad, old ways." She stepped toward the girl.

Signy backed away inside the outer ring. "This is my church, Sister, though I wish yours no disrespect."

Gunnhilde was more than dismayed and, holding up the crucifix on her rosary, she called out, "I abjure you, Satan, in the name of the Father and of the Son and of the Holy Spirit. Leave the body of this, my sister in Christ, and return to the Pit. Go!"

Sorrow darkened Signy's eyes. "I am not possessed, Gunnhilde." She put her hand on the altar stone. "There are no devils here. We are the demons, the evil spirits in this world, and it is we who create suffering and delusion, just us."

It shook Gunnhilde that the Devil was so cunning. Signy sounded like a normal girl, and yet she could not be. Only a possessed soul, in thrall to the Lord of Lies, would seem to speak in this way.

The nun backed away, holding up her cross. "Devil, I know my sister is within this frail flesh. The strength of the Lord will defeat your evil purposes." Turning, she hurried away and, as Signy watched, sped up as if pursued.

The girl knelt and placed Bear's crucifix and the box in the hole she had made. "When will you return, Bear?" This was her own private prayer. "Or must I come to you?" She stared toward the Christian settlement. "Tell me where you hid the coracle. I have looked and looked. Show me, I beg."

Signy raised her arms and slowly turned. Her eyes were closed. She stopped, and sniffed the air like a hound. Her eyes opened. She stared toward the cliffs behind the circle.

CHAPTER 35

A T DAWN on the second day, fourteen ships rode at anchor. Well maintained and sleek, they sat beyond the point where the small estuary emptied into the sea. The river mouth had given the raiding band easy access to the settlement behind it, but now the fleet was stayed to boulders on the shore as the trade goods were assembled.

This was Grimor's raiding band now, and he'd led them for four seasons after killing Reimer. If Thorkeld had not earlier retired to his farm, Grimor might not have been successful, but the old man had gone down to his ax at the end of a bad summer when they'd returned home with little of value in the hulls.

It *was* a young man's game, raiding, and Grimor at twenty-eight or twenty-nine summers was in his prime. He had some years of this work yet before his physical powers declined and it became too hard to manage the men. But he remembered this coast from a season long ago; that had been the year he'd lost his brother, Magni, in one of Reimer's ventures. The boy had been among the first to charge the cliff path on the Christian island, and then he'd disappeared into the flames of the Abbey.

Grimor had always intended to settle that score—to go back to the island and burn it again in memory of his brother. That had been part of the dispute that cost Reimer his life, for the old leader said that pickings in the East were too lean. The people, too, were more difficult and the winds not useful for much of the year. But Grimor knew that Magni's blood would never be appeased until he'd made a proper pyre to his brother's spirit in the place that had taken his body. The Christian island—was this the season to find it again?

He gazed at the sky. He did not like the color of the clouds—wild weather on its way. Perhaps this was the omen he needed; it would be safer for the hulls to run south in front of the storm rather than beat their way north again. But would forty or so seasons be enough to make the island worth another raid?

It was always a problem to assess such things, Grimor knew, and his current company was, on average, young; that meant they were not yet experienced enough to avoid stupidity in the heat of the fight. It was annoying that most of the buildings in the river village had been destroyed, as they had been on the Christian island all those years ago—that was a blunder in both cases. How many times had he said it? Do not burn everything; better to leave something standing and habitable to encourage resettlement.

Raiding was like farming. Burn the stubble, till the ground, leave the crop alone while it grew. Then harvest.

A buffet of wind swirled the plaid from his shoulders. Grimor could smell the storm building from the high east. Time for decisions.

"Edor, hurry it up!"

His chief lieutenant waved from the water's edge and shouted, "Not long now, Grimor, just them to load." Edor pointed. A group of crying women and their children sat on the beach. The leader nodded and turned away, gazing thoughtfully at the smoke still rising from what remained of the village.

Counting those they'd taken plus the dead—the useless women past their physical prime, the oldest of the men, the youngest of the children—there'd been more than seventy people among the houses. Not a bad result in ten years, but then most people thought a river mouth was a good place to live. It was their fate and his luck that people generally rebuilt in places they'd lived before.

Grimor yawned and stretched until his bones cracked, then

tramped across the beach. *Fenrir* bucked against the mooring as waves grew beneath her bow, and he waved Edor over.

"Yes, Lord?"

Grimor pointed at the sky. "What do you think?"

Edor shrugged. "Could get ugly."

"I agree." Grimor nodded. It did no harm to seem to take advice from time to time.

Farther up the beach, a man called out, "Sail. Sail!" The cry was echoed by crew on the other hulls.

Grimor turned and stared out to sea. A substantial ship was making good progress toward them from the south, and a man was standing at the prow, waving.

Edor grinned at his master. One trading vessel against a war fleet. "This man is brave."

Grimor clapped his lieutenant on the shoulder. "Or foolish. Or both. Excellent."

"Lord Grimor? Here is our visitor." Edor's irony was obvious, and some of the crew on *Fenrir* smirked. Grimor glowered. Faces dropped.

Grimor was standing beside the longship's mast. Around him the hulls were loaded and waiting for his command to sail. He nodded to his lieutenant; this would not take long.

Edor ushered the man toward Grimor. Young, with barely a beard, he was dressed well in good, thick wool, the tunic ornamented with expensive braid. His cloak was lined with fur too—another sign of wealth; it was probably only rabbit, but the garment was of good quality.

On the beach, well guarded, was the crew of the ship the stranger commanded. He had run his vessel up onto the beach beside Grimor's hulls as if expecting a welcome.

Leaning on his ax, Grimor glowered. "Who are you?"

The point of Edor's blade just touching his spine, the stranger made a stiff bow. "I am Idorn. Son of Iredern, son of . . ."

Grimor waved his hand impatiently. Edor jumped in. "That is sufficient." Genealogies, after all, could go on all day.

"And what do you want, Idorn, son of Iredern?"

"Lord Grimor, I am an emissary from Solwaer, Lord of Portsol. I have this for you, from my master." The young man swallowed.

Grimor gave the man some credit. He might speak very bad Norse, but he was brave enough to present a scroll with steady hands and a clear voice. The war leader grunted and spat into the tide. "What would I want with this?" He could not read, but he wasn't about to say that to this young fool.

Idorn bowed. "If I may . . ." He went to unroll the parchment and found a knife at his throat. Edor.

Grimor scowled testily at his lieutenant. *Jumps too fast, this one.* "Yes, read it. But be careful, Idorn; my men may not like what you say. They may not like *you.*" No irony here; he prodded the emissary in the chest with a stiff finger. Around him, the crew guffawed.

Idorn's face leached to an uncooked, pale gray, and yet he waited until the laughter died before he cleared his throat and began to read. Another mark in his favor.

" 'To Lord Grimor, son of Ragnar, son of Iarl, son of Othere, son of . . .' " The sonorous genealogy rolled out of the stranger's mouth with skaldlike majesty. Grimor stood straighter. How did he know? " '. . . greeting from your brother, Solwaer, Lord of Portsol.' "

"Brother? I have only one brother, and he is dead."

Idorn's rather harried expression lifted. He said, earnestly, "But that is why I am here, Lord Grimor. Your brother, Magni, is not dead." He waved the parchment.

The silence on the ship changed. It was instantly absolute.

Grimor beckoned Idorn. The youth edged forward a step.

Grimor beckoned again. Another step; only the length of a man's forearm separated them now.

The raider lunged. Two massive hands, two thumbs, gouged into the emissary's neck. The boy was yanked up, and his feet jerked above the deck. As he struggled, his face turned red, then purple, and his eyes rolled back.

Grimor dropped him.

Idorn's head hit one of the rowing benches. He had no breath to howl, but at least he could suck air into his lungs, the sweetest air he'd ever tasted.

Grimor bent down. He said, softly, "Hear me. You live. But if what you tell me is a lie, you will die as will your men, and not quickly."

If the world swum and swung, at least Idorn had not lost all sense. He managed a few words—"It is written"—and pointed at the scroll now lying in the bilges, gently moving back and forth on the water.

"Edor," Grimor growled, and the scroll was picked up and hastily wiped on his lieutenant's tunic. Grimor said, without emphasis, "The ink had better not be smudged." That sparked something of a panic as three men at once tried to unroll the stiff parchment to see if the text was damaged.

Idorn, forgotten for the moment, managed to stand. He touched his throat carefully; he could feel the swelling wheals from Grimor's thumbs. He beckoned one of the crew to him, and in a strangled whisper he asked, "Give the scroll to me. Please. Your lord must hear how his brother came to Portsol."

Edor claimed Grimor's attention. He pointed at the clouds and the ocean. Spray was beginning to fly from wave crest to wave crest out in the sea road.

Grimor nodded. He stared at Idorn. "You shall tell me what is written in your scroll, but out there." He waved toward the sea. "South, Edor. We go south."

Edor cupped his hands and shouted to the nearest hull. "South—pass it on." The word was bellowed from ship to ship as men began to push the hulls off the beach.

Idorn looked pleased. But then he saw his crew hustled onto one of the hulls, and other raiders boarding his own ship. "But, Lord Grimor, I am an emissary. This is—"

"The way it is, my friend. You are my hostage now. But I am looking forward to hearing more. Think well on what you will say."

It was only just the cool side of midsummer when the line of ships was sighted from Portsol.

Solwaer had been thinking about this moment for a long time—much before, in fact, he'd sent Idorn out to search for trouble.

"Bear?" He walked to the berserker's hut at dawn, just after Fiachna had woken him with the news, but the stone shed was empty.

Solwaer turned and surveyed the coast to the north. There they were, beating down the strait between the island and Portsol, the ships formed a flying V—brave sails taut, shields lining their sides—and they were making course for Portsol's harbor. For a moment, even he quailed. Could he really do this?

"What do you want?"

Solwaer swiveled. His eyes widened. Bear had weapons slung around his body—ax, knife, sword, a spear in each hand. They jiggled and knocked as he walked out of the early mist.

Solwaer stood his ground. "There is news, remarkable news." He hoped it was—remarkable, not disastrous.

Bear grunted. "I've seen them. Now we'll find out how good Fiachna really is, and the rest of them." He hefted the ax in his hand, feeling its balance, thumbing its edge. Ignoring Solwaer, he strode to the whetstone beside his door—more work to be done.

"Listen to me, I know who commands these ships."

Bear turned.

"And if I told you . . ." An artful pause.

Bear did not ask the question. The battle to come was already inside his body—each of his muscles tight, getting tighter—but his mind was quiet, detached. Words were irrelevant now.

Those wide, cold eyes made Solwaer nervous. "These ships belong to Grimor. Your brother." He said it helpfully, as if Bear might not remember. "They have not come to fight us."

Bear sharpened his gaze; the focus changed from out on the water. "How can you know that?"

"The ship at the end of the longer line, the trader. I sent that vessel out to find Grimor and bring him to Portsol. I wanted your brother to know you still live."

In Bear's chest, something deep shifted, but he laughed, not a kind laugh. "And you think this is wise? You're a Christian now, Solwaer. Did they tell you about the Devil?"

The Lord of Portsol bent his head. Was he praying? No. He raised his eyes, and they were hard, gray pebbles. "I knew about the Devil long before I met you. More demons will not trouble me. Besides, the Devil loves a bargain."

Bear grunted. "Ah, but what do you have to trade with?"

Solwaer became annoyed as Bear's insolence worked its way under his skin. "You will stand at my back when they arrive to parlay. Remember your obligations."

Bear stared at the ships as they flew on toward the harbor, a morning wind behind the sails. "Fiachna won't like it."

Solwaer shrugged testily. He furled the mantle around his shoulders. It wasn't his best cloak, he would wear that for the meeting with Grimor, but time was passing and there was much to do. "Think of Findnar, Bear, think of your little nun. It's all getting so much closer." He turned to go, then stopped. "Bear!" It was a tricky moment; would his demon follow?

Bear did not respond. The vessel that led the pack, was that his brother's hull? Blood surged, and a chaos of images filled his skull; he ran a finger along the edge of his ax. Solwaer might be wrong.

CHAPTER 36

THEY'D HAD a successful journey down the coast, the ships in Grimor's band. Reimer might have thought the uttermost East and North were less populated—and less valuable to harvest—but unseasonably warm weather in the last few years had changed much. A long growing season is a great inducement, and clans and family groups in search of land had wandered farther north than they might have in less fortunate times.

Farming communities were good sources of slaves, but for luxury goods, and slaves of higher quality, the spreading canker of Christian religious houses were always worth paying attention to. Only three sailing days before they'd sacked one isolated monastery quite easily, and now there was Findnar, temptingly close. First, though, there was Portsol.

The morning wind had dropped as the crews rowed Grimor's ships through the entrance to the settlement's new breakwater. Led by *Fenrir*, they drove those not laden with slaves onto the beach. Whatever transpired in this place, the raiding band would need to return to winter quarters soon to off-load what they'd gathered; space was at a premium in the hulls, and they did not wish to miss the autumn slave markets.

Grimor was first ashore. He'd braced himself in readiness just before *Fenrir*'s keel bottomed on the sloping cove, and now he jumped into the cold shallows. From the shingle he cupped his hands and shouted to Edor as *Wave Biter* followed him in. "Everyone out of the hulls except those with slaves. Stand those off the beach. Six from each ship left to guard in relays; gather the rest here." He pointed at the beach. "This is not a raid until I say it is. Tell them that."

Edor waved; he'd heard. As *Wave Biter* slid up the shingle, he shouted instructions to the next ship's captain, who bellowed to the captain of the vessel beside his until the orders were relayed down the entire line, even to the late-arriving vessel that Idorn had once commanded.

Grimor shouted again. "Bring me the hostage." As a precaution on the run down the coast, Idorn had been tied to *Fenrir's* mast. Bear's brother was a pragmatist; he'd not wanted the hostage jumping overboard in despair once home was in sight—that's what he would have done in the same circumstances rather than face the shame of such an arrival. But Idorn did not think like Grimor. All the youth cared about was survival—and turning what had happened to his advantage. He, too, was a pragmatist, but of a different kind.

The organized chaos of arrival proceeded. The wide, sandy cove was quickly filled to capacity, most of the vessels lying beached, with five standing off behind the breaker line; these were the ships with human cargo.

"Welcome party." Edor nudged his leader.

Grimor turned from watching his fighters gather. He could see their confusion—normally they'd have been into the town by now.

A silent group of men was watching the arrival. They were massed at the beginning of a wooden trackway, which led toward the buildings set back from the shore. All were slung about with weapons, and most carried shields; one was taller than the rest, and he stepped forward.

"Solwaer, Lord of Portsol, greets you through me. He is glad you have accepted his invitation, Lord Grimor. I am Fiachna, son of Fianor, chief housecarl of the Lord Solwaer. He now requests your presence in his hall, where a feast has been prepared in your honor." A certain nervousness betrayed itself in Fiachna's voice.

Grimor turned to Edor. "What does he say?"

Edor shrugged. He turned back to the men waiting silently on the beach. "Form up! No pushing. No shoving!"

Fiachna watched the men from the hulls shuffle into a compact, ordered mass behind their leaders. Each fighter carried at least a sword and a leather-covered shield. Formidable, and silent. Fiachna's fingers convulsed, and the haft of his ax grew slippery with sweat. He tried again, louder; mercifully, his voice did not crack.

"Join us in peace as our welcome guests."

Grimor's men were restless. *Thud, thud, thud,* spear shaft on shield, softly at first, then louder, quicker.

Grimor called out, "Idorn!"

The hostage was pushed forward, and though his bowels jolted in time with the thumps of the spears, hope flickered. Here was salvation; he understood both languages, and no one else, except perhaps Bear, would have that skill.

"Lord Grimor, Solwaer of Portsol thanks you for accepting his invitation, conveyed by me." Idorn raised his voice proudly. "And bids you welcome to his hall, where a noble feast awaits all."

Edor flashed Grimor a glance. He of all the captains understood best how important finding his lost brother was to their leader, but all they had was the word of the hostage that this *Bear* was who he was supposed to be. Was it a trap? Overall, they'd noticed the settlements of this coast had become more professional, better at defending themselves—possibly better at attack also—since the last raids. Portsol could be one of those places. Including Idorn's, there were fifteen valuable ships at stake here, not to mention reputations.

Grimor hefted his ax; he ran a finger along the edge, staring at Fiachna. "Tell them we accept the invitation of your lord, but be very careful, Idorn. Remember we are behind you, all of us."

Idorn gulped. He moved out from behind Grimor and walked to a point midway between the two groups of silent men. Waving vigorously, he shouted, "Lord Grimor asks me to say that he is your friend, and that he comes in peace. He accepts Lord Solwaer's invitation; he and his men will eat in the noble hall of Portsol's Chieftain."

Fiachna frowned as the hostage was recognized. "Idorn? We thought you were dead."

The hostage felt the stares of the men behind him boring into his back. *And I might be soon, idiot!* There were more than two hundred Norse on the beach. His smile was tight. "As you see, Fiachna, I've done what Solwaer asked of me. I've brought Bear's brother to Portsol. I think we should go to the hall now, before everyone gets too excited. Don't you?" Fear made him emphatic.

Fiachna's eyes widened. Fear, by its nature, is contagious.

Pivoting, Idorn beckoned to the Norsemen. "Fiachna, Chief Thane of Lord Solwaer, is honored by your acceptance of his lord's invitation. Your brother will be impatient to see you, Lord Grimor, after all these many years."

"Therefore, I will not keep Magni waiting longer." The Norse leader strode toward the trackway, sword unsheathed in his hand. His men, led by Edor, poured after him, a surging human river.

Ah well, thought Edor, scanning Fiachna and his men. *If it's all a load of bollocks, this lot don't look too difficult.*

He cheered up. Easy pickings were good, but the closer they got to this town, the more prosperous it seemed, even if it was well defended. You couldn't have it easy all the time.

How do you eat safely with the Devil? You smile and invite him to sit where you can see his hands.

So thought Solwaer as Grimor moved toward the honor seat. Behind him, the raiding band strode forward, three abreast. Tough and young, wild-haired, they were well clothed and well fed, and light caught the blue-honed edges of sword and ax. The smell of male sweat was suddenly sharp in the hall, stronger than smoke.

The Lord of Portsol swallowed. Grimor was enormous, just as

his brother was. To avoid the light wheels hanging from the roof, he had to duck his head, and he moved easily, with the grace of a predator.

"Welcome, Lord Grimor, and we welcome, also, your men." Solwaer stood, hands raised high—an honorable greeting and also a demonstration that he held no weapons. Some in the hall thought their lord rose out of respect for the visitors; they were wrong. With the advantage of the dais, Solwaer stood so he'd be taller than Grimor.

"Magni, son of Ragnar, son of Iarl, son of Othere, son of Britwulf Ironhand, brother to Grimor, step forward." Solwaer himself pronounced the invitation.

Bear moved into the light. He'd been standing in the shadows behind Solwaer's seat, watching unseen as the Norsemen strode the length of the hall.

"Magni, do you see this man before me? Do you know him for your brother?" A rhetorical question.

Gazing at Grimor, Bear said nothing. The Norseman's eyes were locked to his.

Fiachna, standing in front of the dais, flushed a congested puce. He'd only just seen that Bear had usurped his accustomed place.

Solwaer lowered his arms. "Come, Magni, let all hear your greeting."

An age of silence stretched. None moved in the hall, or scratched or, even, spat.

Walking slowly, as if in pain, Bear stopped at the edge of the dais. Grimor stood, still as rock. Breath was sucked back, collectively, like wind in the eaves.

"Brother?" It was a whisper.

Bear tried again, louder. *"Brother?"* He used the Norse word.

Idorn was shocked. Drops of water were falling into the beard of the raider Chieftain. *Grimor was crying.*

"He has the look of my father. This is truly my brother. *Magni, my brother, is alive!*" The bellow filled the hall—one man's voice, answered by a roar from many throats.

Bear jumped down into Grimor's arms, and the two men embraced, both crying.

Solwaer's people did not know what was being said, but they understood the emotion. Man turned to wife, friend to friend, comrade to comrade, even the children squealed with infected glee and punched each other among the babble of guffaws and yells of happiness. They were all sentimental people, and in a hard world, seeing such a reunion was like being in the tales of the Gods.

Meanwhile the ale girls filled the skins with new beer and mead as fast as they possibly could, for the drinking was about to start.

"Lord Grimor—and you, Magni—join me here." To demonstrate his superior power in this moment of joy—after all, it was he who had engineered it—Solwaer pointed to the stools now placed on either side of the honor seat. Ostentatiously draped with the finest of winter pelts, they were as large as his, and as high.

The hall was transformed as willing hands hauled trestles and boards to be set along the walls on each side of the central fire pit. The most important men of Portsol and the captains and lieutenants of Grimor's ships would all sit and eat. Women, children, and the men of lesser importance would watch the grandees at the board, though there would certainly be drink for all. As a gracious gesture, those who were seated would also send platters of food around the lesser men—though not the women or children—from which they could help themselves.

It was a miracle, this feast—not least because the women of Portsol had conjured up so many provisions so quickly. It was true Solwaer had been planning for some months, but much of the food had to be prepared very quickly when Grimor and his men actually showed themselves in the strait. And Solwaer's people gave the best of what they had to the men who should have been their enemies.

Roasted lamb and kid and even chickens—luxury food—and fresh fish seethed in milk and fennel were brought to the tables in large vessels of earthenware and iron. There was a cauldron of savory, thick porridge made from oats, wild greens, and bacon; and comfrey and onion fritters piled high on wooden platters next to soft, white cheeses of sheep's milk. And everywhere there were mounds of flat barley bread baked on the stones of the fire pits in houses all around the settlement. These were used to scoop the food to the mouth.

On the dais, as Idorn waited to translate for Solwaer, Grimor and Bear stared at each other and smiled. There was so much to ask, so much to say, and neither knew how to begin the conversation. Bear's Norse, too, was halting, though hearing Grimor shout happily to his men brought words into his head, words he'd not said since he was a cub.

Grimor waved to Idorn. "Ask him, does his face cause him pain?"

Idorn began, "Lord Grimor asks if your face . . ." Bear grinned at his brother—who grinned back—they both had good teeth.

"I understood—enough. Tell him nothing pains me now because he's here."

Grimor, leaning across Solwaer, embraced Bear with a delighted guffaw. "Tell him this was a good answer."

"And tell him that I am a skald in his presence."

The brothers beamed—at each other, at the hall, at the men, the women, the ale girls, even at the children. And the people of Portsol wondered why they'd ever been frightened of Bear, or called him a demon. Plainly, he could be quite nice, provided he liked you.

As the roar of the feast grew louder and the faces of all present flushed scarlet with the good ale and heat, Solwaer began to relax. He signaled to Fiachna, now back in his accustomed place behind the Chieftain's right shoulder.

"Tell the women to keep the beer flowing—not one horn is

to empty without being refilled. And food—tell them to keep cooking."

Solwaer gazed around his hall with pride. The Norse seemed impressed by his community of well-fed, well-dressed people; even the children were free from rickets—that was testimony to the prosperity of Portsol and to his own wealth. Business was yet to be transacted, but that would come, for now he could only pray that the goodwill exchanged in endless toasts would hold until at least tomorrow. "And, Fiachna, I want you to remain alert. Let there be no fights; keep your best men sober."

Fiachna rolled his eyes behind his master's back—too late for that. "See that they keep the peace too." Solwaer waved the chief carl off the dais with shooing motions.

Fiachna was reluctant to leave. He wanted to hear what was said; worse, he could feel the balance of power shifting beneath his feet.

Solwaer smiled as he watched his carl prowl the length of the hall, scowling. It was good to keep his people on edge; in the end, the best retainers were so often the insecure ones.

It was late in the night, and carousing sputtered on. The older men slept where they'd slumped, the women and the children were long gone to bed, but some Portsol girls giggled on the beach with the hard-bodied men from the ships as glowering locals watched in the shadows.

In the hall, Solwaer stood at last. "Come with me, Lord Grimor, and you, Magni. There are things to discuss." He beckoned to Fiachna. "Preside for me."

A stool was quickly placed beside the other three. It was lower, and that did not please Fiachna. As drunk as the rest of them, he was well past surly and heading for rage.

Solwaer belched at the man's sour face. He clapped his chief carl on the shoulder. "Now, old friend, you be the placeholder; they'll obey you, of course they will. Who else would I trust with this? And, remember, no fights. Use this." He tapped Fiachna on the skull. "Not this," he directed, slapping the man's biceps.

One arm slung around Grimor's shoulders and the other around Bear's, Solwaer led the brothers from the hall.

Idorn was unsure of his welcome, but he edged into Grimor's chamber behind the trio. Technically, he was still a hostage—his life forfeit for . . . what? That he did not know, but he'd proved his value today to both Solwaer and Grimor. Did that count?

"Idorn." Grimor was scowling at the frightened chamber slave as she hurried to pour ale for the visitors.

"Yes, Lord Grimor, what shall I say?"

"Solwaer wants something. Ask him what it is." He stared at Idorn with hooded eyes.

Idorn nodded, but his heart ramped up. This was a bald question, latent with menace, and there was the tang of hot metal, suddenly, in the air. He began to sweat.

"Lord Solwaer, the Lord Grimor has journeyed far, and you have brought his lost brother to his heart once more. He thanks you for that most sincerely and seeks to show his gratitude. He asks how that may best be accomplished. He also asks that this conversation be a private one."

Grimor blinked. His eyes became slits. "A lot of words, Idorn."

Solwaer's eyes were half-closed also, but for different reasons. He'd tried not to drink much of the ale for which Portsol was, justly, renowned, but it was rude to refuse a toast, the many toasts, proposed by his guests. Red-eyed and thick-tongued, he frowned at the chamber slave. "You. Go."

The girl blanched. Sober, Solwaer frightened her; drunk, he was utterly unpredictable. She fled.

Solwaer enjoyed obedience—it always improved his mood. "I am honored, but Lord Grimor owes me nothing." He waved grandly. "And yet there are things, important things, that I shall propose for our mutual benefit. I wish to speak of these . . ." He belched; it was all becoming very, very foggy . . .

The Lord of Portsol fell forward right off his stool, a slow, boneless slump.

Idorn grabbed his master just before he rolled into the fire pit. Solwaer pushed Idorn's hand aside good-naturedly. "Just you listen, Idorn. Ears are good." He collapsed sideways, snoring before he hit the floor.

But Grimor was not drunk, and neither was Bear. The elder brother prodded their host cautiously with his foot, and Solwaer twitched like a dreaming hound.

"Is this real?"

Idorn translated Grimor's words without a qualm.

Bear crouched beside Solwaer. He shouted, "Wake!"

Solwaer farted and slept on.

Grimor stood. "Idorn, is there a way out of here?"

"Without going through the hall?" Idorn nodded. He felt along the line of hangings. "Here." A door was concealed in the back wall.

Followed by Idorn, the brothers walked through the darkened settlement. Small fires flickered outside some houses, and there were scuffles and giggles as couples drew back from the light, but the rest of the town slept as they strolled toward the landing beach. Even the sea was quiet, the slump and whisper of the waves enough to cover their words but not hide the meaning.

Grimor stopped. "Is the man a fool, Brother?"

Idorn quickly translated—they all knew who *the man* was.

Bear shook his head. "Solwaer means to consolidate his position as the most powerful man on this coast. He has guile and courage, but desire for wealth drives everything he does, as with all his kind—those who come from nothing. I am the key to the future he craves. So are you, Brother. That is why he asked you to come to Portsol. This could be good for us both." Bear gazed dispassionately at the hostage. "Tell my brother what I have said,

Idorn. Do not lie. I may not speak as fast as you, but I understand much."

Idorn gulped. Words hurried from his mouth.

As Grimor listened, he stared at his brother, trying to sense what he had become. Magni had been a child all those years ago, and it was hard to see that skinny boy in this man of knotted muscle. And more than fire had burned those scars into his face; fury lurked close beneath the skin, a desire for vengeance. That could be good.

Grimor held up his hand, palm out, the classic gesture of peace. "What do you want in this, Magni?"

Bear stared at his older brother. The red stare. "Reparation. There is a girl on Findnar."

"Ah. A girl." Grimor smiled faintly.

"You do not understand." Bear did not expect him to. "You and I will take the island—the Christians have had it long enough— and there will be profit, which we will share."

"With the farter?"

Idorn paused—and then translated the word exactly.

Bear did not smile. "To a degree. There is mutual advantage here, but afterward he will not hold the island or the strait. Those will be ours, our fleet base in the East, and he can expand on the western shore if he proves loyal. I told Solwaer to be careful of alliances; we shall learn if he has listened well enough." His lips curled back from his teeth.

Grimor nodded slowly. "You have fulfilled the promise I saw in you as a boy. I am proud. We will sail the wide seas together, and none shall prevent our passage. They will sing of us two when we are gone. But first we will make children. Many children. You with this girl, if that is your taste, me with fifty to make up for your one." He guffawed and slapped his brother's back.

Idorn rushed to keep up as the conversation flowed back and forth between the brothers. Soon it would be morning, and another day. Was he still a hostage?

CHAPTER 37

O N HIS summer break, Simon liked to sleep in, but this morning, first light found him awake. He was thinking about Freya and about Findnar—sexy girl, intriguing place, and both so full of possibilities.

Drinking with Rob Buchan at the pub had sparked the internal conversation. Simon had not spent much time with his childhood friend since he'd returned to Portsolly. He'd told himself he was too busy, but that was not true. Rob, in fact, made Simon uncomfortable. Their lives had taken such different paths and that was part of the problem. Simon was proud of his success, the result of bloody hard work, where Rob—that lively kid of those distant summers—had morphed into a loser living in the past. Simon felt sorry for the guy because Rob's sense of entitlement trapped him like a fly in a closed room, and it provided neither the will nor the energy to recapture the much-insisted-on status and power of his ancestors. Resentful and bitter, Rob had quickly become tedious, and that "quiet little drink" at the pub had started to feel like a mistake, especially since his old friend could drink for Scotland when someone else was buying. Whisky, too, inflamed Rob's indignation, especially against Freya.

"A backpacker. An Australian! But I've got her measure. She knows she's vulnerable now. More than one way to send that message. She'll be gone by winter." He tapped his nose. "Then I'll drive the price down and buy the island back." Rob snorted. He was pleased with himself.

"Vulnerable?" Simon had stared at him. "You took Freya's boat?"

"Freya, is it?" Robert had lifted his empty glass, waggled it winningly. "And why would I do that?"

"I have no idea." Simon had been impatient. "Just one more. It's late." He'd gone to the bar and when he'd returned, Rob was morose. "More than fifty generations, father to son. All gone. My birthright. But I found the helmet, she didn't. Or her dad. Don't know the island like I do."

"Helmet?" Lying in bed, Simon thought about why he'd asked the question. Having decided Rob was a fantasist, perhaps he'd seemed bored because the response was petulant. "It's true! I'd go over there when Dane was away. He never knew. I'll find the rest of the hoard when she goes and she will, trust me."

"Ah, the hoard." Simon had drained the last of his whisky. "Must go. Lots to do." Rob had grabbed his arm. "Come with me. I haven't shown anyone else. Old times' sake? You can tell me what it's worth."

Why had he gone? Simon threw the bedcovers back and padded to the bathroom in the vestry. Cleaning his teeth, he thought about it. Conscience, the obligation to be polite to a childhood friend, had been laid to rest after the third drink. No, it had been the expression in Rob's eyes. Honest greed.

And there, in the sitting room of the tiny cottage—all that remained of the glory of the Buchans—it truly was. Wrapped in newspaper, hidden in a cupboard among sporting trophies from long, long ago, was an actual helm. Viking era or earlier. After washing himself—no shower yet, that would come—Simon flipped through the shots he'd taken on his phone last night when Rob had gone to the bathroom. Bronze, had to be, and the amount and quality of the ornamentation (gold, couldn't be anything else) was extraordinary. This was the work of a master, a very great smith. At first he'd thought it a ceremonial object and not designed for battle. But the dent in the side said otherwise. Someone important had owned this helmet, and maybe died wearing it too.

It had been after midnight when Simon left Robert's cottage. He'd been glad to go. The atmosphere of unwashed clothes, old dog, and toxic narcissism had become oppressive, as had Rob's increasingly wild schemes for reclaiming Findnar. But the helm had been real, a genuine treasure. Perhaps the hoard, after all, was not a myth.

He knew a lot about himself, Simon Fettler, and thought he'd sorted out the pattern of his life quite nicely. He'd had a lot of women in his life, too, even lived semiseriously with one or two at different times. But he was fussy, fatally so—or so his friends said. And if they were all busy getting married—and good luck to them—Simon still guarded his emotional independence. Yet spending time with Freya on the island—kissing her—and then meeting Robert last night at the pub had set fate's wheel turning. He could feel it—the game changer had arrived. Perhaps this could be the girl, and Findnar the place he was meant to be? The island with such glittering possibilities . . .

Omens. Simon laughed. Was he, after all, superstitious? It seemed unlikely after a life lived, most definitely, in the material world. His was a fortunate existence, one that provided him with pleasure and interest. Didn't mean, though, that there wasn't room for a challenge. A treasure hunt, say, and a very good-looking girl with an interesting edge. These were both challenges undoubtedly. And what was life without the spice of risk? Unlike so many people, Simon Fettler liked change, he really did. He'd always been a rover.

"Hello, Mr. Boyne." Katherine knocked on the office door.

Walter swung around startled. "Miss MacAllister. Something I can do for you?" He was glad of the distraction—finally he'd made a start on filing.

"I'm looking for Daniel. Is he around?"

Walter got up; a man does not sit in the presence of a lady, and Miss MacAllister was certainly a lady. "He's gone to get coffee."

The workshop door swung open, and Dan appeared in the rectangle of light holding two coffees and a brown paper bag.

"Here we go, Dad, got us a treat too." He shouldered the door closed. Then he registered the visitor. "Hello, Katherine."

The librarian nodded to Walter. She hurried toward Dan. "Have you a moment?"

"For you, Katherine, always." He grinned.

"I should like to go to the island. Now." Katherine did her best to sound composed. Her eyes said something else.

Dan blinked; he hesitated. "Okay with you, Dad?"

Walter exhaled. Relief did not begin to describe what he felt about the change in Dan in the last twenty-four hours. "Of course. Denny'll be back soon. Take your time."

Dan's belly tightened. "Right then." He put one of the coffees down, and the little bag of pastries. "You have this, Dad. Just give me a moment, Katherine. Need to load the stuff." As Katherine watched, Dan limped toward a heap of equipment lying beside one of the benches. "Freya needs to shift that bit of stone we found." He dumped coils of slender steel hawser and assorted other equipment onto a flatbed trolley with large rubber wheels, and slung a box of tools, including a battery-driven drill, on top. "Dad, did you move the steel?"

"Stacked it out of the way." Walter pointed.

"Give me a hand?" Father and son loaded lengths of steel on top of the other materials.

Dan opened the workshop door. "After you, Katherine."

It was a clear, high day. Gulls wheeled over the water and dived for scraps in the harbor, and the little port was busy with comings and goings as Katherine automatically slowed her stride to Dan's.

But she was left behind as, pushing the trolley, he limped energetically toward the runabout moored at the stern of *The Holy Isle*.

"Dan, wait." She hurried after him.

"Day's wasting." He was already in the hull. "Can you pass the stuff down? None of it's heavy, just cumbersome."

Katherine and he worked well together. Five minutes and everything was neatly stacked, and the trolley had been loaded too.

"Let's go."

Katherine nodded; she jumped down into the boat. No skirt today. Something had made her wear jeans this morning, and she'd left a key with her neighbor so that Ishbelle and her babies could be fed. Just in case . . .

Compline's back door was unlocked. Katherine knocked. "Freya, hello?" She opened the door, listened for a reply. "Freya?"

"She's not here." Dan stared out over the meadow, shading his eyes. "We'll find her." He nodded at the loaded trolley. "Let's get this to the standing stones. Won't be nearly as hard as hauling it up the cliff, I promise."

With some asperity Katherine said, "Wishful thinking, Daniel Boyne." The beach, not to mention the cliff path, had been a struggle for them both.

"Dan."

He wheeled. Freya was standing in Compline's open doorway. He smiled warmly. "Hiding, were you?" And then he saw how stressed she was.

Katherine started forward at the same moment. "Child, are you all right?" But Dan got there first. He pulled Freya into his arms, holding her close.

She tried to speak calmly. "I saw her, Dan. Last night. I was inside, she was on the other side of the glass, and then she was gone. She looked at me. Right in my eyes. I searched everywhere, and then, back in the house I found, I found—" She swallowed, couldn't go on.

Dan held Freya tighter. "You're safe, that's what matters. No need to be frightened."

"I'm not scared, Dan, it's not that. But each time she's closer, and I don't know what it means." Defeated, Freya leaned against his chest. "But thank you so much for coming back. And you, too, Katherine. At least you're both real."

"Real?" Katherine's expression changed.

A quick glance at Freya and Dan said, "It's a long story, a tale for the fire tonight, Katherine. But we're here to work and the day's wasting."

Freya's expression brightened. "Okay, then. Let's move that stone. It's important, I know it is."

As the pair took hold of the trolley and pushed it toward the meadow, Katherine hung back. She so wanted to ask who *she* was, but did not have the courage. *Michael, tell me what I should say.*

"That's ingenious, Dan. Really clever." Freya stood back to admire his work. It had taken some hours, but a squat, cross-braced tower stood at each end of the trench that housed the slab.

Bolted together from short lengths of steel, a thick arm, also of steel, jutted from each of the towers at head height. Behind a guard, a loop of steel hawser ran through a pulley to form a sling under the stone. A chain-driven mechanism, cranked by hand, would allow the hawser to be ratcheted tight, and then two people working together, one at each end, could raise the stone.

"I played with Meccano as a kid. This is a bigger version—it's all just problem solving, using what's to hand."

If Dan was modest, he was certainly pleased with Freya's response. "Well, I think you're pretty damn clever."

Her fond expression warmed him very much.

"What happens when the slab gets to the top?" Katherine eyed the structure.

"That's the beauty of this." Dan pointed to a gimbal. "Once we've got it above the trench, we unlock the arms and swivel them. Then we drop the slab."

"Lower it, you mean," Freya put in. *Stop bossing the man around!*

He said, patiently, "We lower the slab carefully to one side of the trench. Right—all rigged and ready. Freya, you take that end, I'll do this. Three, two, one . . ."

At first nothing seemed to shift as they pumped the handles back and forth, then, slowly, the slings tightened around the stone.

Dan was breathing faster. "Keep going."

Freya followed his rhythm. Her biceps were burning and sweat stung her eyes as the stone began to move; she gave up trying not to pant.

"You're doing well—that's it—brilliant!" Too close to the edge, Katherine leaned over the trench.

Dan managed a grin. "Thanks, Coach. Careful, though. Watch your step."

Freya bit back a groan. "How far to go?"

From a safer distance, Katherine peered down. "You're about a third of the way."

"We can do it." Even Dan was panting.

"Yes." Freya's teeth were clenched.

"Nearly there—nearly—you've done it!" Katherine stood back as the gray slab rose out of the ground and into the sunlight. And she remembered, finally, to breathe.

The stone lay on the grass, the slings collapsed around it. Out of its resting place it seemed diminished, less formidable.

"And now?" Dan eyed the compressed earth where the stone had lain.

"Guess." Freya handed him a shovel.

Katherine held out a hand. "Me too. I like digging."

"Okay, I'll do the buckets." Freya braced Dan as he clambered into the trench.

Katherine liked the easy way they had with one another now; both seemed so much happier—in themselves and with each other; she'd have to pick her time to tell them.

Freya leaned down over the lip of the excavation. "So, what do you think?"

There was a quiet moment when Dan stared into her eyes until he closed his own.

Katherine watched silently. What was happening here?

"I think . . ." He limped halfway along the trench and measured out one further pace. "Here."

"Like me to start?"

"Back there, Katherine, a pace away from the center on your side." Dan sank his spade.

By the middle of the afternoon, Dan and Katherine were a meter below the former level of the slab. Freya had bucketed the soil away and sifted it—slow work for, so far, no result—but she wasn't discouraged; she was in the zone. And if her arms ached, so did the backs of her thighs and the base of her spine—in fact, she was aching all over. Situation normal.

"Freya."

She dropped the bucket and hobbled to the trench.

"Listen." Dan pushed the shovel blade down. *Thack.* A bit farther along, *thack.* He stared at her.

Katherine said, "Same here." She demonstrated.

"Stone?"

Dan nodded. "Hand me a bucket."

Freya dropped four empty buckets down. They were quickly filled, and an edge became visible—definitely a piece of stone.

"Not as big as the slab or as thick, not remotely." Dan wiped his sweating palms on his trousers.

Katherine brushed loose soil away from her end. She peered closer. "Could this be a lid?" She tapped with a trowel handle.

Freya slid down beside Dan. "Maybe it's a box." There was a buzzing at the back of her skull, insistent as an insect. She bent, touched what they'd found, and the buzz worked up to a cutting whine.

"May I?" Freya picked up a long trowel.

"Of course. It's yours."

It cost Freya an effort to smile, but she picked along the underside of the rectangle with the point of the trowel. "You're right, Katherine. This could be the lid on a cist."

"A cist?" Daniel frowned.

"A stone cist, not a medical problem." Freya eased the trowel deeper and wriggled the point around. "It's a box made of pieces of stone." She squeezed her eyes half-shut against the pain in her head.

"You all right?" Dan was concerned.

"A headache, that's all—not much sleep last night." Freya waved vaguely. "Just give me a minute." She clambered out and sat on the grass, watching as the trench within a trench began to widen and Katherine revealed the form of the cist. They cleared three sides, leaving the fourth embedded in the wall of the trench. Katherine could bear the suspense no longer. "What now?"

White pain pulsed behind Freya's eyes. It was hard to speak. "Lift the lid."

Dan was worried. "You stay there, give yourself a break."

"No!" Freya winced. "Sorry, I want to do this, Dan."

He stepped away reluctantly, giving her room as she slid back into the trench. She took a steadying breath and nudged a crowbar under the covering stone. "I'll try to lever. When I say go, slide your shovels into the gap. Ready?"

Dan and Katherine nodded.

Something hot stung behind her eyes, but with each breath Freya pushed the distraction farther away as she allowed her being, her mind, to sink into the task. Even if she'd had X-ray vision, her sight could not have been clearer now, her hand steadier, as the point of the steel bar found just the correct place—an irregularity where the lid met the wall of the box. As if she were playing an instrument, as if there were a rhythm to all of this, Freya's hand and the steel became one device. She lifted her arm, and dropped it. Lifted again, and down. And . . . the point went in. Again. Farther; the stone began to move.

"Go!" The shovels were in and under, and in unison they lifted as Freya's crowbar slid into the opening. There was a void behind—no resistance—and the bar almost slid from her fingers. "No!"

"We've got it." Dan was straining to hold the lid. Katherine winced. "If it drops, you'll trap your fingers."

But Freya wedged a rock in the gap. "It won't. I promise you." She spoke softly, for she'd seen what lay in the box. *There you are.*

And the pain blinked out.

The skeleton was huddled knees to chin with the hands and arms squashed against the chest. Poignantly, a few dark curls were attached to the skull still, and a scattering of blue beads lay beneath the collarbones.

Freya picked a bead from the dust. "Faience. Valuable. Someone thought she was worth it."

Dan peered at the tiny object in her palm. "She, because of the beads?"

Freya squatted down. "Not just that." She pointed at the skull. "No brow ridges, like the other skeleton. And this is a young adult, too, though older I'd say. At least this girl wasn't murdered."

Katherine stared at the collection of slender bones. This had once been a living, breathing person. "Could be just a large child—the skeleton's small enough."

"But no milk teeth, and the wisdom teeth have erupted too." Freya pointed to the jaw. "They descend any time from the late teens; the rest of the teeth are in good condition though—little wear and none missing—so not old." She peered more closely at the skull. "The sutures are well closed, but they're not obliterated—that happens as you age."

"The body must have been a very tight fit when it was buried, almost squashed in." Dan frowned.

"The fetal position; you see that from time to time . . ." Her voice trailed away as she bent to brush dust from the delicate skull. The skeleton was touching, huddled like a baby.

"Returned to the womb of the earth." Katherine spoke softly, a benediction for the unknown girl.

"Is it a Christian grave?" Dan leaned forward.

Freya shook her head. "No. Wrong orientation, and she was buried inside the standing stones. Not very likely for a Christian woman."

Katherine pointed; there were pottery shards among the bones. "A Pagan grave would explain this, then. A bowl with food for the final journey? A kind gesture." Kindness was important to Katherine.

"But she was buried under a stone slab," Dan said. "That's a lot of effort. They could have just covered the cist with earth and walked away."

Freya looked at him thoughtfully. "You're right, Dan. That is odd."

Katherine glanced at the slab lying in the meadow. "But that stone is marked with a cross; it's all very confusing."

"Another Pagan-Christian grave." Freya shook her head. "This place. Rip up the rule books and start again."

"I'm starved." Freya climbed out of the cist trench with Dan's help. She was filthy; they all were.

"So, I'll cook then." He grinned.

"Again?" They eyed each other, smiling.

"We're putting this back?" Katherine bustled toward the pair carrying the folded tarpaulin.

"Er, yes. Should be okay overnight; it seems fine—at least for the moment—but just for safety." Freya glanced up. It was a perfect evening. Wisps of cloud caught by the declining sun shone pink and gold as the sky slowly changed from peacock blue to milky indigo, the strange half-light of high summer.

She took the tarpaulin and shook it out. "We should be able to empty the grave tomorrow, though. That is, if you'd like to stay, Katherine." She did not look at Dan.

"That would be delightful, if you can lend me a T-shirt." The twinkle faltered.

Freya said, warmly, "I'm sure we'll find you something."

The wander back toward Compline was slow and easy, voices rising and falling in the soft air.

Freya scanned the east. "I haven't seen the comet in a few nights."

Katherine said, lightly, "Been rather wild weather to see anything recently, wouldn't you say?"

"Mild as milk now." Dan stared out over the calm strait. In the faltering light, a lone dinghy chugged past the Portsolly breakwater in the far distance. Someone returning late to Port. Good luck to them.

He caught Freya's glance; he knew where he'd rather be.

"Freya?" Outside the bathroom door, Katherine could hear the water swirling down the plughole.

"Sorry to have taken so long. There's still plenty of hot water."

Freya pushed the door open. She was wrapped in a bathrobe, and her hair, freshly washed, was twisted into a towel. "Your turn."

"I wonder if we could have a chat." Katherine could hear Dan making up the fire in the big room; he was whistling happily to himself.

"Is something wrong?"

Katherine tried to smile. "Not wrong. But there's something I should have said before. I wasn't sure, though, and now you said you've seen, well . . ." She did not have the words.

"Come and sit by the stove."

Katherine nodded gratefully. "I'm sorry. It's not like me to be so silly, but I've been troubled and not sure how to, that is, when to . . ."

Freya unwound the towel and shook her hair free. "Not silly at all. Findnar does this—messes with your head."

"That's why I was trying to tell you what happened," Katherine said. Then she shut her mouth abruptly, as if frightened.

"We have all night." Freya spoke gently.

In the background, behind Katherine, Dan stood silently in the doorway.

"I have never talked of this. Not to anyone." Katherine stared at her hands as they twisted in her lap. She sighed. "The last time your father and I spoke to one another was . . . unhappy—and then he died."

Freya reached forward and clasped Katherine's hands in her own. "Please, if this distresses you . . ."

"It does, but it is a relief to speak of it." Katherine sniffed.

Freya rummaged in a pocket. "Here." She produced a tissue. "It's clean, I promise." She smiled encouragingly.

"You are very kind, Freya. He was kind too." Katherine blew her nose loudly. "But you spoke of seeing 'her.' Was this a pretty girl with dark hair—curly dark hair?"

"Yes." Freya's eyes met Dan's over the top of Katherine's head.

"Your father saw her too. Here on the island. And he said it was the dead come back to life, seeking to tell him something. He seemed completely certain. I have never believed in ghosts, and I told him I thought he might be ill, or suffering delusions from living alone in this place. He would not listen to me, and we quarreled after I asked him to see a doctor. He said I was the deluded one, and that if I would just open my mind to other possibilities . . . *What* possibilities—those that dwell at the bottom of the whisky? That is what I said." A sad little laugh. "We so rarely quarreled, and this was worse for being Christmas—the very day he gave me the crucifix. Christmas affected him, I knew that, though I did my best to help him be cheerful. He missed you, Freya. I would say, each Christmas Eve, Pick up the phone, call her—but he never did. He thought he had no right to disturb your life after all these years. Perhaps I was glad—because I was jealous. I thought he loved you more than me." Katherine tried to smile at Freya, a brave failure. "He was the only family I had and I never saw him again and then, today, you said . . ."

"That I had seen her." Freya expelled a painful breath. Dan limped forward and sat beside Katherine at the table. "I see her, too, and the others, one man in particular."

Katherine's voice cracked. "Others? But I do not see her, or them, whoever they are. Am I the only one without eyes. *Why?*" She was crying, her chest heaving with the effort to contain the sound. "If we had not quarreled, Michael might have stayed with me; he might not have come here that night. He might still be alive, sitting in this kitchen. Why did I not believe him?"

Dan met Freya's glance. *And I might have died, not Michael Dane.*

CHAPTER 38

THE BELL was calling. Prime, the second service of the day, if day this blank dark could be called.

Signy rolled over and slipped from the skins. Fogged with sleep and habit, she knelt beside the palliasse. The air shocked her, and she remembered there was no need to pray. Shivering, she pulled a skin from the bed.

"Signy?" Gunnhilde was in the byre below.

The girl peered down. "What do you want?" She was wary.

"There is danger." An imploring whisper.

"Why?" *Something. Coming closer.*

Gunnhilde twisted her hands together. "I had to confess. I tried to avoid it." She swallowed. "I said I had seen you near the stones and that I was worried for you—which the Lord knows is true. Brother Anselm said he must tell the Abbot and"—she took a quivering breath—"even though I know it is wrong, I have come to warn you." She crossed herself.

Signy climbed down from the loft. "Do you still think I am possessed, Mother?"

Gunnhilde touched Signy's cheek. Tears dripped down the old woman's face. "Promise you will not go to the stones today. They . . ." She stopped, a hand to her mouth.

"They?"

"Our brothers will cast them down."

Signy said, cynically, "They tried once before."

Gunnhilde drew closer. "But an exorcism will be held this

morning." She faltered. "Then they will come for you." She hit her chest with a clenched fist. "This is my fault, my grievous fault."

Signy's glance strayed to a corner of the byre. Leaning against a wall was a large bowl made from hide stretched over a wicker frame; Gunnhilde had not seen it.

The bell stopped. Signy kissed the old woman. "You will be late. Remember me, Mother, in your prayers." She hurried Gunnhilde through the byre.

"Go with God, dearest child." The old nun so yearned to say more; she always did, she always had. She kissed Signy's forehead and hobbled away.

Signy ran to the coracle. It was not especially heavy, but it was cumbersome. Still, she would manage. No choice now.

Cuillin dropped to his knees, cross held high. He stared fearfully at the Pagan temple as, behind him, Findnar's monks also knelt in orderly rows. With eyes as wide as his, they moved their lips without sound as they told the rosary to ward off evil emanations from the stones.

Was it strange to be locked in battle with the Fallen One on such a lovely day? The air was warm, and there was no sound but the twitch of insects. Even the sun, God's comfort to the world, seemed to conspire with Satan, for it picked jewels in the surface of the granite monoliths, lending them beauty.

The Abbot signed a sweeping cross in the air. He would drive away this unnatural, glittering enchantment, and Satan would not beguile him, for he was about God's business.

"Together, Brothers, we shall fight the Prince of Darkness. Rise. Join me!" The monk swept his arms into the air. "That stone"—he pointed, his forefinger a weapon—"their so-called altar; it shall be dragged down and consecrated to Christ in the name of St. Peter, the rock of our Church." He thrust his cross toward the monoliths. "And with God's help and strength, we shall roll the rest into the sea."

Perhaps some of the brothers stared toward the distant cliffs. It was a long way, a very long way.

Cuillin's voice rose sharply. "Evil has returned to the world, Brothers. Last night after Compline, I saw the Wanderer in the sky—a sign of the end-times—and we must act. Salvation, or damnation, is at stake."

Among the monks, Anselm blanched. The wandering star was a most terrible portent, for in the Scriptorium they had only just finished illuminating the great Book of Revelation, the chronicle of what would happen at the end of days. The timing was fearful.

Solwaer woke with a start as something nudged his ribs. Head reeling, he saw what he was intended to see, someone, not something, and felt the boot again in his side.

He sat up quickly. Too fast, the room swayed and tipped. "Stop that."

Portsol's Demon grinned. "Time you were up, old man. Time to plan." Bear reached down.

Hand clasped hand, and Solwaer lunged to his feet as Bear yelled for the chamber slave. Pained, the Lord of Portsol closed his eyes; none of this was good.

A girl hurried in. She huddled at Solwaer's feet. The previous slave was barely alive from the beating he'd given her last night when he woke and wanted water; she'd not brought it quickly enough; her fate was the talk of the village.

"Food." The girl ran.

Solwaer narrowed watering eyes. He coughed; the air was thick with unpleasant smoke, for Bear had kicked the fire into life, feeding the embers dried dung. Standing helped the ale sickness though, and Solwaer croaked, "Be careful, Bear. Very careful." He might have meant the fire.

"It is not my nature to be careful." Bear deliberately used Norse.

"No, it is not." Grimor was at the door. "But you are my brother, you take what you want."

Bear grinned. "Shall I tell him that, Brother?"

"I think you should." Grimor was cheered. Bear's homeland tongue was improving, and that was good; if he was to command a hull in the fleet, he must be able to talk to his men.

"What is this?" Solwaer had slumped to his stool. He did not like conversations he could not understand.

Bear shrugged. "Grimor says strong men do not wait on permission, they take what they want."

The Lord of Portsol looked from one to the other and smiled mirthlessly. "Then it is time to talk. Of Findnar, tell him that."

Bear spoke to his brother. "There is a way onto Findnar out of sight of the cove. It's difficult, but at the right tide with a few men, I can open the cliff gate from the other side."

Grimor nodded slowly. He stared at Solwaer, a long, unsettling look.

Solwaer held Grimor's gaze. Anger helped, though he did not show it. He clapped his hands. "Girl!" The slave scuttled back with a bowl of fresh cheese and barley bread, and an ale jug. Solwaer pointed. The girl unhooked ale horns from her belt and placed the food on a wooden block.

"Go!"

The chamber slave ran.

"Eat, Lord Grimor, and we shall talk." Solwaer deliberately added the honorific.

Bear filled a horn with ale and handed it to Solwaer; then he filled another horn for Grimor, and one for himself. "But first, a toast. To advantage. And to glory."

"To advantage and glory." But new ale did not clear the queasiness of the old. Solwaer belched sour beer and made a business of smoothing his tunic, winning a little time to think. "We have an agreement about Findnar, Bear. I found the men you need, and now you must play your part." A flat statement, quickly translated.

Grimor and Bear both smiled politely.

Bear replied, "And, afterward?"

"Afterward? When I am lord of Findnar, you take what you've been promised and sail away." Solwaer dug a piece of bread into the curds and stuffed it in his mouth, but the smell of the cheese made him retch. He spat the food into the fire.

"Something wrong, Lord Solwaer?" Grimor laughed, a loud snort.

Solwaer curled a lip. It might have been a smile.

Bear swallowed a handful of curds. "But there might be another way, in the future, another path to follow."

Solwaer echoed politely, "Another path?"

"My brother and I can be your allies, Solwaer." Bear's tone was equally courteous. "You do not have enough followers to hold this coast, but we do. And you are a merchant, we are fighters. Each does what he knows best; one protects, one makes money for all. Everyone wins." Bear shot a glance at his brother. Grimor beamed as if he understood each word.

Solwaer stopped himself from nodding too. It was true—an alliance with other powers had been one way he'd seen the future, even so far back as when he'd first taken these once burned and empty buildings with fewer than ten men and renamed the place for himself.

Solwaer knew he was good at trading; men came to him for that—for the chance of prosperity and for protection too. Even some of the original inhabitants—those who'd survived the raids— had crept back once they heard he was in charge. His mother had been a slave here once, and some men remembered that; not many who still lived, however. The ones who'd sneered when he returned were soon disposed of, and the example of a lingering death—he particularly favored flaying—was remarkable for its effect on dissent.

But if Solwaer was prepared to consider this alliance, he certainly disliked the sound of tribute; that part of the deal would need finessing. Still, with the Norse at his back, he could indeed expand his power base up and down the coast. It was better to own half of a very profitable something than all of a smoking ruin.

Solwaer smiled pleasantly at his guests, for that was what Bear had become, another guest. "An interesting proposition, Lord Magni. After we have completed our business on Findnar, we shall speak further." He picked up his own drinking horn, slopped it full, and handed it to Grimor, poured another for Bear and himself. "Translate this then. There's business to be done, and I look forward to our joint enterprise."

Solwaer watched, smiling, as Bear spoke to his brother. Of course, there was also another way of doing things—there was always another way. And, in the end, the choice might be his—if he lived long enough.

CHAPTER 39

FREYA GASPED. She sat up in one convulsive movement. The house was silent, and there was no light. Straining, she listened; there was nothing to hear. Of course there was nothing, she was alone in her bed. Shaking, she reached over to the table. She had to have light. She found the flashlight, flicked it on.

She put a hand to her throat. It hurt as if skin had been stripped from the inside, leaving it raw. She knew what had caused the pain.

They trussed her like an animal—bound tight, knees to chin. She did not scream, but she stared at them, one by one, though they did not look at her as they put her in the grave. She was small, but not small enough. The tallest man pressed her down—and still she was silent. As the food bowl was flung in, and the lid dropped on top, one of the men muttered it was a waste—another said the sacrifice must be worthy or it had no point.

They heard her beneath their feet. Trying to move, trying to get out, at last she called them by name, one by one. That frightened the men.

Earth was brought. It was dumped and tramped down above her head, and they found a stone, too, a big flat one. Heavy and thick enough to hold her beneath the ground, for they did not want her to walk, haunting their dreams. It took six men and poles to roll it over to where she was buried, and then they brought more earth. There was no sound now.

Her legs felt heavy as Freya swung out of bed. Cold plank

floor, socks, sweater on, jeans over pajamas—distractions from shivering.

Feet make no sound, but old floorboards flex. The stair treads squeaked like a bunch of crickets. Censorious. *We see you, Freya Dane, you can't hide.*

Dan was virtuously asleep, an angular shape on the couch—sharp elbows, knees, and shoulders under the blanket. Freya so wanted to wake him, so wanted to talk through this gathering storm, but that was dangerous. If she touched him in this state . . .

She hesitated. Torchlight cast his face in silver. *He's not breathing!* "Dan!"

He jerked. "What? What happened?" He sat up, blinking.

"Nothing. Go to sleep." Freya made soothing sounds, clucks almost, little hushes.

He fell back on the pillow, sighing. "That's good. That's . . ." His eyes drooped closed. Steady and slow, his breathing deepened.

At the door she looked back yearningly. *Get a grip! Leave him be.*

The kitchen was quiet and dark, the fire in the range dead except for embers. Shivering, Freya hurried to the sink. Three pumps and she'd filled a glass, and the taste of the water, this late and this thirsty, was actually sweet. She closed her eyes.

Something squeezed her neck. Dust filled her lungs. She could not breathe! Gasping, she dropped the tumbler, and it broke in the sink, exploded like a tiny bomb, stars and shards of glass. The bony fingers disappeared. Nursing her throat, panting, Freya bent to pick up the pieces.

"Hello?" Katherine was on the landing above; the lamp, held high, splashed her shadow down the stairs.

Freya called out, "Just me, Katherine, getting a drink. Sorry."

"Oh, okay." The librarian yawned; then she went back to the warm nest of her bed.

Freya picked up the flashlight . . .

G

There it was. She could see it. The line in the wall where one kind of masonry ended and something different began. And there were the footprints—this was where they stopped.

A steel table beside the Compactus had wheels and a shelf. Freya pushed it to the wall and placed the flashlight carefully—she must have maximum light for her work.

She weighed the pickax in her hand. The plaster covering the wall was old, its thick surface irregular; clear that first and she would find the masonry beneath.

Minutes later, as she stood among dust and white rubble, her pick found a weakness in the wall. The stone began to fret away in chips and bits under her assault. Then Freya struck hard, a glancing sideways blow, and a sizable lump fell out. She jumped clear and knocked the flashlight to the ground; the beam veered and flashed as it rolled away. She saw the hole she'd made.

"Wow."

"That's one description."

Freya had not heard Dan on the stairs. She stared at him, perplexed. "You were asleep." She swung the tool; it connected, made a good-size gouge.

"What are you doing, Freya?" Katherine appeared behind Dan.

Freya nearly dropped the pick in midswing. She was angry. "That was dangerous."

Katherine flicked a glance at Dan.

He moved closer. "It's very late."

"Chamomile tea? That might help you sleep." Katherine did not know what else to say.

Freya's face was closed and distant, her attention on the wall. "I have to get on."

Dan stared at the carnage. "But what are you trying to do?"

"This, of course. Make it bigger." Freya frowned at the hole.

He tried again. "Why?"

As if Dan was dull-witted, Freya said, "To get through to the other side, of course."

"I can help if you like; it'll be quicker with two."

"If that's what you'd like." She seemed startled—as if an anonymous stranger, in passing, had been unexpectedly kind.

"Okay then." Dan picked up a crowbar.

A pace or two from Freya, he tried to work the steel bar between two stones—it went in only a little way. He began to lever, back and forth, back and forth. "Do you know what you're looking for?" he asked her.

Freya's worried face cleared. "Of course." She swung the pick, and then again; another piece fell out of the wall, doubling the head-size hole. Beside it, a sheet of plaster slumped off the surface, and dust settled all over Freya. A white form with eerie blue eyes.

Dan worked at another block, a big one. "This is a bearing wall for the house above. We'll need a supporting beam here—too dangerous without one; you risk cracking the building."

Freya stood back. "There might be something in the barn." She didn't sound optimistic.

Dan took his chance. "But we don't want to cause structural damage upstairs. That's dangerous, expensive to fix, too, and this is a very old house. For all we know, it's a listed building. This"—he waved at the wilderness of plaster and stone—"might actually be against the law."

Freya stared at him. "Listed?"

Katherine was navigating her way toward them with a tray. "I think Dan's right." She put the tray on the steel table. "Tea?" She handed Freya a mug.

Confused, Freya peered at what she'd done.

Dan picked up the flashlight. "Look there." He pointed at the bottom of the stairs. "And here." The beam played over the surface near the hole. "Massive, massive work. Maybe not Christian. Could even be *pre*-Christian from the size of the stones, unique." A wild guess.

Freya's eyes widened. "Yes, but . . ."

Katherine added her voice. "I agree with Dan. The Abbey ruins will be listed, nothing surer, and the undercroft, too, with this ceiling . . ."

Dan's knowledge of such things was misty at best, but he chimed in. "You really can't hack holes in a registered building, Freya, not without permission from the council and, er, Historic Scotland."

"But I have to do this." Her tone rose.

Dan limped over to her. "It's late—really, really late." He showed her his watch face. "See? After three. Come upstairs. We can talk about this in the morning."

Katherine said, gently, "What a good idea."

Bewildered, Freya stared from one to the other.

Dan stepped closer, but he did not touch her. "Katherine, if you'll help Freya, I'll bring the tray."

Docile, Freya stumbled up the stairs with Katherine, leaving the mess behind.

Dan let the flashlight play over the wreckage. This was not the way an archaeologist worked. And then he heard something, a sifting whisper. Staring, he stepped back. From near the ceiling a crack appeared and, as he watched, it widened and grew until, piece by piece, the remaining plaster crumpled off the walls.

The air was white, thick and dense as a blizzard. Dan stumbled backward, coughing, and then he saw . . .

Embedded deep and near the top of the wall was a huge, single piece of stone. Laid horizontally, it was the size of a recumbent dolmen, and there were hints it was held in place by similarly massive uprights—this was what the destruction had begun to reveal.

The half-exposed structure resembled nothing so much as a concealed doorway—but a doorway made for giants.

CHAPTER 40

I T WAS low water, and thirteen of Grimor's ships stood out in the strait beyond the breaker line—they were waiting for the signal.

From over the strait, they'd heard the Abbey bell toll and stop as distant voices began to sing Vespers. The sound drifted out from the island through the calm night, and it was very beautiful, the deep male note balanced and glorified by the higher female voices.

Grimor, a sentimental man, was moved as they rowed toward Findnar. It was a treat to hear such disciplined, sweet singing.

The chant ceased; now there would be prayers, and more singing.

At last, as Bear had predicted, a small number of lights blinked to life within the other Abbey buildings. This was the beginning of the personal hour—the time in which Grimor would muster the men to the beach. The invasion itself, and the sack, was intended for the last service of the day, Compline.

Now, except for the slop of the waves against the hulls and the stretched creak of rigging, all was silent.

"There!" Idorn was proud of his long sight, but a lantern, waved in the night, is easy to see. Bear had made it to the meadow side of the gate.

Beneath *Fenrir*'s mast, Grimor waved a pale cloth to the next ship in line. It was the signal.

Fenrir slid out ahead of the pack. She would be the first into the cove; that was as it should be. Once landed, Grimor would wait for his brother to call them up the cliff path. This, too, was right—to

Bear should belong the glory of Findnar's unmaking as a Christian stronghold in the East, and the beginning of their joint dominance of this coast.

But Grimor did not see the other ships on the strait side of the sheltering headland.

Not sleek and long like the vessels of the Norsemen, these were broad and slow—traders instead of fighters—and they were fewer in number. But each was a bigger ship and carried more men. Cloaked, still, in darkness, they cut through the calm sea without fuss, and they, too, were steering for Findnar.

Signy had hidden all day in the combe. Hauling the coracle behind her—with some difficulty—she had climbed into the largest of the trees, and from there she'd watched the monks at the circle. It might have been funny once to see them labor to unseat the stones, but today Signy wept. For if the monoliths withstood assault, the monks still had one success—they'd pulled the altar stone down.

Such desecration hurt Signy deeply. Her clan had worshipped here for the whole of their sung history, and now it was defiled. Was there no part of the past that was sacred?

But as the day lengthened, Signy saw the monks trudge away toward the Abbey. They followed Cuillin after he'd shaken his cross at the stones and told them, as if they were living people, that he would return to destroy them yet.

One of the brothers was ordered to stay behind. Signy could hear him. Perhaps the man was frightened, for he sang psalms in a wavering voice as he chipped away at something—*ting, ting, ting*—the sound of a chisel against stone, insistent as birds calling out a warning.

Signy waited. If the sea was calm she would launch her little boat tonight and she would find Bear. She would not allow herself to think further than that—of what might happen if he no longer wanted her.

So often, for comfort, she had relived the few times they had touched each other. And she had remembered, too, when she bled into the earth as the child was expelled from her body. So tiny, so perfectly formed. They'd buried their daughter up there, among the stones.

Misery. And yearning. A veil too thick for even Cruach to pierce.

"Ah, Bear, can you hear me?" It might have been a shout, so great was the clamor in her heart. But Signy whispered the words, her own private prayer.

The bell called—Vespers—and the lone monk hurried away.

Signy climbed down from her shelter. Like a shelled sea creature, she labored across the meadow, the approaching dark her friend. Within sight of the palisade, she hid in the long grass and watched as the gate ward climbed down and ran toward the Abbey.

How to get through? On the meadow side the gate was closed by a wooden bar. Cut in one piece from the heartwood of an oak, it was so heavy four men were necessary to lift it. And, too, a massive haft and staple secured each end.

The service had begun at the Abbey, sound drifting toward Signy in the dark. Vespers was not lengthy. She had only a little time and not enough strength—that was quickly apparent. She could not shift the bar.

If she could not get through the gate, there was only one choice. She must climb over it.

The stairs that led to the wooden walkway above the gate were difficult with the coracle on her back, for she was tired and hungry. But the sky was her reward, for there above her head was the country of the stars where her parents and her child now lived. Signy held up her hands. "Bless me on this journey, Mother and Father, and my beloved daughter. May I know peace as you know peace." There was no time, but this was necessary.

She peered out toward the strait.

The moon was beginning to rise over the lip of the world, a disk of dim gold. Soon the sea road would be thrown down upon the water, the silver path. She had to find a way to get down, but the gate was sheer and she had no rope. Therefore she must jump though it seemed a very long way. The coracle, too, might break if she threw it down. Signy swallowed. Distracted, she stared at the cove. So near and yet . . .

Ships were riding in on the tide. Hulls with shields on their sides, and moonlight found the helmets as the oarsmen bent and pulled. Very soon they would land, and then they would storm the cliff path. The gate was strong, but how strong?

Tears dropped from Signy's open eyes. There was no escape. She had to do it, she had to warn Gunnhilde. She had to warn them all.

The force to run came suddenly. Her feet did not feel the stones in the path as she fled toward the Abbey.

The night climb had been hard. Two chosen companions and him. From Grimor's followers Bear had chosen Edor's steady-eyed helmsman—whip-slight, but strong enough to hold a boat in a wild sea and not old or young. The other was a tall boy who was good with both ax and sword—Bear had watched him at practice. They came from *Wave Biter,* and neither choice pleased Edor since it meant he lost two valuable hands and he'd not been consulted by Grimor. That rankled.

On the chosen day, the three rowed through dusk and on toward night, toward Findnar. Bear knew how to climb the rock pipe from the sea, but the others did not. They'd be fast learners or they would die. He'd found the pipe while looking for somewhere to stow his coracle out of the way of the nosy monks, and he'd taught himself how to climb it, down and up. Perhaps the little craft was there still, wedged in at the top.

The night was calm when they landed on the wave platform

at low water. There was a head of rock there, and to this they tied the hull.

Bear led his companions to the start of the climb. "Listen, and listen well," he told them. "It will save you. Watch where I put my hands and my feet. Use your back to wedge your body while you find the next handhold. I'll drive bolts into the rock for handholds and footholds as we go. Think with each breath that it may be your last."

Bear did not look down, he looked up. When his eyes got used to the dark, faint starlight showed him the lip of the narrow crevasse far above his head. Soon there was nothing but breathing and hammering bolts with the ax and hauling his body weight higher, higher, closer to Signy.

Dressed in leather to save his knees, the helmsman copied Bear silently, move for move. He'd been a good choice. Their other companion, however, confronted with the height of the climb had frozen.

Bear said, "Better you guard the hull." That consideration shamed the boy, and of course he followed—more slowly, but he overcame the fear. This choice, too, was vindicated; the youth would be useful after all.

As Bear heaved himself out of the mouth of the rock pipe, the moon was rising. The coracle had disappeared—that annoyed him. He'd spent long nights making it. But there was no time for regret, for the helmsman was close behind. He could hear the man breathing as he scrabbled the last handholds. Bear leaned to pull his companion up. A grim white face stared up from below—the youth, farther down but relentless. Bear respected that.

"We go to the gate. Follow."

Skirting well clear of the Abbey grounds, Bear ran half-doubled toward the palisade under a rising moon, the helmsman at his heels. He knew the gate, for he had helped forge the bolts that held it closed.

Bear had thought of this moment so many times—rehearsed

each action in his head. This part was easy, and the rest would be, too, if he and Grimor could keep the men in check. And Edor. Edor did not like him.

He grinned. Many men did not like Bear, maybe some did not like Magni either, but they were both Grimor's brothers. He'd have to prove that tonight.

The helmsman breathed easily as they arrived at the palisade, and he said nothing unnecessary. Good signs, both; the man was intelligent and staunch.

Bear pointed to the far end of the bar that held the gate. He mimed hitting the bolt out of the hasp. The man nodded and took out his ax; Bear did the same.

Bolts gone. Now for the bar.

There were feet on the cliff path.

"Magni?" Grimor. A low call.

Bear whispered back, "A moment, Brother." It was odd to be called by his old name but less odd than it had been.

Bear held up three fingers to the helmsman. Two. One. *Heave!*

The bar dropped from the keepers, and Bear stepped neatly out of the way as it hit the turf. He called to Grimor. "Push, Brother."

Willing shoulders pushed the gates apart and in toward the meadow and the Abbey.

Bear stood back and watched the men stream past. They moved silently, the moon finding their swords and axes.

Grimor joined his brother. Bear grunted. He pointed at the waiting men. "They know what to do?"

Grimor smiled with his teeth. "They do. We'll muster here until you send word. How many do you want?"

"Them"—Bear pointed at a small group of fighters—"and the helmsman and the youth." His last companion had just arrived in a hurry.

Grimor beckoned the other men over. "You go with Magni." He glared at one who dared to look cocky. "As few deaths as possible. Do you hear me?"

Bear stared toward the Abbey. Very soon the monastery would assemble for Compline. The lay servants entered the church last—that would be his best chance of finding Signy. He would make sure she was safely hidden, then the other men would be summoned.

Bear rolled his head to loosen the shoulder muscles. *So, Cuillin. The end-time approaches.* He grinned. That was a good joke.

Grimor slapped Bear on the back. "Ready, Brother?"

"Never more than now, Brother."

Hand to forearm, they embraced.

"Brother Vidor?" Signy hurried to the kitchen. It was empty.

A door opened behind her, and a young monk stood there.

Signy ran to him. "Help me, Brother."

The boy gulped. He ducked back and slammed the door behind him.

"You do not understand." Signy rattled the latch. She could hear the novice breathing on the other side.

He yelled, "The Pagan witch! Save me, Brother."

The door was torn open. An enraged monk stood there, carrying a burning torch. The boy cowered behind. "In the name of Christ, be gone, Succubus." The man thrust the flame toward her face.

Backing away, Signy tried reason. "Brother, please. Listen to me."

"Sorceress!" The man feinted forward.

Signy dodged; she was desperate. "They are coming! You must warn the others. Or all of you will die."

Behind the monk, the boy's eyes bulged. He fled, wailing, as the man ran at Signy. "We shall repel the legions of Satan!"

Signy turned and ran.

Owl-light is treacherous for one whose world is blurred. As Gunnhilde groped along the cloister toward the chapel, she heard men's voices. In the personal hour, her place was the nuns' day chamber, and to be caught in an area more commonly frequented by the brothers was unsuitable, old though she was.

Fearful of discovery, Gunnhilde hobbled on until she found the door that led from the outside of the church to the robing room inside. Arthritic fingers prized the latch from its keeper. *Thanks be, Holy Mary!* She was safe.

Opening an inner door to the women's side of the nave, Gunnhilde knelt with some trouble. Compline tonight would have special prayers, she knew—thanks to God for the completion of the great book of the Apocalypse. She could just make out the manuscript lying on the altar, the gilded binding gathering what light there was from the candles left burning.

Gunnhilde crossed herself. For all her grief about Signy, she was under the Lord's protection in this place and she could give herself up to worship. If she was seen, she could justly say this was a moment of private prayer, for there was never enough time to reflect upon her sins.

From long practice, the old woman stilled her mind. It was better, these days, to listen for Christ's voice in silence rather than strain to see Him, even within His dwelling place. Once, as a very young novice, she had caught a glimpse of His glory as a great light—a light that only she had seen—poured from the pyx that stored the Holy Bread. It had happened only once, but in that moment she had known the truth. Her invisible bridegroom lovingly waited for her to join Him, and she so yearned to bathe in that light again, longed to surrender to the radiance. She opened her heart, seeking the comfort of her husband's presence . . .

Something niggled, a formless fidgeting behind her prayers. Gunnhilde's focus dispersed, rippled away like the surface of a lake disturbed by wind.

Voices. She had heard men's voices and they had been whispering. Why would that be so, when it was permitted to speak between Vespers and Compline?

The voice of one who whispers is hard to recognize—almost sexless, nearly ageless—but Gunnhilde remembered something, the language that was spoken. Memory nudged—Bear, as a child, this had been his tongue.

There were strangers on Findnar.

The outer door in the church wall creaked as it opened. Someone was coming.

The only way to leave the church now was through the west door, and to get there, Gunnhilde must hobble the length of the nave. She was dressed in black, and when she hurried away, turning her back on the altar—something she'd never done in all her long service as a nun—she became a shadow among shadows, moving over the earth floor with little more noise than a night breeze or a mouse. As the strangers entered the nave, she was gone.

The rest was not so easy. She heard other voices, those of her brothers and sisters—and the difference was clear.

Gunnhilde tried to run to her companions, but she stumbled. Something was wrong, she could feel it in her head, a terrible ache; her heart, too, was jolting, and there was an immense pressure behind her eyes. Moving was difficult, for her legs were weak suddenly. Was someone shouting—close or far away? Hold on a little longer, just a few more steps. She must find Cuillin, must warn him and . . .

"Mother!"

Gunnhilde was lying beside the path, a black huddle. The voice called her back from the dark. *Signy!* "Help me, child. Help . . ." The words bubbled away half-said, but Gunnhilde tried to make Signy understand. "Cui—the, the men." Her tongue had thickened.

The old woman was a dead weight. Signy could not lift her. "Hush, I am here."

Gunnhilde convulsed against the kind arms of her daughter. She tried to point.

The girl slewed around. A man was running, his sword drawn high; at his back came others. A torch was thrown against the sky. It landed on the refectory roof. Flames spread through heather like a red knife, and the bell began to toll. Not measured, not sonorous, a frightened clamor.

Signy crouched over the old woman as a hand ripped at her clothes. She tried to bite—she had no other weapons—and the man howled. He hit Signy and then pitched over her, pumping blood. She saw the sword in his back.

Another man loomed. He hauled the raider's corpse away; fire filled the sky behind, and heat hurt Signy's eyes. This was death. She would never see Bear again.

Arms scooped her up as light shifted. "Signy!"

She saw his face. Had Cruach sent her comfort as she died?

No. This was Bear, and he was real. He had killed her attacker as the world turned to flame.

Bear was with the raiders.

"Traitor!" Signy knocked his arms away. She stumbled to Gunnhilde, weeping. The nun could not speak, but Signy pulled the old woman up, and as she staggered away she screamed out, "Get away. Go!"

Bear's sword arm dropped to his side. Signy's anguish sliced him open like a blade. Around him, the Abbey burned as fire spread from roof to dry roof. Cinders fell, burning rain. Men ran like shadows through red light—monks and raiders, some the prey, others, predators. Screams ripped the night like cloth.

The raid was out of control. This was not what was planned. *Who had done this thing?*

The bell stopped. There was no one to pull the burning rope.

Gouts of flame—ravenous tongues—reached up into the night. Hot crimson, ice white joined in the cold sky as the stars faded against heat and the risen moon. Behind that silver disk, a white ball moved. It was small, as yet, but it would grow larger in the days to come.

Many of the monks were already dead. Lining up for Compline, they'd scattered into the path of the raiders' swords. Struck down, they littered the ground like straw dolls.

There would be a reckoning later from Grimor, from Bear, but not now, not as the flames and fury took hold and the berserkers became a howling plague of death.

Beside the church a bloodied corpse rose up as Signy stumbled on. Pointing with a scarlet hand, it spoke to her. *"Sanctuary."* Anselm.

Through the blood veil, Signy saw enough of his face to push shock aside. "Help me, Brother. Please!"

The old order of master and pupil was gone. Anselm and the girl lifted the nun, and together all three stumbled toward the side door of the Abbey. It was the last undefiled building left on the island.

Anselm opened the door just a crack. The space behind was empty. Around the church, men roved between buildings, swarming death.

Terror has no words, no plan. Clumsy, silent, they pulled Gunnhilde inside. Beneath the latch they braced a prie-dieu.

Time had come full circle. The two, carrying the third, crept deeper into the body of the church. It was empty, a light burning peacefully before the pyx. There, too, lay the greatest work ever to come out of Findnar's Scriptorium: the Book of Revelation.

Dressed with gold leaf, pages of calfskin vellum—cured by Signy's fingers months before—were pressed between cover boards of whale's ivory. Crystal, chalcedony, and sea topaz graced the surface; the topaz was from the cove where the raiders had landed once again.

The monk moaned at the sight of his masterwork.

"Anselm! We cannot stay here," Signy told him.

Anselm did not hear. Lost to shock and remorse, he knew he would die soon, as would Signy and Gunnhilde. Just as his brothers were dying now.

"Anselm!"

The bewildered monk stared at the girl.

"The west door. Then we run to the combe."

"God is Mercy." Gunnhilde. Her voice brought Anselm back. The nun's eyes were wide; the next world was very near, and just a veil remained, only a veil.

Signy gasped. *"Please,* Anselm."

The brother sighed. "Come, dearest Sister."

Gunnhilde managed to nod as Signy and Anselm swept her up.

In that same moment, Anselm plucked the book from the altar. He cuddled it to his side with one arm.

"Now!" Signy, a scorching whisper.

The three hobbled toward the west door.

They nearly made it.

Behind them, the prie-dieu fell backward as the side door burst open.

Fiachna hurdled the broken prie-dieu. Behind him, like silent wolves, came two more of Solwaer's thanes.

"The altar!" Candlesticks and the pyx, and a great silver cross.

Half-carrying Gunnhilde slowed Signy and Anselm. Her weight, their kindness, brought disaster.

Fiachna saw the trio. "Women!" He threw his ax.

Signy pulled Gunnhilde down. And screamed as Death flew toward her.

The door behind crashed wide. "Fiachna!"

Bear. He'd seen the man enter the church.

Fiachna turned. "I see you, Demon."

Bear roared "Betrayer!" as Fiachna hurled forward with Solwaer's men. Swords whirled in the hot light of the open door.

Bear fought from reflex. His sword so quick it bit and cut. Two of the three died, but Fiachna danced toward him and away. Solwaer's chief carl grinned like a red dog.

"Why?" Bear challenged.

Fiachna laughed. Sweat flew and breath was short. "The game changed. You won't win." A taunt. A thrust, another.

Bear feinted from the carl's blade; the man was better than he'd thought. He sneered. "Envy will kill you, Fiachna, or Solwaer."

"No." The death smile. "And you won't have her."

It was then Bear saw Signy and understood. "She was promised to me."

Huddled with Gunnhilde by Anselm's corpse, his life ended by Fiachna's ax, Signy lifted her head. Bear meant her.

Solwaer's lieutenant howled, plunged forward. "That pledge is broken."

Sword sliced on sword and clashed and slid, Bear's blade against Fiachna's hilt. It broke in a blood fountain, Fiachna's sword wrist, his fingers, shorn like wool.

Bear pressed hard. The knife in his other hand plunged deep in his opponent's guts.

Fiachna screamed, a pig at year-end slaughter. He fell.

A fourth man, foolishly, had his back to Bear. He'd hacked at Gunnhilde trying to get to the girl. The nun's arm flew away, but

Signy had the great book of the end of the world, of the Apocalypse, as a shield. She screamed to Mary. A curse or a prayer.

Bear slashed out, a great unbalanced lurch. In the whirl and
confusion, the half-light, the blade connected with the man's face,
slicing an eye and into a shoulder. The man dropped, blinded. He
died with an arm slung across the nun's body. Bear ran to Signy,
grabbed her wrist, wrenched her up.

He took her from the noise and the death. There was one safe
place they both knew. Chest heaving, he dragged her to the edge
of the stones. "I'll come back." And turned to go.

Signy was staring, wide-eyed. "You won't come back."

Bear leaned on his sword, trying to breathe. "Of course I will."
Flames shot gold in his eyes.

Signy sank to her knees. "I cannot hide. The altar stone. They
took it."

Bear plunged his sword in the turf and knelt. "Hush. This will
be over very soon. And then . . ."

"Then?" She was shaking, dazed.

Bear cupped Signy's face in his hands. The skin was hard, but
his touch was gentle. "Then, we have the future. Life. If you forgive me." He kissed her.

Signy twined her hands in his hair; she sobbed as she tasted
his mouth, breathed him into her heart. "I forgive you. I love you,
I always have."

"Very touching." A sword hilt thumped the boss of a shield—
ironic applause.

In the drifting smoke, making leisurely way toward them came
Solwaer. He'd observed the carnage at the Abbey dispassionately
and decided to keep away from the fury. To find Bear was just
pure, blind luck. Or not.

Bear rose. He glared at Solwaer—the red stare. He pulled his
sword from the earth. "In search of carrion, oath breaker?"

The Chieftain smiled. He held out an open hand. "We are your friends." Men were running toward them, Portsol men. They carried axes and howled like animals.

From the dark side of the stones, a man ran from shadow to shadow.

"Bear!" Signy shouted a warning.

For a moment—only a moment—Bear thought Edor had brought aid.

"Run!" Bear pushed Signy away, his sword held high. Solwaer hung back, watching.

But Signy darted forward, a rock in her hands. Edor dodged as she hurled it. He howled; she'd winged the side of his face. Blood dripped, and he stumbled as Bear pressed forward and the blades engaged.

Men ran toward the fight. Solwaer bellowed, "Hold!" They faltered.

Edor was on his feet but off-balance. Bear drove at him, his sword a blur. The onslaught was vicious, and Edor backed, and backed again. Death came close, closer in that whirling blade. Bear howled victory and lunged, but Edor's sword flashed and slashed Bear's chest. Deep and wide.

Signy saw Bear fall.

"Christ!" In the clamor of the sack, her scream was a knife through smoke. Kneeling, she tried to raise Bear from the ground; blood turned her kirtle black.

Shaken, Edor scrambled up. He wiped his blade and watched the girl cradle the demon he'd murdered, Grimor's brother.

"Magni!" A distant bellow.

Through her tears, Signy saw him first. Fate. She stood.

Bear, eyes turning toward the shadows, reached out, trying to hold Signy at his side. His strength was nearly lost.

Edor swallowed. He rebalanced the sword in his hand as Grimor ran from the burning Abbey.

And stopped. "Magni!" He knelt beside the dying man, half-lifted him from the grass.

"I tried to save him, Grimor. But your brother was betrayed."
Edor turned toward Solwaer.

If Solwaer answered, none heard him.

An angel of destruction, the girl reared up, screaming, "Liar!"
A knife flashed in her hand. Bear's knife.

Edor's sword sliced at the air as the girl dodged beneath his
arm. Her bright, small blade flickered in the light from the fires.

Grimor, defending his lieutenant, surged from the grass. His
fist caught Signy in the side. Gasping, the girl fell back against Bear.

With the last flicker of his life, his breath, Bear flung his arm
across Signy's body. The arm would not do his bidding, but his
fingers found hers, and grasped.

Signy saw the light leave Bear's eyes.

She took his face in her hands, tried to give her breath to that
massive chest. *Bear, come back. Come back to me.*

He had brought her from death once, long ago.

The girl pressed her lips against Bear's, but Grimor's brother
lay open-eyed in those frail arms. Never again would he breathe
in this life.

As Signy keened, rocking Bear in her arms, the war leader knelt
again beside the warm body of his brother.

"Grimor."

He waved Edor away, blear-eyed.

"Pick up your sword, Grimor."

The war leader was confused. Then he saw the truth, saw why
the girl had tried to strike Edor, his brother's killer.

Grimor stood, death incarnate, the sword in his fingers an ex-
tension of his hand.

Edor swallowed; he'd wanted this.

Behind them, Solwaer drew closer.

Grimor taunted, "Foolish man, dead man. Soon you will be
crow food. No Walhal for you."

Was Edor superstitious? "You would have replaced me." He waved his sword at Bear. "But now . . ." He feinted forward, trying for the first strike—a slash, and blood flowed from beneath Grimor's right eye. "I will take the hulls."

"No!" Signy saw Grimor's death arrive.

Solwaer thrust his sword into Grimor's back. The unsullied blade severed spine, pierced lungs, cut heart.

With deep surprise, the Norse leader watched the cold stars slide away as he died.

Edor rallied. Enraged, he rushed to split Solwaer's skull.

"Stop. *Stop!*"

The Lord of Portsol snatched up Grimor's sword and pivoted. "Edor! Think! This was the plan."

Edor shook blood from his eyes. He roared forward.

Solwaer knelt in his path. The raider tripped and fell heavily; winded, he lay gasping.

Solwaer, a foot on Edor's throat, sword poised over his belly, shouted, "Listen!"

The man flexed and struggled, but Solwaer leaned his weight behind the foot. He pushed the sword point through Edor's tunic. It was close, very close to the man's balls. Edor froze.

"Sensible, finally." The Chieftain glanced toward Grimor and Bear. Beyond, the Abbey was almost consumed. Solwaer shook his head. "You did this. Let them loose." He glared at Edor. "Get rope. The Christians who live must be kept together. Leave her." His glance flicked to Signy. "Go—stop the killing." He removed his sword.

Edor rose. He stumbled off, sullen. As war blood ebbed, he stared at the corpses of the brothers.

Something must be saved from Solwaer's betrayal; blood price, at least, must be paid.

Signy, oblivious, knelt beside the body of the man she had so loved. She stared, unseeing, at the comet in the red night sky.

CHAPTER 41

AT DAWN it rained, and the ashes of the monastery leached bitter lye. After the tumult of the night, the day that followed was still and windless, no sound but the calm sea, the shift of insects in the grass. And it was warm, the morning benign, as it had been the first time. That was cruel.

The Abbey was reduced, again, to roofless walls, and there were mounds in the grass. Unrecognizable as men or women, they were lumps among the verdant green—inconsequential. But blackened stone, floorless rooms—these had shocking substance. Bodies are fragile, but stone is presumed to endure.

Signy, in her filthy kirtle, stared out across the strait. Seven nuns and two girls, novices, had survived the sack, and the group were all roped together—hands and necks—beside the rowan at the top of the cliff path. She had been similarly bound but was forced to sit apart from the others. Behind them, the gates within the palisade had been pulled down and lay abandoned. So passed Cuillin's ability to control his world.

Numb and stunned, Signy saw nothing except the gulls as they wheeled and dipped above her head, calling. She would not feel, she would not think, she would not . . . But Bear's phantom hand still lay in hers. There was pressure from his fingers until she sensed the strength begin to fade. "No! Do not go."

One of the nuns bent closer. "Signy, this is our time of trial, we must think on Christ's suffering and—"

Signy jerked the woman's face to hers by the rope at her neck. "Listen to me, Alberga. You are not my sister. Your God has failed us all. He must hate this place to let it burn twice. He must hate you."

The girl drew back, tears in her eyes. The other nuns stared at Signy reproachfully. Cuillin had said she was possessed; this proved it.

Signy turned away, willing herself not to cry. In the east, as she stared into the sun, the circle of stones stood as it always had. They would stand when this agony was long gone.

"That one." She knew the voice. Solwaer. She would not look at the man, but her heart hammered.

Bending down, a stranger blanked out the light of the sun. There was a knife in his hand. As his face loomed into hers, Signy saw the world in hectic color, heard the man's breathing louder than a bellows. Her senses rioted. She welcomed oblivion. She would join Bear, and there would be peace—no more terror, no more suffering. *Please, please, let him be there to receive me.* There was a flash of that other time: she a child, hoping to die quickly as Cuillin tried to lift her up.

But Signy would not close her eyes in submission. Let her killer see she was not afraid. As the knife descended, she stared into his eyes and stretched her throat, exposing its length to that bright edge. The blade was cold as it touched her skin. It sawed, back and forth, back and forth. That was hard to bear.

The rope at her neck dropped away. Her flesh was not touched, and the bonds on her wrists were cut. She was free, but this was a fearful thing—she did not know what it meant.

Solwaer stared at Signy. He took an inventory of her body, piece by piece, and she remembered, ah yes, she remembered when Bear had been taken by this man.

"Sister Signy. Or should I just call you Signy?" Solwaer held out a hand as if today were a cheerful festival and she a bashful village girl. "Come. You have been distressed enough. I will protect you."

She caught his odor. Smoke, sweat, and wet wool. Yet there was a softness in his eyes, as if he truly understood what she was feeling.

Signy almost laughed. She had seen him, she had seen this man stab Grimor with dispassionate accuracy. Protect her?

Solwaer's dirty hand cupped Signy's chin. "I want only the best for you." He turned her head gently, so that she was forced to stare into his eyes.

She flinched from what she saw there.

"Do you understand me?" He spoke loudly, saying the words with extra care. His other hand now grasped her waist. He might speak like a thoughtful lover, but that hand was hard and possessive.

Signy frowned as if confused.

Disappointed, he yelled. "Idorn!"

"Here I am, Lord." The translator hurried forward, sheathing the knife that had freed the girl.

The last day and night had shifted Idorn's world. After these anxious days standing between Grimor, Bear, and Solwaer, his allegiances had been sorely tested, especially when it seemed the brothers had the upper hand. But this was the moment to demonstrate loyalty to Solwaer; in times of chaos, great opportunities existed. "What do you need of me, Lord?"

Solwaer waved toward Signy. "Tell this girl I will protect her, that she is not to fear. Say I can give her a good life if she obeys me."

Idorn nodded, though the request made him anxious—he had only a few words of the southern tongue the girl most probably spoke, and none at all of Latin.

With many smiles, bowing low to Solwaer, Idorn tried to mime a strong man protecting the weak; he patted the muscles of Solwaer's arms and pretended to rock a baby. That confused the nuns, and Signy too. Then Idorn danced around Solwaer, clapping his hands and simpering—a pantomime of delight. He encouraged Signy to dance, but she folded her arms as he capered.

Sweating slightly, Idorn stopped, his brows raised inquiringly. Did the girl understand? No. She seemed puzzled. He sighed; not intelligent, then. That surprised him—she had a clever face.

Solwaer was impatient. "Take her to my vessel, discreetly. Hide her there—she is not to be harmed. And . . ." He stared at Idorn thoughtfully, for a long, unnerving moment. "Accomplish this and the future will be interesting." He punched the younger man in the shoulder. "The raiders are not to have her. See that she is well guarded, then return to me at the Abbey. There is much to discuss with Edor."

Relieved and intrigued, Idorn gestured courteously for Signy to precede him toward the cove. She did not move, and the nuns watched the interchange openmouthed.

Solwaer turned back and spoke sharply. "She's frightened. You'll have to do better than that. Win her trust. Do it quickly, I need you." He strode away.

I need you. Idorn closed his eyes. He could almost taste the future. Fiachna was dead, and Solwaer had no chief carl . . .

Idorn made his face merry, in the way all women seemed to like. He beckoned invitingly. "You are safe, lady, truly. Just . . . come with me now." He mimed rocking the baby again, pointing toward the cove and nodding with great energy. Eventually, the girl moved toward him.

"Signy! Do not leave us." The youngest of the group, Witlaef the novice, called out. She was only a child and crying piteously, as were the others.

Signy closed her eyes, tried not to hear, but that was impossible.

"Idorn." She addressed the man by name. "I will go with you, but only if they come as well."

Idorn should have been angry, but curiosity won out. "You knew all along." His first instinct had been right—this girl *was* clever—and desperate. That was good. If she became Solwaer's favorite—perhaps even more than a concubine—an alliance could advantage them both. "But I have no instructions from Solwaer." He nodded toward the frightened huddle of women.

Signy sighed impatiently. "If you want me to help you"—Idorn looked at her sharply, perhaps this girl was too intelligent—"you must help me first."

Solwaer had said, "Win her trust." The charming smile dropped from Idorn's face. "Quickly then, all of you."

Signy helped Witlaef stand, and the others followed, though it was awkward. Their neck ropes made it hard to move as a group.

Idorn was starting to sweat. He knew he was resourceful, but how was he going to hide so many sobbing women?

Two equally large blocks of stone had been placed on either side of a fire pit dug in the meadow near the stones. One had a cross carved in it—the Norse gave that to Solwaer—and now he and Edor sat staring at each other, waiting for the interpreter.

During the morning some order had been brought to the island. The bodies of the slain fighters had been laid out in the grass—the raiders in one tidy row, the men of Portsol in another. Together in death, as was fitting, they were decently supplied with weapons, their own or others lent by comrades.

Close to thirty monks remained alive from the sack, chief among them Cuillin. The monks had been made to kneel—roped and bound—before the Abbey's ruined west door. They were all exhausted, filthy, and frightened, and Solwaer thought them incapable of resistance, especially since, when Cuillin had tried to lead them in prayer, he'd been smashed in the mouth with an ax shaft. The monks went quiet after that.

Idorn felt some pity for the brutalized Abbot. Yes, life had made him a pragmatist, but as he hurried past the kneeling men toward the talking place—worried he'd taken too long with the women—he understood how shocking it must feel to be deserted by your God.

"Idorn!" Solwaer bellowed his name.

"Here I am, Lord." The translator increased his pace, but he did not run—that would have been undignified; he might be a man of substance soon. "I tried to hurry, Lord, but the girl . . ."

Solwaer waved an impatient hand. "Stand behind me. Tell them I am ready to talk."

Idorn bowed to Edor, and the business of ordering the island and dividing the spoils between Solwaer and Edor began.

First it was agreed that a pyre would be built and the dead raiders burned with the sacrifice of several animals from the Abbey flocks. The Portsol dead would return in the town ships this very day, and the corpses of the murdered monks and nuns would be thrown into the sea from the cliffs.

Grimor and Bear, however, had been laid out apart from the others, and each was covered by a mound of shields. The brothers would be silent witnesses of the negotiations between the victors, their successors.

Edor gestured toward the shields. "Grimor and Magni died fighting for this place. They must be honorably buried and a stone raised up recording their names and deeds, for these will be sung by our people forever. Tell him that." The fighter spoke without irony.

Spear shafts began to beat against the shields of the Norse, softly at first, then louder and faster. The raiders approved of their new leaders' decision.

Solwaer raised a hand. "Lord Grimor was my friend and Lord Magni the Bear was my honored carl. These noble men will indeed be honored by us all. Their valiant deaths deserve all that we can give so that they will be remembered. I salute the courage of our heroes!" He stood and bowed to the dead men beneath the shields.

"I honor all who fought here!" Another bow to the corpses of the fighters in the grass.

"We will avenge you all." Solwaer glared at the monks, who shifted apprehensively. The spears thumped harder, for the Norse appreciated oratory and ceremonial revenge. Both were pleasing to the Gods.

Over the din—as an afterthought—Solwaer shouted out, "And my former chief carl, Fiachna, will be buried with Grimor and Magni. He, too, died nobly. We also honor his courage." Solwaer bowed his head sorrowfully. A pleased cheer from his own men rewarded him. The Portsol fighters, too, liked homegrown heroes to talk about in their cups.

Solwaer held up his arms for silence. "And I ask the blessing of the Gods. Hear now what I say." He gathered himself and turned to face the sun. "In the name of the great Lord Jesus, and of the mighty All Father Odin, and of Cruach. Fathers all, you have guided me, your son, to a great victory, and I rejoice, as do my allies also."

Apparently only mildly interested in Solwaer's words, Edor lounged on his stone seat. The presumption of this man was boundless, but he was certainly cunning. Let Solwaer have this moment; he, Edor, would be content to wait on a better time to act. Words meant little when swords were sharp.

But Solwaer was not finished. "And I call on our Gods to witness these, my acts and intentions today, and those of Lord Edor also. All that I do, I do in your names." Some of his men might think of themselves as Christians now, and the Norse had their own barbarian Gods and rites. Worshiping Cruach was a hangover from the old days, when he'd grown up the despised son of a slave in the old clan settlement, but by claiming the support of these Gods, he seized fate in his hands and took the initiative from Edor. In the end, he did not care what any of them believed so long as he was obeyed. "Midsummer Day approaches quickly, and by that time, we will have built a great burial chamber in which our heroes shall lie. Fortunately, we have enough slaves." Solwaer stared at the monks.

The Abbot bowed his head; he would not allow Solwaer to enjoy his despair.

The Chieftain lifted his arm, a sword in his hand. He waved it above his head. With a roar, the fighters raised their weapons.

Edor, cheering with the rest, knew he'd lost round one, though the tomb would bolster his prestige as well as Solwaer's. He glanced at the brothers; perhaps he owed them that at least. Blood price.

CHAPTER 42

DAN LAY beside Freya on the single bed. She was deeply asleep, and his arm, under her head, was numb. Gently, he eased it out and flexed his fingers to get the blood moving. Freya shifted, and her eyelids flickered.

Dan stroked her cheek. She muttered and half-smiled.

What was it about this girl? Like a gale she'd swept through his life and taken all certainty away. A few days, that was all it had been—less than two weeks. Could life really change so fast?

Freya fidgeted. She was frowning. "No. I said no!" She half sat up.

Clearly, she was still asleep, but he engaged her. "No?"

"No," she echoed, sighing. "Not now." She snuggled into the pillow again.

Dan smiled. She always knew her own mind, Freya Dane, even in sleep. Had she been sleepwalking last night, or was that something else? His money was on something else, but eventually Katherine and he had persuaded Freya to go back to bed. He'd tried to stay awake beside her—chastely lying on top of the covers—just to make sure she didn't take off again. But of course he'd gone to sleep, waking cramped and crammed against the wall. Freya might have thrashed around, but she hadn't left the bed.

Dan propped himself on one elbow. There was a mystery to Freya's face. Asleep, without those vivid blue eyes challenging life, challenging him, she seemed much younger—and so vulnerable.

The desire to protect—even to protect someone as spiky and well defended as Freya Dane—was a deep surprise to Daniel

Boyne. He'd like to get used to it—the certainty that she'd run to him when she needed shelter, between the rounds of sparring. Sparring was quite good fun with this girl. Dan smiled.

"Why do you look so cheerful?" She was staring at him.

"Free country, isn't it?" He pushed her hair back.

"Sometimes." She sighed happily and cozied up against him. "You're not under the covers."

"I am not."

"Why?" She struggled to sit up.

Dan tried to create more room, fluffed a pillow for her back. He said, solemnly, "I am a Scot, and we have hardly been introduced."

"Have you been here all night?" Her eyes were serious, but there was devilry in the depths.

As gravely, he replied, "I have. Well, if you call four hours a night. But what a pleasure it was."

Freya giggled. "A pleasure, you say. What sort of pleasure?"

"Contemplative." He smiled broadly.

She yawned. "Sounds way too monastic to me. Must be this place."

Dan put an arm around Freya's shoulders and pulled her close. "Do you remember much of last night?"

"Of course. Katherine talked about Dad seeing the people here, then we had dinner. After dinner she showed us the last diary entry. The Pagan prayer. Very odd. Do you think, could it be possible . . ." Her eyes were suddenly huge.

Dan nodded. "It would be remarkable if it could be proved. That the girl in the grave wrote—"

"The diary! Yes, but it seems just too much of a coincidence—doesn't it?"

"You'd know that better than me, Freya."

She pushed back the covers and swung out of bed, in knickers and T-shirt and nothing else. "We'd have to get dating evidence. We've got the bowl from the grave, and her bones and the diary itself. It's possible, I suppose; there is that cross on the stone—she might have been the nun."

"That wasn't a nun's grave, however." Dan, before he looked away, saw that Freya's legs were as he'd thought they might be—long and strong and lean. Warmth flooded his belly. He leaned back against the wall, eyes half-closed. "You're a handsome woman, Freya Dane."

She paused in the act of pulling on her jeans. "Have to get dressed. No time for flirting."

She seemed happy rather than embarrassed, and he grinned amiably. "But I have to practice or I'll never get good, will I?"

She giggled, dragging a brush through wild hair.

Dan said quietly, "What else do you remember, Freya?"

She stared at him from the scrap of mirror next to the window. "About last night? Well, after the diary, we all went to bed. Very chaste. You to the couch, me up here, Katherine to Dad's room."

Dan limped to stand behind her. He put his hands on Freya's shoulders and, head beside head, they stared at each other. "How did I end up here, on your bed?"

She looked puzzled. "This is embarrassing. I don't know."

Dan allowed his hands to roam, the curve of each shoulder, down her arms. "It was not for the reason you might expect, though I will admit, before I tried to sleep on that damn couch, I was sorely tempted."

"You were?" Freya leaned back against him, her throat a beautiful, supple column.

He nodded thoughtfully. "I was." Watching her in the mirror, he stroked the tender skin.

"What happened then? Don't stop." She tipped her head against his shoulder, her eyes half-closed.

Dan sighed. "Oh, I must, or we shall both be distracted. There's something you have to see."

⌕

They lit the wall as brightly as the combined resources of the house would allow—all the candles, the flashlights, and the lamps—but nothing was quite enough. The dark lodged very deep in the corners of the undercroft, even on a bright day.

"I don't know what to say." *I did this?* Freya stared at the carnage.

Katherine said, firmly, "Somnambulism. You cannot control a thing like that."

Dan was staring at the massive pieces of stone embedded in the wall; last night's final impression held. He pointed. "So, what does that remind you of?"

Freya stepped back. She searched for words. "I . . . it looks like a lintel. The lintel over a door."

"I agree." Katherine almost spoke to herself.

Dan limped to stand beside Freya. "Any other thoughts?"

"I still cannot believe this, but what's done is done." She touched his arm. "And I want to know what's on the other side."

"All right with me." Dan picked up a masonry ax.

"And me." Katherine hefted a crowbar.

An unspoken signal, and all three stepped forward.

For some hours they worked in near silence. The dust was pernicious, but Freya found face masks and they kept going, focused on the task of breaking through.

"Can you hear that?" Daniel tapped the head of his ax against the wall—a hollow tock-tocking. "We're close."

Tension ramped up as they all concentrated on a small area where the structure of the wall seemed weak.

Katherine wiped her sweating face. "It's odd, don't you think? Monumental masonry like this under an ordinary house."

"*Odd* isn't the word I'd use." Dan had chipped around a lump of rock, trying to ease it from the wall.

Freya caught her breath. "I suppose, as a long shot, it could just be a bricked-up chamber of the undercroft. Some sort of store-room, maybe."

Dan scoffed. "Lot of trouble to go to."

"Depends what they were storing." This from Katherine. "Watch out!"

Dan's rock fell with an abrupt *thud*. They all stood back coughing as the dust slowly cleared.

There was a hole now—a big one—all the way through the wall. Dan poked a flashlight through the opening. "You have to see this."

The women crowded close. Freya yelped. "There's a passage!"

There was, long and wide, and light bounced off the walls—Dan was too excited to hold the flashlight still—displaying massive stones, stacked one on top of another to form each side of the tunnel. Overhead, the roof was made of long stones laid like logs alongside each other.

"But . . ." Katherine was awed. "They're just enormous. Where did they come from? Who *put* them here?"

"The tools you'd need to work those things . . ." Dan's voice trailed away. Ahead, beyond the reach of the flashlight beam, light was swallowed whole.

It's a passage tomb, Dad. A big one. You talked about a tomb. Dialogue with the dead—this was the right place for it, no question.

Responsibility hit Freya, a tangible jolt. She was an archaeologist, and people waited their whole professional lives for a fraction of what she'd been handed in this place by her father. And she hadn't even recorded what they'd been doing—she'd just been hacking into the stone like a navvy, with no more thought in her head than breaking through. Mortifying!

"Can you both stand back, please?" Two baffled faces turned toward her. "I'm sorry, but this is just so potentially important. It needs to be documented properly."

Dan leaned on the pickax. "A bit late for that, isn't it?"

Freya rubbed gritty eyes. "I know, but something sane has to be taken from this situation."

CHAPTER 43

CRUACH HAD thrown a golden road across the water tonight—a road that reached all the way from Portsol's harbor to Findnar's cove. Shimmering and changing as the sky was bled of light, that glittering path showed Solwaer his destiny—the joining of these two places in him, and his descendants.

For now there was also Findnar, defensible Findnar with its sheltered cove. This would be his second domain, the natural fortress of the trading empire he would build.

Out of this new alliance with Edor, he would control much more than his eyes could see. *Not bad for the hungry son of the slave woman.*

But first, the bond must be made solid. The burial of the brothers with Fiachna would help. That would go down in legend—his legend—since the tomb of Bear and Grimor would be lavishly equipped.

Of course it would cost more than a pang when he surrendered some of the fine things he owned, and it would cost Edor dearly, too, for an entry into joint lordship of the sea would not come cheap. However, with another good season, this large outlay should be recouped without trouble.

Solwaer shaded his eyes. Edor's ships and his own were blocked from sight by the edge of the cliff, but he could just make out the monks in the fading light—their black robes stood out against the green of the meadow. They were clearing the entrance to the Pagan tomb that lay beneath the swell of rising ground.

Solwaer guffawed. Christians preparing the main chamber of a heathen burial place to receive new occupants? He could hear the old Gods laughing, though the monks tried to pretend they were dead.

This had been his decision. With limited time before midsummer—the most propitious time to bury the brothers—but also a recognition that the bodies would stink very soon, Solwaer and Edor had agreed that constructing a new tomb was unrealistic.

Findnar had always been a sacred island, since well before the Christians came. Generations of important local men had been buried here, but only the hereditary shamans of this coast knew where to find their tomb. Solwaer was their successor—he was the Knowledge Keeper now. That was because of the girl. She'd told Idorn about the tomb—burrowed into rising ground and well concealed by what seemed a natural fall of rock—and he had told Solwaer.

Why would she want me to know this thing, Idorn?

She loved Bear, Lord. She wants him to sleep with her ancestors since, under other circumstances, they would have married.

Solwaer frowned. The girl mourned for Bear, but she was his now and, if she was wise, she would recognize that fact quickly. He did not wish her to grieve. He preferred cheerful bedmates, and he hoped Signy was young enough and intelligent enough to learn what was required of her.

Of course, it would advantage him locally—and her too—if the daughter of the last shaman became his concubine. If she pleased him, he might make her one of his minor wives.

She was waiting on his ship. A pleasant thought. He intended to enjoy their first night together, and Idorn had been instructed to set up a tent at a discreet distance from the fighters' camp. The translator had also been told to find something pretty for the girl to wear, even if he had to go back to Portsol to get it.

Solwaer yawned. It had been an eventful few days, and he was tired. He walked across the meadow in the long shadows, gazing appreciatively at his new possession. On a still night, this really was a very pretty place if you ignored the burned buildings. A useful view, too, from the cliffs. Any approach across the strait would immediately be seen.

Solwaer paused. He gazed at the line of toiling monks. More than half were working in the inner chambers, and it would be dark there by now. Yet leather buckets of bones and rubble were still being passed hand to hand to the last monk in line. Standing on the cliff's edge, he emptied the buckets into the sea below. *Not many ancestral bones left now, Signy.* He laughed as another skull sailed out into the sky and down.

However, the monks remained a problem. Since his baptism, Solwaer had made sure the settlements up and down the coast saw him as an honest *Christian* trader now—a man of peace. He did not doubt the loyalty of his own men where his reputation was concerned, and no one would believe what Edor might say about him, but the monks from the Abbey, particularly Cuillin, knew the truth about the raid.

Of course, too, they now knew the location of Bear and Grimor's grave. *Sorry, Fiachna, you too*—he kept forgetting his former chief carl.

Solwaer came to a decision. In this instance, the magnificence of the gesture, the economic sacrifice, would serve only to increase his reputation; no, *his legend* . . .

Solwaer ambled toward the monks. Frightened, they increased their pace of work, for the whips of their overseers had shredded cassock and flesh alike.

"I pray for you, Solwaer," Cuillin mumbled—he had few teeth left in his broken mouth.

"Do you, Abbot?" Perhaps the Lord of Portsol was amused.

The monk straightened. "I pity the suffering that will come to you. There is a place in Hell for apostates."

Solwaer laughed. "This God we spoke of once or twice"—he winked at the Portsol men guarding the monks—"perhaps He does not exist—or He's weak, very weak." Solwaer waved a contemptuous hand over the laboring brothers. "Why does He not protect you better?"

Cuillin held a bucket filled with Pagan bones. He dropped it deliberately. "God requires us to bear your horrors so we may emulate His suffering. He died for you, Solwaer; He died for your sins, innumerable though they are." The Abbot's voice boomed, scaring birds into the air. "For I say that you are damned and I say that your bones will never rest peacefully within His kind earth." The monk flung the bucket toward the cliff in a violent arc. Holding up his arm, he advanced on Solwaer relentlessly. "Your soul will writhe in a lake of hellfire, and your blood will boil in your veins, for *you* brought fire and blood to this holy island." Cuillin began to sign a great, sweeping cross in the air.

That was too much.

With a roar, Solwaer charged and, shoulder down, he took Cuillin in his bony midriff; knocking the monk to the ground, he kicked him where he lay. The brothers rushed to protect their abbot, and most unchristian punches were thrown as the melee developed.

But the Portsol men had axes, knives, and swords and, most of all, whips. The unequal contest claimed two lives.

At the mouth of the Pagan tomb, Solwaer shouted, "Shut them in. All of them. No food tonight. Let them think about the power of real Gods."

The Lord of Portsol stalked away. A lake of hellfire? Rubbish. He was always the victor because *he* had luck and the Gods, *all* the Gods, were on his side. Now, too, he had a shaman's daughter. What more protection did he need?

Something came at him out of the half-light, a white shape. For one paralyzed moment he thought it was Bear's spirit. Like a stone down a well, Solwaer fell to the turf, hiding his head. Something brushed his skull, and all the hair on his back stood up, stiff as pigs' bristles. He felt the air move as the thing passed on. And when he dared to look he saw the truth—it was an owl; a bird had unmanned him.

Had they seen? Solwaer stood warily. But the light was mostly gone and his men too busy herding the monks to witness what had happened. His breathing calmed.

This was a good lesson, because an owl symbolized good luck, his unfailing luck. Solwaer thought of the Shaman's daughter; yes, she was part of his luck. He smiled.

"Brother! Wassail." A yell.

Solwaer turned. Edor was waving to him from the gathering place, an ale horn in his hand.

"Idorn!" *Where was the man?*

"Here, Lord." The translator had been trailing Solwaer at a discreet distance. He hurried toward his master.

"What did that barbarian say to me?"

"Lord Edor offers ale and food, my lord, and he called you brother."

Solwaer snorted. "Brother. Ha!" He was annoyed now. He craved oblivion in the arms of the girl—he'd earned that—and another night of drinking held no appeal. He grunted. "Is the tent arranged?"

Idorn nodded. "It is. And I have found clothes for the girl—a very nice dress. It was on one of the Norse ships and—"

"I don't care where you got it. Was she pleased?"

"Oh, yes. She asked me to thank you, Lord Solwaer." Idorn lied unflinchingly. "I've had her washed, too, by the nuns. I think she looks very pretty."

Solwaer shot Idorn a hard glance.

Aware he'd strayed into delicate territory, the translator said,

"As I'm sure you will see for yourself very shortly, Lord. She is eager to please you." He tried to sound sincere, but it had been a difficult afternoon. Signy had not been cooperative.

"She is to be guarded at the tent while I confer with Lord Edor; he can do it." Solwaer pointed at one of the Portsol men. "You will stay with me." He raised an arm to Edor, calling out, "I am coming, Lord Edor."

It had been a long night, too long. Light had only briefly dipped from the sky into milky gloom, and now, all too soon, the sun had returned, and it hurt. It was hard, sometimes, not to take such things personally.

Solwaer rolled over, squinting. Was Cruach angry? Perhaps these spears in his eyes were punishment for linking the name of the mighty Sun with all the other Gods. A moment's bravado in the full flight of the speech yesterday, and now he had something else to worry about.

Time to face the day. Solwaer managed to sit up gracelessly—more a roll than anything else—and stared around the talking place. It seemed he must have slept beside the fire trench with some of his men, and Edor was snoring among his followers on the other side. They appeared to be breathing, though Solwaer had some dim recollection of a fight between the Portsol men and the Norse some hours back. A fight in which he and Edor had jointly intervened and, of course, peace had demanded more ale be drunk.

Solwaer grimaced. It would be a slow start to the day, but that was not to be the worst of it—he'd still not enjoyed the girl and, in this state, doubted he'd be capable for some hours. A concubine had dared to mock him once after he'd found himself unmanned by ale; once, and no more than that, for life had not been pleasant for the girl afterward. But he had time enough to enjoy this one properly—all the time he might want. An incautious nod and his skull pulsed, the pain too big to be contained behind his eyes. Solwaer groaned; focus was impossible, and his mouth—he hawked up sour phlegm and spat into the ashes—his mouth tasted of sulfur and bile. He heaved himself to his feet and kicked Idorn where he lay.

"What?" The man woke, wild-eyed. Groaning, he, too, leaned over the fire trench and retched into the ashes. Perhaps that gave Solwaer a little pleasure, but not enough.

"There's work to be done. Wake the others."

"Yes, Lord." Idorn stood too quickly; the horizon tilted, and the sun wove a giddy arc in the sky. Stumbling away with half-closed eyes, he paused here and there to shake ungrateful men to their senses.

Solwaer sighed. This would be an important day and another big night afterward. But then . . .

Though work had progressed well on the clearing and refurbishment of the tomb, not all was as it should be.

Death, as life, throws up politics, and finally, Solwaer faced the truth. He could not have everything he wanted—not if he wished to control the direction of the larger game.

He forced himself to sound reasonable. "We have two things that must be resolved, Edor. First, the work on the tomb must be finished today. Then we will light the pyres and place Grimor and Magni in the chamber tonight. We cannot wait past that."

Edor, playing at knucklebones, frowned. This, at least, was true; the corpses of all the dead were besieged by flies.

Solwaer continued, "Then there is the matter of the slaves and the overseers. Mine and yours."

Since he had claimed Grimor's place, Edor had been presented with nothing but problems. He was tired of sitting around on this island, talking as the good weather wasted away. He threw the bones on the ground. "You can't just kill them all, Solwaer. That's very expensive."

Solwaer stopped pacing around the dead fire pit. "Do you trust your men?"

"Yes." *Mostly,* thought Edor.

"Will you trust them when they see the treasures we place around the brothers?" *And Fiachna.* "And Fiachna?"

"Whatever you do, *we* do not plunder the graves of our comrades." Edor's face was sullen.

Solwaer tried another tack. "You trust your men, and that is good. I certainly trust my own." So much for disposing of the Portsol overseers, but there were only a few of those; they could be dealt with later. "I do not, however, trust the monks. Once at the market . . ." He left that thought hanging. "Bear—that is, Magni—and Grimor must have attendants. What I am proposing would serve the purpose, and it would be a most kingly gesture. Men would remember, after you are gone, how you honored these noble brothers."

Kingly, an enticing word. Generosity was the mark of greatness—wasn't that what Grimor always used to say? But Edor shook his head, his face a bland mask. "So, no income from the monks. And the nuns won't be worth much. A scrawny bunch."

Solwaer rolled his eyes. Idorn had told him, finally, where the nuns had been hidden, and he'd pretended to be angry—to make sure his translator did not make another important decision without his approval—but he'd been pleased, secretly. At least their value had been protected. "You know they'll do better when we fatten them up. It's all in the presentation."

Edor stared at him. "You kept one for yourself, I hear, the girl Magni wanted." He paused, conscious of an advantage at last. "Solwaer, this will be a long and prosperous relationship. We raid, you trade, and Findnar becomes the base of our venture. Yes?"

The other man nodded warily.

"If I agree to give the monks to the brothers, I think this girl goes with them. We both make sacrifices. Mine is greater."

"How is that? We both lose jointly the value of the monks, and I fail to see—"

Edor held up his hand. He said patiently, "My loss is greater than yours because Grimor, who was more than a brother to me, was murdered. By you. I saw it. If I told my fighters, they would not be happy." The hypocrisy was shameless.

Unguarded words jammed behind Solwaer's teeth. He contained them, but only just.

Edor allowed himself to sound magnanimous. "Come, why squabble over something so small? Bear's spirit will be greatly appeased with the girl as a companion."

Solwaer forced himself to think. Normally he did not permit sentiment to interfere with business, but this was different. Personal considerations aside, the girl had a political value that might repay risk and long-term investment. Bear's ruined face flashed into his mind. *You're dead. Go away.* Signy was also beautiful—an impressive addition to his household—and she was the daughter of Portsol's former shaman. With these advantages, she would give him children who might be worthy to carry his name and his goods into the future. The only son he had now from his chief wife was not at all like him; his mother called him *sensitive*. Yes, he needed more boys, proper boys, and Signy would bear them. That said, she was just a girl, and there were always fertile girls around.

He eyed the grinning Edor, a smile securely in place. "I'll give you my answer tonight." He forced respect into his voice and was rewarded by the younger man's smug expression.

Solwaer's own smile grew wider. *Let the idiot think he's won. And we'll see who comes out ahead in the end.*

CHAPTER 44

ANYONE HOME? Hello . . ."

All three heard the voice and the footsteps overhead. Dan wiped his eyes; the dust was irritating. "Who's that?"

Freya dropped the pickax and hurried off. "Simon Fettler."

"Who?" Dan's question was redundant.

"Freya, there you are." Simon sauntered down the stairs. He paused on the last step, amused. "My, my, what have you been doing?" His eyes swept past her to the brightly lit wall and the yawning hole. "Hello there, Miss MacAllister. Working hard, I see." A cheery wave.

Embarrassed by her appearance, Katherine nodded. She put the crowbar behind her back.

"Hi, Simon." Freya stopped a pace or two away from the visitor. She didn't care what she looked like, but the man was a heritage architect and the place looked like a war zone. "Nice to see you."

Simon switched his attention back to Freya. "I've brought something for you." He held up a tablet computer. "Plans. As I promised." His eyes widened further as Dan appeared from the tunnel behind the girl.

Freya brushed dust off her clothes. "Great. Let's go upstairs. I'm sure we could all do with a break." She sounded jumpy; she *was* jumpy. "After you."

Her visitor turned on his heel. "Excellent."

Freya called out to the others, "I'll stick the kettle on. Come up when you're ready."

Dan nudged Katherine. "And Simon is . . . ?"

"Too nosy by half." The librarian looked grim. She tried to pat her hair into some kind of order as she strode toward the stairs. "He bought the church."

"*Nosy*. What's that supposed to mean?" Dan hobbled after her; standing for such a long time had stiffened his bad leg.

Katherine stopped at the foot of the stairs. "I forgot to tell Freya. Mr. Fettler's been in and out of my library these last couple of days. He's been researching the island. Tried to pump me, too, about Michael's work." She'd been so discreet about her relationship with Michael Dane—how had he known?

"And?"

"*And*, I'd say he's too interested." Katherine's tone was grim.

"In what?"

"The past."

"These are really lovely." Freya watched as Simon clicked through image after image. "So many possibilities—just fantastic."

"I'm glad you like them." He clicked to another. "As I said, your house is interesting, and that makes it an added pleasure to work on." He stared at her, bright-eyed. "Plaster suits you, by the way." A teasing smile.

Freya leaned closer to the screen. "Is that the undercroft? Wow." She spoke quickly.

"It really would make the most amazing apartment—great self-contained tourist accommodation with its own entrance downstairs. Unique. People will pay for high-end experiences in this part of the world. It's not all about B and Bs. Could be a handy source of income for you."

She sat back. "It's certainly novel—if I could just get people to walk up that path with their bags." Freya went to say something else but stopped. "I'll think about it."

"Think about what?" Katherine joined them.

Simon half-rose as the librarian sat. "Renovations—and something else. I almost forgot." He hit a key. The image of a crane came up on the screen, and he pressed the Play arrow. The crane animated, lifting a stone slab—he'd even drawn the circle of stones in behind.

Dan entered quietly. He stood behind Freya's chair. "Ingenious."

"Yes, it is, Simon, it's great"—Freya tried not to look uncomfortable—"but actually we've already managed to raise the slab."

"Really?" Simon pressed Pause.

Freya ducked her head. "Yes. Dan came up with something—a surprise. He's a boatbuilder." She tried not to sound guilty; that made it worse. "Sorry. I should have let you know."

Dan leaned forward across the table and held out his hand. "Dan Boyne."

Simon hesitated. "Oh. Well, that makes sense." He went to take the offered hand, just as it was withdrawn.

With a charming smile, Simon broke the awkward moment. "Still and all, glad to hear it worked. Great outcome. You must be happy—all three of you, I mean." A smile for Katherine.

Dan pulled the chair out beside Freya. He took some time to sit down.

Simon observed the performance and asked, politely, "And did you find anything?"

"You mean under the stone?" Dan's tone was neutral.

"No." Katherine jumped in.

Freya glanced at the librarian, astonished.

Simon got up, uncurling his long frame. "Well, can't be lucky all the time, I guess." He extracted a sheaf of papers from his pack. "You're busy, Freya, so I'll leave these with you—a printout of the drawings. Take your time. I'm happy to talk further when it suits." He waved vaguely toward the undercroft. "Have fun with, whatever."

Freya got up hastily. "Thanks so much. Very kind of you to take the trouble to come all this way." She ran up the steps to open the back door. "You've included an invoice for your time, I hope?"

Simon bent under the lintel. He paused and dropped his voice. "Don't worry about money. If you like the ideas, there's always a way to find what you need."

She looked at him cautiously. "A way?"

"To finance things. I don't know if your father ever found anything here, but if he did, there's a market for real antiquities. I've got all sorts of contacts. Let me help you. I'd really like that."

Freya stiffened slightly.

He sensed her hesitation, but Simon's smile was genuine. "Look, just a thought. Don't be offended. The art market's booming. People are frightened to put their money into the stock market, for instance, or buying houses. In troubled times, unique objects outperform other investments; that's well known. You should think about it."

"I will. Thanks again."

Simon nodded. He went to go, turned back. "By the way, next time you're in Portsolly, a working dinner might be nice; when you've had time to look at the house drawings properly."

The pause was telling, and the beginnings of a blush. Simon watched as Freya forced a smile.

"That's a kind thought."

He waved dismissively. "No pressure at all—just let me know what suits." He strode away.

Freya closed the door on his back and leaned against it.

Dan stared at her. "You know what?"

She went back to the table. "No—what?"

"He's after something."

Freya said nothing, just stared at her hands, nicked and battered from the work.

"And he didn't ask," Katherine chimed in.

Two pairs of eyes swiveled toward her.

"What we were doing." She gestured. Their clothes and faces might have been dipped in flour. "Don't you think that's odd?"

CHAPTER 45

Idorn waved the sentry away and pulled back the opening of the tent. It was warm inside, pungent and gloomy, daylight shut out by the badly cured skin walls. His eyes adjusted. The interior looked pleasing, though, considering what he'd had to work with; he'd even found sheepskins to strew over the grass as well as a number of hangings, not that Solwaer would care.

"Hello, Signy."

"What do you want?" The girl was standing as far away from him as the space allowed. She did not sound welcoming.

"It is close to evening."

"I know that." Signy raised her chin. She stared at him steadily.

Idorn cleared his throat. "I see you've been given food." The charred haunch of something, perhaps a rabbit, lay on a wooden platter. The meat was untouched, and flies buzzed around it, disturbed by his entrance.

"I am not hungry."

"You should eat to keep up your strength."

Signy laughed heartily. "Why?"

He admired the defiance and felt some pity for the useless courage that drove her spirit. But despite what Edor had proposed, this girl might survive, still, if she allowed herself to be pragmatic. "I have good news, as you will see. By the way, you look very nice. Did I say that yesterday?" Idorn meant it. She might be too slender for his taste, but the girl looked so different for being clean. A captive had left the ocher-dyed tunic on one of the raider hulls; the color suited Signy, and the dress had pretty blue cord sewn around

the hem and the neck, which was flattering too. He'd even managed to find a shift, and the flash of white linen at the throat was
pleasing against Signy's tawny skin, while the wide belt cinched
her waist in a way that displayed the slight curves of her body very
pleasingly. Had it been the nuns or Signy herself who'd tied her
hair back in the white kerchief? In the warm afternoon, dark curls
had escaped and clustered softly around her brow. His task was
made so much harder by the girl's appeal.

He forced himself to sound cheerful. "My lord wants you to
witness the ceremonies. I've come to take you to him. And at first
light in the morning, Bear and Grimor will be sent to their Gods."

"In the tomb?"

Idorn nodded. He was economical with the truth; he did not
tell her about the ancestors' bones.

"Very well, I will come with you." As if Signy had a choice, she
walked toward him and paused not an arm's length away. "Well?"

Idorn pulled back the flap of the tent and motioned her through.
In his heart, he was troubled that his master now owned this girl.
Solwaer did not deserve Signy—so finely made and graceful—and
more than one man turned to watch her as they walked through
the camp together.

But Signy saw nothing and no one. Tonight, as last light faded,
Bear and his brother would be laid inside the tomb, and when
dawn entered the passage and shone through to the chamber
within—Cruach's blessing on their faces for the last time—the
brothers would be sealed away. Forever.

It seemed to Signy that time had ceased to be, that she would
walk this path forever and never suffer the pain of arriving, of seeing where he was to lie without her as long as the moon hung in
the heavens. Tears dropped into the dust at her feet. Idorn, close
behind, heard the swallowed sobs.

Rounding the last part of the path to the talking ground, they
smelled smoke—and something else. Flesh was burning. This was
the cremation of the raiders ahead of the inhumation of the broth-

ers. Once the fire was lit, fat dripped from the ripe bodies, and the pyre became an inferno, a storm of flame.

Men from the boats and Solwaer's followers stood back. Red-faced from the heat, they stared somberly into the heart of the fire. They'd been promised beer, but not until the pyre burned down, and without ale or war blood, it was sobering to watch this roaring beast consume a comrade's body. The smell reminded far too many of pork meat roasting.

"Solwaer?" Idorn approached his leader warily. "Here is the girl."

Men were turning to look; some smirked as they approached.

The Lord of Portsol swung around. To honor the dead, he was wearing the torque Bear had made and a wolf-trimmed cloak, because the full pelt—head, tail, and claws—made him seem broader, more substantial. But so close to the fire, the heavy garment was a burden. Sweat dripped down his neck, and irritation was the result, especially when Edor asked him something and Idorn was not there to translate.

But Solwaer forgot bad humor when he saw the Shaman's daughter. When he'd last seen her, Signy had been dressed in blood-stiffened rags—she was very different now. Face impassive, right hand on the hilt of his sword, he beckoned her to approach.

Signy was the sole woman in this gathering of men and, since he was her master, Solwaer had expected she would bow to him, at least. Another woman might have knelt humbly at his feet.

But Signy did neither of these things. Unblinking, she stared into his eyes as she advanced, and surprise made him look away. He covered the moment with a laugh, turning toward the men. "A spirited slave. Is that a good thing?" There was a ripple of laughter from the men. Some things crossed all language barriers.

Edor watched for what would happen next.

"Show me." Solwaer waved a languid hand—he might have been inspecting livestock. "Turn." There was an edge in his voice. Men had gathered behind him. "Do it, slave."

Signy's eyes widened. She lifted her head proudly and turned in a circle.

Solwaer grunted. "Again. Slower. Hands above your head. Now!" His voice was a lash.

Signy flinched.

The men laughed, not unkindly. It was to the girl's credit that she was embarrassed—a harlot might have enjoyed displaying herself.

Signy's breathing slowed, and she closed her eyes. From long training, she took her spirit away to the place that prayer provided. But who would hear her prayers in this moment? Bear.

She raised her arms high and trancelike, solemnly, turned as stiffly as a statue might. *Bear, protect me.*

Solwaer frowned, but he had made his point. He commanded, she obeyed. "Idorn!"

"Yes, Lord?"

"I am displeased by this girl. Take her back to my tent." He did not call her Signy—slaves had no personal possessions, not even names.

Signy shouted at Solwaer, "Idorn said I could witness the ceremonies. You told him." This loss, a final sight of Bear's face, was too much.

Solwaer turned his back on Signy. He would not dignify her defiance with a response. "Translator, Lord Edor asked me a question."

Idorn was harried. He clamped his hand across Signy's mouth, muttering, "Be still. Please." He raised his voice as the girl struggled. "Yes, Lord."

Edor threw the last of his mead in the grass. "I was asking, is the girl a virgin?"

Solwaer laughed uproariously. "Is she a virgin? I have yet to find out. It is a meaningless state for a slave."

"But not for a shaman's daughter." A voice spoke up beyond the fire.

There was no answering laughter from the Portsol men this time, only a muttering silence. All knew it was dangerous to challenge the power of a shaman, even a dead one. *Especially* a dead one. To damage a shaman's kin was to invite reprisal.

Solwaer glowered at the crowd—it had to be a Portsol man. Who else would have known?

He spoke loudly. "Come, Edor. We have beer, and there is good Portsol mead. To your fighters! To their journey!" No translation was required.

Hastily, a full horn was passed to him. Solwaer held it high so all could see. With a sweep of his arm, he threw the contents into the white heart of the fire. There was enough liquid to create an impressive hiss.

That lifted the spirits of the gathering, and a rain of ale followed, so much that smoke lifted toward the faint stars.

Idorn used the moment. He dragged Signy away and, when she would not walk, he slung her over his shoulder. Good-humored laughter followed. Who had not had trouble with women refusing to obey?

Away from the fire, Signy kicked herself free, and they both tumbled into the grass. Idorn, after a difficult day, was sorely tempted to lie beside her, if only for a moment—it might be dark enough. A foolish thought, and he knew it. He stood and reached down to help the girl. She ignored him.

"Come on, Signy. This is silly."

She would not look at him.

Idorn grew angry. He raised a fist. Perhaps he should hit her. She might obey him then.

But Idorn sighed. Brutalizing girls was Solwaer's style, not his. "Be reasonable, Signy. Get up. Please. You'll just bring me more trouble."

"I would rather die tonight than let that man have me."

Idorn said nothing. Signy might say such a thing but, in the end, she would have to acquiesce. Women were tough creatures, in his observation—tougher than men, he sometimes thought.

He bent down. "Here."

Signy hesitated, but she grasped his hand.

"That's better." Idorn pulled her toward the makeshift camp. "You must be there when he arrives. Welcome your master properly, and he will treat you well."

This was good advice, and he, Idorn, had a job to do. That should have been enough. But seeing the abject slump of Signy's shoulders, he experienced complex regret. He knew what Solwaer did to women who displeased him.

Midsummer nights in the North are strange. An eerie half-darkness lies across the sky, and the stars are faint and weary, the color of milk, when they can be seen. So it was on this night. The world hovered between light and dark as they wheeled, faint and cold, above the face of the earth.

But the comet was larger than any of the stars. Close to the end of its journey, it approached the size of half the moon, and soon it would be swallowed by black eternity as it was slung out once more, beyond the bowl of Earth's blue sky.

Some hours had passed, and the pyre had burned to ash.

At Edor's signal, men lit torches from the embers, and soon a double line of flaring light showed where the path, beaten out by the naked feet of the monks, led down from the meadow to the entrance of the tomb.

Somewhere, in the distance, a slow thudding began. A single beat, it was joined by others as the procession began to form at the top of the cliff. The ash shafts of spears, the leather-covered shields, these were the drums.

But there were other noises, a creaking, grinding rumble, and the sound of men running and shouting to each other.

Solwaer waited, standing beside Edor. He knew what was coming. They both did.

"There." Edor pointed at the dark shape.

At first it was hard to make out the detail; then a dragon's head reared up and cut its shape from the material of the sky. The dragon's body came after as the ship, rolling on logs laid under the keel by the Norsemen, slid down her carefully managed path. They'd cut a road from the meadow to the cliff terrace at a gentle gradient, but it was not enough. The fighters barely held her as the vessel gathered speed on the downhill run.

"She's running off the logs!" In the prow, Idorn screamed the warning.

Only because the ropes and the men were very strong did they arrest the momentum of the ship, turning her at last in a wide curve toward the grave mouth.

Fewer men, less strength, fewer logs, and she would have veered away, ripped the ropes from their hands and tipped over the cliff. But they managed it.

Edor and Solwaer stood like rocks. They'd both seen the near disaster, but neither moved—that would not have been dignified.

Now the mastless hull, stripped of her oars though with shields still lining the sides, rested before them as men braced her on either flank, breathless from the effort.

Edor and Solwaer bowed their heads in respect for the ship and her passengers. The drumming ceased.

In a loud voice, Edor spoke. Idorn translated from beside the dragon's head; height was an advantage—his voice carried well to the waiting men.

"Tonight, Midsummer Night, we honor Grimor and Magni, sons of Ragnar, son of Iarl, son of Othere, son of Britwulf Ironhand. Their deaths in this place have brought us much grief and, here, they lie before us as they begin their voyage into eternity."

Tears were coursing down Edor's face, and Solwaer had trouble controlling his own rush of feeling. Funerals—they were always hard.

"Brothers in life, reunited only to be torn apart again, they are our brothers, our kin. Their last earthly dwelling place is this great ship." Edor waved at the hull that had been wrestled by the Norse across the meadow.

If that had been testing, the journey of the vessel up the narrow cliff path had been blood-sweatingly difficult. Just as well one of the smaller, narrow vessels had been chosen.

"They died for us, and we will never forget our deathless heroes." Edor paused, overcome.

Around him, torchlight shone on wet cheeks, damp beards. From a man of few words, this was a moving speech. Even Idorn had to blink tears away, nodding.

But Edor did not care. Howling a battle cry, he ran forward and clambered up the side of the ship, hoisted on willing shoulders.

Before him, beneath a pall of crimson wool—one of the hangings brought over from Solwaer's hall—lay the corpses of the brothers. Side by side on a thick bed of meadow herbs and grasses, they had been raised on a platform constructed where the mast was usually stepped. Both bodies had been washed in sour wine, to preserve them as long as possible, and dressed in the finest tunics that could be found. In the stern of the ship, Fiachna's body lay at their feet.

Edor prostrated himself and knocked his head against the edge of the wooden bier. "We ask that your journey is swift. We ask that the joy of the afterlife is greater than any happiness you experienced in this life. We honor you."

Screaming the last words, he leaped from the ship, his fall broken by willing arms, and, like a man possessed by the Gods, he ran with a lighted torch to the gaping entrance of the tomb. "Bring them!"

Tough arms and broad shoulders, strong legs and backs slabbed with muscle, all were pressed into service as, slowly, the ship traveled into the dark of the chamber beneath the hill.

Solwaer stood back, holding his torch high as grunting, heaving men strained to roll the vessel along the passage toward the inner tomb. It was a long passage, but there was enough room, just.

Edor and Solwaer both breathed in—it was purely a reflex action—and as Grimor's corpse passed by, the Lord of Portsol stood back against the rock wall. He grasped the cross he wore around his neck; he had Thor's golden hammer on a thong too—extra protection and in honor of his new partners, the Norse. It was as well to have such things to ward off danger, especially as, sometimes, a corpse sat up in the presence of its killer.

There was still a faint glow in the sky as the vessel, with its cargo, was positioned. The monks had been forced to gather stones from the burned buildings to brace the hull and then, lit only by flame, they would build a wall between the chamber and the passageway.

In Solwaer's judgment, the Gods of the Norse had overcome the Trinity. It was fitting, then, that part of the substance of the destroyed Abbey should hold up the vessel that would carry the brothers to Walhal.

His thoughts wandered under the waning influence of the beer. Too much and he always felt sad and, these days, old. Drinking all night was something he'd once done with impunity—not anymore. Now he needed a soft bed and the girl who waited for him. The last would provide something he'd long delayed claiming—and the first would send him to oblivion, when he was ready, if only for an hour or so.

Peering into the milky gloom, Solwaer held the torch higher. What was keeping them? His mind drifted to the first time he'd seen Signy. That surprising display in the church. He'd not known who she was then, for Signy had not been born when he'd run away from her clan. But he remembered her father. The Shaman had been good to his slaves. A sign of weakness.

A shout, and he jerked back to the present. A cart creaked down the slope, pulled by the strongest of the monks, Cuillin among them.

Solwaer was not without pity. As the sweating men pulled the heavy vehicle toward the entrance, he acknowledged—but only to himself—that this must indeed be a bitter moment. The monks had been forced to load this vehicle with grave goods for Bear and his brother—including a silver cross from the Abbey's altar that lay, glinting, on the top of the hoard.

That cross had caused another dispute with Edor. Solwaer had wanted it for his church, but he'd given it up—making much of the goodwill. In return he'd kept the great manuscript of Revelation that had survived the burning of the church. He'd decided not to sell the book; tomorrow it would go with him to Portsol to adorn the altar of the church he would eventually build.

Now he watched the wagon roll toward them with some regret. *Bear, I hope you know what I'm doing for you.*

All the grave goods had come either from Grimor's ships—objects acquired in the earlier raids of this summer—or from among Solwaer's possessions. The large silver platter, for instance, and the massive bronze bowl with a frieze of horses running around the lip—they'd both been his. The bowl he'd traded years ago for six slaves, but he still thought he'd had the best of the bargain. Its previous owner, a man with a face the color of copper, had told him it was made in a place where the sun was hotter than fire and all the people black as bog water.

Solwaer was proud of the riches they'd put together. As the cart finally passed by, firelight played across the treasures piled high above the sides. This generosity would be spoken of long after he and his children were gone. Men flocked to a leader lavish with favors; this investment would return to him many times in the years to come.

Soon, now, all would be in place, and then he could snatch an hour or so with the girl. She was one treasure he intended to have a little use from.

CHAPTER 46

Y OU KNOW what will happen, don't you?"

"What?" Freya blinked sweat from her eyes. She'd got over being exhausted hours ago.

Dan pointed at the opening—it was big enough to squeeze through now. He glanced at Katherine. They were all so covered with dust-bloom they might have been stone themselves. "Once we enter, there's no going back."

Freya stared into the passage. "What time is it?"

"Past midnight."

"Give me a minute before we go through." She picked up the camera. "Just a bit more documentation."

Without proper lights, she had to improvise. "Dan, can you shine your lamp from over there, please?" She pointed to the top of the opening. "And, Katherine, from the other side? Thanks." Minutes slid by as Freya shot angle after angle.

Dan said, "It's moments like this I wish I smoked."

Adrenaline kept Freya moving. "Nearly there." She took a last photo and put the camera down very carefully. She wasn't frightened anymore. "Ready?"

"After you." Dan swept the girl a bow. The atmosphere was lighter—perhaps they'd reached the silly side of tired.

Freya pointed a flashlight, and the beam played over the edges of the opening before she ducked and disappeared into the dark. Her footsteps become fainter until they stopped.

"I don't believe it."

Dan and Katherine shared a look. She said, "You go."

The opening was tight. Energetic wriggling, and Dan was through.

Reverse birth, thought Katherine, *that's what it looks like.*

As Dan limped toward Freya, he took in the massive structure of this passageway, so wide his hands could not touch either side. So high . . .

He stopped. His face dropped. "No."

Freya nodded. "Yes. Katherine, bring the picks!"

In front of them, blocking the way, was another wall.

Time evaporated. Freya blinked away the grit—her eyes felt raw. "Maybe we should stop, get some sleep. We're working like slaves." Part of her so, so wanted to give up and just lie down.

Katherine was breathing hard, but she mustered a smile. "Slaves don't have a choice."

Dan leaned on his pick. "We're closer than you think. We can do it."

"You wild, crazy, optimistic kid. I love you for that."

He grinned, white face, white teeth. "Promise?"

They'd started at the top of the wall this time. Though the blocks had been laid without mortar, rubble had been rammed in against the ceiling; it wasn't hard to shift, but there was a lot of it, and the wall proper was proving stubborn.

Dan tapped against a big block of stone a little above his head. The sound was dead. "But listen here . . ." He knocked the pick head close by. "It's not all uniformly thick. Thrown up in haste, is what I think."

Freya straightened her back. She stretched like a bow. "Similar to the other wall. Okay. Another half hour—that's it."

Dan nodded. "One last go?"

She nodded, hefting the pick. "Yep."

The two picks swung, almost in unison. And again. Toward

the top, a gap began to open as rubble came down, more and more of it.

Freya stood back. "Careful, Dan. Don't want to do more damage than we have to."

Dan offered a crowbar. "Your turn, then." Eyes dark in a white face.

For one last time, adrenaline obliterated exhaustion. Freya chipped away with the point of the metal bar, opening the gap, making it wider, deeper. It was exhausting work, and she spat grit as she dug, her biceps aching fiercely.

"I'm through!" She pulled back the bar. "It's another void. Truly."

Time became water, dripping slow. They worked in careful relays. Chipping, levering, chipping again. Soon, Freya knew, only will would keep them upright.

"Let me." Dan took over. "I'll try to hook the block out." He inserted the head of the pick and pulled with both hands.

The block came out, and brought the wall with it.

Dan launched himself, pushing Freya backward, landing on her chest so hard, breath was driven from her lungs.

"Freya!" Katherine rushed forward; she stumbled and nearly fell on the rubble. Dan had protected Freya's head, but a falling block had caught him on the shoulder, and there was blood on his shirt.

Gasping, Freya wriggled from underneath. "Are you all right?" She touched him, and her hand came away wet and red.

Dan coughed. He tried to sit up and winced.

Freya was shaking, hands over her eyes. Katherine pulled the girl into her arms and held her tight. "There, hush. Dan's okay. You are too."

"Thank you, Katherine. I mean that."

The librarian nodded. Brushing dust from her face, she noticed Dan. He stared through the hole transfixed.

Katherine touched Freya. Still dazed, she swiveled—and stared.

The women helped one another to stand. In the breathing silence, Dan's flashlight slowly showed them wonders.

The ship was entire, almost as she had been when first brought to this place, though the stones placed under her keel had formed a cradle as the oak planks slumped. But her shape was clear, and the dragon's head reared proudly, just as it had on the sea that still washed Findnar's shores.

The chamber of the tomb was large and so high, the corbeled roof was twice a tall man's height and more above that snarling mask. Off to each side there were other openings—a series of smaller caverns half-glimpsed as light splashed like water over the walls.

"It's a tomb complex." Freya's voice shook.

They went forward through the opening, one by one. The beam of the flashlight caressed the hull. It lingered on the oak of its planked sides, the round shields still resting against the flanks of the ship. The desiccated air had preserved the wood, but boiled leather, the covering of the shields, had rotted long ago.

Freya stood on her toes. "I can't see inside!" The sides of the vessel were too high.

"Easy fixed." Dan limped away and returned, clasping a block of stone. He put it down, trying not to wince.

Freya was immediately worried. "Dan, I'm so sorry. You're in pain; we should go upstairs and—"

He put a finger to her lips. "Step up, Miss Dane."

She took his hand and gently kissed his fingers. "Katherine, you go first," she said. But she was staring at Dan, and he at her.

"No." Katherine's voice was firm. "Though I am grateful for the invitation." Dignified. Holding up.

Freya stretched out her hand. "Come on. You, too, Dan; all of us together."

Dan pulled another block forward. "Ready?"

Freya nodded. At first, she could not make sense of what she saw; then, from beneath the bloom and felt of dust, color seeped from the deep past.

"It's cloth. There's actual cloth! I think it's a pall." Freya was almost whispering; this was a holy moment.

Dan held the flashlight steady. "There are bones underneath." The light dimmed. "Come on." He shook the flashlight—the glow flickered and intensified. "The battery's giving out; we won't have much time."

Freya leaned forward, trying not to touch the sides of the ship, trying not to breathe moisture into the air. "Two skeletons?"

Katherine was finding it hard to speak. "Look. They're still wearing clothes."

Freya's voice cracked. "I wish Dad was here."

Katherine's glance was fond. "He *is* here because you are."

Light, ever fainter, traveled on over occluded shapes—the hills and valleys of a secret landscape. Something glimmered. Dan pointed silently—a wide collar of gold lay beneath one of the skulls where bones had collapsed.

"And the platter—look at the platter. It's enormous, bigger than the Mildenhall find." Katherine's face was alight with joy and awe.

"And what about that bowl? Has to be bronze." Freya was lost in contemplation. The frieze of horses, nose to tail, had run in the dark for a thousand years with no one to see them.

An enameled pommel glimmered. "Is that a sword?" Dan pointed.

Taking the flashlight, Freya leaned closer. "My God—weapons, and they're still absolutely recognizable." The pommel had a sword blade attached, and there was an ax, two axes, and at least one battle helm.

"I can't wrap my head around this. Bronze I can understand, but for forged iron to have survived as anything more than rust, the air must have stayed dry. We must be deep under the hill behind the house."

The hit of terror was like deep, cold water. Freya couldn't breathe; she was far beneath the surface of the earth.

"What's wrong?" Dan grabbed her hand.

"I'll be fine. It's just . . ."

"Claustrophobia—that's what you called it last time."

The flashlight beam veered wildly.

Simon Fettler. Dust danced like snow as a pallid line cut his body from the dark; outside the tunnel, light was rising. Dawn was close.

Their visitor sauntered forward. "This looks interesting."

Dan tensed. "What brought you back, Fettler?"

Simon smiled apologetically. "Oh, I just don't like being left out."

Katherine's eyes fired. "Told you he was nosy." This was addressed to Dan, and not in a whisper.

Freya said hastily, "Come and have a look if you like, Simon. Just, please, cover your mouth."

Standing beside Dan, the curve of Freya's waist was a neat fit for his good hip. She felt his arm edge around her. "We need to seal the entrance very soon—the moisture in our breath is dangerous. And please don't touch anything."

Simon asked politely. "Find something else?"

Freya was nonplussed. "I'm not sure what you mean."

Unseen, a long finger of sunlight crept along the tunnel behind them, gilding their backs and spilling along the walls of the tomb.

Freya turned. She yelled, "Look! Look at the light!"

The flare was intense as the heart of the sun beat into the burial chamber—brilliant, molten gold.

Dazzled, the three did not notice what the fourth was doing.

Simon Fettler was taking pictures.

CHAPTER 47

SOLWAER WAS angry, righteously angry. The girl was the cause.

"Idorn!"

Solwaer's new chief carl—announced after the burial ceremony last night—had been waiting outside the tent because dawn was near. Relieved, he lifted the entry flap. He had not wanted to wake Solwaer, but they must be at the cliff top before light entered the passageway in the tomb, so there was little time. Stepping forward, the cheerful greeting died in his mouth. By rushlight he saw Signy crouched in a corner. Her shift had been torn from one shoulder and the pretty dress flung to the floor. There were bruises on her face, but a knife glittered in her fist. Bear's knife.

Solwaer glowered. "Dress me."

Idorn said nothing. What was there to say? Offering a clean linen shirt, he winced.

There were slash marks scored across Solwaer's trunk; they had bled, and his undershirt was stuck to the skin.

"Do you want me to . . . ?" Idorn couldn't bring himself to say, *Should I wash the blood off?*

"No." With one brutal movement, Solwaer ripped the garment over his head. Some of the surface cuts bled. He roared, rounding on the girl. "You did this!"

And then something remarkable happened.

Signy jumped up and spat directly into Solwaer's eyes. "I curse you. My father curses you. My ancestors curse you." Her eyes flamed with rage to match his.

Solwaer, Lord of Portsol, shied back as if she'd hit him.

Never was a man dressed so quickly.

Idorn, nearly gibbering with what he'd seen—Solwaer would not forgive him for witnessing this humiliation—pulled the shirt, the tunic, the trews, the leggings, and the shoes onto his master as if by magic.

Portsol's Lord stalked to the tent's opening. As he lifted the blanket, he turned. "Bind her. And a gag." Perhaps he saw Idorn's reluctance, so quickly suppressed, because he yelled, "Do it."

Only then did he look at Signy and smile. "Perhaps you will be a bride today, the bride of a dead man. But you already know what that's like. A cold bed will be yours, Signy." He'd forgotten that slaves had no names.

She swallowed. "I will lie gladly with Bear in the tomb of my ancestors."

Solwaer snorted a laugh. "Ancestors? The monks threw their bones off the cliff, all of them. My orders. Oh, nothing to say?"

Signy drained white.

Solwaer strode forward, staring into her eyes. "And I shall choose where you lie. It will not be with him." He wheeled. His finger stabbed Idorn's chest. "She is not to kill herself. On your head." He was gone in a whirl of plaid and sweat.

All the fury leached away, and Signy became an empty thing.

Idorn took a step toward her. He had to do this.

The girl raised her head. She'd brought Bear's knife to her throat and, as the tears she'd not shed during the last terrible hours became a torrent, her hand trembled. Idorn twitched the blade away and captured her bruised arms.

Signy whispered, "Please, Idorn, do not let him win. Let me die."

He held her, almost as a lover would. "Hush, little Signy, hush. First we must dress and . . ."

She slumped against him. "Will you give Bear the knife?"

"The knife?" Idorn hedged. The carved hilt was handsome, and besides, the brothers were well supplied with treasure already. Bear did not need another knife.

"It was the first thing he made. It is all I have to give since I shall not lie beside him." She did not beg; that would have shamed Bear.

Reluctantly, Idorn nodded. It was a little thing and a kindness. He tried to be gentle, too, as he bound her, but in the end, that was not possible. The ropes must be tight and the knots strong, though he did not think she would try to run away. Not now.

It was done. Cruach bathed the faces of the brothers in his light for the last time as they lay among their splendor, the otter-handled knife close now to Bear's hand. The monks were driven like animals by the overseers as, faster and faster, the two walls were built—the first inside the tunnel, the second at its mouth, the walls that would seal the grave for all time.

The work, even with so many, would take the whole Midsummer Day to accomplish, since some of the monks were too weak to lift the largest stones, even when six or eight worked together. But Cuillin was tireless—by his example he led them.

"For our Lord, my brothers, we bear this, for our God. Say after me, Our Father, which art in Heaven . . ."

In this way the monks worked steadily, chanting prayers that took them into an otherworldly state in which hours passed like mere moments.

They had almost finished when Cuillin stumbled and dropped a rock on the naked feet of a Portsol overseer. The whip of the agonized man caught the Abbot full across his face.

As he fell in a red fog, Cuillin understood, at last, how it must have been for Bear—how much he must have suffered as a boy.

And in that epiphany he saw, too, how he had broken that long-ago child's soul. Bear had never allowed Christ to enter his heart, for he, Cuillin, had driven the boy's natural love away into a dark, distorted place governed by rage and lust for the Pagan girl—pretty little Signy. The girl who should never have been a nun.

And he, Cuillin, had unleashed a force that had destroyed them all.

And there was worse than this.

Bear had perished as an unredeemed, barbaric Pagan, his soul consigned to the Devil for all eternity, because of the pride of the man who should have been his spiritual father.

He, false abbot, false priest corrupted by worldly pride, must now endure what was meted out by the savage Norse and that treacherous apostate Solwaer, because he had failed Bear and he had failed all those in his care. Atonement must be made for what he had done.

On his knees at the closed-up entrance to the tomb, Cuillin called out, "Bear, Bear, can you hear me? Forgive me, dear child, in the name of Christ."

The monks trembled; under the power of the whip, their Abbot had become insane.

But Cuillin had not finished. "I have sinned most grievously against you, Bear, and for this I accuse myself. Mea culpa, mea culpa, mea maxima culpa." Cuillin knocked his brow on the rocks before the tomb, crying out the words most piteously as blood ran into his eyes.

The brothers dropped the stones they were holding. Oblivious to the whips of the overseers, they knelt around their fallen leader, crying out as he did. If Cuillin collapsed beneath the weight of punishment, how could they endure what must be endured?

Solwaer yelled at the overseers, "Stop them!"

The Portsol men shrugged. They were three against thirty, and the monks had formed a human knot, linking arms together like some writhing, many-legged animal.

"Edor!" Solwaer bellowed and kept bellowing until the leader of the Norse arrived.

Edor was sullen from a mighty headache, a relic of the beer and the smoke. "What?" He saw the problem, and his eyes widened. The monks had gone mad.

Solwaer pointed. "They have done all they'll ever do." He drew a finger across his throat. "It is time."

Reluctant to the end, Edor finally nodded. Yesterday some of the monks had been made to dig a pit beside the entrance to the tomb.

Edor cheered up. If this was finally the end of the Findnar adventure, he could put to sea in his hulls. His hulls—that had a fine sound. He stared at Solwaer. "And the girl?" He mimed breasts and pointed toward the tent.

There was another pit. This, smaller and deeper, had been dug in the innermost stone circle. The monks had lined the sides with stone.

The Lord of Portsol flexed his shoulders; they pained him. "I agree, Edor. Yes." He nodded without regret.

The Norse leader pointed to the monks and then toward the pit that had been dug for them.

The overseers looked at each other and then at the knot of howling madmen. Lunatics, it was said, are very strong.

The men of Portsol and the Norse dragged the monks, flailing, to the pit, though it took many to accomplish this task. There they stripped them of their clothes; naked they would go into the earth as, naked, they had been born.

But the girl was only a girl. She could not protest as she walked gagged and bound to her grave, pricked on by spearpoint; Solwaer had commanded it, though some muttered, saying it was best if her sacrifice, at least, was willing.

"Brothers, our martyrdom is upon us. We die for Christ. Rejoice and be glad, for He will shortly welcome us to Paradise." Cuillin knelt on the edge of the greater pit, hands decently covering his genitals. One by one the brothers knelt beside him as they began to sing.

Their overseers were greatly relieved—the Abbot's words and actions seemed to calm the monks. The raiders on the beach heard the chanting too. The sound was eerie, coming and going on the wind, the voices of ghosts. But soon the chant sputtered, grew less, less still, until, at last, only one voice sang on . . .

Idorn stood behind his master as Signy was brought forward to the smaller pit. To Solwaer would belong the honor of signaling her burial, since she was his slave.

But Solwaer was tired and, yes, even sad, for this process gave him no feeling of fulfillment or release. Standing above the grave that had been prepared for her, staring down upon her own grave goods—a little barley in a simple bowl waiting beside the opening in the earth—Signy seemed frail and small, shivering as the wind whipped at her pretty dress.

Weary with this festival of death, Solwaer wanted it finished. "Edor, I will speak with my slave. As men say, it would be better if she was willing." He signaled that the gag should be removed. "Signy, there is a chance you will not die today."

The girl spat the cloth from her mouth and stared at him steadily. She said nothing.

"I ask one thing only. Take back the curse." Solwaer was superstitious, but superstition was the sister of caution, and that was the secret of his many successes.

For one unsettling moment Signy gazed at Portsol's Lord. Then she said, "I have seen you break faith before."

The man found he rather liked her hard certainty, for she dared to bargain with him at the edge of death. An unusual woman. But she knew the truth about Grimor and about Bear, and all women gossiped, especially the ones with a grudge. "Raise the curse and you will see."

Before she looked into the pit at her feet, Signy smiled, and that was unnerving to all who stood there. "My father was a shaman." Her eyes were glittering, bleak pools as she scanned the small crowd of men. "He taught his sons to follow him, but I learned well from his example also." Her glance, a blade, peeled the skin of Solwaer's soul. "You do not mean for me to live, Solwaer; this is a lie. For that I curse you again, sleeping and waking, in your walking out and in your returning." She raised her voice. "You will never sleep without monsters in your bed and your mind, and you will die without children. With my death, you condemn them. No sons will follow you." The last words were a gathering scream of power.

Shaken, Solwaer pushed Signy to the ground, his foot on her neck. "Idorn!"

Others rushed to help, for such defiance in a slave toward her master was unseemly.

It was quick, since she was, finally, one girl and there were many men.

And so they trussed her, tied her in the form she'd once had inside her mother, head to knees, as she went to her new, dark birth. And when she called out their names from inside her tomb, they placed earth on her and then a stone, a large stone marked with a cross. As it dropped and she felt that final weight, she screamed out, "I am Signy. Remember me."

Cuillin, awaiting his own end, heard the noise. It had distracted the men with the axes and the swords, but some of Signy's tormentors laughed, and that piercing sorrow was the last thing the Abbot ever knew.

CHAPTER 48

L IGHT BLINDED them. It blazed through the ancient air, and for one flickering moment, the burial ship burned as the benediction of the sun for the first time in more than a thousand years touched silver to silver, gold to gold as the shining net spread farther, wider, until, at last, it found the skulls of the brothers, filling the empty sockets of their eyes.

And, as quickly as it had come, it shrank away, leaving the chamber and the passageway to the soft gray of morning.

Freya was close to speechless. "That was . . . it was . . ."

Katherine said, softly, "To have seen such a thing, after so many centuries." She, too, groped for words.

Dan touched Freya's shoulder. "We should seal the chamber?"

"Wait. Katherine, look." Freya was leaning forward, pointing. "Is that . . . ?"

They stared at the bones of a skeletal hand. "I think it is." Once a knife had lain close beside those fingers. The blade was gone, but the haft remained, an otter-handled knife.

"Could it be . . ." Freya hesitated.

"Perhaps it's a coincidence." Katherine's attempt at reason.

"But she *described* the knife—and he made it; her friend." Freya took a deep breath. "This is him, it must be." She turned to Dan, eyes shining.

"And the girl under the slab?" Dan stared at her.

In a daze, Freya nodded. "She's our writer—the one we've been seeing. She showed us how to find the ship and her grave."

Simon, forgotten by them all, stared from Dan to Freya. "Showed you how to find the ship?" He laughed. "What is this?"

Dan stepped between Freya and Simon. "Shame you have to go. Must do it again sometime." His tone was polite; his eyes were not.

Simon's expression darkened, and Freya said, quickly, "Can you find some tarps, Dan? We'll need gaffer tape too. Please."

Dan's eyes were dangerous, and he was simmering as he stalked away, but he did what she asked. Simon he ignored.

"Sorry to hurry you out of here, Simon, but Dan's right. We should leave."

"I remain curious, though." Simon stepped back from the long-ship.

Freya, utterly weary, shrugged. "What about?"

"Why didn't you tell me what you were doing? I really could have helped." His smile was rueful. "Said that before, I think."

She looked away. The kiss. It had led to expectations and that was her fault. "Well, it all just sort of happened."

He gestured at the fallen rocks in the passageway. "Just like that?" A little less rueful.

"Yes." She was short. Simon might be kind and attractive, but she actually owed him nothing. "That's the truth. Now, if you don't mind."

"Okay. Understood." He said nothing more as he strode from the burial chamber.

Freya called after him, "I'd appreciate keeping this confidential, Simon." She hurried forward a few steps. "Simon?" He must have heard her.

Katherine joined her. "Well, really. Manners."

Freya mumbled, "He's a nice man actually. He was just upset about something."

Dan returned. Grinning, he handed Freya a tarpaulin. "I'm thinking he's big enough to get over it without you holding his hand."

CHAPTER 49

THE CHURCH was certainly a fine building, the largest in Portsol—even bigger than the rebuilt hall—though it was dark inside. *It was a pity then,* thought Idorn, *that the old bastard hadn't finally lived long enough to see it finished.*

Idorn stood with the men to one side of the altar as the priest intoned the funeral Mass. He smiled at Isolde, standing with the women. *Not much longer.* His wife was in the pride of late pregnancy and found it hard to stand for very long. This was their first child, and they were happy together though, sometimes, another face swam through his dreams. *My name is Signy. Remember me.*

The priest censed the congregation. "In the name of the Father and of the Son and of the Holy Spirit, we commit the body of our brother Solwaer, Lord of Portsol, to the earth."

Idorn was the only person in the church who understood what the man was saying. Latin was useful in trade, and he'd acquired working knowledge of the language in the last year from this same priest. Clergy had become valuable clients again, though Findnar would be a long time rebuilding.

There was a closed stone coffin—more of a box, to be accurate—before the altar. Solwaer had been frightened of dying, and only Idorn knew that it contained one or two things the priest would not like. They'd had to fold the old man's body to get him in there, but he'd asked for that too. Perhaps Idorn knew why. *Too little and too late, Solwaer. You'd better hope the Christians aren't right about Hell.*

Idorn sighed. They were here today because the old man had

given up. The raid on Findnar had signaled some years of prosperity in Portsol, but Solwaer had never seemed to enjoy it, and he'd taken to his bed after his only son drowned in the strait last year and his chief wife, the mother of the boy, killed herself.

Deep in the winter dark, just after the Christ-mass. What had the boy been doing out there on the water? He'd taken Solwaer's new ship—the one with the finely carved steering rudder—down with him, as well as too many youths from Portsol. How do you put a price on that kind of loss? The ship and the boys. He must have been testing his strength as all young men do, but death stalks vainglorious fools.

Lucky for Idorn, of course. He, rather than Solwaer's reckless son, was standing here now as the new Lord of Portsol. Maybe Signy's curse had found the boy and drowned him?

Idorn crossed himself quickly. *Lord, protect my child from harm and Isolde, in the birth to come.* In so many ways, he hoped they had a daughter.

He knelt as the congregation was censed again. On and on the service went, and Idorn's mind drifted. He wondered, sometimes, if Signy had cursed him, too, cursed him with her memory so that no other woman was ever quite enough.

Idorn crossed himself again, more slowly. The past was the past; it could not come back, and ghosts did not walk. Personally, he did not believe in spirits, but Solwaer, of course, was superstitious to the last. He'd made Idorn promise one last favor. It seemed a waste, but he would do as he'd been asked; he would honor the deathbed promise. Solwaer's torque and arm rings, the ones Bear had made, would be thrown into the marsh on the island, asking release for Solwaer's soul from Signy's curse. *Won't do any good, old man. Signy didn't care about gold anyway, and you can't buy salvation.*

Then, of course, there was the stone outside the burial chamber on Findnar. *Grimor and Magni, sons of Ragnar, lie here. Solwaer made me.* The old man had been quite specific. Idorn had been practical; he'd had the runes carved on the back of a tumbled stone from the standing circle. Signy's people had already used the front—that seemed fair to him, for it had been their clan tomb too. He'd made sure that the stone was well buried as, of course, was the entrance to the tomb. The slaves who'd done the work, and the carver, had all been killed; perhaps he'd learned something from Solwaer.

The congregation was muttering. They were restless, for they'd been promised a feast when the service was done. If the priest would just stop droning on, Solwaer would be gone for good and they could all get on with life. The old barbarian and the old ways. Strange to think of the brutality they'd all taken for granted as the only way life could be. With the exception of sensible lapses, Idorn knew he was a leader of a different kind—he was grateful for what he'd been given, and he'd defend it, if he had to, but war was wasteful. Religion, on the other hand, settled life down for everyone because with it you knew where you stood. Perhaps, in the end, all the ceremonial nonsense made sense for this alone.

The priest signaled the congregation to rise. At last, he led them down toward the crypt as six men of Portsol shouldered the stone box and followed behind.

The newest Lord of Portsol held out his hand to his wife. They were the chief mourners, since none of Solwaer's legitimate blood family survived. Isolde leaned on his arm. *Nearly there,* he mouthed, and she smiled at him trustingly.

Family, land, children—in the end, these were all that mattered, the here and now. The past was the past, and the future would take care of itself.

CHAPTER 50

W E NEED to give them back."

It was late morning; Freya, Dan, and Katherine were together at the grave in the circle of stones. Freya had the crucifix in her hand, and the little lead box with the diary was inside.

"I agree," Dan said, though he sounded uncertain.

"So do I." Katherine did not.

Freya looked from face to face. "And I think we must take her to lie in the hull. They should be together. That's what she's been trying to tell us, and Dad, too, I'm sure of it. Finding this"—she held up the crucifix—"started it all. Sometimes, just saying this stuff, it feels like I've taken drugs, and not in a good way." She smiled an apologetic half-smile.

Katherine nodded thoughtfully. After they'd cleaned up yesterday—the luxury of hot water and clean clothes—she'd been told the whole story—the details of Freya and Dan's visions—over eggs and bacon and a good deal of coffee. "Extreme exhaustion *can* be compared to hallucinogens, I often think. A very similar effect."

Freya and Dan stared at each other, and back at Katherine.

The librarian cleared her throat. "Or so I've heard. But I support what you'd like to do, Freya. It seems right."

"Dan, what do you really think?" Freya was better able to read him now.

His eyes were troubled. "Of course it's the right thing to do. But these finds—this grave, the ship, maybe even the girl you found who was murdered—they're important. Especially in context. And . . ." He stopped, at a loss.

Freya sagged. "I know. We have to inform Historic Scotland, and things should not, ordinarily, be touched. But someone has to keep faith with that poor girl." She rubbed her eyes. The elation of yesterday had gone because she was troubled about Simon. That whole experience had been upsetting. She'd tried to call him several times, but he'd not called her back.

Katherine coughed. "If I may make a suggestion?"

"Of course. Please."

"I think there is no harm in restoring the crucifix and the diary—the last prayer included—to this girl. If she is who we think she is, she has a right to these objects because they were hers. As to moving her, why not think about that when you're a little more sure about what you will do with the other finds? She's waited a very long time; a few more weeks will be neither here nor there."

Freya brightened. "Dan, what do you think?"

"It seems verra sensible to me. Verra."

Freya laughed. That naughty glint was back in those gray eyes, and she felt a whole, whole lot better.

It was a nice day, and Simon closed his eyes as he tipped his head back, the sun warming his throat. The churchyard was peaceful; perhaps that helped.

A shadow fell across his face. He opened his eyes. "Rob, thanks for coming." He picked up his laptop, making room on the bench.

"You said it was urgent." Robert Buchan sat. He stared at the church. "For the life of me, I don't know why you bought this church. Lot of work for such an ugly building."

Simon shrugged. "Just my bit of the past—we suit each other somehow. And it's what I do. Work." A wry half-smile.

Robert sniffed. "Not all so lucky, are we?" A tone between offense and gloom.

"Luck is a capricious mistress, Rob. And cruel sometimes. Unfortunately, I've got something to show you." Simon flipped open the laptop and pointed to a file on the desktop.

"What?" But Rob took the computer and clicked obediently. And almost dropped it. "Where did these . . ." His tone was half-strangled.

"Keep going. There's more. Lots more."

"That bloody girl!" Rob bubbled with fury.

"Pretty, though." An image of Freya clicked on screen. Gilded by the light of that midsummer dawn, she standing beside the longship.

"The hoard. She's found it." Robert was almost crying. "She's got no right, not to this."

Simon was surprisingly gentle. "Time to walk away, Rob. Freya owns Findnar. Accept it, or I think the past will consume you. More than it has already." He gestured at the images. "I'm doing you a favor. And you still have the battle helm. Sell it. Start a new life. Really."

"Easy for you to say, this isn't your home." Robert's face was a sick yellow.

Simon stared at the restless sea. In the misty distance, Findnar rode the horizon. *Never say die.* He flicked Rob a glance. "We'll see. But you know what they say in Hollywood. 'They won, we lost. Next.' So, why don't I get us a beer and we can discuss what to do with your helm. I know people who know people." He strode off to the church, tipping an imaginary hat to Michael Dane. "Dr. Dane, you have a remarkable daughter."

Left to himself, Robert Buchan glared at the headstone. "There's another word I'd use."

But when Simon returned, the graveyard was deserted and his laptop was gone.

With the tarpaulin peeled back, the grave seemed very small. Dan eased his way into the trench, followed by the women. The three stood around the stone box in silence; it was the evening of a perfect day.

After a moment Freya held out her hands. "I'd like to say something." Dan and Katherine linked their fingers through hers. "We do not know your name, but we know who you are. You were treated with great cruelty and profound injustice, but you have returned, and we have found at least some part of your story. Now we know where your man is buried, and though we do not understand what has happened, we know your love for him was and is very real." Freya stared at Dan as she talked to the girl in the grave. "And I am grateful. I know so much more about love now because of you—love of family, the passion lovers share and how that endures. These things are real, and faith must be kept; that is why we have brought your possessions back to you." Freya held the crucifix in her hand, and the two little boxes. "You found us, and now we hope you can rest."

The three bent down; between them, the lid began to shift.

On the far side of the stone circle, out of the east, the chop of rotor blades cut the air as the rushing *pffwopp, pffwopp, pffwopp* grew louder.

Freya glanced up as they wrestled to move the lid. She saw the insignia on the side. "That's a news chopper! They're filming us." A cameraman was shooting from the opened doorway.

"Freya." Dan's voice cut through, she heard Katherine gasp.

"What?" Freya had to shout—the chopper was directly above— and her hair flew around her head in a furious cloud.

And then she looked down.

The grave was empty.

CHAPTER 51

IT WAS a warm day, the autumn air flushed and ripe, when the gathering assembled on the island.

Walter had taken charge. The Boynes had brought a small diesel generator over, and it would supply the power they needed.

"Mum, like to do the honors?"

Elizabeth Dane smiled at her daughter. "I would." She flicked a switch, and strings of lights blinked on in the undercroft.

"Face masks, everyone." Walter was handing them around.

Katherine stood beside Elizabeth. The older women smiled tentatively at each other; they'd had their fair share of being organized by Walter today—maybe that was some kind of bond.

Dan limped to Freya's side. "So, does someone cut a ribbon?"

"Damn. Forgot. Not a ribbon kind of a girl." Freya smiled at him warmly. "And I'd just like to say, that is, Dan and I would like to say, how much we appreciate everyone being here today."

She put an arm around her mother's shoulders. "Mum's come a very long way. And thanks, Walter, to you. Katherine, of course— that goes without saying."

Katherine flushed happily.

"And you, Dan. We wouldn't be standing here without you— your loyalty and your kindness, especially over the last few weeks . . ."

Dan's face darkened. "As if I was going to tell those idiots anything."

Walter grumbled, "All that nonsense on TV. You'd think they'd have better things to do."

Katherine nodded. "Not to mention the tabloids."

Freya winced. All that crap about "The Lost Hoard," and "Freya Dane, Treasure Hunter." They'd even chased Elizabeth through a shopping mall in Sydney and pestered three former boyfriends for details of their love life. Freya still didn't know who'd tipped them off. Dan, of course, fingered Simon. Who else could have taken the photos that had created all the frenzy? Shots of the ship and the treasures it contained had splashed on the news and gone viral on the Web, and for the last few weeks journalists had made Freya's life a misery. And then there was Historic Scotland; that had yet to be sorted out, and things were delicate.

Freya was still deeply confused. She hardly knew Simon. What motive could he have for making her life so difficult? It just didn't make sense. "Well, after all that fuss and silliness, I want you, the people I love, to know and see the truth." One by one, her warm smile embraced them all and lingered on Dan.

"Walter and Mum, you are about to see what's been glimpsed only once before in our time, just a few short weeks ago." Freya led them toward the entrance passage. She and Dan had cleared the rubble and dust from the undercroft, a huge job, but the tunnel remained sealed, just as they had left it on that Midsummer Day.

Dan climbed a stepladder with some effort. "Ready?"

Freya nodded.

He began to peel the well-taped plastic sheets away from the wall.

"So, where are you up to?" Walter gestured toward the tomb.

Freya shrugged. "Still negotiating, but I'm insisting on a number of things."

Katherine eyed Freya. "Can you do that? I thought a treasure trove . . ."

"Is the property of the state. Yes, it is, but this is a bit complicated. In the end it would be a PR disaster for them if they tried to force their way onto private property, so we need each other.

Besides, soon the weather will keep interlopers away until spring. Some of those journalists don't like cold water." Freya's laugh was grim. "Here we go. Watch your step inside the passage, though, there's rubble everywhere."

Holding lights, the visitors squeezed through into the passage and walked to the tomb chamber. Elizabeth stopped. Awestruck, she clutched Walter's arm. "Freya, I don't know what to say."

"I know, Mum, I know."

"It's better than the pictures, Dan." Walter had found his tongue. He patted Elizabeth's hand absently; they smiled at each other, both of them dazed.

The ship lay just as Freya, Dan, and Katherine remembered, but brighter illumination showed them so much more. The mass of objects was overwhelming, and it would be a life's work to assess and understand what lay before them.

Elizabeth walked to the stern of the vessel, and Freya joined her, tucking a hand through the crook of her arm as her mother wiped her eyes. "I am so very sorry Michael did not live to see this." Freya cuddled her. "That's very generous, Mum." She hesitated. "We've never really talked about why he left, not really, but I think I know."

Elizabeth Dane stared at her daughter. "Tell me, because I've never understood."

"He didn't know it, but he had to come here. He had to come to Findnar. He belonged here, truly, because there was unfinished business. That's what I think."

"Unfinished? But what do you mean?"

"Dan?" Walter called out to his son; he was staring down at the bier. "I thought you said there were three skeletons—one in the stern and two under the pall."

Such a casual little sentence. Freya stiffened.

Dan limped forward. "Yes, Dad."

Freya joined them. "Three men, from their size."

Walter said happily, "But there's another skeleton under there. I can see why you missed it; you have to look really carefully." He stood back.

Walter was right. The dome of a fourth cranium, a small one, was visible beneath the pall. It lay between the skulls of two of the larger skeletons.

Dan touched Freya's arm. "That's his skeleton, isn't it? The one on the left."

Dry-mouthed, Freya nodded. "Yes." There was the otter-handled knife.

Fascinated, Walter peered at the delicate bones that lay between the larger skeletons. "The phalanges of the middle one"— he pointed—"they've mingled with the ones on the left. The big chap with the knife. Katherine, what do you think? Maybe it's a kid."

The librarian caught Freya's glance. "No, not a child. These will be the bones of a woman. Quite a small woman."

EPILOGUE

T HE GREAT equinoctial gale battered the front windows of Compline, wind and rain assaulting the old house with useless fury. Nights were drawing in, this was fire and red wine weather, but at Michael's desk Freya was absorbed in working on her thesis.

"Time to eat." Dan caressed her shoulder.

She leaned back trustingly, put her hand on his.

"So, how did you know it was me?" He bent. "Might have been anyone." He kissed the hollow of her throat.

"Because I have faith." She turned in his embrace. "Mmmm, something smells nice."

"That will be the cassoulet. Table's set, wine's open and breathing, just steaming the greens. Come to the kitchen, Freya Dane."

"Cassoulet? I thought it was you, Dan Boyne."

"You can't have one without the other." He grinned. "And if you don't eat soon, you'll fall over. Bread and jam staggers, that's what you'll get, and then where will you be?"

She giggled. "Bread and jam what?"

Dan said solemnly, "What Walter used to tell me. Very serious condition indeed when you work too hard; come on, it'll keep till morning." He held out a hand.

Freya took it and got up.

"I know it will, it's just that I've done so much reworking of the thesis since we found the longship, and that means there's so much more to do." She followed him to the kitchen.

"But all of it good, you said." Dan flourished a tea towel at the kitchen table. "Sit." He pulled out Michael's chair.

Freya meekly sat. "Yes, it does feel better now. The crucifix has given me a whole new way to approach the topic. So much more real this time, not just theory, and I'm really enjoying the writing." She looked surprised. "Who'd have thought that?"

Dan brought a Le Creuset pot to the table and removed the lid. "Duck and pork, best mashed potatoes, and green beans *plus* a pretty nice bottle of Tasmanian pinot noir; should be good."

"But where did you find the wine?"

He splashed some into her glass. "Not Portsolly, that's for sure. To us." He lifted his glass to Freya.

She lifted hers. "To us." They drank happily. "Whatever happened to the man who couldn't cook?"

"He learned." Dan busied himself serving the food.

Freya glanced around the candlelit kitchen. On the dresser were a number of cookbooks, and a couple of favorites were starting to look well used. "I love this house and the fact that we live here together. Thank you."

"No need for thanks." His glance was shy.

Freya put down her knife and fork. "Yes, there is. You saved me, Dan."

"We were both lost." He reached a hand across the table, and she took it. "Getting cold, though."

"What?"

"The food."

Freya laughed out loud. She ate with relish. "This is very good."

"Don't sound so surprised."

The silence between them was easy and companionable until Dan said, "By the way, I heard something interesting today in Port—about the fuss."

Fuss was their word for the media frenzy that had visited Findnar like a sudden storm.

Freya said accusingly, "You've been to the newsagent."

He laughed. "You're right, and I cannot tell a lie."

"And so?"

"So." Dan sat back. "It wasn't Simon."

"Then who?"

"Robert Buchan."

"Him!"

"Yep. Seems he left the cover sheet behind. He uses the news-agency fax from time to time because he doesn't own a computer. It was a contract with a picture agency for images of 'The Findnar Treasureship.' "

Freya's eyes darkened. "He got the pictures from somewhere, though."

Dan nodded as he filled her glass again. "And that will be an interesting conversation when we have it with the man."

"I don't think I care. I hope it made him happy." She held the wine up against a candle flame, admiring the color. "We." She glanced at Dan. "And will we have longer together than they did—or my parents?" Freya was without defenses.

"Yes." He leaned across the tabletop and cupped her face in his hands.

"Yes. Just that?"

"We've been given this chance, of that I am verra sure."

"I'm never sure of anything." The half-laugh broke.

"Yes, you are. You trust me as I trust you. *Creideas* in Gaelic, and this I swear—I will never desert you, Freya Dane. If I go, I will always return. Look at me."

Freya was brave. She lifted her eyes to his, and Dan was smiling.

"We have been given to each other. There's completion in this."

She was shaken. "You really believe that?"

"I do."

Her eyes were enormous. "And is the slow wooing therefore finished?"

"It is." Daniel Boyne leaned forward. "I love you, Freya Dane, and there is no more to be said."

ACKNOWLEDGMENTS

This book was a long time coming, and now that it's finished I owe thanks to so many people for their patience.

I am fortunate indeed to have such understanding publishers. Judith Curr at Atria Books, Simon & Schuster in New York; Carolyn Caughey, Hodder Headline in London; and Lou Johnson, Simon & Schuster in Sydney have been saintly indeed, waiting for this one to finally land.

This is a story I've wanted to write for a very long time. And when, first time around, *The Island House* (then called *Freya Dane*) just would not behave itself and I put it aside at second draft to write *The Dressmaker*, I still knew that, one day, I'd finish it. Perhaps my characters drove the process. I don't think I did, but they and I got there in a photo finish at last.

I've had so much help along the way. When it was time to start on this manuscript again, Nicola O'Shea, my Australian editor, read the story as it returned to life and provided great, great advice. That forensic eye is priceless when I'm lost in the bog of my own making and half-formed characters go missing along with the plot.

And Sarah Branham, too, my kind editor from Simon and Schuster in New York—though kind does not mean indulgent here, it means bracing and clever—has an overview second to none. I hang on tight to that first feedback from Sarah because it always sets me straight and fills me with courage. And, more recently, Larissa Edwards, at Simon and Schuster in Sydney, has been a wonderful and warm support as we've begun our working relationship.

Others I must mention. Suzanne O'Neil gave me great advice, too, through the first couple of drafts; Tina Gitsas was encouragement itself when she read the story; and Franscois McHardy believed in the book, too, from day one. Alexandra Arnold, in Sarah Branham's office, was just absolutely tireless in sorting out problems—especially the dramas of getting manuscripts back and forth between New York City and the wilds of Tasmania at the height of the December silly season. Thanks, too, to the talented Evelyn Saunders, who supplied me with invaluable research during the writing of the first draft. Everything from how oil rigs are run in the North Sea to countless facts about the Vikings and a great deal more besides.

And where would I be without Rick Raftos, agent and friend of such long standing? Can you believe I first talked to you, Rick, in 1984 when I was a starting-out producer and wanted to work with one of your star writers? No. Neither can I. So long ago, and the wheel has turned full circle. I call myself a writer now, thanks to you and to Rachel (Skinner) also. She it was who rang me from your office after reading the first hundred pages of what, eventually, became *The Innocent*. "Get off your bum," she said. "There's a book here." And so there was.

But living day to day with a writer is, I think, a difficult thing. In writing mode, you're just as likely to share the house with a ghost as a wife; a shadow of someone who barely talks, bumps into walls, looks vague when addressed, and stops cooking (and I like to cook). So, finally, this is to thank first, last, and always Andrew

Blaxland. Tolerant beyond all understanding when you, also, have too much to do, you take care of me when I'm not safe to be let outside and so many other times as well.

How fortunate I am to be married to you.

With love and gratitude.

Posie

POSIE GRAEME-EVANS

Tasmania, 2012

The
Island House

POSIE GRAEME-EVANS

A Readers Club Guide

INTRODUCTION

Freya Dane, a PhD candidate in archaeology, arrives on the island of Findnar off the northern coast of Scotland. After years of estrangement from her father—an archaeologist who recently died—Freya has come to the island to find out more about him and his work. As Freya explores the island and her father's research, she discovers much more than just the roots of Findnar's history. In AD 800 a young girl named Signy from the local Pictish tribe is taken in by the surviving members of the Christian community who have settled on the island of Findnar. As Signy grows up behind the walls of the monastery, she finds herself at the center of the clash between the island's three religious cultures—caught between her adopted Christian faith, her native Pictish religion, and the Viking man she loves.

Alternating between present-day and ninth-century Scotland, *The Island House* is an intertwined story of fascinating discoveries and two women connected to each other over centuries.

QUESTIONS AND TOPICS FOR DISCUSSION

1. Reread the opening passage, which describes the brothers' burial chamber: "The dead must have attendants in the next life and, too, sacrifice paid the blood debt of betrayal. Murder, unappeased, makes the dead malevolent." (p. 1) What tone does this preface set for *The Island House*? Who do you think is the "attendant"?

2. Freya describes an "unholy trinity" of anxiety, fear, and yearning that have followed her since childhood. (p. 7) How do these feelings influence her actions throughout the novel? What motivates Freya's character? Do you think this "trinity" still defines Freya by the conclusion of *The Island House*?

3. How does the "Wanderer comet" influence both Freya and Signy's lives? Reflect on instances in the novel where the comet is mentioned. What do you think "the Wanderer" might symbolize?

4. Freya reflects early in the novel: "Perhaps, in the end, there were no accidents." (p. 32) How is the theme of destiny and fate played in *The Island House*? Do you agree with Freya? Why or why not?

5. Freya and her father both longed to rebuild their relationship, but never made the first step to reconnect. What stood in the way? Why do you think they never reached out to one another? How might Freya's discovery have been different if her father was still alive?

6. Dan was initially withdrawn and hostile toward Freya. What caused him to open up? How do Dan and Freya transform one another? What do they learn from each other?

7. Is Signy's loyalty to her family and need for a deep religious faith greater than her love for Bear? Is she the author of her own tragedy?

8. Why does Signy become a nun? Why does she remain devoted to the Christian lifestyle, even though she struggles to fit in? What does this say about her character? What finally causes her to turn away from her adopted faith? What was her breaking point?

9. What was Simon's motivation for taking the pictures? Do you believe he ever had legitimate feelings for Freya? Or do you think he was using her?

10. *The Island House* alternates between the present day and AD 800. Did you relate to or have a preference for one storyline more than the other? If so, which one? How did the two women's stories

parallel each other? Do you think Freya and Signy would have understood each other if they both lived in the same century?

11. Both Freya's and Signy's lives change dramatically over the course of *The Island House*. Reflect on each character in the opening pages of the novel. How did each evolve or mature as characters?

12. There are many religious and supernatural elements in the novel—from Signy's ancestry as the daughter of the Pictish shaman to Freya's discoveries on Findnar. Discuss each character's relationship with their faith. How does religion affect their lives, and those around them? When is religion a source of comfort? A source of contention?

13. Discuss the ending of *The Island House*. How do you think Signy's bones ended up on the ship with Bear's?

ENHANCE YOUR BOOK CLUB

1. Freya's father, Michael Dane, has only one word carved on his gravestone: "Scholar." Freya wonders to herself, "How could a life be summed up in just one word?" (p. 123) If you had to pick just one, what word would you use to describe Freya? Signy? Yourself? Your fellow book club members? Discuss this concept and your chosen word at your next meeting.

2. "Freya" is the Norse goddess of love, beauty, fertility, and destiny, while "Signy" is the name of heroines in two connected legends from Scandinavian mythology. Divide your book club into two groups: one group that will research the goddess Freya and one that will research the importance of Signy in Scandinavian mythology. Have each group present their findings at your book club discussion. Do you see any parallels with what you found in your research on Signy's and Freya's characters in *The Island House*?

Finally, research the origins of your own name to share with your book club.

3. Get a feel for a coastal Scottish town by watching the movie *Local Hero*, starring Burt Lancaster. The 1983 film is one of Posie Graeme-Evans's favorites and was partially filmed in Pennan, a town located in northern Scotland. The town and beautiful landscapes featured will help you visualize the setting of *The Island House*. Visit www.undiscoveredscotland.co.uk/pennan/pennan/ for more photos.

4. Author Posie Graeme-Evans drew inspiration for *The Island House* from the Scottish landscape during research trips in 2006 and 2011. Real standing stones on the island of Orkney—the Ring of Brodgar—and at Callanish on the Isle of Lewis provided reference for the ring of stones on Findnar; both sites are over five thousand years old. Neolithic passage tombs at Maes Howe (Orkney) and Newgrange in Ireland were also influential in her descriptions of the tomb of Signy's ancestors on Findnar. View pictures of these remarkable and mystical places and learn more about Posie by visiting www.posiegraemeevans.com.